THE ENGLISH GERMAN GIRL

THE ENGLISH GERMAN GIRL

A Novel

Jake Wallis Simons

Skyhorse Publishing
A Herman Graf Book

To the children who escaped from the Nazis on
the Kindertransport, and to their families.
And to my own children, Libi, Isaac and Imogen.

I catch sight of my face in the mirror of a shop, and am horrified to see that I am smiling. You can't help smiling, in such beautiful weather. The trams are going up and down the Kleiststrasse, just as usual. They, and the people on the pavement, and the tea-cosy dome of the Nollendorfplatz station have an air of curious familiarity, of striking resemblance to something one remembers as normal and pleasant in the past – like a very good photograph. No. Even now I can't altogether believe that any of this has really happened.

—Christopher Isherwood

PART ONE

31 January 1933, Berlin

I

The grand city of Berlin lies milky in the morning light. Amid the avenues and alleyways, the tram stops and department stores, a little girl by the name of Rosa Klein hurries through the freezing air to buy some rolls for breakfast. She turns onto the Wilhelmstraße, a trail of vapour from her mouth lingering in the air beneath a canopy of tram cables, and, a little breathless, reaches the Konditorei and heaves at the heavy door. A little bell chimes, and a cloud of delicious, moist scent blossoms into the street, floating like a blessing towards the dogs scrounging in the gutters. Rosa enters the bakery, a Reichsmark note clenched in her fist like an autumn leaf, brimming with pride; she is not usually allowed out alone, after all she's only nine, but there is not a crumb of bread in the entire apartment, and she was awake anyway, and Mama decided that it's time for her to spread her wings, or at least start to unfurl them.

In the Aladdin's cave of browns and golds, with mirrors multiplying her every move, Rosa Klein approaches the counter. The steely-eyed Fräulein in a black-and-white uniform cocks her head curiously, twisting a paper bag in pink, chapped fingers. Rosa smiles politely but no such smile is returned; instead the Fräulein rearranges the Mandeltorte, shuffles the Apfelkuchen and wipes down the surfaces, which are already spotless. Only then does she acknowledge the little girl in the blue felt hat, raising her eyebrows the tiniest of fractions. Rosa smiles understandingly, for the Fräulein is clearly a very busy lady, asks for a dozen Schrippen rolls and presents her Reichsmark note. The Fräulein speaks not a word as she slots the rolls into a bag, places them on the counter and activates an ornate cash register, which rattles, whirrs and produces a single ring. Then suddenly she says, wait a moment, and reaches for her lapel where there glints a small golden pin. A deft movement of her fingers brings it away from the fabric, and she places it on the counter, gesturing for the girl to take it – Rosa, confused, accepts the gift, enacts an awkward bow and makes her way to the door. She heaves it open, the bell chimes again, and a bracing gust of air freshens her face; she responds to the Fräulein's salute by mumbling Heil Hintern, as her big brother Heinrich taught her, then hurries from the Konditorei, clutching the Schrippen, into the wintry watery light.

As she runs home with the Schrippen in her satchel and the lapel pin cold in her palm, and her curls bounce like the hair of a clown from beneath her blue felt hat with the big flower on the side which Papa says butterflies will land on come summer, a shadow passes across Rosa's face. How clean the bakery was, how spotless; it made her feel dirty just for being there, just for breathing, just for having hair, just for being composed of flesh and blood rather than perfect surfaces and pure, moist bread. As for the Fräulein, well she fitted right in, cool as the stainless-steel trays, manipulating the loaves with fingers mercury-cold, her white cap like an ice-cap upon the undulating straw-coloured waves, her apron white and starched and stiff against the creaseless black of her skirt. Yes, that bakery is beginning to seem a little sinister, and so, come to think of it, is the Fräulein, although it isn't so nice to think like that, she should always think the best of everybody, or that's what Mama says at least.

As she turns onto the grand boulevards of Tiergarten and her nose grows pink and chilly, she feels a little confused because the symbol on the pin in her palm has appeared all over Berlin since yesterday. In practically every window it stares, an angry swirl, spinning mechanically in its pure white disc in the centre of a scarlet rectangle, hundreds of them, like wheels in a vast machine, row upon row spinning all along the Tiergarten, even hanging from the lamp-posts, and when she gets home she will want to know the meaning of this! She takes a short cut and is cast into shadow as she veers down an alley, the slopey floor clip-clop-ping its response to her flapping feet; then she emerges once again into the light, arrives breathless at her front door and rings, and rings again, until finally the door is opened by Frau Schulz, and Rosa cries, Schrippen im Anmarsch! Schrippen im Anmarsch! Here comes bread! and hurries up the polished staircase to give it to her mama.

Frau Schulz shivers, rubs her shoulders and shuts the door against the biting Berlin air. Rosa takes off her little coat and flings it over the banisters, and the maid gathers it up for her, following her pattering patent shoes into the spacious, high-ceilinged, high-windowed apart-ment, full of air and light, with a fine fire roaring in the fireplace, and rugs imported from the Orient stretching luxuriantly underfoot, and blond oak panels lining the walls to chest height. The breakfast things are all laid out beautifully, gleaming even, reflected in the mammoth gilt-edged mirror above the fireplace. Rosa hands the rolls to her mama and climbs up onto one of the high-backed chairs with the stripes that she likes, looking intently at Papa, and what she really wants to know is:

—What is the meaning of this?

She holds out her hand, displaying the pin like a golden bullet; but Papa is not paying attention, he is talking to Mama, who is standing with her hands on the back of her chair, rolling her eyes.

—Come on now, Otto, she is saying, come on.

—But it's just not possible, says Papa. The man is a hypocrite. However can he remain in his position as if nothing has happened?

—Ah, stop being so anxious, replies his wife. Wilhelm is nothing but an honest policeman. Politics has nothing to do with his job.

—Of course it does, Inga. The police force is riddled with politics. You saw how they behaved during the riots on the Fasanenstraße. It's a matter of principle.

—Really, Liebling, really. This will not last, that's what everybody is saying, you said so yourself. You shouldn't worry so.

By this time Rosa is sitting on her father's knee, her dress tumbling in a fan over the edge of the seat, tugging at his slippery necktie, and he is benignly swatting her hands away.

—Well at least now we have Schrippen, he says, a morning without Schrippen is almost as bad as a morning without tea.

—I need an entire pot of coffee this morning, says Inga, after last night.

Last night – suddenly Rosa remembers. It had been forgotten along with her dreams, but now it all comes back. Woken by a commotion outside, she got up, straightened her nightdress and padded along the dark-wooded hall into the drawing room. Papa and Mama were standing side by side at the window, their hands clasped behind their backs, gazing down at the Wilhelmstraße, where a flickering ocean of flaming torches could be seen, and marching music and drums could dimly be heard, together with the roar of massed voices. Papa passed his hand over his sleek hair and said: one cannot pretend that this new Reichschancellor is not bad news, but in reality, my dear, he is only a figurehead, he cannot survive very long. At this point he drew the curtains in a strange sort of way, and Mama lit a cigarette; Rosa got a funny feeling behind her knees and crept back to bed, where she burrowed into the blankets and, to the sound of her parents' voices, fell into a fitful sleep.

—Was it a fire last night, Papa? she says.

5

—It was nothing, Püppchen. Your mother and I just stayed up too late, talking.

—Why? says Rosa.

—Because to talk, says her father, is good for the soul.

He lifts Rosa from his knee and places her on a chair.

—There, he says, have one of your Schrippen. Now, has anybody seen Heinrich? It's not like him to miss breakfast.

—I think he came back late last night, Liebling, says Inga. Ah, that boy.

—How late? says Papa. I'll get to the bottom of it when he deigns to make an appearance, that's for sure. And here he is missing the Schrippen. Frau Schulz, the tea please? And a pot of coffee for my wife.

—Hedi, says Inga, come here! Oh, Hedi, please. Be a good girl.

Hedi, being quite good but only two, slips from her chair and toddles off after Frau Schulz on her short plump legs, her little white dress ruffling in all directions like a moving heap of doilies, and Mama strides up behind her and gathers her squealing into her arms and returns her to the breakfast table, pfumpf on her nappy. And Hedi slips down again and makes for the hall again, and Mama, slightly impatient now, gathers her up once again and firmly places her at table, ignoring her yelps and fixing a puff pastry Schillerlocke in her hand.

As Papa reaches for the silver teapot with one hand and smooths his moustache nattily with the other, and the sun falls upon his slicked-back hair, his eye is caught by the glint on Rosa's palm – finally – and he notices what is lying there – finally – and he takes it from her and gets to his feet. Dropping his napkin to the carpet he crosses to the fireplace, holding the pin delicately before him in long, surgeon's fingers.

—Where did you come upon this little thing, Püppchen?

—From the bakery Fräulein.

Her father pauses.

—You must not go back there, he says.

—Why?

—No questions now. Frau Schulz, place the Schrippen in the fire.

—In the fire?

—We have some Schillerlocken, do we not? That will do. And some green herring or something, I don't know. Just bring whatever we have for the moment, yes, Frau Schulz? And hurry please, Rosa needs to go to school.

Frau Schulz, looking somewhat bewildered, gathers up the Schrippen and takes them through to the pantry.

—Don't you think you may be over-reacting, dear? says Inga in a low voice. Rosa did purchase the Schrippen specially, you know.

Klein turns to Rosa, sees her anxious expression.

—Püppchen, next time you see such a Hakenkreuz, close your eyes and have nothing to do with it, do you hear?

—Yes, Papa. But what does it mean?

—Sit up straight, Püppchen. No questions now.

Well, all this seems like madness to Frau Schulz, but then this type of madness has become commonplace in the household of late. First it was the newspapers: Herr Klein instructed her to cancel his beloved subscriptions, every one, saying the papers contained nothing but nonsense cover to cover, and she said, are you sure, even the *Berliner Tageblatt*, and he snapped at her, yes, Frau Schulz, I am quite sure. It was unfathomable – to think of it, Herr Klein without his newspapers! More curious still, he ordered her to set up a subscription with the *Jüdische Rundschau*, even though he cannot stand that newspaper, he had been saying so for years. He is losing his mind, in Frau Schulz's opinion. How about last week: she was walking down the hall towards the kitchen late at night, getting a drink of water, when she heard a strange noise from the drawing room, so naturally she went to investigate. The door was ajar, she put her head round it and who did she spy but Herr Klein, alone, hunched over on the floor, shirt all untucked and with no collar on even, a cigarette clamped between his teeth, a screwdriver in his hand, dismantling the wireless, yes, dismantling the wireless! And burning the walnut casing in the fire. Very methodically and everything, in his surgeon's manner, but there was something frightening about it, breaking up the wireless, now what will she have to listen to in the long evenings when the children are in bed and Herr Klein and his wife are at the theatre? She has never been one for books, and these days everyone should have a wireless, should they not? Then Herr Klein looked sharply up from the screws and walnut panels on the floor and saw her, he looked as if he was going to scold her, but he said, Frau Schulz, dispose of this dreckige Goebbels' Schnauze, would you please? And, ignoring her alarm, he strode past her and slammed the door to his study, to work on his book no doubt, he is obsessed by that book at the moment, and the smell of cologne and cigarette smoke hung in the air, and more than a little Schnaps, as well as a positively poisonous feeling. What language, she thought to herself, dirty Goebbels' gob indeed, not the kind of phrase that she was accustomed to from Herr Klein, but

7

what was she to do? So she cleared up the remaining bits of her poor precious wireless and went directly to bed.

Frau Schulz: she has been working for the Kleins for several years now, with her starched apron that never stains and her widely spaced grey eyes. She is, Otto Klein felt at first, too angular to be a maid, maids should be softer, more homely, and Frau Schulz is not soft or homely in the slightest, but she is extremely competent, she runs the house like clockwork. Yes, the only thing that stands between Frau Schulz and the Aryan ideal is her chestnut hair, several shades away from blonde, which she wears in a propeller bow, black for weekdays, white for weekends; she is a woman whose attractiveness is eclipsed by her preoccupation with getting things done. Yet that is a good quality in a maid, in Klein's opinion, you don't want one who gets above her station. Often when he visits his colleagues to play a rubber of bridge and is exposed to the sorts of maids that some people are forced to put up with, he thanks his lucky stars for Frau Schulz.

The children like her too, particularly Rosa, who is terribly fond of the maid, which at times seems to bother her mother, who appears to feel a little dethroned, shall we say, but in Klein's opinion there is nothing to worry about: better a maid she loves than a maid she loathes! And Inga, reluctantly, tends to concede at this point, in the face of such irrefutable male logic. But there is enough to think about at the moment without worrying about maids and servants, there is an overwhelming quantity of work at the hospital, and several colleagues are now card-carrying members of the Party – the expressions they wear in the corridors, it is practically laughable – no, it doesn't help, this political madness that is blighting the proud face of the nation, the sooner it passes the better. But where on earth is Heinrich?

Heinrich is, somewhat guiltily, allowing himself to wonder what it would be like to kiss Frau Schulz. Lying in bed, he calls through the door, I will be there directly, just give me a moment. These illicit thoughts make him feel rather schmutzig, but he can't help but wonder what her mouth would feel like upon his own, ach, it makes him feel sick to consider it, incestuous almost, kissing the maid Frau Schulz. Yet at once somehow attractive. Then again the fantasy collapses in the face of reality, for when he lays eyes upon her he realises that he would not like to kiss her in real life, not at all, with her dry lips and unnerving stare. It was Klaus who put these ideas into his head, he is always talking about her, in fact he is obsessed, the only reason he comes to visit is to stare at Frau Schulz as she comes in and out with tea, his mouth slightly ajar like a lizard. Heinrich can still recall the expression on his face when she dropped a spoon and bent over to retrieve it – his eyes bulged like eggs and he gulped visibly, it was funny, of course – ach, to hell with Klaus after last night, the coward, and now Heinrich has a splitting headache to show for it, and there is blood on the pillow, and he does not know how to explain it to his parents.

—Goodness gracious, Heinrich, what on earth happened to you? says Inga, alarmed.

—It's nothing, Mutter, just a graze. I took a tumble playing handball and—

—Where were you last night? says Klein. You came in awfully late. You gave your mother and me cause for concern.

—I was just visiting Klaus, Vater . . .

—Fighting again, says Klein.

—Of course not, Vater. Just playing handball. Are there no Schrippen this morning?

—No, this morning there are Schillerlocken. You won, of course.

—I did my best.

—Liebling, you should not encourage him, says Inga.

—I was referring to the handball, says Klein.

—Ah, says Inga, come on.

Klein glances at the grandfather clock and gets to his feet, taking a final gulp of tea.

—I must go, he says, time waits for no man. I will be a little late this evening, dear, I am meeting the publisher from the Jüdische Verlag, I have to submit to him the manuscript. Those green herrings were perfect this morning, Frau Schulz. Goodbye everyone, goodbye.

—Can you teach me to ride my bicycle after school, Papa? says Rosa, and Papa promises that he will and leaves the room. Already his thoughts are with his work, and it is a relief when, after a smooth journey, he arrives a few kilometres north, in the district of Wedding, where his beloved Rudolf-Virchow Hospital is located.

2

This week Klein has an extremely full schedule; there are several patients still in the hospital whom he operated on last week, and more operations scheduled over the coming days. And he senses that his position is increasingly under pressure; he must fight to keep his job, prove himself, demonstrate that he is first and foremost a German and a doctor and an accomplished surgeon, and not Jewish in the sense that the Ostjuden are Jewish, indeed, far from it, far from it.

On a normal day his first task would be to complete a round of his patients in the wards, striding with squeaking soles over the shiny green floors, stethoscope bobbing, pausing to read a chart, or take a pulse, or enquire after a particular patient's bowel movements overnight. This is his favourite part of the job, at these times he recalls just why he trained as a doctor – the patients rely on him, and he is confident of his ability to help, and this puts a power in his voice, a certainty in his stride, and as he strokes his fingers across his natty moustache and peers at them with his sharp, clever eyes, their poor heads sunken in the pillows like potatoes, he can see that his mere presence is bringing comfort. His patients have become accustomed to these morning rounds; it brings stability to their day knowing that their doctor will be there every morning with his imposing gait, cheery belly-laughs, fingertip knowledge. But this morning, as he enters the wards, they are being visited already by a younger doctor with circular wire-rimmed spectacles and a wave of blond hair swept back across his head. Klein approaches and politely enquires what is happening here – the man introduces himself as Dr Möller, informs Klein that the head physician, the Chefarzt, wishes to see him and turns his back.

Unnerved, Klein makes his way to the head physician's office, takes a seat in the uncomfortable wooden chair and waits nervously, telling himself that he has nothing to hide; and then the Chefarzt himself enters, does not offer him a drink, does not enquire after his family, sits down and begins his speech: in the hospital we are attempting to create an Aryan atmosphere, but you are not being sacked of course, after all you saw action as a Frontkämpfer during the war, we are just changing your position in the hospital, for the good of the patients you understand, who will be best treated by a Volksgenosse, a national comrade, and at all times the well-being of the patients must be foremost in our minds. The sun pricks on the Chefarzt's lapel, on a small golden Hakenkreuz pin; he never used to wear it, or not in Klein's presence at least. The Chefarzt, reiterating his point, says that sadly Klein is ein Deutscher aber ein Jude. Klein nods, mouth opening and closing drily, and, most uncharacteristically, cannot think of a thing to say. He clears his throat once or twice and strokes his moustache, trying to muster his sense of authority, trying to get his bearings; but still no words come, so he backs out of the office and closes the door behind him.

As he makes his squeaking way back to his own office, trembling and pale, he is aware of Dr Möller's upright figure striding towards him, white coat whipping against the metal legs of the beds, clipboard perched jauntily against his hip, his circular lenses white in the light, and the two men ignore one another, icily; Klein, his moustache bristling, holds his head higher as Dr Möller's stony visage glides past his ear like a ship. Then he is back in the privacy of his office – he shuts the door heavily and stands there for a moment clenching his hands to his temples. Suddenly, with rapid movements, he crosses to his desk and pulls out one of the drawers. It shoots from its socket and tumbles onto the floor, spilling neatly piled papers and stationery across the carpet. He kicks the papers into the air, falls to his knees, picks up a handful of pencils and begins to break them into halves, and quarters, and eighths, it doesn't take long before not a single pencil remains intact. Then he sweeps the debris back into the drawer, crams the papers into the wastepaper basket, pours himself a shot of Schnaps and throws it down his throat; finally he collapses into his chair and gazes at the ceiling, massaging his forehead. Gradually his agitation settles and he tries to marshal his thoughts. This is not something that he cannot endure. He did not survive the war, battle to the very pinnacle of his profession, just to be discouraged by the prevailing idiocy of the times. He will lie low, bide his time until it passes. He gets to his feet, removes his white coat and hangs it on the peg, loops his stethoscope into a ball and pushes it into the pocket. Then he sits at his desk again, spreading his long fingers on the green-topped surface and staring at them in silence, his white coat hanging on the back of the door like a ghost. From the window, street sounds break the quietude: motorcars backfiring, trams jolting, shouts, laughs, barks, conversations, snatches of music, and if Klein were to get to his feet and look out of the window he would behold Hakenkreuz after Hakenkreuz, as far as the eye can see. But he does not; he remains sitting at his desk in silence, staring at his hands. Somebody has put a pile of paperwork, three fists in height, on the desk of the obliging Herr Doktor Klein, who will have lots of spare time now that his schedule has been cleared of patients. And of course, your salary will be altered in line with your new position, it is only a token alteration, a small reduction, you do understand, Herr Klein, we must keep in mind at all times that this is for the good of the hospital, for the good of the patients, and the well-being of our patients should be our foremost concern, should it not?

There is an urgent knock at the door and Klein calls his permission to enter; a white-coated figure rushes in and closes the door hastily behind him.

—Herr Doktor Klein. May I have a word?

—Of course, Doktor Fehr, take a seat.

—I see you are not wearing your white coat and stethoscope?

—It seems there is no need at the moment.

—They have taken your patients away?

—For the moment, yes.

—Me too.

Oskar Fehr removes his spectacles and places a thumb and finger on his eyelids. He is a senior doctor, an ophthalmologist, a surgeon even, not as accomplished as Herr Doktor Otto Klein but distinguished none the less; normally he is industrious of activity, deliberate of movement and intense of disposition, yet this morning he is in a state of distress.

—Because of our racial origin, he says, a little pointlessly.

—I would suppose so, Klein replies.

—This can't do. This can't do. These are our careers, Doktor Klein. We are Germans. They have cut your pay?

—A little.

—Me too. Those Hurensöhne.

—Doktor Fehr, calm yourself. You still have your private practice. Would you like a glass of Schnaps?

—Not for me. I cannot drink in the morning, you know that. Yes, my private practice, I still have that. Would you care to join me for lunch, Herr Doktor?

—Yes, that would be grand. Shall we say half past twelve?

—I have a mountain of paperwork to do. An absolute mountain. Do you think this state of affairs will be permanent? My wife is talking of emigration.

—Doktor Fehr, it will not do to panic. I'm sure this madness will blow over. Haven't you read Artur Landsberger? Almost fifty per cent of doctors in Berlin are of Jewish origin. They can't do without us.

—Yes, yes, of course, you're absolutely correct. I suppose this represents the worst of it.

—Let's hope so, says Klein, smoothing his collar.

—It's not unbearable, of course, says Fehr. It's just the humiliation of it. Such a humiliation.

—Just focus on the bigger picture, replies Klein. This will all be over before long.

—Yes, you are absolutely correct. Very well. I shall make a start on that paperwork.

—That sounds like a good idea.

—Goodbye, Doktor Klein.

—See you at lunch time.

The door closes smartly, Fehr's footsteps squeak away and all is still once more. That's the habit of an officer, thinks Klein, to keep a level head and inspire others with confidence, regardless of the fact that one may be falling apart oneself.

3

As Rosa sits in her classroom next to her best friend Frieda Fischer, the teacher's voice washing around her, she thinks about how she went out this morning, by herself, for the first time, reliving each detail proudly. Usually she goes with Mama to buy the groceries, and when it comes to buying bread Mama prefers to shop not in the upmarket Konditorei, but in the Jewish quarter, the Scheunenviertel, which is some distance from their apartment, but Mama says it is worth the journey to support the impoverished Ostjuden. Not that Mama cares about God as such, pfui, she is an atheist, and Rosa has heard her declare it many times to anyone who will listen, and even some who won't, that is the sort of person Mama is; as she always says, I am someone who is more impressed by Goethe than by God, more enamoured of Bildung than of the Bible, more Mozart than Moses, and always will be. Nevertheless she wishes to support the Jews in some small way, even the Ostjuden, who, with their hunched backs and their papery skin, and their inability to understand proper German Hochdeutsch, appear like people from another age, different from the respectable reformist types who frequent the Spandauer Viertel.

But Rosa loves the Scheunenviertel. She loves wandering through the teeming streets with that strange mix of feelings, carrying her little shopping basket daintily by her side, holding Mama's hand, placing one square heel clip-clop in front of the other; and she always feels inexplicably warm, as in the thermal springs in Wiesbaden where the family spend their Christmases, only the Scheunenviertel warmth comes from a geyser hidden deep within.

Now Rosa is no longer in the classroom, she is in the Scheunenviertel, holding Mama's hand, tingling as she gazes up at the ribbed golden dome of the Neue Synagogue, resplendent against the blue ribbons of sky, looking more like a sultan's palace than a Jewish house of worship, whose three thousand seats are all filled, every one of them, on the High Holy Days; Mama says that she set foot inside the synagogue once herself, though not for religious reasons, no, she was attending a benefit concert for the Youth and Welfare Office, for Mama is an opera enthusiast as well as an atheist; Hermann Jadlowker, the renowned Kammersänger, was performing, supported by Albert Einstein on first violin. Mama has long been a fan of Einstein, both his physics and his music, and of course his dashing hangdog eyes, those deep sorcerer's orbs that gave a racing pulse to every woman in Europe, before, that is, he emigrated to America.

So Rosa and Mama, walking on, pass the Rabbiner-Seminar on the Artilleriestraße, where the black-hatted orthodox rabbis, behind closed doors, learn and debate and sing and dance in great chaotic rings, you can hear them, glimpse them through the windows; and on the Große Hamburger Straße they pass the Jewish schools, busy with fresh-faced, red-cheeked young boys and girls learning Hebrew and Bible studies and German and mathematics; and they pass the Israelite Hospital on the Elsässer Straße, where everything is run in accordance with Talmudic law, and smells of chemicals that make you feel a little faint; and finally the Alter Jüdischer Friedhof, with its sombre, dignified rows of gravestones, some newer, some older, some overgrown, some with dates as ancient as 1672. Rosa knows how to find the grave of Herr Mendelssohn, Papa takes her to see it once in a while, deep in the farthest corner of the ceme-tery, all overgrown with ivy, you have to pull the leaves away to see the name, barely visible, there it is – Moses Mendelssohn – all the more mysterious as the slab has, through the ages, been all but worn away. They place pebbles on the grave, according to tradition, and back away in silence. Papa knows the location of this gravestone because he knows everything, because he is a Frontkämpfer, and has been awarded medals, has an Iron Cross 2nd Klasse, and he fought at Arras in 1917, and lived to tell the tale, lived to show his daughter this most remarkable grave, and she, in time, will show it to her own children, or that's what Papa says at least; and she would be able to find the grave now all by herself, if she wanted to, probably, only she wouldn't, because it's ghostly there in the Friedhof.

Frieda Fischer nudges Rosa – the eyes of the class are upon her, and Klara Neumann is openly smirking. Falteringly Rosa tries to decipher the equation on the blackboard, kicking herself for having been lost in such an elaborate daydream. After a slight pause, however, she is able to answer the teacher's question correctly. The snickering dies down, the lesson drones on, and outside the window a flock of sparrows whirls in the sky like poppy seeds. She must be sure not to lose her concentration, her marks in mathematics have been good, only she has to try harder than other people because she is not good at mathematics naturally, as Heinrich is, maybe she can get him to help with her homework again this evening, if he's not at handball practice. She can't wait for school to finish, to go home and ride her bicycle with Papa; perhaps she will manage to ride by herself tonight, without Papa holding her! Then she will cycle to school in the morning and home again in the evening, she will be the only one in the class to have a bicycle, and everyone will want to have a turn, the whole class, the whole school even, and then we will see what Klara Neumann has to say, whether she asks to ride it too or sits in the playground alone.

Rosa turns from the window and looks across the classroom at Klara Neumann, who catches her eye, and for once the other girl is the first to look away. Already Rosa is feeling empowered by the bicycle nestling under its sheet at home in the stairwell, a trusty steed awaiting the return of its mistress. Yes, Klara, she may be eine Jüdin but she is the one with a bicycle. Rosa turns the page of her textbook and furrows her brow, enough daydreaming, she must concentrate or she will get into trouble, yet a shimmering excitement is building in her tummy, and she simply can't wait to get home.

4

The sun climbs in the sky above Berlin, masked by a white blanket of cloud. Sizzling incandescent lamps gleam in hundreds of polished shop windows where wax figures pose in suits, overcoats, skirts, shoes. A blotchy-aproned man wearing a leather hood strides across the pavement, a yellowing carcass moist and heavy on his shoulder, heading for a butcher's red shop. A postman crouches at a bright blue postbox, positions his sack and pulls the lever, netting a cascade of letters. A tram takes a curve a little too fast – the bright-buttoned conductor leans out over the stern and jiggles a cord until the pole is back on the overhead wire. A white-capped baker's boy glides by on a tricycle, dusted with flour like an angel; a woman in a fur coat waits to cross the road, cradling a dog in her arms.

In one of the Konditoreien on the Alexanderplatz sits Inga Klein, opposite her old friend Berta Krützfeld. The tea scalds Inga's tongue but she doesn't show it, instead she replaces the cup upon the saucer and smiles across the table at Berta, reproaching herself inwardly for being so stupid as to take a sip of tea immediately after it was poured. They are sitting in window seats, enjoying some light refreshments before the matinée performance at the Volksbühne. Inga takes a bite of Dobostorte to muffle the sting of the burn on her tongue and gazes out at the teeming crowd of grey-trilbied men, fur-muffled women, peacock policemen and surly street vendors, all pink-faced and hunched against the cold. But inside it is warm. Light piano music bubbles in the background like an Alpine brook, mingling with the clink and chink of porcelain and the polite joviality of conversation. Inga's eyes focus on her friend across the table. Berta is wearing a darling lilac hat, and Inga is mildly jealous; as if reading her mind, Berta removes the hat and places it on the chair beside her, ah, just look at the way she is eating that Dobostorte, I don't know how Inga can possibly maintain her figure.

—What a lovely brooch you are wearing, Inga. Is that emerald?

—It is, yes. It was a birthday present from Otto.

—Oh, he is a dear, is he not? says Berta, taking a sip of tea. And how are the children?

—Yes, all right. How are Walter and Artur?

—Both fine. Inga, you seem somewhat distracted. Are you ill?

A narrow red rectangle is visible at the top of the Konditorei window, rippling in the wind outside. Berta places her cigarette holder between her painted lips and blows a thin line of smoke towards the ceiling. Inga takes a sip of tea and studies the steam as it curls soothingly upwards; then she too lights a cigarette.

—I am a little worried about Heinrich, she says. He returned awfully late last night, with a graze on his forehead. He has been getting into fights.

—How old is he now? Ten? Eleven?

—Pfui, Berta! He is thirteen, you know that.

—Ah yes, of course. How time flies. So. It is completely normal for boys of his age to have fights from time to time, is it not? says Berta, philosophically.

—Yes. Yes, of course. I don't know. It's just . . . it must be difficult for him at school.

—Why?

—With our racial background.

—Yes, of course. I can understand that, but don't go blowing it out of proportion, says Berta. The main thing is that he does well in his studies and becomes a fine, upstanding gentleman.

—I agree, says Inga. I know it's silly but I am afraid.

—Have you considered sending him to one of those Jewish schools? suggests Berta. I think there is one on the Große Hamburger Straße, or somewhere in Mitte . . .

—I don't think so, Inga replies. The quality of the education will surely not be as fine as in his present school. And he is becoming quite a sportsman. I suspect that Jewish schools may neglect physical education.

—I don't see why that would be the case. I think it might be worth looking into. After all, you said yourself that he is not comfortable at the moment.

—It's not that, it's just . . . but I am making a problem out of nothing, says Inga, passing her hand across her brow. It must be almost time for our play, is it not?

—Indeed, says Berta. Let's go. I cannot eat the rest of this Dobostorte. It tastes like leather, you know, she says, replacing the last crumb of cake daintily on her plate. Nothing can compare, Inga, to your homemade Dobostorte. Your cook is so very talented.

—Why don't you and Wilhelm come over for dinner one evening? says Inga. Otto hasn't seen you for a while. I shall have Cook prepare you as much Dobostorte as you can eat. Are you available tomorrow?

—I'm sorry, we have another engagement tomorrow. Now, we're running late, says Berta hastily. Let's head for the Volksbühne.

—Very well. Shall we say Thursday?

—Come along, we'll miss the play, says Berta again. We still need to travel all the way to the Horst-Wessel-Platz.

—Don't you mean the Bülowplatz?

—Yes, yes. The Chancellor has renamed it.

—Well it is the Bülowplatz to me, says Inga sharply. Now where is that Fräulein? We haven't paid yet.

—Oh goodness, I completely forgot.

Inga stubs her cigarette out in an ashtray, raising her hand and craning her neck to catch the attention of the Fräulein.

—Heavens, where has she got to? she says, irritably. So then, Thursday evening is convenient for you? I will instruct Frau Schulz upon my return, and . . .

—Inga. Please. Let me be honest with you. It is very kind, but . . . I must decline. We can't come over to visit you for a few months or so, says Berta. Until things have died down.

—Why ever not? says Inga.

—Please don't take it personally, my dear. It's Wilhelm's job, you see. With this new chancellor and the political climate, it is just not possible for high-ranking police officers to socialise with Jews.

—Even Jews with whom you happen to be old friends?

—Especially with Jews with whom we happen to be old friends.

—I see.

—I am sorry.

—Of course.

—Now don't be like that, says Berta breezily. These are not our rules, you understand. First and foremost you are my best friend, and neither Wilhelm nor I give two hoots about the odd Jewish relative here or there.

—Come now, Berta.

—Oh, Inga, you're not *that* Jewish. Look, what I'm trying to say is that we're friends and that's what matters, even if you happen not to have completely Aryan racial origins. But you must appreciate: we must act pragmatically in times like these. Only last year Wilhelm celebrated his twenty-fifth year in the police. He's got a very high profile these days. His position would be in jeopardy.

—And he still wishes to maintain his position, asks Inga, recalling her discussion with Otto over breakfast, given the current political climate?

—What other job could he possibly do, after twenty-five years? says Berta. Come now, Inga. Wilhelm is a servant of the law, that's all. If he were to resign, he would surely be replaced by a Nazi. Better for a compassionate man like Wilhelm to command the police for the Jewish locality than some boorish sausage-eating Nazi. Wouldn't you say?

—Of course, says Inga weakly. It's just a shame, that's all. I never thought politics would drive a wedge between us.

—Oh really, says Berta, it's hardly a wedge. We can still see each other, yes? We can go to the theatre and go shopping and go for strolls in the Tiergarten as we always do. Wilhelm can be a boring old goat anyway, especially on social occasions. We can have more fun by ourselves, girls together. Now let me pay the bill and let's go to the theatre and say no more about it. Fräulein? Fräulein!

As Inga pulls on her gloves, hugs her mink collar high against her cheekbones and steps onto the hard pavement of the Alexanderplatz, her mind wanders, and turns to dark things. Snap out of it, Inga, you are letting your silly imagination run away with you, just look at Berta's lovely lilac hat, and the play will certainly be fabulous. We are fighters, Otto and I, no strangers to hard knocks. We have been through difficult times, ten years ago I was selling socks and jumpers to make ends meet, but now I have three healthy children and a wonderful home, and we have food in our bellies and money in the bank, and this bitter winter will give way to spring soon enough.

5

The Tiergarten is all but deserted. Klein's favourite gold wristwatch glints greenish yellow in the glow from the lamps which are embedded in the elms that line the park; he raises it, checks the time, curses breathlessly to himself as he jogs along. It is unbearably cold and gloomy out here, but Klein is a man who understands the importance of keeping promises to one's children. Rosa's bicycle is big for her, but he reassures her that this is a good thing, it means it will be of use for many years to come, and mein Gott it certainly cost enough; it is a solid German bicycle, stocky, heavy, black in colour, its tyres plump and deeply grooved, brakes on the front as well as the back, three gears to choose from and the air of a proper work-horse. Rosa looks somewhat incongruous atop the machine, gripping tightly the ridged handlebars as Klein steadies the beast by holding the saddle springs, jogging along in his rakish spats, looking for the right time to let go; Rosa is a flash of colour, a jockey on a powerful thoroughbred, clad in her favourite polka dot frock that sweeps out in two arcs on either side of the crossbar and billows in the air behind; and from Rosa's collar peeps a crumpled piece of newspaper, which was Klein's idea; he is of the opinion that a layer of newspaper against the skin offers a great amount of insulation to the wearer, even if it is rather crackly and leaves a mirror image of the headlines across the body once removed; so long as you spread the newspaper over your whole chest before putting on your outer garments, you are guaranteed not to catch any form of cold, guaranteed. Even so, Klein was not happy about Rosa removing her coat given the temperature, but his daughter absolutely insisted, claimed she couldn't ride the bicycle properly with her coat on, and the exercise would keep her warm, and it's not really that cold anyhow, and she is wearing a great deal of newspaper, and please Papa please, and Klein beseeched her to be sensible, she would catch her death of cold, and in the end they arrived at a compromise: so her coat is off, hanging over Klein's arm as he hurries after the bicycle like a beggar, but her blue felt hat, scarf and mittens are still firmly on – Klein, strict as he is with Heinrich, always finds himself compromising with his Püppchen whenever she asserts herself. And Rosa is secretly glad of the mittens at least, for she can feel the chill on her knuckles even through the weave of the wool.

—Don't let go, Papa, I think I almost have it, but don't let go, I will crash if you do; shall I go between the trees or around them? Papa? Papa?

Rosa takes her eyes from the path before her and glances over her shoulder to see her papa shrinking in the distance, and she screams a scream of excitement, she is riding all by herself, and she must have been for some time because Papa is far away, so now she must focus, the rotation of the pedals is powering her along, and how will she stop if she needs to stop, that is the question, she doesn't think she can stop, so focus, keep upright as Papa told her, and make sure she doesn't hit a tree, and she is really riding, all by herself, but she needs the lavatory.

She picks up pace down the hill, blown by the icy wind, the sensation is stunning, being in control of your direction, your destiny, with the power of speed beneath you, exhilarating; suddenly she loses control, can no longer direct the heavy hurtling machine, has to hold on tight and hope for the best, and then the bicycle slows and she is master once more, and she pedals again to see how fast it will go, and then loses control again, closes her eyes tight until the speed falls away; she tilts her body to the side and the bicycle curves to the left, sailing like a ship. Now she can see her father again, standing under the incandescent lamp lighting a cigarette, watch me Papa, watch me; she pedals harder to reach him and hopes that he will be able to stop the bicycle when she arrives, because she jolly well can't stop and if Papa wasn't there she would be sitting atop the bicycle all night, all day, doing figure-of-eights, infinity signs, forever.

Klein sucks on his cigarette and pulls his scarf tighter, watching his daughter gliding around the park like a bird of paradise. He is feeling rather more Jewish than usual today, he reflects. Ever since the conversation with the Chefarzt he has been feeling like a lowly Betteljude, as if he should be speaking only Judendeutsch, dressing all in black and eating nothing but boiled fish. So he has formulated a speech which he will have on hand to deliver to the Chefarzt as soon as the opportunity presents itself: Herr Hoffmann, can you point to a single instance in my career when my professional conduct has been anything less than impeccable? As you rightly assert, we must consider the well-being of the patients first and foremost; and, I can assure you, cardiac patients would rather be treated by a renowned, experienced surgeon, albeit of Semitic origin, than by a more junior doctor of Aryan descent. That is what he may say, given the opportunity. He was too dumbfounded to articulate his reaction earlier, but he will not let that happen again.

Klein's day was spent on paperwork, which was intensely frustrating, but after work he was cheered by his meeting with the publisher – what an honour to contribute to his book, indeed, what an honour to be included in it! For several weeks, late into the night, Klein has been working on his entries for Siegmund Kaznelson's project, a vast, meticulously detailed encyclopaedia of prominent German Jews and their achievements over the past two centuries, entitled *The Jews in German Culture*; Klein has been requested to compile the medical component of the book, and to this task he has applied himself wholeheartedly, with great energy and dedication. He took particular care over composing his own entry, reworking line by line, word by word, oscillating between bashfulness and self-aggrandisement until he settled upon: *Dr Dr Otto Klein (1896–), surgeon and physician of Berlin, awarded the Iron Cross 2nd Klasse for bravery at Arras in April 1917, holder of a doctorate in medicine and another in chemistry. For the latter he studied in Munich under the Nobel Prize winner Richard Willstätter, author of the introduction to this volume.* Yes, the blend of bald fact and modesty reads very well, thinks Klein to himself, and it was good to mention the Iron Cross; he counted the number of words in Willstätter's own entry, deducted five and took that for his own quota; this, he felt, displayed a certain humility, as everyone is aware of the long-standing feud between them, and even today Klein loathes his old mentor, the way he pontificates about plant pigments and chemical enzymes through his ostentatious bushy moustache; but at times like these, Klein understands, friends are more valuable than enemies, particularly the great and the good, and particularly when they live in Switzerland, as does Willstätter, who emigrated in protest against Germany's treatment of her Jews.

Rosa wobbles a little and rights herself, and Klein calls out to her some advice: practise using the brakes! Left for front, right for back, and never use the left one alone! There, she is getting the hang of it.

When they met earlier that evening, the publisher Kaznelson was scruffier than Klein remembered. His wiry dark hair was dishevelled, there was a shimmer of bristles upon his chin and he was smoking incessantly. Klein had been looking forward to their appointment, after a day like today a good old chat with a well-educated man about Kultur would be a welcome panacea for this dreckige Betteljude who has spent the day tarnishing the hospital with his unwanted presence. They met in a cramped beer shop on the Rosenthaler Straße near Wertheim's department store, just down from Fabish & Co – a far cry from the Romanisches Café, but conveniently located for both of them. Together they sipped light beer from glass mugs, and Klein snacked on a small plate of meat – Kaznelson declined, being subject to the kosher code – and they conversed for an hour or so, overshadowed by a sky-blue 'Löwenbräu' sign with the winking lion and tankard of beer, puffing on Kaznelson's flat, gold-tipped, Egyptian cigarettes. Kaznelson displayed a publisher's passion for his new book, said it was taking shape very nicely indeed, this encyclopaedia of prominent Jews is just what is needed to combat worrying trends; Klein responded by pointing out that this very beer shop was near the site of the ancient Rosenthaler Gate, through which Moses Mendelssohn entered Berlin in 1743, subject to a Jewish tax at the rate of Polish cattle, yet in a few short years he had become the most respected intellectual in the country. So the two men traded ideas for a while, the conversation drifting towards the subject of the avant-garde, the beer lightening their heads.

And when they bade one another farewell Kaznelson shook Klein warmly by the hand and disappeared down the narrow Sophienstraße, Klein's manuscript stuffed under his greatcoat, turning his head away from the graffiti scrawled on the wall; and Klein looked left and right and sneaked back into the beer shop for a swift glass of cognac before remembering Rosa's bicycle lesson and, rubbery-legged, catching the tram home.

6

—Frau Schulz, that was the doorbell. I shall take over with Hedi. Thank you.

As the sound of the doorbell fades and Frau Schulz goes to open it, Inga finishes fixing the safety pin in Hedi's nappy, pulls her little dress straight and sets her upright. With a squeal of delight, Hedi immediately makes a run for the hall. Inga gets up wearily, scoops up her daughter and places her amongst her toys; with a burble Hedi gets to her feet and totters towards the hall again. Inga sits her down amongst the toys once more and waves Gigi in the air. The doll catches Hedi's attention and she makes a clumsy grab for the big china head, and the distraction tactic has worked again, for the moment.

The windows are rectangles of black in the warm yellow light. Inga stretches to ease the stiffness in her back, draws the curtains and glances at her watch. The days are certainly showing no sign of lengthening, she thinks, and already she feels as if it has been winter for ever. She crosses to the fireplace and stokes it gingerly with the poker; this is the servants' job, stoking the fire, look, now she has soot on her hands. The matinee was not a performance of exceptional quality and she spent most of the play reeling from the revelation that Wilhelm and Berta Krützfeld no longer think it fit to set foot inside the abode of Otto and Inga Klein, who are now classified as artfremd – inappropriate – on account of their racial origin. But now she is thinking of it again, and she had promised herself not to do so; truly it will do not a bit of good to dwell on it any longer.

—Madame?

—Frau Schulz?

—There is a Frau Werner waiting for Madame in the drawing room.

—Frau who did you say?

—Frau Werner, madame.

—I am acquainted with a Frau Werner?

—Her son Rudi is a classmate of Heinrich, madame.

—Very well. Please sit here with Hedi and I shall come at once. Ensure she does not become over-exuberant again, remember how long it took you to calm her last time.

—Very good, madame.

Inga crosses to the gilt-edged mirror and adjusts her hair, then pinches her cheeks and smooths her collar. She draws herself up, aligning her posture, then lights a cigarette and walks deliberately through to the drawing room. As she passes the grandfather clock it chimes the hour, giving her a slight fright, what is wrong with her this evening; and as the sound of the hour fades she pushes open the heavy door and enters. In the centre of the rug stands a tall, well-dressed woman with wispy hair and very pale skin, still wearing a pair of leather gloves. On her lapel glints a little golden pin, and Inga's heart quickens. Beside her slouches a plump lad of Heinrich's age, with an unruly shock of ginger hair, staring glumly at the carpet. The boy is flushed and nervous, and the chandelier above throws a dappled light upon them.

—Ah, you must be Frau Klein.

—Frau Werner, I take it?

—Indeed, and my son Rudi. A pleasure to make your acquaintance, and my apologies for appearing at such a very late hour.

—Please, the clock has only just struck eight. Ah yes, I remember you from parents' evening. Can I offer you a cigarette? Some soda water? Cognac perhaps?

—A little soda water would be fine.

—And for you, Rudi?

—Rudi will not drink anything, thank you, Frau Klein.

—Very well.

Inga spurts some water from the siphon into a glass and hands it to her uninvited guest. As she does so, she glances at the woman's lapel pin: a little brooch in the shape of a rose. Relieved but not completely at ease, Inga twists her lighted cigarette into a holder and holds it at a sophisticated angle.

—Please, take a seat, she says.

—We were hoping to address both you and your son together. Would this be possible?

—I should think so, Frau Werner. If you'll excuse me, I will see if he is available to join us.

—Thank you.

Inga once again enters the hall. She can hear the soft sound of Frau Schulz singing to Hedi and feels a twinge of jealousy; she passes the grandfather clock and makes her way to her son's bedroom, experiencing more than a measure of confusion. How odd for this lady to appear at this time of night, and what on earth could she want with Heinrich? The door opens and her son emerges, a pencil between his teeth and smudges beneath his eyes, his hair standing on end, the scabbed graze on his forehead exposed; at his mother's request he smooths his hair, puts on his jacket, tidies his shirt and accompanies her into the drawing room where he stands stiff as a board upon beholding the figures before him.

—Ah, Heinrich, says Frau Werner. I have brought my son here in order to make a statement to you. Rudi?

—I apologise for calling you . . .

—Stand up straight, Rudi.

—Calling you names and chasing you and fighting you yesterday. It was inexcusable and I ask . . .

—Look him in the eye, Rudi.

—And I ask . . .

—Louder, Rudi.

—And I ask for your forgiveness.

—Come now, Frau Werner, says Inga, surely it takes two to fight.

—I am not to blame, Mutter, says Heinrich.

—Heinrich!

—He is right, Frau Klein, says Frau Werner, your son is innocent. Rudi is a good boy but he has been influenced by some unsavoury elements at school and thought it would be amusing to taunt the class Jew. Such cruelty is inexcusable. What say you, Heinrich? Are you able to forgive and forget?

—Ach, very well.

—Now shake hands and put it all behind you.

Heinrich clasps the boy's hand. Rudi's face has flushed as red as his hair, yet his eyes are inscrutable; Heinrich's skin creeps and he withdraws his hand sharply; Rudi scratches his nose and returns to his mother.

—Now, Heinrich, go and continue with your homework, says Inga.

Frau Werner finishes her soda water and gets to her feet.

—Does Heinrich suffer much of this sort of abuse? she asks in a low voice.

—I . . . I am not sure, replies Inga, he rarely speaks of it.

—Perhaps you should consider moving him to a Jewish school. I hear that some of them are really rather good.

—Yes, the idea had occurred to me.

—I will not go to a Jewish school! comes Heinrich's voice from the hall.

—Pfui, Heinrich, I told you to continue with your homework.

—I am not going to a Jewish school, says Heinrich, and I don't want to be Jewish and I don't care about Rudi and his friends and if they come near me again I will murder them.

—Now stop that at once, Heinrich. Come back here, Heinrich. Heinrich!

—I think it is time we left for home, says Frau Werner hastily.

Inga shakes hands, pauses, wrings her hands, makes her way smartly down the hall and knocks on Heinrich's bedroom door. There is no response. She calls his name repeatedly, then tries the handle; the door opens easily, Heinrich's desk lamp shines on pages of mathematical calculations, his chair is lying on the floor, the curtains are drawn, and her son is nowhere to be seen.

7

The grandfather clock counts off the minutes, and Inga is approaching a state of panic. Frau Schulz is fretting on the fringes of the room and offering her drinks all too frequently, and as the pressure becomes unbearable and the panic reaches fever pitch there is the sound of voices downstairs; Inga rushes to the door and flings it open, rests her hands on the slippery banister and peers down the stairwell, and her heart almost stops – for there, seen from a bird's eye view in the dim light of the entrance hall, is Otto returning from the park at last, flanked by Rosa and her bicycle on the one side and Heinrich on the other. They appear in good spirits as they cover the bicycle with a sheet and climb the staircase, Otto lagging behind to check the postbox before joining his children; when eventually they enter the room it is as if the apartment has once again returned to life. Otto is laughing, unwinding his scarf, clapping his hands together and warming them by the fire, Rosa is clutching at her mother's elbow and is platzt with excitement, saying that she can now ride a bike all by herself and she isn't even cold because of the newspaper and oh Mama you should have seen and can you take me out tomorrow please, and Frau Schulz disappears to make tea for the weary adventurers. Heinrich is sullen, slinking from the room, and Inga feels a heat, almost a pain, in her stomach, yet she is lost for words in the cheerful atmosphere; Otto calls him back and Heinrich, prompted, mumbles an apology to his mother, then walks straight towards his bedroom. Inga is about to follow him when her husband holds her back.

—I fancy it is better to let things be for a while, Inga.

—Where did you find him?

—Rosa and I bumped into him on the Dorotheenstadt and he explained everything. He assured me that he will not run away in such a manner again, and I take him at his word. Do you know, he is considering taking up boxing? I suggested he join a youth group, the Kameraden or something similar. Nothing too Zionist or retrogressive. It might help.

Inga sits heavily at the dining room table, and Rosa, noticing her mother's mood, goes to her room and begins to prepare for bed, passing Frau Schulz with a steaming silver teapot. She hears the unmistakable sound of Papa removing his coat and hat, he always makes that strange grunting noise; she is glad that the fire is high and that Papa is able to get properly warm, his nose had gone as red as a cherry by the time they arrived back at the apartment. When all is in order in her little room Rosa snuggles herself into bed; she doesn't want to interrupt her parents to kiss them goodnight, she knows that once they have finished their conversation they will come into her room and kiss her on the forehead and tuck her in. In the meantime she is content to lie in the darkness and listen dreamily to their muffled tones, the treble and the bass of their voices, one, then the other, then both together, then a pause, then one, then the other, the floorboards vibrating when Papa speaks. Family life is filled with crises such as these, they are inevitable, but they are never serious; Papa and Mama always sit down and have a discussion late into the night, their voices like a duet from here in her room, and things are always resolved by the morning. Rosa drifts off, and as she sleeps she dreams of riding her bicycle through Berlin all by herself, alone, going round and round in the darkness upon rapidly spinning wheels.

23 December 1935, Berlin

I

Otto Klein rotates his wrist a quarter-turn, angling his watch face towards the dim light above his desk; he notices the chalk on his fingers and wipes them carefully on a handkerchief. Only five minutes remain until he can release the first group. He looks out of the window at the school gate and can see nobody gathered outside; it looks fairly safe but appearances are so deceptive these days – what's that – no, just a cat, maybe, or a dog. He is on edge. It has been utterly black outside since four o'clock, and bitterly cold at that, and the children are desperate to get home, but safety must come first, and since they started releasing the children at intervals there have been fewer attacks. The twinkling silver baubles around Berlin would be terribly pretty. He used to take Rosa and Heinrich out to see the seasonal decorations, that's impossible of course this year, perhaps once again in the future; this dim light above is making him feel rather tired, it aggravates the darkness by seeking to dispel it, but now only five minutes to go, four actually, another minute has slipped by, he can hear nothing but the buzz of this infernal light. Whom shall he release first?

—You boys on the front row, yes, you five. Pack away your books. You may go.

—Yes, sir.

—Thank you, sir.

Now there is noise – no voices, no laughing or talking, only floor-boards creaking, desks closing, they are well behaved, these boys, which makes the job bearable. He resisted teaching in his former life, used to avoid at all costs the lecture hall, repelled by the tedium of it, the very idea of repeating the same facts and figures to wave upon wave of half-interested students used to fill him with horror – and here he is a schoolmaster, in a schoolroom, who'd have thought it would come to this?

—You boy, Pfeifenkopf, put down your work. You may leave along with the others. Hurry along now, boy, catch them up.

—Very good, sir.

Ah, little Bernhard Pfeifenkopf, so scrawny and tiny, his clothes are practically ragged, he needs a good hot meal and some proper fresh air, and to run about in the park or something, although in all probability his spectacles preclude any serious physical exertion. The boy must surely get bullied, his very name lends itself to bullying, a ridiculous name. According to Pfeifenkopf, it goes back to the giving of surnames to Jews in Austria in the last century, his grandfather was called to the police station to be named and happened to be smoking a pipe at the time. What a sense of humour, those Austrian policemen, hilarious. Klein understands that Pfeifenkopf's parents have fallen upon hard times, that following the Aryanisation of their factory they have turned to selling soap for a living, though one wouldn't know it from the state of their progeny's face. And they receive supplementary income from Jewish Social Welfare, or so he has been led to believe.

Klein can see through the window little sprites, little shadows, keeping to the walls, that is good to see, and they are going three this way, two that way, which is probably a fine idea as well, they are ingenious, these children, he will say that for them, they are able to think for themselves, to a certain degree at least; and there goes little Pfeifenkopf, sidling off alone.

Klein is exceptionally tired today, he is glad that school is breaking up tomorrow for the Weihnachtsferien holidays, just one more day to get through then no school until January, that is one advantage of being a schoolmaster, he supposes. Today is a Monday, only the beginning of the week and already he's exhausted, there was no time to relax over the weekend, especially Sunday, which he spent in the Scheunenviertel, in the musty corridors of the Central Jewish Offices at the Oranienburger Straße 31: the place was packed with people seeking emigration advice – everyone apart from Klein, that is, who was only seeking a loan. He will have nothing to do with the emigration hysteria that is gripping the Jewish community, his memory is not so short; only twelve years ago inflation had spiralled into the millions, Inga was forced to knit socks and gloves to sell, and money had to be spent immediately, before it lost its value. On the morning after payday he would get up before dawn and take his entire wages to the wholesale market where the entire sum would be spent on non-perishables, tins, hundredweights of potatoes, soup cubes, spongy hams, great fat cheeses, all piled higgledy-piggledy into a handcart, for within a few days the entire month's salary would not have bought a cinema ticket; everyone thought the world was coming to an end, yet now it is almost forgotten; Klein is convinced that in just the same way this current unpleasant episode will pass.

When he arrived at the Oranienburger Straße, sombre hordes were clustering in thick brown lines around the building, pouring in a great queue onto the icy pavement and past the Neue Synagogue, which was looking magnificent on that clear winter's day, its dome a drop of molten gold. He queued for an hour, his trilby pulled low on his forehead, nuzzling into his scarf, his nose cherry-red above the frosty natty moustache, his numb hands poking like sugar mice from the sleeves of his overcoat. Eventually the pressure became too great, the queue burst and seethed into a disorderly crowd, so Klein pushed his way through, squeezed into the building through the narrow entrance. Then came the corridors, teeming with people hurrying this way and that, pressed in packs around offices, glancing in all directions, clutching sheaves of papers, or trailing after officials in the flickering electric light. Klein, losing his bearings, was borne along in a sudden slipstream of teenagers, had to lay a hand on the doorframe and prise himself away from the Youth Aliyah classroom; he slipped down a dingy metal staircase, emerged into a throng on the floor below, pushed his way through a cluster of men with string-bound files, and finally, above a shifting sea of hats, a sign came into view: the Central Office for Jewish Economic Aid. It took an hour for Klein to lever his way into the office and a further half-hour of jockeying before finally he could sit on the battered leather-capped chair in front of the desk and raise his eyes to look someone in the face.

The man behind the desk looked familiar, and after a few seconds Klein placed him: Ludwig Altmann, the organist from the Neue Synagogue, whom he had met at a lecture that Inga had forced him to attend; the two men had sneaked out and struck up a conversation over a cigarette on the synagogue steps. Altmann recognised him immediately, shook him warmly by the hand, his broad face lighting up like a Chinese lantern; then it dimmed, the strain returned, he dipped his pen excessively in a pot of lavender-coloured ink and scratched Klein's details on a sheet of foolscap, and the second of the 'o's in 'Otto' pooled, causing a major kerfuffle with a sheet of blotting paper. Klein was sweating now; he removed his spectacles and passed a handkerchief over his face; the blare of voices all around was interfering with his thoughts. He loosened his scarf. The conversation was fragmented, punctuated by interjections from anxious people, and somebody jogged the table and another blot appeared. Klein had to raise his voice above the din, and Altmann craned his neck to hear him, but the upshot was yes, in all likelihood he will indeed receive a loan, it is understood that he has incurred many expenses while changing careers and addresses and so forth, he will be contacted by letter in the near future, next please!

The way out was worse than the way in. No sooner had Klein raised himself from the rickety chair than three men were competing for it, he was spun by the crowd away from the desk and once again found himself buffeted here and there by the mob, his legs were rubbery and he had to get some air, he squeezed his hand upwards through the tightly packed shoulders and tilted back his hat; and it was then that it came to his attention that somebody was calling his name.

—Herr Doktor Klein! Doktor Klein!

It had been a long time since Klein had been called Doktor. With an effort he turned and squinted in the direction of the voice. Somebody was waving a bowler hat in the air.

—Doktor Klein! Over here! Herr Doktor!

Klein recognised immediately the silvery crown of Doktor Oskar Fehr projecting half a head above the crowd. Klein waved, briefly, and continued to make his way towards the exit, but the crowd-tides turned and he found himself at a standstill; before long, having found a swifter current, Fehr appeared beside him.

—Doktor Klein, I say, I haven't seen you since our hospital days. What are you doing here?

—Everyone in Berlin is here, said Klein, why should I not join them?

—Not holidaymaking in Wiesbaden this year, Herr Doktor?

—Not this year.

—My God, I have never seen such crowds. Have you come to visit the Emigration Advice Centre?

—No, I am . . . making a social call.

—I see you have not managed to obtain one of these. They are in short supply, you understand.

Fehr parted his greatcoat to reveal a pile of battered-looking books, each as thick as a fist, cradled in his arms like an infant. He pulled one out, awkwardly, and pressed it to Klein's chest.

—Here, I already have two Chicagos.

—What's this?

—It's a Chicago – I have a New York, a Chicago and a Washington, but here is an extra Chicago.

The crowd moved and Fehr was carried away, calling over his shoulder:

—Look under 'Klein'. Write to them – they might help you emigrate. Farewell, Herr Doktor, and good luck! My kindest regards to your family. Good luck!

And then he was gone, leaving Klein further encumbered by the telephone book, as a result of which it took him another hour to get out of the building, so that is why today, standing in the gloomy schoolroom, he feels deeply tired, and his mind, like a compass needle, turns towards the bottom drawer of his desk, in the depths of which there nestles an amber lozenge of Schnaps; no, he mustn't put his job in jeopardy, no, it will be worth the wait, he can taste it now, that dry tartness on the tongue followed by the candle in the throat, ah.

2

Rosa looks up at the black sky, listening to the regular tick-tick of her bicycle as trams and cars whirr past. Gone are the days when she would cycle through the city for pleasure, barely can she remember a time when she would ride freely in the streets, in the parks, for enjoyment. Pushing her bicycle, she passes a bundled-up group of children singing Stille Nacht, heilige Nacht; she lowers her eyes and crosses the road, avoiding unnecessary attention. A few steps behind are Heinrich and his two friends, both of whom are leaders in his youth group, the Makkabi Hatzair. Jizchak is tall, like a bending stalk of corn, with a gentle smile, bulbous nose and round-glassed spectacles; he is a favourite amongst the children he leads, loved for his bottomless generosity. Edith is diminutive, mischievous, loved for her dry Berlin charm; she wears her hair pulled back in a clip, emphasising her spectacled, good-humoured face. Here on the streets, however, they are both hunched into their overcoats, hats pulled low, walking swiftly.

—Pull your scarf tighter, says Edith, you are exposing the collar of your Kluft.

Heinrich looks down to see the blue collar of his Makkabi uniform poking from his scarf like an ear, and tucks it back into the folds. He and Edith have just returned from the public library where they have been fixing pharmaceutical warning stickers to Nazi books, and writing anonymous letters saying 'The Jews will be your downfall? Let's hope so' to post to the authorities. Jizchak does not approve, thinks they are taking unnecessary risks, but Edith says it's pinpricks like these that maintain the spirit of resistance. As they approach the corner of the Danziger Straße the sound of baritone laughter can be heard. Jizchak looks up the road and sucks his teeth; a group of brown-shirted men – SA – can be seen gathered by a newspaper kiosk with a red glass case displaying copies of the Nazi weekly, *Der Stürmer*. Jizchak hurries up to

Rosa and takes her by the arm, sending her heart all of a flutter – she was twelve last month – and steers the little group across the road, behind an advertising pillar covered with cinema programmes and posters announcing executions. Rosa glances around nervously, knowing that they are making themselves a target standing about like this, but she can see the men on the corner and knows that the alternative would be even more risky; after a time the men move off and with a sense of relief, but without a word, they continue their journey.

—And how was school, kleine Rosa?

—It was fine, Jizchak.

His hand is still on her arm.

—What have you been studying of late?

—Biology.

Heinrich, now walking a little behind, is still buoyed by the memory of Shabbat, the day before yesterday, which he so very much enjoyed. Shabbat has become his highlight since he joined the Makkabi; every week there are activities, and singing, and dancing, and prayers, and good friends; he feels at home amongst the Chaverim and Chaverot, people who have something to really strive for, united by their yearning for a homeland. It was the first night of Chanukah, and they celebrated in the woods, hundreds of people came, they spent the day practising their Hebrew and learning about farming and Herzl; and in the evening Heinrich was given the honour of leading the prayers to conclude the sabbath. The group gathered in a big circle in a clearing under the stars and sang together a hymn, the prophet Elijah, the returning Elijah, may he soon come back to us, and as they were singing, swaying as one body, Heinrich stepped shakily forwards, took the brimming goblet of wine in his right hand, the cool liquid spilling like tears over his fingers, and began the prayers, falteringly, in Hebrew – behold, God is my salvation, I shall trust and not fear, my God is my might and my praise, you can draw water with joy from the springs of salvation – and more wine was dripping from his fingers, and more, and then he lifted the box of spices, said the prayer and inhaled the fragrance to soothe the soul as the sabbath departs, then the spices were passed round the Chaverim and Chaverot, still standing in a circle round Heinrich in the moonlight; finally he plunged the plaited candle sizzling into the pool of wine and everybody cried, shavua tov! a good week! and shook hands with one another, particularly with Heinrich who had led them in prayer, his hand was pumped so much it hurt, shaking hands with the left hand which comes from the heart. Then there was Horra dancing round the

34

camp fire, great spinning circles, round and round, one circle this way, one circle the other way, and songs about Jerusalem and hope, showers of orange sparks cascading upwards from the bonfire in the centre, singing and clapping intoxicated, deeply and joyfully into the night.

—Truly, your Hebrew has improved, Heinrich. I was most impressed at your Havdalah reading last Shabbat.

—Thank you, Ewo, but I think it's because I have such a good teacher.

—What a charmer, no? But thank you.

They continue along the wide pavement of the Prenzlauer Allee, Rosa's bicycle gently ticking, the lamp-posts pooling light at intervals. A commuter tram struggles past, its antenna fizzing on the overhead wire; through its windows Rosa sees a forest of arms suspended from the overhead straps, surging back and forth. The conductor stretches a grey-mittened hand to reaffix the green cloth curtaining the lower half of the door, and for a moment catches Rosa's eye – then the tram is obscured by a cluster of Christmas trees for sale. Something flies through the air and lands sizzling at her feet. She looks up; the driver of a beer van is hanging out of his window, looking at Rosa strangely, blowing the last traces of cigarette smoke from his nose. There is a sound of jingling as he pulls away, bottles tinkling and jumping in their cases behind him.

They walk on in silence. As they cross the Stargarder Straße, Heinrich suddenly comes to a standstill, his head poised as if catching a scent.

—Heinrich, says Jizchak, come on.

Heinrich gestures for him to be quiet. A sound can be heard, a noise that doesn't belong. He listens. From the bustle of the street two voices gradually distinguish themselves – an undulating, high-pitched cry and a lower one. Then they are gone and the bustle continues.

—Did you hear that? he whispers.

—What? asks Jizchak curtly.

—Someone's in trouble. A Jew.

—Your mind is playing tricks. Come on, Heinrich.

Heinrich turns away and, as if hypnotised, begins to walk down the Stargarder Straße.

—You're hearing things, says Jizchak. Come on. We must keep moving.

Without a word, Heinrich sleepwalks into the darkness, and as he does so a high-pitched scream can be heard above the noise of the traffic.

—Heinrich, calls Rosa, come back!

She props her bicycle against the wall and begins to follow her brother, but Jizchak grabs her by the arm.

—You must get back on your bicycle and ride all the way home, he says. Rosa? Do you hear me?

—Jizchak, let me go. He is my brother. We can't leave him.

—Nobody is leaving him. I will go after him. Rosa, hurry now. Edith, take her.

—But Heinrich—

—Don't worry about Heinrich. I will look after him, I promise. Quickly now, off you go. Rosa, trust me. Run along now. Off you go. Edith, take her. I said go.

Reluctantly Rosa allows Edith to lead her back to her bicycle. She looks over her shoulder; Jizchak has pulled his collar around his ears and is disappearing into the shadows after Heinrich. She tries to run back, but Edith's firm hand presses her towards the bicycle.

—Come on, my dear, she says, Jizchak will look after him. Everything will be all right. We need to get you home.

Against her instincts Rosa finds herself mounting the bicycle on trembling feet. Edith climbs onto the handlebars, and Rosa pedals away, wobbling slightly until she picks up speed.

—Not too fast, Rosa, I fear I shall take a tumble.

—Just hold on, Edith, hold tight.

—You're drawing attention to us by riding so fast. I'm not even sure that bicycles are permitted for Jews any more. Please slow down.

Rosa makes an effort to slow the bicycle and glances around her. Heads are turning all along the pavement.

—Shall I stop?

—No, carry on, says Edith. Just not too fast. Try to appear jolly, as if we are having fun. It is Christmas, after all, is it not? And we are nearly at the Grellstraße.

—I want to go back to Heinrich.

—We can't risk losing you both. Keep your eyes front.

3

Several hours earlier: the door swings open, throwing a triangular shadow against the grey corridor wall with its hairline cracks and peeling paint. At first nobody from the apartment emerges, then there is a scuffling sound, and a slight moan, and then Inga appears, carrying Hedi in her arms – at the age of four Hedi is a little old, really, to be carried, but otherwise it will take forever to leave the apartment, and the night draws in so early these days, they only have an hour or so of sunlight left in which to visit the park. Inga checks she has the keys and pulls the door awkwardly to. She is tired – she has been working all morning, washing shirts, hanging them to dry in the bedroom, ironing, folding, packaging, addressing the packages so that they are ready for Rosa to deliver. And now she must spend some time with Hedi, who has been quiet and sullen all morning. Inga has tried to make the most of her own ageing wardrobe, her hat is pinned to the side, and she wears an old mink stole smelling faintly of onions which she holds to her nose as she passes the communal latrine on the landing. Her coat hangs loosely from its shoulder pads, and above the collar her face is gaunt. With another moan she lifts her daughter once more and clomps asymmetrically down the stairs, eventually emerging into the weak light on the pavement, where she sets Hedi on her feet, takes her hand in tautly gloved fingers and walks slowly in the direction of the park. She pauses by a postbox, slides a letter from her pocket and holds it poised in the rectangular mouth; Mr and Mrs Kremer, 15 Paget Road, Stamford Hill, London; Otto's cousins, a begging letter. Inga draws a breath, lets the letter fall and continues, with Hedi, on her way. Otto does not know about this letter, he refuses to discuss emigration even for a moment. It was just the same in '23, Inga was knitting to make ends meet and she pleaded with him to try his hand at the markets, for although the country was in poverty there was wealth to be had in shares, if one was canny enough one could make one's fortune, boys of sixteen were becoming rich beyond their wildest dreams while their parents hanged themselves in their attics. But Otto refused, pride prevented him; a Prussian Frontkämpfer does not profit from speculation, he said. Looking back she can understand him better, his steely high-mindedness, his refusal to accept that the stuff of nightmares was already in motion, every day, around him. So now the struggle is similar: when she thrusts her arm into a sack of dirty linen, submerging to the shoulder, she is thinking of survival, just survival, the survival of her family, nothing nobler than that. And Otto? Well, Otto.

From a window somewhere drifts tinny march music, and despite herself Inga glances around to make sure that a mob is not heading in this direction. The sky is perfectly white and the air is strangely still as they walk. Hedi is in a quiet mood again; Inga is beginning to wonder about this girl, it cannot be natural that she barely says a word, and she seems tired all the time, withdrawn. She must mention it again to Otto, though he will probably scold her for fussing about nothing. She must try to keep her engaged.

37

—So Hedi, was Kindergarten nice today?

—

—Look, Hedi, a duck.

—

—Duck, Hedi, duck. Quak.
—Duck.
—Yes, Hedi, very good. Duck. Duck, duck, duck, quak, quak, quak.

—

—I am sure there are many, many ducks in the park. I say, what on earth has happened to Gigi's head?
—My dolly.
—Yes, I know, just let me see . . .
—My dolly, my Gigi.
—Her poor little head is cracked. And her eye is all pushed in.
—My dolly!
—But this is frightful. How did this happen, Hedi?
—Go away, naughty Mama.
—Pfui, now that is no way to speak to your mother, little miss. Say sorry.
—Naughty Mama.
—If you say that one more time we shan't stay in the park, we shall go straight home. Is that understood? Is that understood?

—

—Now come along.

As if there was not enough to worry about already. Oh, it is cold, at least Hedi is snug in her coat. But she refuses to smile, or talk, or be a child at all, really. Herr Schwab's shirt needs to be washed a second time, that beetroot stain just hasn't come out—

—Hedi, put that down, we don't pick up sticks, you should know that by now, we don't know where they've been.

—

—Now you may run about on the grass with Gigi, and Mama will sit down for a while. But do not stray out of my sight, do you hear?

There she goes, walking away like an old lady, and just four years old. Ah, the worry, with every child there is a worry, hundreds of worries in fact. And now where to sit? This question is a loaded one thanks to Heinrich and his newfound Zionist zeal. Heinrich, you imp, you have made everything into a political issue, even the question of where to sit – do we or do we not use the Judenbänke? Discuss. Heinrich argues that we should ignore those Jewish seats, we have our values, we have the beauty of nature, such seats are nothing to us; and yet where else to sit? On the Aryan benches? On the grass? It's all very well for Heinrich, he is young and fit, he can sit on the grass with no problem at all, not so for a lady, especially with a four-year-old. Surely it makes no difference, the park is all but deserted anyway, too cold for most people. It is perishing, indeed. All right, Heinrich, you win – on the grass. On the cold, frosty grass. Ah.

Inga gathers her stole around her ears, a solitary speck in the centre of the park, the white domed sky keeping a vigil overhead. She watches Hedi playing – no, not playing, if she were to play it would be wonderful, she would be the happiest mother in the world to see her little daughter play like other children. Hugging her arms around herself, Inga sings softly the Chanukah prayers she has been practising: thus we kindle lights to commemorate the miracles, wonders, salvations and battles which God performed for our forefathers. When Otto returns tonight from work they will light the menorah, it is the third night of the first Chanukah of their life, a substitute for Christmas this year. Inga has been studying the festival with Rabbinerin Regina Jonas at the Neue Synagogue, which she has begun to attend regularly; it may be some distance away from the Kleins' apartment but in Inga's opinion it is well worth the trip, it was love at first sight back in 1930 when she visited for the Einstein concert, the building is so very beautiful, with its intricate baroque masonry and opulent dome, and they organise fascinating lectures and events for Jews like Inga, Jewesses rather, who know next to nothing about Judaism. And the community is so welcoming, particularly Rabbinerin Regina, Inga warmed to her immediately, loved the idea of a female rabbi, for – as Regina put it – why should the men have all the fun? From the beginning Regina took Inga under her wing and became a real pillar of strength, what with Otto's job situation, and the apartment situation, and the Frau Schulz situation, the list just goes on and on. Inga was an atheist to start with, still is in a way, but that does not preclude ritual and culture, there is no point in allowing scepticism to shackle one, to stifle new experiences. The synagogue is a welcome dimension to life in these dark days, it helps her to feel that she is not alone, that others are sharing her burden; one gets so accustomed to feeling like an outsider, being part of a group again is intoxicating.

After a time the light begins to falter and evening begins to tinge the white sky. Inga struggles stiffly to her feet, gathers her chilly daughter to her and walks the deserted streets in the direction of home. She does not try to engage Hedi in conversation, is content instead with the deafness of the streets. They walk cold across the flagstoned courtyard and climb the stairs, footsteps echoing several times, looking forward to the relative warmth of home. As Inga raises her key to the latch, her feet brush against a parcel on the doorstep; she looks down, sees a sizeable cardboard box bound with string. Her gloved fingers drift to her mouth and trace around her lips. She swings the door open and, uncertainly, lifts the box inside.

4

—Here we are, Rosa. You're home.

—Do you think my brother—

—Don't worry about your brother. Jizchak will make sure—

—But Jizchak doesn't know how to fight.

—He's clever, he doesn't need to. Go on, now. Go inside. Heinrich will be back soon, I promise.

Reluctantly Rosa waves a brief goodbye to Edith, opens the narrow wooden door to her apartment block, stows her bicycle and walks across the courtyard, her footsteps echoing on the cracked flagstones. Light glows from snugly curtained windows in the tenements, and the smell of cooking fattens the air. Edith is right, surely she is right, Rosa is panicking unnecessarily, Heinrich will be fine, between him and Jizchak they can surely deal with anything. Suddenly, from the other side of the courtyard comes the sound of jolly voices – she raises her eyes and sees a group of lads approaching, jingling cylindrical tins, collecting for Winterhilfe; her heart quickens. They are wearing the brown uniforms of the Hitlerjugend.

They haven't seen her yet; Rosa glances swiftly left and right, then slips through a doorway and crouches in the stairwell, in the shadows, out of sight, watching. Such camaraderie they exhibit, these Nazi boys, such confidence; there is a hierarchy in their world and they are at its zenith, with their clean red armbands and neatly combed hair, and pins and badges and epaulettes, their patent boots striking the flagstones defiantly like the beats of a tightly skinned drum. They glow, these boys, there's something about them, like gods almost, like angels.

The group marches past the entrance to the stairwell, a band of boisterous voices and tucked-in shirts, filled with the Christmas spirit; first two pass, then one more, then another two – but the last one pauses in front of the stairwell, his breath clouding round his head. The voices of his companions begin to recede yet he stands there unmoving, a shadow falling across his face; as if made of stone, he turns his head to face the stairwell, then his shoulders, then his whole body; he takes a step towards the entrance, then another, then a third, and now he is covered in shadow. Rosa shrinks back against the wall, clutching her arms around her legs, crouching, finding the darkest place she can, like an insect. He takes another two steps forward and is obscured from view by the stairs. All is still. Rosa strains her ears but can hear only a door closing several floors above, the muffled voice of a child, footsteps in the distance, the sound of water through pipes. Nothing out of the ordinary. Nothing else.

There – a sound from behind the stairs. Rosa's breath is short and gasping, she feels light-headed, she is panting almost, like an animal almost, like a small scared mammal. No noise again, perhaps it is safe. And then two patent boots appear, and the shadows slide off brown-uniformed shoulders as the boy steps quietly into view, a trail of cloud streaming gently from his nose. Rosa cannot help but glance up to his marble face and look into his unblinking eyes; he holds in front of him a collection tin, adorned with a Hakenkreuz and a sprig of holly. He takes a step closer and Rosa slides herself as tightly as she can into the corner, there is no way she can escape, and she cannot make a sound, her throat has clamped shut. He looks at Rosa unblinking, at her face, into her eyes, expressionless, and his hands hover around his belt. A distant conversation can still be heard, the water in the pipes can still be heard, another door closes, another child speaks. Rosa hears the sound of trickling liquid; her legs go warm, then icy cold. The boy looks at her, unblinking, motionless, noiseless; then, very slowly, his legs, then his shoulders, then his head turns away from her, the two lamps of his eyes breaking from hers and sweeping towards the courtyard, and he disappears from view once more behind the stairs; then she sees him strolling casually into the courtyard, calling to his friends to wait, and she listens as his footsteps fade and disappear. For a long while she waits, crouching, her breath slowly becoming regular, the feeling returning to her face. Finally she pushes herself to her feet, takes off her shoes and creeps up the stairs to her family's apartment, frozen-legged, exhausted and ashamed.

5

So finally Hedi is playing in her room, and Otto and the children are not yet back from school, and Inga has a few minutes' peace; time in which to cook. The latkes are sizzling in the pan, all that grating has made her

41

fingers ache, she hopes she has the proportions right, onion to potato and so forth. If there is one thing she hates in life, it is cooking, but it is one of those things that must be done, it cannot be avoided, maybe she will improve with practice. The important thing about latkes is that they are fried, oil being the symbol of Chanukah. Rabbinerin Regina explained: in 175 BC, the Greek king Antiochus IV, lord of Syria and successor to Alexander the Great, oppressed the Jews and sacked their temple; ah yes, there it is, the first latke, and it seems to have turned out fine, very nice in fact, oh dear, it's fallen apart, let's put it to one side and try another. But the Jewish rebels, led by Judah Makkabi, defeated the Greeks in combat and reconsecrated the Temple. Another failure, two crumbled latkes, maybe she will serve mashed latke, pretend it's a delicacy, let's try another, a little more oil. After the battle it emerged that the Temple's stock of sacred oil had been vandalised by the Greeks and there was only one phial remaining, just enough to fuel the sacred candelabra for a single day; but miraculously it burned for an entire eight days, enough time for more to be pressed and prepared. Thus we kindle lights to commemorate the miracles, wonders, salvations and battles which God enacted for our forefathers, ah. Inga imagines Judah Makkabi to look like Rabbi Warschauer, the second rabbi at the Neue Synagogue, for despite his wispy beard and fine-boned face there is a hint of steel about him when he preaches from the pulpit. Mind you, even Rabbi Warschauer is no match for the synagogue ladies. Every week he demands that they leave the flamboyant hats and dresses at home when attending the synagogue, for it draws unwanted attention, but does anybody listen? That would be like requesting a flock of peacocks to fold their tails. Each week the rabbi peers up at the ladies' gallery from the pulpit and shakes his head in despair, begging them once again to next time please wear more sombre apparel; he must know his words are falling upon deaf ears, but pleads again and again none the less: this isn't like Inga at all, she actually feels tears welling in her eyes as she recalls it, the heroic Judah Makkabi and his band of Jewish warriors, refusing to submit. She hopes to hear from London soon, she hasn't been in touch with the Kremers for years, but family is family, surely they will have compassion, which reminds her, where on earth are Rosa and Heinrich, it is getting late and they promised to be home in time for supper and candle-lighting, ah yes, the trout is ready now, and the vegetable stew, and the asparagus, Otto will be overjoyed with the asparagus, and Rosa could do with getting a bit fatter, not to mention Heinrich – where can they have got to?

—Rosa? Rosa, is that you?

—Yes, Mama, it is.

—Ah, thank goodness. You are late home this evening, I was worrying. Heinrich is not with you?

—No, he is with Jizchak. He said he would be back soon.

—Ah yes, Jizchak, of course. Would you mind helping me in the kitchen? I am cooking latkes, for Chanukah. I wish to have them ready by the time Papa returns.

—Yes, of course. Let me just wash my face.

—There are many deliveries to be made this evening, Rosa. Rosa?

Rosa wedges the bathroom door closed with a bucket of firewood. Amid the smell of boiling laundry she peels off her clothes, placing wet things on one side and dry on the other. It is so cramped in this bathroom, she cannot even stretch her arms out properly to remove her shirt. She sees herself blushing scarlet in the mirror even though there is nobody to see her, she feels stupid and ashamed. Her teeth are chattering, she must be colder than she thought, her skin is rough with goosebumps. She struggles out of her clammy knickers, places some firewood in the oven-heater and lights it, blowing and stoking until the flames take to the wood and begin to lick upwards; then she closes the little iron door and waits for the water to heat up, the tiles chilling her feet. She does not look in the mirror, she averts her eyes then reaches up and turns the glass on its chain so that it faces the wall; now she is truly alone, not even a reflection for company. She takes a little water from the tap and spreads it between her thighs to alleviate the discomfort, pressing her legs hard together, then picks up the waxen pebble of soap and rubs it between her hands as if for warmth – but what about Heinrich? She knows that he can fight, he protected her on several occasions at school – but what if they overcame him this time? What if more of them arrived and outnumbered him, what if he was badly beaten, what if his bones were broken? What about Jacob Ehrenfreund, who tore down a Hakenkreuz and was beaten so brutally that he had to be taken to a mental institution; or what about the Chaver from Leipzig who refused to trample a Torah at Bomsdorf and was shot? What if Heinrich, even as she awaits the warming of the water, lies dead on the icy Berlin pavement, blood and mucus mingling around his nose, fingers twisted and snapped . . .

—Rosa! Whatever is the matter with you? Are you all right in there?

—Yes, Mama, I think the water is warm now.

—Why ever are you warming the water?

—I just need to wash my face. Is Heinrich back yet?

—No, darling, not yet.

6

Jizchak slips down the Stargarder Straße, eyes darting left and right, desperately looking for Heinrich; the night is clear and he finds himself counting the stars of Ursa Major, he learnt to recognise constellations from his father. The street is quiet, and not a soul can be seen, there is no sign of Heinrich anywhere, Jizchak considers calling out but thinks better of it. He walks on.

Then he stops walking. Halfway along the street a steel bin has been upended and lies on its side, rubbish has spread onto the pavement, the bin is rocking very slightly back and forth. Not far away, in the very centre of the street, a single, empty shoe lies with its sole tilted towards the night. Jizchak is about to shout Heinrich's name, but stops himself.

Suddenly there is a noise. He stops, bird-like, listening, something wooden is collapsing, a fence perhaps, followed by cries of surprise and some shouts; the commotion seems to be coming from an alleyway across the street. He takes his hands out of his pockets and approaches the alleyway, sees Orion suspended overhead, automatically counts its stars. As he draws near he hears a confused, muffled noise of grunting, pounding, vomiting, gagging; then there is a long, gurgling, choking sound, a moan of agony and release.

Jizchak hurries into the darkness, aware of his own footsteps, and there, in a patch of moonlight, he sees Heinrich locked in a lumbering embrace with a larger man. Their movements are fatigued and heavy, drained by the fight, they seem to have lost even the strength to speak; they lurch from side to side, hunching against the walls, making slow attempts at strikes. For a moment Jizchak glimpses the white oval of the other man's face, the eyes screwed shut, the mouth a black inverted moon. Jizchak does not know what to do but he knows he has to act; amazed at his own actions, he grabs the man by the collar and prises him away from Heinrich. The man looks up, half-moon widening. Jizchak, powered by adrenalin, swings his fist in an arc and strikes the white oval with surprising force; the head bounces and there is a dull clang as it hits an iron drainpipe; the moon snaps shut and spills blood, the man skids noiselessly to the floor. Heinrich recovers his balance and stamps on him with startling venom, once, twice, three times; Jizchak grabs him, pulls him away. The man lies still.

—Heinrich, don't, you'll kill him. You'll kill him.

—You dreckige coward, shouts Heinrich at the prostrate figure, you puppy, you coward, we will murder you.

In a nearby window the curtains part; a woman's slender hands lower the catch, and the curtains are drawn again.

Heinrich falls to his knees amongst the bins, and for the first time Jizchak notices another figure crumpled there in the shadows.

—Are you hurt? says Heinrich, out of breath.

—Not badly, comes the reply.

Jizchak walks over; a teenager sits with his head in his hands, his face bloodied and swollen.

—You need a handkerchief, says Heinrich. Here, take this. What's your name?

—Pfeifenkopf, sir.

—Sorry?

—Pfeifenkopf, sir. Pfeifenkopf. My name.

—Well, Pfeifenkopf, you'd better run along, if you don't want any more trouble. You can run, can't you?

—Yes, sir.

—Just get home as quickly as you can, yes? And Pfeifenkopf? Emigrate to Palestine, do you hear? Join the Makkabi Hatzair.

—Yes, sir, thank you.

—Now off you go. Run along.

Pfeifenkopf clutches Heinrich's handkerchief to his face and hobbles off down the street, his shirt torn and dirty; he glances warily left and right, slips down an alleyway and disappears into the shadows.

Heinrich and Jizchak look at the man lying unconscious on the cobbles, his face dark with blood, cursed by his injuries, as if he might come alive with supernatural strength at any moment.

—Ach, I'm bleeding, says Heinrich suddenly.

In a daze they make their way back to the Prenzlauer Allee. Within minutes packs of men will be prowling the streets, hunting them. Heinrich is shaken, crazed with adrenalin, clenching and unclenching his fists. Jizchak, shaking all over, can only think of one thing: a woman's pale hands stretching through the curtains, lowering the catch on the windows.

7

—Good evening Inga, sorry I'm late, says Klein.

—Liebling, you're back, wonderful. Are you drunk?

45

—Of course not, of course not. I am awfully hungry though, ravenous. Something smells sublime in here. May I just . . . I don't believe my eyes. Is that truly asparagus? But the season ended many months ago. And – tomatoes in the stew? Where on earth did we acquire all these Aryan vegetables? And trout?

—I found it in a box on the doorstep.

—Who sent it?

—There was no note but the address is written in Berta Krützfeld's handwriting. Isn't it good of them?

—I'm not sure good is the word, this is the first we've heard from them in over a year. But this food is absolutely divine, I'll give you that. Real Aryan food, indeed! Such a feast calls for a real celebration. I must have a little glass of something, to lubricate the machinery so to speak. Are the children home from school?

—Everyone but Heinrich.

Klein pauses by the drinks cabinet.

—Where is he?

—With Jizchak, apparently. You'll have to ask Rosa.

There are three soft taps on the bedroom door, and Rosa knows who it is at once. She places Gigi carefully on the desk, tells Hedi to keep an eye on her, opens the door and gives Papa a kiss. He enters the room in a cloud of pipe smoke, kisses the air above Hedi's forehead, then sits down and takes her onto his knee. The room is dimly lit apart from a strong desk lamp which makes the desk as bright as an operating table; on the desk lies Gigi, a tube of Heinrich's UHU and an assortment of tools and implements.

—Good evening, girls, what is going on here? Pfff, pfff.

—I am the dolly doctor, Papa. I am performing an operation on Gigi to make her all better.

—Let me have a little look, I am a surgeon after all. . . I say, that does look nasty. But I can see that Rosa is doing an excellent job. I think you may be a more skilled surgeon than myself, Püppchen.

—Thank you, Papa.

Klein lowers his voice and leans forward.

—Rosa, I wish to ask you a question and I want you to be honest with me. Is Heinrich in trouble?

—

—I thought as much. Rosa, you must tell me everything.

—It's nothing, Papa. Jizchak is with him.

—What happened?

—It's nothing, I mustn't worry you, it's nothing.

—Then tell me.

There is the sound of somebody hurrying into the apartment. Doors open and heads appear, Inga's, Otto's, Rosa's. A figure stands in the hall, hunched awkwardly, smoothing his hair with his palms: Heinrich.

—Heinrich, says Rosa, you're back!

—Yes, kleine Rosa, I'm back.

—Are you all right?

—Of course. I'll just get ready for dinner, and then . . .

He disappears into the bathroom and locks the door behind him. Rosa pauses for a moment, her eyes closed, weakening with relief; then she gathers her strength and walks through to the kitchen, followed by her father, leaving Hedi sitting on the bed with her mended doll.

—What is wrong with Rosa and Heinrich this evening, says Inga, they both have the most unhealthy attraction to the bathroom, like a pair of bluebottles.

—I'm sure nothing's wrong, says her husband, it's the weather. It's perishing outside. I should like to have a nice warm wash myself.

He exchanges a glance with Rosa.

—Yes, says Rosa, Papa's right. It's freezing outside, really freezing.

Hedi, sitting on her bed, looks at Gigi's porcelain face, at the dark crack from the crown to the jaw passing through the broken left eye, encrusted with icicles of UHU. She puts her pudgy finger at her crown and traces a line down her own face, then pushes at her eye; the harder she pushes the wilder the patterns become. She watches galaxies of red and black dust exploding on the inside of her eyelids, then a series of red and green flashes, then a never-ending procession of cubes rushing towards her; she releases her finger and opens her eyes, slowly the black clouds part until she can see clearly again. That is what Gigi sees, because Gigi has a bad eye, and Hedi wants a bad eye too, and Gigi is a Jude because she is bad, and she has a bad head because Christine Bauer threw her out of the window and that is what happens when you are a Jude, and Christine Bauer has a unicorn, and Bärbel Koch says that Herr Hitler is going to finish the Juden, Hedi saw a picture of Herr, and he looked all white, and Hedi wants a rabbit, and a horse, and she likes Papa's moustache better than Herr's moustache, a lot, and wonders if Herr will throw Gigi out of the window? Yes, and Bärbel Koch will help throw her out and Christine Bauer will laugh and laugh because she will be so happy, and Hedi knows Christine Bauer will be so happy because she pinches her, and so does Bärbel Koch, and so does Netti Huber and Edith

Weber and Ida Lehmann, and when she is finished Frau Fuchs will be happy too, because she laughs when Hedi is pinched, and she won't let her have a bandage and she will make her stand in the corner, and when she is five she wants a bicycle like Rosa and she wants to meet Santa Claus and she will ask him for a bicycle like Rosa's and a cloud.

Heinrich is standing in his bedroom in front of the mirror, examining a graze on his shoulder, when his father knocks. He pulls his shirt on to conceal his bruises and opens the door; his father enters in a cloud of pipe smoke.

—Good evening, Vater.

—Good evening, Heinrich. May I come in? Pfff, pfff.

—Of course.

—Now I understand you have been in another fight this evening.

—Ach, Rosa.

—No, not Rosa. Vater knows everything. Now, I have brought you this. You should carry it under your arm on your way to school and back. Don't let Mutter see it.

—*Der Stürmer*? Honestly, Vater, I would rather . . . I do not even wish to touch it.

—Heinrich, be practical. It's only a newspaper, and it could help you avoid a lot of trouble.

—I will not hide like a rabbit.

—Heinrich, you are fifteen years old. I am nearing forty, and I am your Vater. You will carry a copy of *Der Stürmer*, it is necessary for your own protection. You may place a Jewish newspaper inside it if you wish, that is up to you.

—I will never carry it. I will stand and fight.

—Keep your voice down, your mother will hear. Look, Jews need to know when to keep quiet and when to fight. We have only had civic equality in Deutschland for sixty-five years, before that we suffered abuse for centuries. But it has always got better. It won't last.

—I cannot be patient, I will not. This is no way to live. While I have breath I will stand and fight. I have nothing to lose, none of us do.

—Heinrich, the legislation of the Nürnberger Gesetze makes the Jewish position final. Things may not be pleasant, but they cannot very well get worse. We have survived for generations in such circumstances, and we will survive many more generations to come. One day, when you are older, you will see that I am right. We must think in the long term.

—I will not be here in the long term. I am going to Palestine.

—Palestine, eh? Well in the meantime, you will carry *Der Stürmer*. Is that understood?

—Ach, says Heinrich, accepting the newspaper.

—Excellent. And do not breathe a word to Mutter, yes? Now put it away, it must be time for candle-lighting.

The family stand to behold the spectacle of Inga lighting the menorah, slowly, with dignity, singing the prayers and lighting one, two, three candles for the third day of Chanukah, and the yellow light casts flickering shadows over her face, which bears an expression that is rather intent for an atheist; Otto holds Hedi quietly in his arms and Rosa and Heinrich stand together, watching the small candelabra with its little swaying flames. There is something rather melancholy about them, so tiny, surrounded by so much darkness.

—Blessed are you, the Lord our God, King of the universe, who wrought miracles for our forefathers at this time of year.

As she chants the prayers Inga wonders when would be the best time to tell her husband that she has written to the Kremers in London; and Heinrich wonders if it would be possible to change his name to Judah, after all Jizchak Schwersenz changed his name so why can't he do the same; and Otto wonders how much asparagus the Krützfelds gave them, and if there is any left for another meal, and how on earth does Wilhelm, that coward, manage to grow it in the winter, even with a greenhouse; and Rosa wonders which route would be best to take to school tomorrow; and Hedi wonders if one were to collect all the melted wax that drips off the candles could one make an elephant, because elephants are big and they have sad eyes. And the night draws in, and the family draw their woollens around them, for they tend to feel the cold these days; and they very much look forward to the hearty meal that, for once, awaits them.

9 November 1938, Berlin

I

Polizeiobermeister Wilhelm Krützfeld sits for several minutes, staring straight ahead, a troubled expression on his face, his head like a tortoise's protruding from the steep collar of his jerkin. He consults his pocket-watch, replaces it, then continues stiffly to sit in his chair, at his desk, in his office, which is unremarkable save for the extensive collection of potted plants and flowers which cluster in the corners of the room. Flowers are, as one would imagine, an unusual feature in the office of a Polizeiobermeister, especially in such quantities. Each morning he arrives half an hour early to water them, talk to them, play them a little Mozart; but since last night, when the execution of Jewish prisoners at Buchenwald began, the Polizeiobermeister has had more on his mind.

Silently he sits, his fists resting on the edge of his desk, his polished buttons glinting like berries. He is feeling his age tonight, one month from today he will be fifty-nine, just a hair's breadth away from sixty. He seizes a pen and begins to tap it on a sheaf of paper nervously, end to end, end to end, end to end, leaving barely perceptible indentations, end to end, end to end, end to end. On the paper is typed a list of names and addresses, in alphabetical order, including: Familie Klein, Otto, Inga, drei Kinder, Beeskower Straße 53, Prenzlauer Berg, Berlin. The clock strikes the hour, the chimes syncopating with the taps of pen on paper, end chime to end chime to end chime to end chime to end. Still the policeman sits.

Enough. He opens a desk drawer and retrieves his Luger, which he snaps firmly into his holster. Then he strides over to the hatstand, throws his blue-grey trench coat bat-like over his shoulders and presses his cap on his head, pulling its patent peak low, the police insignia glinting in the light. Then he sweeps from the office, folding the list of names smartly into his pocket.

As he swings the car door open he notices passers-by reacting, notices the expressions on their faces, how they cast down their eyes and turn up their lapels and scurry furtively from him. Things were never like this, he thinks, before; we policemen used to be seen as the champions of the just, protectors of the defenceless, upholders of the law, yet these days people turn from us in fear; if he had known, all those years ago, when he first joined the force, that it would one day come to this! Last June he and his colleagues were informed by Doktor Goebbels that the common law no longer applied when dealing with Jews, and this evening they have been ordered to withdraw all officers from the streets, to stand aside, so that the Jews will, for once, taste the unbridled force of popular anger. And now here he is, alone, with a list in his pocket and bullets in his gun, the servant of an ever more maddening master.

The Polizeiobermeister's gun-handle presses awkwardly into his kidney as he sits in the driver's smooth seat; he readjusts it with impatience, drops his hat roundly on the passenger seat, fires the engine and steers onto the Dircksenstraße. Afternoon is being overpowered by evening and it has been a dark afternoon at that, thinks the Polizeiobermeister as he guides the clattering black car north towards the Arbeiterviertel, through the Berlin traffic with its moisture-spotted windows. The city is a cauldron tonight, the tension simmering, almost unbearable, yet on the face of it everywhere it is business as usual: the pockets of SA men smoking their lung torpedoes, the groups of girls walking gaily to a dance, the children being led by the hand, the trams and newspaper vendors and vagabonds, the beleaguered shop assistants and shifty-looking Jews in threadbare felt hats, carrying bronze-topped canes.

Polizeiobermeister Krützfeld parks outside the cream-coloured tenements, sits for a moment with the engine running, one hand resting on his Luger, the other playing with his hat, rolling his tongue in his mouth, absentmindedly reading a billboard by the side of the road, Becker-Fiebig, Building Contractor, Berlin W 38. Then all at once he exits the vehicle, consults the list of addresses, pushes through the wooden doors of Block 3, strides across the courtyard towards the staircase and disappears into the shadows.

The events that have led to tonight began just a few weeks ago. Thousands of Polish-born Jews were torn from their beds in the middle of the night, rounded up by the Gestapo and driven away, the streets black with crowds shouting Juden raus, Juden raus, Juden raus; they were driven into Poland and dumped in the wilderness of the borderlands. Having nowhere else to go, they have been there ever since, sheltering in disused barns, scavenging for food, deserted by the world. Amongst this unhappy group was an elderly grocer by the name of Zindel Grynszpan, who had lived in Hanover for twenty-seven years; he was beaten by a soldier and would have met his end had not one of his sons dragged him away to re-join the panicking throng.

Zindel Grynszpan had another son by the name of Herschel, a narrow-faced seventeen-year-old boy with raven-black hair and a troubled manner. Unable to finish school and expelled from several institutions, Herschel had been mooching around Europe for years and was currently living in Paris. When he received word of his family's fate, he was enraged. Armed with a gun that he had procured from a disreputable dealer with a knotty moustache who ran a shop on the south bank of the Seine, he took the Métro to the Champs-Élysées and paid a visit to the German embassy, where he told the gendarme at the door that he must deliver an urgent document to the ambassador. To Herschel's surprise he found himself being ushered into the office of the hapless Third Secretary Ernst vom Rath. Herschel was instructed to wait, the five-bulleted gun lying undetected, heavy and silent in his pocket.

Now Ernst vom Rath, despite working for the diplomatic corps, was no Nazi; indeed, he openly displayed Jewish sympathies, and the Gestapo had been trailing him for weeks. Yet as he entered the room, hand extended, Herschel drew his gun, screamed, you filthy Nazi Boche, and pulled the trigger. Two bullets hit, three missed, and then his gun was empty, the door burst open and a gendarme rushed clumsily in, pistol drawn. Herschel was dragged away, his slight frame buckling, leaving the Third Secretary slumped over the desk, his life-blood flowing from him. Back in Germany the Jews as a race were blamed, Berlin simmered with a lust for revenge and is due to boil over tonight.

The Polizeiobermeister climbs the stairs to the Kleins' apartment. People are closing their doors as they glimpse him, not as young as he was, these stairs will be the death of him, and these communal latrines really do stink, not too many more to go, ah so, apartment Klein, it smells of boiling laundry, the paint is peeling badly, my they have gone down in the world. Now to knock on the door, ha, knock is not the word, funny how he has got used to raising his fist like this and thumping on the doors of perfect strangers, it comes naturally to him now, to break the unspoken sanctity of another man's door with heavy violent thumping – there, the scrape of chairs and hushed voices, now is the time to thump again, don't give them a chance to hide or escape, and now is the time to shout, this is the police! Open the door immediately, Jews! and thump again. Now the door is creaking slightly beneath his fist, it is thin and worn, this door, not hardwood that's for certain, and, as expected, a child starts crying within, their little daughter no doubt, in Krützfeld's experience a child's cries make the parents act unpredictably, so he must thump again, and again shout, open up, Jews, open up! Now someone is finally coming, yes, the click of the latch, and—

—Wilhelm?

—Silence, Jewess, stand aside.

Wilhelm Krützfeld strides into the Kleins' apartment, shouts again at Inga and slams the door behind him, loud enough for the neighbours to hear. Then he stops, stands in the middle of the room and for several seconds gazes at the Kleins. Gradually his face, mask-like, changes, and he turns from one to the other, showing them each a faltering smile. Heinrich, is that Heinrich? Much older, sullen-looking, wiry; and that must be Rosa, emerging from her room, goodness hasn't she grown, she is practically a woman now, rather sad-looking, aren't they all these days, isn't everyone; and little Hedi; and Inga, aged beyond her years, she never used to wear a headscarf, he almost didn't recognise her; and finally Klein himself, tumbler of Schnaps in hand, some things never change. And all around them is hanging laundry.

Without a word Krützfeld removes his hat.

—Wilhelm, is it really you? says Inga. I can't believe my eyes.

—I'm sorry for the crude entrance, says the Polizeiobermeister awkwardly, but these days, you understand. My wife sends her best regards. She talks of you often.

—Have you lost your mind, says Klein, banging on our door like a madman? Scaring the children?

—My apologies, Klein, but things have changed. It has been a long time.

—Indeed, says Klein, I almost didn't recognise you. You're looking very well.

—I need to speak to you as a matter of urgency, says the Polizeiobermeister.

—Sit down, says Inga. Let me get you a drink. Brandy?

—I shouldn't. I'm on duty.

—Pfui, nonsense. Our brandy is cheap, but nevertheless.

Inga crosses to the drinks cabinet. Krützfeld sits at the table and looks at Klein, stretching a smile across his teeth.

—So, Klein, he says. You look well. Older, but well.

Klein does not reply. He turns to Rosa and Heinrich who are standing uncomfortably side by side:

—Rosa, go and play with Hedi in her room. Heinrich, go to your room as well.

—Why not let them stay? says Krützfeld.

—Yes, I would rather stay, Vater. I am eighteen, says Heinrich.

Klein gives his son a piercing glare, and Heinrich stalks from the room saying ach, very well, very well.

There is a pause.

—That is a grand uniform you have, says Inga, handing Krützfeld his brandy. Are you a major now?

—Polizeiobermeister, says the Polizeiobermeister, chief of the sixteenth precinct at the Hackescher Markt. I was promoted in the spring.

—Berta must be very proud.

—Indeed.

—Naturally, says Klein.

The three of them sit at the table in awkward silence. There is the sound of water gushing noisily through the pipes, and shadows cast by haphazard rows of laundry move drearily on the ceiling. A threadbare pair of trousers hanging on the side of a door drips regularly on the floorboards.

—It has been ever such a long time, says Inga, at last. How many years? Three? Four?

—I've lost count, says Krützfeld.

—Five years, says Klein. Now enough of this charade. If this matter is so urgent, spit it out.

—They have been sending us food parcels, says Inga.

—Look, Klein, I have come with your welfare in mind, Krützfeld interrupts. If anyone knew I was doing this, my career would be destroyed.

—We wouldn't want that, says Klein.

—Liebling . . .

—Just tell us why you're here, says Klein. We don't owe you anything.

—Direct as ever, says Krützfeld. Very well. You will be aware, of course, that Herr vom Rath died this evening.

—Goodness, says Inga, alarmed.

Krützfeld is inscrutable.

—And this does not mean good things for you, he says carefully. I must tell you, the police are being withdrawn from the streets tonight.

—Withdrawn? Why? asks Inga.

Krützfeld says nothing, and through his silence Inga understands the answer to her question.

—I have come to help you, says Krützfeld.

—You are a little late, says Klein.

—I don't have much time, says the Polizeiobermeister, I must be frank. Your family is in danger. Your names are on the list.

—There is a list? says Inga.

—Come now, says Klein. Do you expect us to die of fright just because of the feeble threats of a second-rate policeman?

—This is not a threat, says Krützfeld, it's a warning.

—It is quiet outside, Klein replies, gesturing generally towards the window, there is no sign of disturbance. I have the distinct impression we are being lied to, Herr Polizeiuntermeister, the distinct impression.

—Liebling, says Inga, her voice wavering.

—You're seeing a liar where there isn't one, Klein, says Krützfeld, displaying a professional patience. You can trust me. Vom Rath is dead, you can confirm it yourself by listening to the wireless. See, I have no men with me. Nobody knows I am here. As I told you, the police have been withdrawn.

—As you told us, as you told us, says Klein. We Jews have been told a lot of things recently, Herr Polizeiuntermeister, by people like you. But be careful, change your clothes before you go drinking with your Gestapo friends. I have heard that we Jews have a stench.

—Liebling! Inga exclaims.

—You are drunk, says Krützfeld. Please. When they are breaking down your door, it will be too late.

—Breaking down our door? says Inga. What shall we do? What can we do?

—Don't panic, says Krützfeld, I have prepared everything. You must split up, it's only logical. Inga, you take Hedi and go to the railway station, as inconspicuously as possible. There you must mingle with the crowds until the morning when you can make your way back home.

—Will the violence be over by then, asks Inga, are you sure?

—So I believe. And if it is not I will come and give you further instructions. Now, Heinrich and Rosa must hasten to my house. The address I have written here. There is a shed in the garden where they can hide until morning, or whenever it is safe. It can be accessed by a side entrance. It is small but there should just be room for two. For goodness' sake tell them not to show their faces, or come anywhere near the house itself.

Krützfeld passes a scrap of paper to Inga, on which his address is written.

—So you expect us to run away and hide like rabbits? says Klein, his eyes piercing points of steel.

—Not at all. I have a different plan for you, Klein: I will arrest you.

—Arrest me?

—Yes. I will take you to the station and lock you in a cell for the night. You will come to no harm. Then, in the morning, or whenever it is over, I will release you.

—Have you lost your mind?

—Not at all. We must act. Quickly now. You must all be out of the apartment within ten minutes. Get your coats and hats.

—I suppose you wish to handcuff me as well?

—That would be sensible, yes.

—Ha ha ha! He takes me for a fool!

—I must get you out of harm's way, Klein. I promised my wife.

—Do you really think I would be tricked so easily? I thought you knew me better than that, Herr Untersergeanten. Do you think I haven't realised this is nothing more than a ploy to seize our apartment, our property, our silver? Ha! You will not arrest me without a fight. You are nothing but a common thief.

—Liebling, says Inga, if Wilhelm wanted to arrest you he would have done so already.

—You're not punishing me, says Krützfeld. You're punishing yourself.

—Oh, now a sermon from a greedy policeman, says Klein. You are humiliating yourself, Wilhelm, you are debasing yourself. A common thief.

—Klein, don't make me use force, says Krützfeld.

—There's a snake in this room, a reptile in a uniform, says Klein. You will never seize my property without a fight. I am a Frontkämpfer. You will have to shoot me first.

Krützfeld rolls his eyes and thumps the table in frustration.

—We are both Frontkämpfer, Klein, in case you have forgotten. I cannot dally here forever trying to win your trust and I am too old to be insulted by a drunk. If I stay any longer I will be in danger myself. Just remember our friendship and come with me. He presses his hat onto his head.

—All my friendships are dead, says Klein, you have shown that over the last five years and you are showing it again tonight.

Krützfeld softens his voice.

—Klein, I am asking you one more time. No, I am begging you. Come with me. Once I have gone your fate will be sealed.

—Nothing would please me more, Herr thief, says Klein.

—Mein Gott. Inga, if your husband does not regain his sanity, at least you and the children may be safe. Do as I have instructed, it is for your own good.

—I will, says Inga.

—You will not, says Klein, draining his glass.

The Polizeiobermeister avoids Klein's eyes, pulls his cap down on his brow, pushes his way past the hanging laundry and strides out of the apartment.

It all happened so quickly, yet as Krützfeld crosses the courtyard, rubbing his hand across his face, he tells himself that he has done everything humanly possible, everything within his power, to help these people, that no more could reasonably have been done to protect them. He dreads what his wife will say, she was very fond of the Kleins, especially her old friend Inga. He tosses his hat onto the seat and slips behind the wheel of his car. His Luger presses into his kidney and he adjusts his holster irritably. Before pulling away he lights a cigarette and inhales, deeply, to the bottom of his lungs.

2

Hedi, in her bedroom, wails into the night. Rosa takes her in her arms and rocks her to and fro. In the sitting-room, Inga speaks.

—Otto, are you mad? Now what shall we do? She gets to her feet and stands in the middle of the room, her arms folded across her chest, clutching the scrap of paper.

—That was a trap, replies her husband. He struggles up from the sofa and crosses uncertainly to the drinks cabinet. Wilhelm Krützfeld has evil in his eyes, he says morbidly.

Inga turns off the electric lights, then crosses to the window and opens the curtains.

—Liebling, you see? A fire on the horizon.

—That is not a fire, grunts her husband dismissively.

—It is a fire. I am sure it is a fire.

Klein rolls his drink in his hand and taps his fingernails against his teeth. So? he says. A fire in the city of Berlin. This should make us worried?

—I have a bad feeling, Liebling, in my stomach. A bad feeling, like I'm going to be sick.

—Have a drink.

—That fire.

—Have a drink.

The door half opens. Heinrich slinks through like a stray cat and asks:

—Has he gone?

—Heinrich, get back to your room, says his father, still rolling his glass in his palm.

—Judah, Vater, call me Judah. That is my name now.

—Heinrich, I won't tell you again.

Rosa pads into the room, her eyes darting anxiously from one person to another.

—Mama, what is going on? she says. Will somebody please tell me?

—It is nothing, Püppchen, Klein mutters. Just a misunderstanding with an acquaintance. Now go back to your room.

—But Judah is not in his room.

—He is just on his way, is he not, Heinrich?

—What shall we do, Liebling, what shall we do? says Inga. Vom Rath has died, it's a disaster. Wilhelm said they will break down our door.

—Nonsense. I am perfectly capable of protecting my own family. Anyway it is dangerous outside, especially at night. We would stand more chance of getting attacked in the street.

—But what if he is right, says Inga, what if they have a list?

—We have locks on the door, do we not? her husband replies. Do you really think we would be safer walking the streets?

Inga unfolds her arms, clasps her fingers several times by her sides and strides from the room.

—Inga, where are you going? Klein goes after her, followed by Heinrich and Rosa. Where are you going? Are you losing your mind?

Inga enters Hedi's room and plucks her from the bed. The rest of the family crowd in behind her as she gets Hedi dressed.

—But Mama, protests Hedi mildly, I don't want to go out.

—Don't argue, little madam. Get your gloves and coat this instant.

—Inga, this is absurd, says Klein.

—You should take a suitcase, Mama, suggests Heinrich. It will help you to blend in.

—Good idea. Would you please get me one from my room?

—You will do nothing of the sort, snaps Klein. Get back to your room, this instant. Heinrich?

—Where are you going, Mama? asks Rosa anxiously.

—Your mother is going nowhere, says Klein. Now get back to your room, both of you.

—Come now, Hedi, and put your scarf on too, says Inga, undeterred.

—Inga, you are not leaving this house. Nobody is leaving this house. I forbid it.

—Liebling, if you must commit suicide, don't take us with you, says Inga. Now, we don't have time. There – look. Another fire.

—That is not a fire.

—Of course it is a fire. Oh, thank you, Judah.

—Not at all. I filled it with a few woollens.

Inga takes Hedi's arm in a firm grip and leads her through the laundry to the front door. Then she turns to her older children.

—Now Judah, Rosa, listen to me, she says. You must leave the apartment and go to the address written here, the Krützfelds' house. There is a side entrance and a shed in the garden where you can hide. Take some warm clothes and remain there until morning. And do not show your face, or go near the house. Do you hear?

—Can they be trusted? says Heinrich, taking the scrap of paper.

—Just do it. Do you hear? snaps Inga. Liebling, I think you should accompany the children, now that you have refused Wilhelm's first offer.

—I shall accompany nobody. This is farcical.

—I beg you. Please, for the sake of the children. For the sake of the children. Ah, Heinrich, try to take your father with you, please. Now I must go. God bless you all, and I shall see you here tomorrow. Come along now, Hedi, we are going to the railway station. Come along.

There is no time for tears, embraces, goodbyes. The door closes and Inga and Hedi are gone. Klein drains his glass and crosses to the drinks cabinet. He pours himself a measure of Schnaps, spilling a little as he does so, the lip of the bottle clattering against the glass. Heinrich and Rosa sit at the kitchen table, Rosa tapping it compulsively, Heinrich pounding his chin with his fingers.

—I say, says Heinrich, is your old bicycle still downstairs?

—I suppose so.

—Stop laughing, this is serious.

—I am not laughing, says Rosa, I am just nervous.

—You must take it and ride to that address, as Mama said, and sleep in the shed for the night, says Heinrich. I will get some food for you to take.

—I can't. Bicycles are verboten. If I am caught it will be terrible.

—You will not get caught. Just pull your hat down, avoid Jewish areas and stick to the back streets. And if anything happens, ride as fast as you can.

—And what about you?

—I will take Papa and go a different route. We will meet you there. It is better if you go by yourself, you will attract less attention.

—I'm not sure I can still ride a bicycle.

—What nonsense, of course you can, says Heinrich, showing her a smile. When you get to the house, hide the bicycle in the bushes and settle down in the shed. Now hurry along and put some warm clothes on. I will get you some food. The sooner you go, the safer it will be.

—Mama said we should go together. I do not want you to fight, Judah.

—Who said anything about fighting? Papa and I will leave a few minutes after you and make our way directly to the house.

—Another fire.

—No, that's the same one. Go on, hurry up.

Rosa takes the scrap of paper and places it carefully in her pocket. Then she goes to her room and puts on two jumpers, for it is cold outside; she catches sight of herself in the mirror and stops for a moment. Her face is taut and her eyes are dry and dark, like chestnuts. She looks older, somehow, so much older, who would believe she is only fifteen, look at her, haggard, that is the word, and now she is to ride off in the middle of the night on a verboten bicycle. She pulls on her hat and winds her scarf several times round her neck, then goes back through to the kitchen where Heinrich is packing some food into a canvas bag. Opposite him sits their father, sipping from another glass of Schnaps and trying to smooth his hair; his collar is undone and hanging down his shirt.

—So you are leaving me as well, Püppchen? he says.

—I think it is for the best that we go separately, says Rosa unconvincingly. Better to be safe. But I will see you there.

—There is nothing to worry about. Can you hear anything? Attackers? Crowds? Sirens? Anything? No reason to flee like rabbits.

—What about the fires, Papa? says Rosa.

—Heinrich, you should go with her. It is not safe for a girl on her own, girls cannot fight, eh?

—Papa, I will be fine, retorts Rosa, a little too strongly. I will have my bicycle. If anything happens I will just ride away.

—If only it were that simple! exclaims her father in sudden despair.

—Rosa, says Heinrich, there is no time to waste. I will look after Papa. Take this, it's only bread and cheese but it will keep your strength up. Good, you are warmly dressed. You must go.

—Very well.

Rosa embraces Heinrich, holding him tight, she feels like crying, only her eyes are dry as chestnuts; she wishes more than anything that he was coming with her, and suddenly she hates her father for being so weak. Then she tells herself now is not the time for such thoughts, and she turns to her papa and embraces him as well; the Schnaps is warm on his breath. Then she turns and walks backwards out of the door, allowing it to click shut in front of her face.

3

Outside in the corridor it is very cold, and Rosa can smell the communal latrine. She stops for a moment, carefully listens: nothing out of the ordinary, nothing at all, just the occasional car trundling by, the occasional voice from a neighbouring apartment, the occasional whisper of a draught round her ankles. It is hard to imagine that anything will happen tonight; why should it? She decides to return to the apartment, she puts her hand on the handle, but then something makes her stop; she turns and makes her way down the stairs, and as she reaches the bottom her legs feel weak. Suddenly she feels the urge to escape, to run, to put as much distance between herself and this apartment as possible. She is short of breath already, and the ride has not even begun.

Under the stairs she struggles with a moth-eaten sheet until her old bicycle is revealed in a cloud of dust. Then she manoeuvres it from under the stairs. The saddle is mildewed and there is a black layer of grime on the handlebars, but apart from that the bicycle seems quite serviceable. Remarkably enough, the tyres are as hard now as they were three years ago, how different things were then, how different. She wheels the bicycle to the doorway, gathers her skirt and mounts it. Then, slightly wobbly at first but with growing confidence, she rides across the courtyard, pushes her way through the wooden doors – the street is deserted – looks left and right and, heart thumping, raises her body to a stand and brings her entire weight to bear upon the pedals, which are a little stiff. They start to rotate, then faster, and as she picks up speed she lowers herself to the saddle and takes a rest from pedalling, allowing the bicycle to carry her along in the old way, the way it used to.

As Rosa rides, her breath creates little double clouds which stream off on either side and disappear in the gloom behind. The street, everything about it, she knows in detail: the cobbles sunken in tar, the iron railings which she would be tapping were she walking, the walls of faceted sandstone blocks with regular stepped entrances; yes, even by night this is familiar, even on such a night as this, even, indeed, from this height, for Rosa is elevated to an unusual degree on the bicycle, and even at this unusual pace. Nothing is particularly out of the ordinary about Berlin tonight, she thinks as she turns, uncertainly, onto the Prenzlauer Allee – when you haven't ridden for a while straight lines aren't a problem but corners can be somewhat tricky. Groups of people are milling about the streets – packs of SA men in their coffee-coloured shirts and caps, clusters of office workers in sombre overcoats – yes, nothing out of the ordinary at all, surely this evening will become one of those family stories that are laughed about in years to come. But she keeps riding, does not turn back, speeds up, pedals harder. A tram draws alongside, lit from inside like a lantern, its antennae buzzing on the overhead wire, it is empty apart from the conductor, slouching in his uniform and stifling a yawn, and, on the back seat, a man in a derby hat scratching his back with a rolled-up newspaper; it passes and the street is hers once again.

The shops are all closed, their wares lit against black backgrounds behind highly polished Kristallglas. Rosa sees her reflection in these windows, in this glass, flicking in and out of view between cars, pedestrians, tram stops, advertising pillars, charting smooth lines across black-slabbed roads in the centre of a wide street scene. Far off, behind the buzz and groan of the traffic, marching music can be heard – Rosa steers her bicycle carefully across the tramlines and turns onto the Sredzkistraße, away from the sound of the music until it is no longer audible. A van rattles by carrying a group of SA men smoking cigarettes, they are singing loudly a Nazi song and banging on the side of the van: Wenn's Judenblut vom Messer spritzt, dann geht's nochmal so gut, when Jewish blood springs from the knife then things are twice as well. Rosa turns onto the Rykestraße and pedals down it, picking up as much speed as she can, rattling on the cobbles, recalling Heinrich's advice to keep away from main roads, seek out the shadows, avoid busy areas and those frequented by Jews. She can feel her breasts jerking uncomfortably and reduces her speed, pressing gently on the brake, the back brake, not the front brake, that much she can remember at least. The streetlights are dim here, all the windows are curtained, thin pencil-lines of light appearing in the gaps between them; this area is more deserted than the rest, the houses have a strange sense of being barricaded.

Suddenly there is a great deal of noise. Rosa sees a cloud of sand falling into the road and bouncing on the cobbles like salt. Not sand, broken glass. In the next second a dark bundle lands heavily on the cobbles with a curious skidding crunch: a tailor's dummy, Rosa thinks, like the one Mama uses. She clamps her fingers on the brakes and veers the handlebars to the side; the bicycle lurches across the road, then wobbles and rights itself. A cacophony of shouts and screams breaks out and Rosa looks back over her shoulder; in the diminishing distance she can see two men in black uniforms, their faces cast into shadow by the peaks of their SS hats, walking over to the dummy and rolling it to the kerb – it comes to rest, a white forearm protruding upwards and arcing onto the pavement. Rosa stands on the pedals, turning them as fast as she can.

Without warning, all around her, doors open, and neighbours emerge, hurrying into the street, men still chewing with their napkins round their necks, women buttoning their coats, children holding toys scurrying behind; at the same time more people appear from other parts of the city, trotting round corners, groups of three, five, twenty, jostling and laughing and craning their necks, in hats and caps and scarves. Everywhere are schoolboys, many carrying bricks, some with planks and hammers, and one, for some reason, a broom; then there are SA men, big and broad and pink-faced, most with their brown shirts neat and pressed, but some untidy, untucked; then scores of others, following keenly, the sort of people you would see in the bank, or the library, or the post office, men with collars turned up, women with fashionable hats and gloves, mothers lifting children high above the crowds to give them a better view. People mill about, breathing into their hands and rubbing them for warmth, many smiling broadly, nudging and giggling as if sharing a secret. Rosa is forced to slow down and dismount. She wheels her bicycle through the swelling crowd, trying to keep to the shadows as inconspicuously as possible, while further down the street more breaking glass can be heard, and cheers and laughter, and a woman weeping, and piercing screams, and shouts, and laughter, and the clatter of bricks against walls.

Rosa's hands are numb and she feels as if she is floating, as if the world is pulsating in time with her thumping heart; the crowd is pressing in on her, she tries to catch her breath but cannot, she knows from experience that walking against the flow will give her away, so she allows herself to be carried by the current, tries to smile like the others, appear as if she too is enjoying herself. The screams get louder, from many throats now, unseen in the buildings, and the sound of shattering glass, and male shouts, and doors splintering under heavy blows; then an orange light is thrown into the darkness, Rosa looks up and sees flames darting from a triangular roof, in the centre of which is a stone Star of David – of course, she is in the Rykestraße, she has ridden to the very steps of a synagogue, why didn't she think, she must have been sleeping, straight to a synagogue, how stupid! There are more screams, and the smoke rises, and a cheer goes up from the crowd, together with a brief chant of 'Raus mit den Juden', which develops into 'Raus, raus, raus, Juden raus'. Everyone is jostling to get a better view, and Rosa jostles as well, looking for a means of escape. Then, seeing her chance, she threads through the crowd and turns down an alleyway, wheeling her bicycle casually, forcing herself to walk as if she is a normal German girl.

A young woman steps out in front of her, arms folded. Rosa stops, catches her eye, starts, looks away, steers round her, tries to walk on; but now she fears that there will be trouble, for in that brief moment when their eyes met Rosa recognised Krista Schwab, from her old school, unmistakably, looking almost the same as all those years ago, if slightly plumper and taller; and it is likely that Krista has also recognised her. Suddenly she feels as if she is itching, her whole body is itching, and she can't help but glance over her shoulder. Krista is gazing after her, her face bleached orange on one side from the flames, and she has not unfolded her arms. For a moment Rosa considers stopping, acting as if she has bumped into an old acquaintance in a café, just a normal German girl. But then Krista opens her eyes wide and, her arms still folded tightly across her stomach, lets out a piercing shriek:

—A Jew, a Jew! A Jew, a Jew! Throw her on the fire! Throw her on the fire! Let her burn!

Rosa recoils in alarm and almost overbalances, but manages to mount the bicycle and starts to pedal away. It takes an age for the bicycle to get moving, it seems so heavy, she heaves against the pedals, and still Krista shrieks, unremittingly, without pausing for breath, her arms folded tight across her stomach, a Jew, a Jew, a dirty Jew, throw her on the flames, and Rosa strains at the pedals, and there are shouts behind her, something smashes to her left; there is the sound of pounding feet, and she looks over her shoulder to see the silhouette of a man giving chase, flames illuminating the cobbles behind him. She swerves, almost loses control, then lowers her head and rides as fast as she can. The man is still in pursuit; suddenly he is alongside, jacket and tie whipping out behind. She glances over and sees his face white against the darkness, wide eyes and wide grin, and she pedals some more and he clutches her sleeve, pulling the handlebars out of alignment; the bicycle swerves again, he tips his head back and spits in her face, she screams and the bicycle veers away, out of his grasp; it weaves and almost upends, but Rosa rights it, and the man falls behind. He makes a last-ditch attempt to catch her, takes a final grab at the saddle, his fingers grip the bicycle but then break away; he slows down, Rosa speeds up, the gap between them widens: Judensau! Judensau! Something hits her on the shoulder, she gasps but pedals on, faster and faster, veering around corners, not knowing where she is going, away from the crowds, away from the noise and the flames, into the darkness, the night.

A silence falls over the city again and Rosa can hear herself breathing. She turns in her saddle and can see no sign of pursuit, and the crowd can no longer be heard; she has left them behind, she is safe, for the moment. She slows the bicycle to a regular speed and tries to calm her racing heart. This part of the city seems so foreign, nothing is familiar, but at least there are no crowds here, the streets are deserted, even quieter than usual. She must concentrate, that was a stupid mistake, could have been the end. She must keep calm, keep riding, clear her head, think rationally, nobody can see that she is Jewish if she rides her bicycle as normal, at a normal pace, and keeps her head up, acts cheerful, she is normal, a normal German girl. The road beneath the wheels slips by like a conveyor belt, the tyres thrum and the cogs and chain clank drily in the darkness; perhaps she is not moving at all, perhaps the world is moving around her. Just keep going, keep going, everything will be all right if she keeps riding as normal, there is nothing to give her away.

Suddenly, without warning, the pedals freeze solid and the bicycle loses momentum. Rosa brings her whole weight to bear upon the pedals but they do not budge. There is nothing for it. She guides the bicycle into an alcove, dismounts on trembling feet. In the corner she crouches and peers at the cogs and the chain, biting her lip; the alcove smells of urine and is gritty with grime underfoot. Her mouth hangs open, her eyes strain against the dark: the chain has come off the central cog and is wedged impossibly tightly against the frame. Rosa presses it with her foot but it cannot be shifted. The smell of urine lingers bitterly in her nostrils. She pushes her hat up to her hairline, leaving a webbed indentation across her forehead.

A voice comes from the street, a woman's:

—Excuse me? Fräulein? Are you all right?

Rosa stiffens, half turns towards the pavement, pulling her hat swiftly back down.

—Yes, fine, thank you, she replies. Just a little bicycle trouble. I can fix it myself.

—Are you not in need of help? I know a little about bicycles. I have three brothers and they are obsessed with them.

—You are most kind but I can manage. I am fine. Please. Rosa forces a weak smile and looks briefly up. The woman on the pavement is unremarkable, of average height, hair drawn back in a propeller bow beneath a beret; she is wrapped in a coat with a high collar and her hands are deep in her pockets. There is something about her . . .

—Good Lord, it couldn't be, could it? Klein? Rosa Klein?

—I . . .

—My, how you have grown. How you have grown! But do you not recognise me?

—Frau Schulz?

—Yes, your old Frau Schulz, your old, faithful maid. Kleine Rosa! I haven't seen you since you were a little girl. How old are you now, eighteen?

—Fifteen.

—My, my, fifteen, fifteen! What a coincidence, what fun.

A gust of freezing wind blows into the alcove, and Frau Schulz draws her collar higher around her cheeks.

—It is awfully cold, she continues. What are you doing in this part of town all by yourself?

—Nothing.

—Nothing?

—Just riding my bicycle.

—Your bicycle, I see. You should be careful, Rosa. Jews are forbidden to ride bicycles, were you not aware? I believe that a reward would be due to whoever hands you in to the Gestapo.

Rosa tries to swallow, her throat a metal tube, dry and unyielding.

—I was not aware that bicycles were verboten, she says.

—It is not safe for a Jew to be in the street, you know. Tonight.

—I . . . was unaware of any danger.

—Unaware! What do you think that noise is? Haven't you been listening to the wireless? I don't know where I would be without my Volksempfänger. Well, thank goodness we bumped into each other. This is a happy coincidence, would you not agree?

—Yes, Frau Schulz, indeed. Now I think I should get on my way.

—Your bicycle is broken.

—It is not a serious fault. The chain has come off, that's all.

—That is easy to fix. Here, let me.

Within seconds Frau Schulz has upended the bicycle and is fiddling with the chain, her hands protected from the grease by a handkerchief.

—It's a little neglected, isn't it, she says. Hasn't been oiled, that's why. The maid braces herself against the wall and prises the chain free. Ah: there. Good as new.

—Thank you so much, says Rosa. Now I must go.

The maid lifts the bicycle onto its tyres but does not let go of the handlebars.

—I am concerned for you, Rosa, she says. You shouldn't be outside tonight by yourself, especially on an Aryan bicycle.

Rosa moves to take the handlebars, but Frau Schulz does not release her grasp.

—Where are you going, asks the maid, surely not home?

—Nowhere.

—Come now, kleine Rosa. I know you haven't seen me for many years, but I cared for you as a child. You can trust me.

—Please let me have my bicycle. I need to go.

—Do not be in such a hurry, my dear. This bicycle may be the death of you. Where are you going?

—Please give me my bicycle.

—Rosa Klein, I can see you have lost none of your stubbornness. Why so suspicious? I'd have thought you could trust me. Many of my neighbours were Jews. I only want to help.

Rosa looks intently at Frau Schulz, trying to read the expression in her eyes, but it is dim in the alcove and her face, sunk in its collar, is cast in shadow. Rosa twists her fingers uneasily on the handlebars, unsure of what to do, undecided. Frau Schulz is probably harmless. Rosa is still shaken by the incident on the Rykestraße, perhaps she is being too suspicious. It is the general condition of life as a Jew at the moment that makes for suspicion of everyone, even of childhood maids. Frau Schulz, noting Rosa's silence, speaks again.

—Believe me, she says, if I had wanted to turn you and your bicycle in to the Gestapo, I could have done so by now. Now tell me where you are going and I will give you back your bicycle.

—I'm sorry, Frau Schulz. I just want it back.

The maid lowers her voice to a tender purr.

—Kleine Rosa. It was most painful for me when I was forced out of your family, for economic reasons, as your Vater so eloquently put it at the time. I gave the best years of my life to you. I have never had any children of my own. And now you don't trust me.

Rosa's conscience is activated, automatically, like a bicycle that can be ridden by anybody, regardless of their intention. Words flash unbidden into her mind: ungrateful, suspicious, cynical, joyless, unfair, that is what she is, how she is acting, Frau Schulz is only trying to help, this is no way to treat her. Fighting her instincts, Rosa forces herself to smile; but her mouth is dry and no words will come. Frau Schulz speaks again in even more gentle tones.

—I will ask you one final time. Then I will give up and leave you to your own devices, alone on a night like this. Are you going to trust me? Or humiliate me further?

—Frau Schulz, please, I must apologise. At times like these Jews are predisposed to suspicion . . .

—Naturally, I quite understand. Very good. Now where are you going?

—West, to the suburbs.

—Where exactly?

—I have the address written down. I am seeking refuge with a friend of the family.

—Let me see that piece of paper. Ah, I know the area well. I happen to live nearby. Another coincidence. Come now, let us go.

Frau Schulz returns the scrap of paper to Rosa, adjusts her beret and pushes the bicycle into the street.

—It is dangerous for Jews to ride bicycles tonight, kleine Rosa, she says. I shall wheel it for you and we will walk together. Nobody would mistake me for a Jew.

—I don't want to inconvenience you. I can easily go alone.

—Not at all. It isn't more than a few miles. It is the least I can do, I am going that way myself. Come now, enough silliness.

The maid pushes the bicycle briskly away, and Rosa hurries to catch up with her, glancing over her shoulder; then they fall into step.

—Is this really the best route, Frau Schulz?

—Of course, of course. Where is your family living now? I assume no longer in that lovely apartment by the Tiergarten.

—In Prenzlauer Berg.

—The Arbeiterviertel? Really? That must be . . . quite a change for you.

—One gets used to things.

69

—Of course. I have some friends in the Arbeiterviertel. What is the name of your street?

—The Beeskower Straße.

—Ah so, I know it well. My friends live in that area exactly. What apartment and block?

—Block three, fifty-three.

—A good number, fifty-three, a good number.

Goodness, what about her family? Rosa has been so preoccupied with Frau Schulz that she hasn't spared them a thought. A bitter guilt rises in her stomach, and she clenches her fists in her pockets.

4

Never thought I would be glad Hedi is so withdrawn, thinks Inga; tonight, for once, her disposition is a blessing, she attracts no attention at all, and there are enough people on the concourse for us to remain anonymous. It isn't too cold either, especially bundled up like this.

They sit for ten minutes on one bench and then move to another, sporadically around the concourse, meandering occasionally out of the station and back again, onto the steps and round the clock tower, back into the station, avoiding the ticket office, and around the concourse once again. The departures board ripples in great yellow waves and flicks up platform numbers and destinations, making Inga feel sick, must be bad for the eyes or something, and she has this nausea inside her anyway, sick all the way to the bones. There is a hubbub of voices, everything as normal, nothing unusual, apart from the fact that there are few Jews about, fewer than usual, Inga and Hedi may be the only ones in fact; my God, she thinks, Wilhelm's idea seems to be working, my God, it seems to be working. Please, my God, preserve us, protect us, shelter us all from harm, Rosa and Heinrich too, and Otto of course, in your mercy and compassion keep us all safe.

Inga hopes Rosa and Heinrich are safely at the Krützfelds' and she hopes Otto went with them. Surely he did, Heinrich will have found a way to get him out of the apartment, he is a shrewd boy, and devoted to his father, by now they will be safe, she hopes, hopes against hope, really, for hope is all one has left at times like these, hope. Hedi, are your hands cold? Do you need to go to the bathroom? Very good, so well behaved. Inga could never have done this with Heinrich at this age, or Rosa come to think of it. Hedi is so compliant, Inga is grateful for that, a blessing. There, on the other side of the concourse – a pair of SS men, striding purposefully at a diagonal, don't look, Hedi, don't look, must fix your scarf, there, and your gloves, there, wait: now carry on, another nervous circuit. Inga is feeling sick from her own heartbeats, she wonders if that's a medical condition. Get out of here, those images, like a madwoman, she can't stop these pictures of the family, dead; begone, foul thoughts, begone. The time – that cannot be correct, God the clock is crawling, eight hours to go at least, more probably, how can it be humanly possible to keep this up for ten hours? And Hedi is looking tired already, this is madness, as Otto said, madness, madness. And the rest of the family, what could be befalling them even now as Inga strolls around the concourse in blessed anonymity? Yet it is quiet here, nothing out of the ordinary, perhaps Wilhelm was wrong, panicking, or over-reacting, there may very well be nothing to worry about in the first place. However will this end, O Lord, however will it all end?

Above the high-roofed railway station clouds are beginning to collect in the darkness, overlapping and merging like a soapy sea, blocking the star-peppered clarity of the sky above. Beneath the cloud line street-lamps thread about the contours of the city, twinkling in their thousands around Berlin; the railway station glows dully in the dark.

There is a commotion on the edge of the concourse. A drunken man in a frayed cloth cap is paying unwanted attention to a woman with a suitcase who is leading a child by the hand. The woman is hurrying away, trying to shrug the man off while retaining her composure, but he will not be deterred. He is accusing her of being a Jew, bellowing, Jude Jude Jude, measuring her nose with clumsy fingers. Her hat almost falls off. Her little daughter is pulled about like a toy on a string. The SS men outside the ticket office laugh uproariously, the comedy, the entertainment. The woman slips from the station and disappears down the steps, the night closes behind her, and the drunken man, a little dizzy, slumps on a bench. A chuckling SS officer strides over, clicks his heels, claps the man on the shoulder and offers him a Reichsmark note.

5

They walk on in silence for a long time, the maid wheeling the bicycle a little in front, Rosa following behind. She does not recognise the area, can only follow Frau Schulz obediently round corner after corner, down street after anonymous street. Frau Schulz certainly seems to know where she is going; Rosa is sure that without her help she would be hopelessly lost by now.

The night deepens and they proceed into the outer suburbs where the streets are increasingly deserted, less well lit. The sound of crowds can be heard again, maybe a few blocks away, maybe further, and a gang of schoolboys runs past them, laughing, carrying fistfuls of watches. From time to time Frau Schulz disappears in the darkness, and Rosa has to hurry to catch up; she feels giddy, bites the inside of her cheek to keep alert. There is a red glow above some buildings further ahead.

—Frau Schulz. Look up there.

—What do you want?

—There, a little further along.

—There? Oh, the watchmaker's must be burning. Or the furniture shop, perhaps, on the Kastanienallee. The German people are teaching the Jews a lesson. We must avoid that area at all costs. Come, let's go this way.

The watchmaker, Rosa thinks, the furniture shop, the Kastanienallee. As she follows the maid in silence she sinks into a somnambulant daze, regarding the streets, the buildings, blankly. The cold soaks into the deepest recesses of her being, bringing with it a smothering numbness. She loses track of time, looking down at her feet and biting the insides of her cheeks.

—It is getting late, Rosa. Are you tired?

—A little.

—I am tired too. I live only a few minutes from here. Why don't we go to my apartment, sleep there for a few hours and continue on our way when rested? You will be safe at my house, at least for a while.

—I would rather carry on, says Rosa weakly.

—Rather carry on? What about me? I have given up my evening to ensure your safety.

—I did not ask you to do so. I did not need a guide.

—You say that now that we are out of the city. But I kept you away from the mobs and the burning synagogues. Without me you would certainly have been caught. And you are not safe yet, kleine Rosa. Not safe at all.

—You're right. I am grateful, says Rosa.

—I have even lost money, you know, says Frau Schulz. I was on my way to work when I met you. And now I may lose my job.

—You never told me that.

—Of course I didn't. I am not looking for recognition or reward. I am only being a good Christian. You are like my own child, you know. All I ask is for a little rest, a little sleep. Nothing more.

—I'm sorry. If you are tired, you should rest.

—Very well, we will rest, if that's how you feel. My apartment is on the next street.

They walk a little farther until they come to a park. On the corner is a turn-of-the-century apartment block, typical of the area, with a half-pyramid of stairs leading to a door flanked by iron handrails and blank-eyed lions. Frau Schulz carries the bicycle up the steps without the slightest difficulty, unlocks the door and leads Rosa inside, their footsteps echoing conspicuously in the night-time stairwell. Inside, the building is an example of shabby splendour, adorned with plaster mouldings, mirrors and a highly polished banister. The wallpaper is missing in patches and has been darkened over decades as if by smoke; the carpet is faded and thin in the middle, and worn strips of brass line the edges of the stairs. The muffled noise of the crowds is just audible, swelling and surging like the sound of the sea. Frau Schulz removes her beret and ushers Rosa up the stairs in front of her, hands spread out to touch the banisters on both sides. Rosa finds herself being shepherded into a neat gas-lit apartment that smells weakly of wood smoke. The door opens on a sitting room containing a table, two chairs arranged symmetrically, a sofa covered with a burgundy blanket, a fireplace, a wardrobe, a dressing table – that burgundy blanket, Rosa recognises it from years ago, it used to lie on Mama's armchair in her bedroom, how strange that it ended up in Frau Schulz's apartment, perhaps it was hers to begin with, or maybe Mama gave it to her when she left, who knows. And there is a doorway hung with a curtain of multicoloured beads, through which can be seen glimpses of a cramped kitchen cluttered with pots; another door, ajar, leads into a darkened bedroom.

—Can I offer you some tea?

—No thank you.

—Very well. Make yourself comfortable in the bed. I will wake you when it is time to set off again, says Frau Schulz maternally.

—But it wasn't me who wanted to rest. It was you.

—Yes of course, the maid says lightly. But first I must oil your bicycle, it is in a terrible state. And I have to light the fire. It is cold in here, don't you think?

Rosa takes off her hat and scarf, feeling, for a moment, like an eight-year-old again, under Frau Schulz's orders, only without the higher authority of her parents to appeal to; go to bed, you must be up for school tomorrow morning, very well, she will go to bed. She walks tiredly into the bedroom, is pleasantly surprised by the comfortable-looking bed with its patchwork quilt and fat cotton pillows. Wearily she drops her hat and coat upon a rocking chair in the corner, draws the curtains on the night, lights a stubby candle on the bedside table; with the curtains lying softly against one another, the noise of the crowds is diminished to a whisper. Without removing her clothes, she climbs gingerly into the bed. The sheets make a pleasant rustling sound, they smell of her childhood, perhaps it's Frau Schulz's soap; she stretches and snuggles into the pillow, for she is, in the end, rather tired, her body begins to relax and despite herself she falls into a doze, the butter-coloured candlelight softening her features, go to bed, very well, go to sleep.

There is a noise. Someone has entered the room. Rosa sits groggily up. She has no idea how long she has been sleeping; the candle is still lit, it can't have been very long.

—My dear Rosa, I thought you were tired, says Frau Schulz. Why ever are you not yet asleep? Rosa does not answer. The maid drags the rocking chair in front of the door, blocking it. Leaning over the bed, her face made ghoulish by long shadows, she moves to blow out the candle.

—No, please, don't, says Rosa. I don't like the dark. I will be afraid.

—Nonsense.

With a brisk puff the maid blows out the candle and the room is plunged into darkness. The wind rubs against the window, creaking the glass in the frame.

Rosa peers wide-eyed into the blackness, trying to see where Frau Schulz has gone. She could be anywhere, could have left the room, or be squatting in the corner, or hiding under the bed, or right in front of her face, holding a knife in the air, who could tell. Rosa does not dare speak out. As her eyes get used to the dark she gradually makes out the maid's silhouette, sitting in the rocking chair blocking the door, swaying to and fro, to and fro, like a caged animal. The movement of the chair has a hypnotic effect; after a time the darkness draws Rosa's consciousness inwards and sleep begins to overtake her, despite her best efforts to keep her eyes open.

—Are you awake?

Rosa awakes. Frau Schulz is whispering in her ear; she can feel the maid's breath soft on her cheek.

—Are you awake?

The breath of the maid is almost ticklish. An unpleasant shiver ripples through Rosa's body but she manages to keep her eyes closed, does not answer, tries to breathe normally; the maid repeats it once more, and then a silence falls, an interminable silence, masking who knows what actions. Rosa worries that her heartbeats are audible; she lies still as the dead and forces herself to breathe deeply, regularly.

There is a noise. Rosa opens her eyes the tiniest of cracks and sees the silhouette of Frau Schulz gently edging the chair away from the door. Then, quietly as a huntsman, the maid leaves the room. There is a gentle click as the door is locked behind her.

Rosa sits up, her hair standing in a pile on top of her head, red creases scoring her cheek. The room is profoundly black, and she is afraid; she sits for many minutes, making not a sound, straining her ears for a noise, a clue, something from the silence. But nothing is forthcoming, the silence is not broken. She swings her legs round and slips out of the bed. She must do something, she knows not what. She stands up and listens once again, then sits on the bed and listens again. Still the smell of Frau Schulz's soap lingers. She gets to her feet, crosses to the window, parts the curtains, peers down: the street is empty, dotted with regular pools of light from the streetlamps. A dog prowls along the kerb. Far below, a figure emerges from the apartment block, hurrying down the stairs – Rosa raises herself on her toes – it is Frau Schulz, her coat collar drawn up high against her cheeks, her beret on her head, her arms wrapped tightly around her body. She appears in a state of some agitation. She glances over both shoulders, then hurries off down the street, breaking from a walk into a run and back again; she turns a corner and is out of sight.

Like a plague, a bad feeling spreads throughout Rosa's body. With uncertain fingers she fumbles for the candle; she strikes a match, and a sphere of light sifts into the room. There is not much wax left, perhaps enough for a few minutes. It is cold, she is shivering. She reaches under the bed for her shoes, her hand brushes against something leather; she draws the object out and is surprised to find herself holding a man's boot, black, knee-length and highly polished, smelling of cigarette smoke and grease. She drops to the floor and searches under the bed, but her shoes are nowhere to be found. Her coat and scarf are gone as well.

She crosses to the window and tries to open it, but it will not budge. Not that it would make a difference; the apartment is several floors up. She crosses to the door and rattles the handle, then throws her weight upon it and heaves with her shoulder, this is so strange, trying to open a door that is locked, so strange that she has been locked in.

Rosa sits back on the bed, pushing her fingers through her tangled hair, her stockinged feet treading on each other. As she glances round the room, her eyes fall upon a squat-looking hand iron, the kind that Mama uses to iron clothes for the customers, the sort that has a considerable weight. Rosa gets to her feet and picks the iron up; then she swings it and strikes the door. A small dent is left in the wood, that is all. She strikes again. The dent deepens. Then she strikes again, and again, and there is a splintering sound, and once again, and again, and the paint chips away, then, finally, one final strike, with all her strength, for all she is worth, and the door bursts open, splinters spraying onto the carpet. Rosa drops the iron on the floor, picks up the stub of candle on its little plate and hurries into the sitting room, heart pounding. Her shoes, where are her shoes? And her coat and hat? She searches the room, quickly, on the sofa, on the dressing table, a dim orb of light accompanying her – in her haste she collides with a chair which falls clattering to the floor. Finally she opens the wardrobe, and there, neatly hanging, like a museum piece, is her coat, the hat rolled up in the pocket and the scarf draped around the collar, just as Frau Schulz used to do when Rosa was a child, and there, on the wardrobe floor, her shoes. Rosa bundles herself up hastily then walks towards the door, carrying her shoes. As she does so something on the floor catches her eye: a scrap of paper, *her* scrap of paper, with the Krützfelds' address written on it. Rosa snatches it and crumples it into her pocket. Then the candle splutters and burns out, and blackness once again descends.

Suddenly she freezes. Footsteps can be heard coming up the stairs outside the apartment, as well as hushed voices, a woman's and a man's. There is nothing she can do. The footsteps arrive at the door – then fade away and spiral up to the floor above. Rosa slips out of the apartment and pads noiselessly down the spiral staircase, seeing herself reflected many times in the mirrors round the stairwell. Arriving at the entrance to the apartment block she puts on her shoes and opens the door a fraction. The street is deserted and there is no sign of her bicycle anywhere. She hurries down the stairs, past the blank-eyed lions, and disappears into the night.

6

Yes, Hedi, it is getting late; of course she hasn't complained but she is tired, a mother can tell these things, her little eyes are rimmed with red, and she is stumbling slightly as she walks, for the umpteenth time, around the concourse. Earlier, Inga feared they were looking suspicious, so she extended the circuit to include the surrounding roads. It is quiet on the streets, so quiet, as if the colour has been permanently drained from everything forever, yet Inga can tell that something out of the ordinary is happening. Half an hour ago another group of brownshirts passed, one of them scrutinised Inga and Hedi but they didn't stop, his pockmarked cheeks, couldn't have been more than eighteen, a child really, they seemed so excited, very boisterous, possessed by an unusual mood. And the SS are walking more briskly than normal if that's possible. Then there was that horrid little man who prowled over, made a great show of examining Inga's nose, almost gave them away, she managed to shake him off in the end, he must have been drunk.

What's that, little one? Very well, let's return to the station and you can go to the bathroom, you are doing very well, only been once so far this evening, and you must be very thirsty, there has been nothing at all to drink. Mama's hungry, didn't notice that, you must be hungry too.

So: here they are again, this accursed station, greeted yet again by that sickening yellow board of destinations, departures, arrivals, all the numbers blurring together, fewer now than there were before. Inga supposes the last trains are approaching, soon everything will stop and then what will they do? This plan of Wilhelm's may not have been very well conceived after all, before long it will be quite deserted, and then where will they go?

Yes, Hedi, very well, the bathroom, in you go, Mama will come too, lock the door behind you, goodness it's draughty in here, all right, let's help you with your coat. There now, no need to rush but please do be quick. Ah, these images of the family, suffering, dying, get out, get out. Perhaps . . . it's a crazy idea but madness is everywhere tonight . . . yes, the broom cupboard, let's see – Mama's still here, Hedi, just a moment – it is unlocked, very dusty, those are cobwebs lurking in the corner, like nets; not pleasant exactly, but it might be worth a try, it can't be any more dangerous than being outside, and there is enough space for two, space to lie down even, but it is so cold in here, as cold as outside. Hedi, come along now, yes, in here, let's make some space, these brooms haven't been used in a long time, covered in cobwebs, this is an adventure isn't it, all right, let's pull the door to, slide a bucket against it, very good, now the main thing is not to make a noise, we must be quiet as mice, Hedi darling, yes? Quiet as mice, little mice. Come here, come under here. Yes, you are tired, so is Mama. There we are, not too bad. Let's hope nobody opens the door. Maybe we can get a little sleep.

7

The air is bitter and the streets are deserted and Rosa makes her way along the road in the shadow of the tenements, unsure of where she is, unsure of where to go. Her eyes flit nervously around, looking for any sign of Frau Schulz, or those devilish schoolboys, or anybody – anyone could be a threat to her now, all it would take would be one person to see her and raise the alarm, and then what would she do, she is vulnerable, without her bicycle she would have no means of escape. Her hopes of passing as a normal German girl are dashed, for what would a normal German girl be doing slipping through the shadows alone, on foot, on a night like this? The tenements stretch high into the grey-black heavens, the trees form a canopy above, Rosa feels tiny, and slow, as if for all her efforts she is barely moving at all. A figure peels out from the shadows ahead, a bearded man with a hat, hunched and glancing about him; he ghosts across the road and disappears into an alleyway, followed by a second figure, and a third, then all is still again. Rosa turns a corner, a dog prowls alongside her on the kerb for a while, then glares at her maliciously and disappears into the gloom – should she try to find her way home? That may be fatal, Mama said people were going to break down their door, what if she were to go home and— But she feels so helpless out here in the open, so unprotected, and so cold. Can nowhere be safe? Perhaps she should try once again to find the Krützfelds' house, though Frau Schulz knows the address and may have alerted the authorities, and Rosa doesn't know how to get there anyway, she has lost her bearings. If she went towards the centre of the city she could find her way from there; but that's where the big Jewish shops are, on the Alexanderplatz, the Unter den Linden, the Kurfürstendamm, she cannot imagine what the scenes are like there now. She decides to find a place outside, pass the remaining hours of the night in a dark corner somewhere, make her way home at dawn.

The sky stretches overhead like a dark, smeared window, huge and opaque, with no stars; on the horizon several fires ebb, but these streets are empty and quiet, for the moment. Further up the road there is a small park, next to which can be seen, behind a fence, a shadowy bridge over a railway track. Rosa glances over each shoulder and slinks along the flowerbeds towards the fence; she finds a gap, crawls through, then scrambles down the bank to the track.

It is darker down here than on the streets; foliage obscures the moon, and she must strain to see anything at all. Around the base of the bridge nettles grow bushily, and rubbish lies rotting; there are probably rats. Driven by tiredness she feels her way underneath and squats with her back against the wall. The air is dank and freezing, pitch black; Rosa's eyes open wide, involuntarily, yet still she can see nothing. This is a good place, nobody will find her here. She wonders if Frau Schulz is looking for her, if anyone saw where she went. She wonders if Mama and Hedi made it to the railway station, if Heinrich persuaded Papa to leave the apartment – they might be in the Krützfelds' shed at this very moment, unaware that the Gestapo is closing in, perhaps she should go there to warn them, but by the time she arrived it would probably be too late. Ah, it is possible that Frau Schulz didn't inform on them at all, it is possible that Papa and Heinrich will be safe. How she wishes she had the bread and cheese that Heinrich packed for her, which she left in Frau Schulz's apartment.

Suddenly there is a scuffling sound. Rosa starts and peers into the darkness; her eyes are adjusting to the gloom but still nothing can be seen. A whisper comes from beside her, startlingly close:

—What are you doing here?

Rosa scrambles to her feet and looks around, in vain. She thinks she can make out the figure of a man standing over her, his hat pulled low over his pale face, but she cannot be sure, the shapes keep moving in the blackness.

—Who's there, she says, who's that?

—Get out, comes a different voice, this is our place. Find your own place. You'll give us all away. Get out.

Rosa looks round for the second speaker but still nothing can be seen. She opens her mouth but cannot make a sound; she backs away, stumbles out from under the bridge, scrambles up the bank and, heart pounding, makes her way back to the street.

She hurries along the empty, echoing streets, from time to time passing apartment blocks with fresh graffiti on the walls, windows broken. As she walks visions of her family crowd into her mind. What must be happening to them now? She tries not to dwell on this morbidity, envisions them all together at the dinner table, at a time when all of these troubles have passed; they will have moved back into their old apartment, and Papa will be back at the hospital, and they will be eating well again, and going to Wiesbaden on holiday again, and this night will have become nothing but a half-remembered dream. Borne on these thoughts she walks for a long time, her senses attuned to signs of danger. Eventually she finds herself approaching the Arbeiterviertel, finally she knows where she is and she feels strangely exhilarated; these streets she has walked many times, these grey Berlin pavements with their wrought-iron lamp-posts and rows of inscrutable buildings. As she nears the Beeskower Straße she slips into the alleyways behind the tenements, picking her way through dustbins and brooms, nobody ever comes this way – was that a shout? No, just a trick of the mind probably, carry on, almost there, turn left between these buildings, and now she can see across the road her apartment block – it looks as if there are people standing in the road outside, not a crowd as such, just a line of people. She has to get closer, but carefully.

She creeps to the end of the alleyway and looks out; the Beeskower Straße is filled with a strange quietude. Outside her apartment block, in the middle of the street, illuminated by the grey light as it edges towards dawn, stand ten or fifteen men in a line. None are wearing hats, few are wearing coats, some are wearing jackets, but most are in shirtsleeves or pyjamas, and one is barefoot, his hair ruffled from sleep. Their eyes are downcast, or staring straight ahead, there is something ridiculous about them, as if they are playing a game, except for their awful expressions. Those wearing shoes have had their laces removed; the leather tongues hang limply forward. A lorry is reversing towards them, exhaust fumes slipping round their ankles. Black-uniformed SS officers guide the driver towards the kerb, stride briskly up and down the line. The wind flutters the clothes of the men standing to attention, disperses the exhaust, and still they do not move; the tenement block, their homes, stand behind them, metres away and yet unreachable.

Eventually the lorry is parked and the rear doors open. The SS officers start herding the men on and they clamber awkwardly aboard, pulling each other up by the elbows, blows falling upon them. In the windows of the apartments faces can be seen, families watching, and as the lorry starts to fill up clusters of people appear at the doors of the buildings, huddling in dressing gowns and blankets.

There: three from the end, a man standing very erect, his chin jutting defiantly outwards, his natty moustache bristling, strands of hair falling over his forehead, in nothing but shirtsleeves yet showing no signs of cold, collar hanging down his chest and open cuffs hiding his hands. Next to him is a boy of eighteen, his eyes fixed on the ground between his stockinged feet, shoulders hunched, shirt-tails flapping in the breeze behind his legs; they turn and follow the others towards the lorry. Papa and Heinrich look so different in this state of disarray, from this distance, but they are recognisable none the less – before Rosa can call out, before she can move, someone grabs her from behind, lifts her bodily from the ground, strong fingers clamp her mouth closed, she kicks and thrashes, her face is pressed against a heavy trench coat smelling of petrol and cigarettes. The figure waves to the officers in the street and they acknowledge him, laughing, for he has hunted down another; shut up, Jew, he says, halt gefälligst den Mund. Rosa squirms and glimpses his face, black against the moonlight, a peaked cap low on the forehead, insignia glinting, she struggles again but cannot break free. The man drags her back down the alleyway, laughter can still be heard from the officers in the road, did Heinrich see her, did Papa? She hears a commotion in the street but it fades, she is dragged further down the alleyway, she can hear the man panting, his fingers are biting into her arm, he is mumbling, shut up, Jew, shut up; then they emerge from the alleyway, and he pushes her against a motorcar, and she gasps for breath and stares up at him.

—Shut up, keep quiet, he says.

—Leave me alone, cries Rosa, get your hands away.

—Calm down, he replies, I am a friend.

Rosa stops struggling and looks up into the man's face; there, beneath the low patent peak, above the high trench-coat collar, nestles the bony white face of Wilhelm Krützfeld. The policeman relaxes his grip.

—What are you doing, says Rosa, what have you done to Papa and Heinrich? What have you done?

—There was nothing I could do for them, says Krützfeld, passing his hand over his eyes. I came back to try again, but it was too late. What are you doing here? Why are you not at my house, in my shed? You would be safe there.

—What will happen to them?

—They are being interned. I promise you, I will do my best to get them freed. But for now we must make sure you are safe.

—Safe? How can I be safe? How can any of us be safe? Nowhere in the entire city is safe.

—Get into the motorcar, says Krützfeld.

—What?

—I will take you to my police station. You will be safe there. Quickly now. Lie on the back seat and don't make a sound.

Krützfeld swings the car door open with the manner of a man who expects to be obeyed.

—I will go and find Mama and Hedi.

Krützfeld rolls his eyes impatiently.

—They are still in the railway station. They are safe. I looked in on them only half an hour ago, he says, hoping the girl will believe him. Now hurry up, into the car.

—Then I will go to the railway station and join them, says Rosa boldly.

—You will attract unnecessary attention, says Krützfeld sharply, it will endanger you all. Look, come with me. Tomorrow we will find your mother.

—But she has been outside all night. It is not safe, especially with my little sister.

—Very well, says Krützfeld, I will see you safely to the police station and then I will go and find them. All right? Now get in the motorcar.

—You will bring them to the police station as well?

—Yes.

The motorcar sinks under Krützfeld's weight as he collapses into the seat, adjusting his gun, and slams the door; the engine clanks into life and the car moves off. As it heads towards the heart of Berlin, nothing can be seen on the back seat but Krützfeld's blue-grey trench coat, shadows passing across its velvet collar and epaulettes, light glinting on its parallel lines of metal buttons; an observer might wonder why the Polizeiobermeister is not wearing it, the night is certainly cold enough. But when spread out flat it is larger than it looks, and just adequate to conceal the frightened girl who hides beneath it.

8

For a long time the motorcar winds through the backstreets of the city, streetlights reflecting in its black bonnet, its round headlamps shining in the half-light. Krützfeld drives without speaking, grinding the gears and rubbing his temples, his jaw set. After a time he lights a cigarette, breathes the smoke in deeply, his brow furrowed, smoke collecting in wisps against the roof. A group of Hitlerjugend boys are walking in the middle of the street. They see the police car and hasten back onto the pavement; Krützfeld glares at them and steers the car towards the Scheunenviertel, past rows of shops with Hebrew nameplates, and glass spreading into the street, and wares hanging out like fish guts.

As they approach the Oranienburger Straße, the sound of chanting and breaking glass swells beneath the noise of the engine, and the smell of burning fills the air. Under the suffocating trench coat Rosa tenses. She forces herself to remain still, straining her ears, listening for clues, wondering where they are, what is happening outside. The motorcar slows down, weaving round obstacles in the road, the din is getting louder, the stench more acrid. Rosa feels as if the sides of the car are paper-thin; at any moment they will be ripped open and she will be snatched, dragged away, thrown into the fire. Suddenly it lurches to the right, bumps over the kerb and grinds to a halt; there is the creak of the handbrake being applied, and the sound of the door opening. The car rises as the Polizeiobermeister, grunting, climbs out, slamming the door behind him.

Rosa dares not move. She tells herself Krützfeld will return, but the seconds pass and there is no sign; he has gone, he has deserted her. The noise of the crowd becomes louder, more agitated. Something hits the roof of the car. Rosa slides along the seat, pushes herself up on her elbows, edging out from the trench coat like a tortoise. She lifts her eyes to the window and at once she knows where she is: before her towers the magnificent Neue Synagogue, Mama's favourite place in Berlin, dignified like an elder statesman, its golden dome sitting like a crown upon its head. Around its walls a seething crowd has amassed, hurling stones and bottles and bricks, swarming about the great stone entrance. From one side of the synagogue, where the weekday prayer room is located, a pillar of smoke rises and flames can be seen at the windows. Across the street fire engines are parked, the crews sitting casually on their vehicles, ready to act should the fire threaten Aryan properties. And in front of it all, on the pavement, stands the imposing figure of Krützfeld.

The Polizeiobermeister, leaving the car parked hastily at an angle, fixes his cap on his head with a flourish and surveys the baying crowd. It is a large crowd, and a violent one, comprising mainly the Hitlerjugend and stormtroopers from the SA. The Polizeiobermeister knows how to deal with crowds. He takes in a deep draught of smoky city air; this is his district, the synagogue is in his jurisdiction, and now that he is on his feet, with the wind on his face and his cap pulled low, he has not the slightest pang of fear, despite being an old man, so vastly outnumbered. Deep within him a fury is smouldering, an anger that leaves no room for cowardice. He looks at his reflection in the car window, sees Rosa, glares at her sternly; she shrinks out of sight and lies still. Krützfeld straightens his back, opens the latch on his holster and pushes his way into the crowd – suddenly he is back at war, back at Arras, shoving his way through the German trenches, past the dead and the dying, the shell-shocked men convulsing, the troops going over the top, and his feet fall firm on the pavement. Above his head, and above the heads of the crowd, the golden dome of the synagogue shines into the sky as night gives way to the dull strains of morning; beside it is the thickening column of smoke. Krützfeld pushes roughly past layer after layer of hollering Berliners; many start to object but fall silent when they see his uniform and the expression on his face.

Rosa lies back on the seat beneath the trench coat, wondering what is going on. Then, without warning, the noise from the crowd comes to an abrupt end. Rosa raises herself on her elbow. From the car she hears nothing but a lone voice bellowing and the sound of muted panic; she strains her ears but cannot make out the words. She pushes herself up, peels back the trench coat and looks out of the window. At the top of the steps, framed by the magnificent doorway, stands Krützfeld, his gun in his hand, jutting it at the people below him like a sabre. With every movement of the gun the crowd surges backwards, revealing first the steps, then patches of the pavement; then the people begin to scatter. Krützfeld descends the steps to chase them, clearing the street in rings around him, dispersing the mob, jabbing with his gun, a Moses splitting the sea. As he comes closer Rosa can finally make out what he is shouting: this is a landmark, a protected municipal building, opened by Otto von Bismarck himself! Anyone who touches it will be shot! Get out of here, get out! Get out!

As a group of Hitlerjugend boys flee, they drop a burning torch on the pavement. Krützfeld sets about it furiously with his boots, stamping and scuffing, burning embers flurrying into the air around him, momentarily he is transformed into a mythological creature, illuminated by amber flashes, surrounded by flame; then the torch is extinguished and he kicks it aside, strides up and down the road, chasing away the last pockets of people. The fire crews have not departed, they sit perched on their vehicles wearing expressions of bemusement – Krützfeld turns his wrath on them, bellowing from below and striking their vehicles with the barrel of his gun. Their bemusement turns to fear; upon his order they unfurl their heavy hoses and train them on the synagogue, arcing ropes of water into the smoke. The fire has not yet fully taken hold of the building, it does not take long to extinguish; Krützfeld waits until the job is done then waves the fire crews on. They reel in their hoses, start their engines and rumble hastily away. The Polizeiobermeister glances up and down the empty street like a huntsman. Then, looking up at the synagogue, he fixes his gun back in his holster and fastens the latch. A minute passes, then another, as he stands alone on the pavement, dwarfed by the elaborate building. The smell of smoke begins to disperse, gradually replaced by the fresh dewy scent of morning. Water runs onto the pavement from the blackened and sodden weekday prayer room; it runs like tears along the Oranienburger Straße, pools around Krützfeld's boots, trickles gently into the gutter. Finally the Polizeiobermeister turns on his heel and returns to the car.

For a while longer he sits with the engine running, keeping a watch on the synagogue as dawn begins its final approach. Finally, satisfied, he steers the car slowly back onto the road and motors the short distance to the Hackescher Markt police station, lighting another cigarette.

9

On the outskirts of Berlin there is a place called Sachsenhausen. Beneath the blank sky you are marched down the main road with the camp on your left, watchtowers protruding like buttresses from the perimeter wall. Eventually you arrive at the mouth of the camp, outside which lies the SS casino, a large green building that the prisoners have nicknamed das grüne Ungeheuer, the Green Monster. You pass through the perimeter wall and are lined up facing a squat, white building crowned with a clock tower. In the middle of the building is a tunnel accessed by a wrought-iron gate bearing the legend *Arbeit Macht Frei*. On your left is the luxury bungalow belonging to the camp commandant. Your head is shaved, and you are given new clothes. After a time you are herded through the gate, past the window behind which an SS officer observes you, along the tunnel, and out into the open again. Then you are in the camp proper. Lethargic black birds hop heavily about; several of them have skin diseases and the feathers on their bodies have dropped out. Before you is the roll-call square, the Appelplatz, around which is a semicircular track. The surface of the track is a patchwork made up of many different surfaces, tarmac, slate, gravel, mud; this is where they test the army boots, they run the prisoners round the track and see how long it takes for the boots to wear thin. In the centre of the Appelplatz is the gallows, which once a year is exchanged for a Christmas tree. You see a line of prisoners squatting in the Sachsenhausen salute. All around the perimeter wall stand thick beautiful trees, bunched behind the watchtowers outside the camp. To your right, the dungeon block, with its three poles on which prisoners are hung by the wrists. To your left, the sanatorium and morgue. On the far side, the execution trench. And fanning out from the centre, in great semicircular rows, cabin after cabin, triple bunks, hard slats, draughty, leaking, lice-ridden, to which a twilight army of prisoners retreat, exhausted, each night.

All the way to Sachsenhausen, as Heinrich holds his hand like a child, and the other Jews speculate with each other as to their fate, Klein curses Wilhelm Krützfeld under his breath.

10

The police station is deserted. Krützfeld leads Rosa quietly through the rear entrance, along dismal corridors with narrow wooden floorboards and grey, scarred walls, leaving a trail of cigarette smoke in their wake. Faint sunlight filters through the windows, filling the building with an eerie glow; down corridor after corridor they walk, their footsteps resounding louder than usual. Finally he ushers Rosa into his office, closes all the blinds and locks the door behind them. Then he collapses heavily into the cracked leather seat behind his desk, rubbing his eyes between thumb and forefinger.

—Herr Krützfeld, says Rosa.

—Don't say anything, says Krützfeld, just keep quiet. I need to make a telephone call. Please take a seat.

He picks up the receiver and dials a number, reading it from a notebook on his desk.

—Frau Warschaur? Wilhelm Krützfeld speaking. I'm sorry to call at such an hour. Yes. I trust you are . . . good. Now, did your husband receive my message in time? The night train? Very good. Ah, to England, excellent. Let us hope that his journey is without incident. Not at all, I wish you all the best. Goodbye.

Replacing the receiver, the Polizeiobermeister looks at Rosa as if for the first time.

—Now, Klein, Rosa Klein, yes. Give me a moment to gather my thoughts. Then I will go to the railway station to find your mother and sister.

He crosses to the drinks cabinet, pours himself some brandy and tilts it down his throat, his shadow falling across the large-scale map of his precinct that hangs on the wall behind his desk. Then he takes a wine bottle from the drinks cabinet and holds it up to the light; it is filled not with wine but with water. Meditatively, the Polizeiobermeister walks around the room, pouring water into the scores of plant pots that clutter the room, on the desk, in the corners, on the filing cabinet, on the shelves. Then he replaces the bottle carefully in the drinks cabinet, hangs his trench coat over his shoulders like a cape, and without a word leaves the office, locking the door quietly behind him.

Some time later the key turns in the lock again, this time awakening Rosa from a slumber. For a moment she does not know where she is. She is still in Krützfeld's office, but the light coming through the blind on the window is brighter now, and birds can be heard outside, and the occasional sound of traffic. The Polizeiobermeister enters the room and closes the door behind him. In the daylight he looks older than his years; his hair seems whiter than before, deep lines score his forehead, and his trench coat is badly creased.

—I'm sorry, he says, I couldn't find them. It doesn't mean anything, you understand.

He crosses the room and, without taking off his trench coat, sits heavily behind his desk. The leather chair creaks, and all is quiet.

—Did you truly search everywhere? says Rosa, surprised at how tiny her voice sounds.

The Polizeiobermeister shrugs and rests his head in his hands. Once again a discomfort, like an illness, spreads through Rosa's body.

—I must go, she says weakly.

The Polizeiobermeister is about to reply when the telephone rings, startling them both. He clears his throat and answers.

—Polizeiobermeister Krützfeld . . . Oh, good morning, Herr Graf von Helldorf . . . yes sir . . . Well, it is a protected building, so I . . . ah, so. Very well, one hour.

He replaces the receiver, his eyes fixed vacantly on the telephone.

—I'm afraid I shall have to motor you home, he says. I have a meeting in an hour.

—Can you leave me at the railway station?

—I will take you to your apartment. If you want to go to the railway station later, that is up to you. I'm sorry I cannot do any more. But I will do everything in my power to return your family to you.

—Thank you, Herr Krützfeld, says Rosa, the words catching in her throat.

—Yes, yes, follow me.

The Polizeiobermeister leads Rosa out of the office and along the corridors of the police station. It is busy now, and many heads turn as they pass, watching darkly, saying nothing. When they reach the car Krützfeld tells Rosa to sit up straight, for concealment is no longer necessary. From that moment on he says nothing more; for the remainder of the journey they sit in silence, Krützfeld smoking cigarette after cigarette as he guides the car north, to the Arbeiterviertel.

Finally they arrive at the Beeskower Straße and the Polizeiobermeister draws the car to a halt. It is a morning like any other and the street looks exactly the same as usual. Rosa opens the door and climbs out.

—You will keep in contact? she says.

The Polizeiobermeister nods and swings the car round; it grinds away down the street, disappearing round a corner, and Rosa is left standing in front of the tenements, small and helpless and alone.

Steeling herself, she passes through the double doors and walks across the flagstones of the courtyard. Now there is evidence of the events of the night before: the door of the Lichtensteins' apartment is hanging on its hinges, there are jagged holes in several of the windows, and amidst a scattering of shattered glass an almost black stain has marked indelibly the flagstones. As Rosa approaches her stairwell she can smell fresh bread; Frau Brandt at number two must be baking. Amid the sound of birdsong she climbs the stairs, as quietly as she can, her hand brushing lightly the banister, her breathing loud in her ears.

Finally she arrives at her apartment. The door hangs open like a flap of skin, surrounded by a corona of splinters. In a neighbouring apartment somebody turns on a wireless, sings the first line of a song. She slips inside without touching the door, her feet creaking on the floorboards.

Inside lies a scene of devastation. Broken furniture is intertwined with laundry, the tables and cupboards have been overturned, windows and mirrors are smashed, picture-frames hang at crazy angles. It is as if her apartment has been removed, replaced with a scene from an earthquake or a hurricane, and as she moves from room to room, gazing in disbelief at the ruins of her life, she is struck by the childish thought that she might stumble upon a fairytale door leading to her proper apartment, the one she left only hours ago, still intact and neat and familiar as ever, with her parents, her brother and sister, still there.

As she nears her parents' bedroom, she hears a noise – only a slight noise, but one that doesn't fit. Heart pounding, she approaches the battered bedroom door and pushes it nervously open. The morning sun streams through the broken window, illuminating another ransacked room; wardrobes lie face down on the floor, drawers gape open, twisted clothes are everywhere, the bed has been upended and thrown against the wall. She gasps and her hands fly to her temples, for there in the centre of the room, kneeling on the floor, tired and pale but otherwise unscathed, is her mama, clutching an exhausted Hedi in her arms, the contours of their bodies traced by sunlight from the broken window. Inga's mouth opens and closes, but no sound comes out; Rosa rushes to her, and they clasp each other close for a long time in the morning sunlight.

10 November 1938, Berlin

I

Rosa and Inga pass the day without daring to leave the apartment, moving quietly from room to room, keeping away from the windows, salvaging what they can of their belongings. Most of the customers' laundry is found to be intact, dirty and crumpled, but intact. The day is dull and cold; an icy wind whistles through the broken windows and passes in chilly channels through the apartment. Inga boards up the windows with pieces of shelving, then spends a long time fixing the front door as best she can, painstakingly, using the tools that Heinrich keeps under his bed, which have remained somehow undisturbed. For a long time Hedi sits quietly in the corner of her bedroom, clutching her dolly Gigi, who has escaped, so far, unharmed. Rosa is able to find some bread in the chaos of the kitchen and they eat it together, sitting at the remains of the table, which they prop up with a stool and a pile of books. They talk: in hushed tones they exchange their stories, Rosa telling her mother about Frau Schulz, and Herr Krützfeld, and seeing Papa and Heinrich being taken away, and Inga telling her daughter about the railway station, the drunkard, the SS, about walking for hours on end around the concourse and the streets, snatching a few hours' sleep in a broom cupboard, then, at dawn, finding a circuitous route home. And they worry about Papa and Heinrich, where they might have been taken, how to find out about their well-being. Once they discover that Papa is a Frontkämpfer they will surely release them at once, whatever could the Gestapo want with two innocent and law-abiding citizens? And they discuss, repeatedly, emigration, agreeing that as soon as it is safe to go outside they should start applying for visas, for the only choice now is to leave as quickly as possible, regardless of what Papa might say. The day wears on and nobody comes to visit them, none of the neighbours, Jewish or Aryan, and neither do they leave the apartment.

Night closes quickly, and they dare not use the electric lights. What little bread is left is given to Hedi, who then is put quietly to bed and falls immediately asleep, clutching her dolly. Inga finds a box of Shabbat candles that haven't been crushed and lights one of them in the kitchen, then she and Rosa sit at the table drinking water from cracked glasses, speaking again and again about Papa, about Heinrich, worrying what fate may have befallen them, whether it would be safe to enquire at the police station, when it will be safe to go outside, and their faces have the graininess of sandstone in the candlelight.

An hour later, when their whispers have fallen silent, and they sit without speaking over the diminishing candle, there is the quietest of knocks on the door. They freeze for a moment; and then the knock is heard again, a little louder, and a high-pitched voice saying Inga, Inga, are you there?

Inga crosses to the door and whispers, who is it? and the reply comes, Berta, Berta Krützfeld, please open the door at once. Inga ushers Berta in; she is carrying a cardboard box, she puts it down, and they embrace.

—So you are here, says Berta, thank God you are here. Darling, you look so different, I almost didn't recognise you. So thin.

—Come through to the kitchen, we have a candle, says Inga.

—Goodness, your poor little home, says Berta.

In the kitchen she greets Rosa, embraces her and sits at the table, looking around in disbelief, not removing her shimmering fur coat and hat.

—I cannot believe it, I just cannot believe it, she says. Do you mind if I smoke?

—Pfui, of course not, says Inga.

Berta places a cigarette holder between her painted lips and lights a cigarette with a match.

—I can't stay long, she says, too dangerous. But Wilhelm said I must come. We've kept away for five years, but last night changed everything.

—Any news? says Inga anxiously.

—Well, our dear Goering made a speech on the wireless this evening telling people to go back to normal, Berta replies. To stop rioting, I mean. And that's excellent news of course. This whole episode has been horrid, from what Wilhelm tells me. Four Jews were lynched in central Berlin, I'm told, and lots of others were killed. The caretaker of the synagogue on the Prinzregentstraße was burned alive with his family. Many have committed suicide. And apparently over three thousand men have been arrested and sent away to prison camps. The city looks as if it's been through a war or something, there's broken glass and burned-out buildings everywhere, Israel's Department Store on the Alexanderplatz is absolutely wrecked, I don't know where I shall go for my perfume now. The shopkeepers have been cleaning it up today, but the Jewish community has been issued a fine of a billion Reichsmark to pay for all the damage.

—A billion?

—So I hear.

—My God. But what of Otto and Heinrich?

—Wilhelm has been making enquiries, says Berta, he has not given up hope.

She blows a thread of smoke straight upwards. It winds in wisps around the pipes and pools along the edges of the ceiling in the honeyed candlelight.

—Does Wilhelm have any idea what happened to them? asks Inga.

—Sachsenhausen, says Berta shortly, but they are both still alive. That's all he's been able to discover for the moment.

Inga gives a short sigh and crumples back in her chair; Rosa unfolds her arms and begins to rub her temples.

—Has anything happened to Herr Krützfeld? says Rosa. I thought he might have been in trouble.

—Oh that, says Berta, maintaining her insouciant manner, there was a meeting with old Graf von Helldorf. Wilhelm said that the tone was amicable. After all, Wilhelm has been privy to one or two of his indiscretions over the years. It'll be fine.

—I hope so, says Rosa.

There is a pause.

—Now, Berta continues, I should tell you this. Jews have now been banned from all grocery shops, so you won't be able to buy any food.

—No food? says Inga. But how will we live?

—I've brought you some supplies – she gestures towards the box – but it's going to have to last two weeks, I'm afraid, Wilhelm said to make a delivery more often would be too risky. So you'll have to ration it, and I'll see if I can't bring a greater quantity next time.

—Very well. Goodness, not allowed food.

—Now, you mustn't leave your apartment except on urgent business, for a week or two at least. I tell you, it's horrendous out there. There are Jews crawling all over the city, creeping in search of food. They're in the alleyways and back streets, cowering from every lighted corner. The men cannot return home for fear of being arrested, and they're afraid to sleep under the same roof for two nights in a row, so they're left wandering the streets and the parks. It's just frightful. People are still being arrested and beaten and things. So you must lie low.

—Yes, says Inga, we will. Thank you so much, Berta. You're a real friend, taking such a risk on our account.

—Nonsense, says Berta, you would do the same for me. Speaking of which, I think I should go. I mustn't tempt fate. I shall see you again in two weeks' time.

—Do be in touch sooner, says Inga, if you find out more about Otto and Heinrich.

—Of course, Berta replies. Goodbye, dear girls. Au revoir.

Angling her cigarette holder in a clandestine sort of way she leaves the apartment, creeps down the stairs and slinks across the courtyard, making sure nobody is watching. When she is safely back on the street she breathes a sigh of relief and walks swiftly towards the tram stop, gathering her fur coat high about her neck, looking forward to the warmth of home.

When Berta has gone, Inga opens the box. It contains a selection of gleaming tins of food, as well as bread, cheese, vegetables and dried meat; combined with the food that they can salvage from the kitchen it should be just enough for two weeks, if they're careful. Inga and Rosa allow themselves to taste a little of the cheese before putting the box away.

—I refuse to believe we can no longer buy food, says Rosa. Surely somebody will sell to us.

—We should try to get a little sleep, says Inga, it must be getting late.

—I'm jangling all over.

—Me too, says Inga, but we must try.

—No matter what Frau Krützfeld says, says Rosa, we need to start applying for visas.

—I agree, says Inga, so let's get some sleep. We'll start in the morning.

2

Over the next two days Inga spends her time trying to trace her husband and her son, pursuing visas at various embassies, and struggling to revive the laundry business. She enlists Rosa to help; day by day they take it in turns to brave the streets, joining the hundreds of sombre Jews at the embassies, waiting for hours on end in dimly lit rooms, hoping against hope for a change of fortune. Jews cannot queue on the pavement any more, it is too conspicuous, so they are packed into waiting rooms, and when these are full the doors are closed and nobody else is admitted. Gradually Rosa and Inga discover the rules of the game; even if you are fortunate enough to obtain a visa for some far-flung place, that alone is not enough. An exit visa is also required, as well as a transit visa, a valid passport, a substantial sum of money and the tickets for the journey. All these documents have a limited period of validity, and some depend on others being issued first, and each member of your family must have a separate set of paperwork, and all must be presented together; Rosa and Inga fill out form after form, wait in unmoving queues, discuss endlessly the application procedures and requirements of different countries, the comparable merits of Mexico, Argentina, Shanghai; and all the while they are plagued by a constant anxiety, worrying about Papa and Heinrich.

On 12 November, while talking in hushed tones to a woman in a queue at the British embassy, Inga finds out that a Jew was trampled to death near the Kurfürstendamm the day before. On the fifteenth, while in the waiting room of the Chilean consulate, Rosa hears a rumour that Paraguay has relaxed its entry restrictions; she hastens to their embassy immediately, only to find that the rumours are false and the doors to the embassy are closed. On the sixteenth, Inga writes again to the Kremers in London, appealing to their family bond, requesting their urgent assistance to get passage abroad, to England or to anywhere. On the seventeenth, they hear reports that almost twenty Jews have committed suicide since 9 November. At home, whilst restoring order to the bedroom, Inga stumbles across her husband's Iron Cross 2nd Klasse, in a walnut display case lined with green velvet; and she finds his pipe and tobacco, places them back in the kitchen drawer for when he returns. A few regular customers begin to arrive with their sacks of dirty clothes, and a little money starts to trickle in. None of their letters to the authorities asking for information about Otto and Heinrich receive responses. Hedi spends hours playing with pots and pans under the kitchen table, day after day, never seeming to tire of it. Inga recommences her weekly appointments with Rabbinerin Regina Jonas, studying Hebrew and Torah and prayers and, despite the danger, starts to attend synagogue once a week. Night after night sleep remains elusive; they snatch an hour here and there, dream of queues and waiting rooms and visas, awake in fear at the slightest noise and are left sleepless for hours.

On 21 November they hear that the last of the Jewish shops have been shut down permanently. Berta's box of food is almost empty, the two weeks are almost up, still there is no sign of her and no news of Otto and Heinrich. By the twenty-fourth Inga is convinced that something has happened to them, and Berta as well, and that it is just a matter of time before the net closes in on them. But there is simply no way of knowing. She leaves the apartment first thing in the morning, for it is her turn to go into the city, telling Rosa that today she is trying Uruguay and will be back for supper, God willing. As she crosses the courtyard and steps onto the Beeskower Straße, rain begins to fall in dull sheets, her overcoat spills water from the shoulders as she walks, and her felt hat darkens by several shades. She takes the back streets, as usual, but instead of following her usual route, today she does not head west towards the embassy district; instead, praying, she walks south, in the direction of the Scheunenviertel.

Inga has not been to the Scheunenviertel for many months as it is unsafe, an obvious target, she is afraid of what it must be like these days, how it must have changed, whether any Jews are left there at all. When she arrives, she discovers that her fears were well founded. The place is almost unrecognisable, deserted. Curtains are drawn, and many shops and buildings are boarded up. Avoiding the main thoroughfares, she skirts the Große Hamburger Straße and takes the Sophienstraße, where the gutters are overflowing and the water laps over her shoes, which are stout but sodden, waterlogged by now. She turns onto the Rosenthaler Straße, and her heart quickens as she catches sight of her destination: the square-windowed police station at Hackescher Markt.

Before entering she waits for a few minutes across the road as the rain raises millions of watery flowers on the pavement around her, existing only for a moment and then gone, tiny watery flowers that appear and disappear in the blink of an eye, again and again, mesmerisingly. Then she steels herself and steps through the rain to the concrete entrance, her hands in the pockets of her overcoat, approaching metre by metre until, all at once, she is inside, feeling out of place, a dripping wet female in a bustling police station of uniforms, brusque voices, comradely laughter.

She follows the signs on the wall, ignoring the glances, trailing a double line of water-spots from her overcoat along the narrow floor-boards. She arrives at the door of an office inscribed *Erkundigungen*, enquiries. Without giving herself the opportunity to lose her momentum she knocks firmly, and immediately a voice calls for her to enter. The office is exactly as she would have expected, with its filing cabinets, notice boards and photographs of men in police uniforms along the wall. Behind the desk is a balding officer with a steep collar that looks a little tight. He raises his eyebrows and beckons her in.

—Name?

—Inga Klein.

The officer peers at her closely, framed by the map on the wall behind him as the rain beats against the window.

—Do you have identification?

—Please, I wish to speak to the Polizeiobermeister Krützfeld.

He smiles.

—On what business?

—A personal matter.

—Well, I am sorry to tell you that Krützfeld is not here today.

Inga looks at the officer, startled. She has prepared herself carefully but failed to anticipate that. An ambiguous expression is masking the officer's face, and she cannot read his eyes.

—Please, when will the Polizeiobermeister be here? she says.

His face shifts into another, equally ambiguous expression; Inga looks away, trying to organise her thoughts, to think of something to say. When she looks back the officer is leaning back in his chair, his hands behind his head.

—May I help?

Inga takes a deep breath.

—I wish to enquire as to the well-being of my husband and son, she says, who were interned in Sachsenhausen on the ninth of November. My husband is a Frontkämpfer. He was awarded the Iron Cross. And my son is only eighteen.

—Juden, says the officer enigmatically.

—I'm not lying, he's a Frontkämpfer, says Inga, rummaging in her bag. Just a moment.

She places a walnut display case symmetrically on the desk, and opens it. The officer leans over and peers into the glass; the reflection of his face falls over the medal pinned onto green velvet.

—Impressive, he says in a tone of voice that is impossible to decipher, then he slides the medal back towards Inga and sits back in his chair. Do you have an exit visa for your family, he says, or a ticket on a ship bound for a distant land?

—We have applied for many, says Inga, I am sure that something will be issued soon.

—But nothing has been issued yet?

—Not yet, but—

—Then nothing can be done, he says abruptly. He leans forward and lowers his voice.

—Frau Klein, if you want your husband back, secure him a visa. Juden are not wanted here in Deutschland. So do please come back when you have a visa for a distant land. Now let us end our conversation here, on good terms.

Inga backs away from the desk, turns and hastens out of the office, her shoes making a squelching sound, closing the door a little too hard behind her. As she hurries along the corridor, pushing past blue-grey policemen's shoulders, the *Erkundigungen* door opens and the officer's head appears.

—Frau Klein, he calls after her, grinning, your medal!

Inga hears him but does not turn back. She reaches the entrance to the police station, turns up the collar on her overcoat and plunges out into the rain.

3

In the evening, when Inga arrives home, still soaked through, frustrated by another day spent in vain in an embassy waiting room, carrying her hat and running her fingers through her rain-tangled hair, she is surprised to see that Rosa is in a better mood; she welcomes her mother into the apartment with something approaching her old enthusiasm.

—Hello, Mama, did you have any luck today?

—I'm afraid not. You look cheerful.

—Berta visited earlier.

—Berta?

—Yes. She and Herr Krützfeld are both fine. Look.

Rosa gestures behind her to the kitchen where another of Berta's boxes stands, its bounty spread all over the table, meat and bread and vegetables. Hedi is sitting on the floor, carefully eating a small piece of bread.

—You see? says Rosa. Berta brought much more this time, true to her word.

Inga follows her daughter into the apartment, past rows of hanging laundry, kissing Hedi and struggling out of her sodden coat.

—And she didn't mention Otto?

—No, Rosa replies, now here, look, have a bit of Damenkäse, can you believe she managed to find Damenkäse?

—We shouldn't, we should save it.

—We will save the rest, just have a taste.

Inga takes a small bite of the buttery cheese, and a wave of soft pleasure flits momentarily through her, causing her to sway on her feet, almost to stumble.

—Tasty, isn't it? says Rosa. Here, have some more.

—Pfui, Rosa, stop being so indulgent, says Inga sharply, this has to last for two weeks at least. She sneezes.

—Oh, says Rosa, have you been wet all day?

—I'm afraid so, Inga replies, I hope I am not coming down with a chill.

—Do you feel ill?

—A little hot and cold, says Inga and sneezes again.

Behind the boarded-up windows of the apartment, night is slipping across the sky. The atmosphere inside darkens, and Inga, peeling off her stockings in her bedroom, calls out:

—Rosa? Please would you light a candle or two?

—There are not many left, comes the reply.

Inga wraps herself in a dressing gown and leaves the room, suppressing another sneeze.

—Why don't we use the electric lights? says Rosa. I'm sure it's safe now.

—I don't know, says Inga worriedly.

—If you look out of the window you will see other lights.

—Ah, very well, says Inga.

Within a minute the lights are blazing throughout the apartment, and Rosa busies herself preparing the supper. From the bathroom, Inga can be heard sneezing and splashing water in the sink. Rosa is overcome by the luxurious food that she is able to cook, she has the entire palette at her disposal, all the colours and textures and flavours.

The windows steam up, and the apartment, which is blazing with light, fills with delicious aromas. Then there is a heavy thud on the door. Rosa stops still for a moment, aubergine sizzling in the frying pan. There is another thud.

—Rosa, calls Inga from the bathroom, can you please bring me a towel?

Rosa creeps across the apartment, turning off the lights as she goes, and shepherding Hedi into her bedroom. Then she opens the bathroom door a crack; in an instant Inga understands something is wrong.

—Open up, comes a man's voice, I know you're in there. I can smell the food.

The voice ends with a gravelly chuckle. Rosa feels her way to the cabinet and lights one of their last Shabbat candles. Then she carries it over to the door and says:

—Who is it?

—Herr Gruber, don't you recognise my voice? Herr Gruber. Now open up.

Rosa exchanges glances with her mother and opens the door halfway. In the doorway stands an ogre of a man with florid cheeks, wearing a worn pair of braces that strain at his trousers.

—Good evening, says Inga, to what do we owe the pleasure?

—The pleasure? Ha, snorts Gruber, this is my building, I can do as I please.

He nudges his way into the apartment and stands, hands on hips, in the gloom.

—Turn on the damned light, won't you?

Inga nods to Rosa, and she turns on the light. Gruber squints, rubs his eyes and proceeds to light a wrinkled cigarillo, puffing smoke in gritty clouds round his shoulders.

—What can we do for you, Herr Gruber, says Inga levelly, have we fallen behind with the rent?

—Rent's up to date, Frau Klein, up to date. Mein Gott, something smells delicious. What is it?

—Just our supper, says Rosa respectfully.

—Just nothing, says Gruber, it smells like heaven itself. Bring me a plateful.

Rosa hurries into the kitchen and returns with a plate of food; Gruber accepts it and, without sitting down, begins to eat, scooping the food into his mouth with a piece of bread, cigarillo smoke wafting from his nose.

—Very good, very good, he says, now how about some beer?

—I'm afraid all we have is brandy, says Inga.

—No beer? You Jews make me laugh. Very well, brandy. He coughs noisily as Rosa hurries over to the drinks cabinet.

—Now, he says, you must be out within two weeks.

—Out? says Inga. Out?

—Out, says Gruber, chewing. I've got nothing against a tenant so long as they pay the rent, whether they're a criminal, a pimp or a Jew.

—Why then?

—It's the law. It has been since the twenty-first of November. I'm a bit late. Ah, thank you, darling.

He accepts a glass of brandy from Rosa, drinks it in a single draught and winces.

—What swill. It's true what they say about the Jews. You've probably got the good stuff under lock and key, haven't you? Only for your brethren?

—No, Herr Gruber, that's all we have, says Rosa.

Gruber laughs in an exaggerated way.

—Anyway, two weeks, he says, finishing the last of the food, stubbing his half-smoked cigarillo out on the plate and dropping it onto an armchair.

—Herr Gruber, wait a minute, says Inga. You don't understand, my husband and son have been taken to Sachsenhausen. If we move house then when they are released they will be unable to find us.

—I'm crying, says Gruber, walking towards the door, I'm really crying.

He makes a whining sound in the back of his throat, which then becomes an unidentified tune as he walks out of the apartment without closing the door and descends the stairs; his footsteps fade away, and all is silent.

Inga turns off the electric lights and kindles the candle again. Cigarillo smoke lingers horribly in the air.

—What shall we do? she says, and sneezes.

—Two weeks, says Rosa, how can we find somewhere in two weeks?

—We need to think, says Inga.

—Is it really true that Jews can no longer be tenants? says Rosa.

—Anything is possible, Inga replies, ah, this makes things difficult. She paces around the kitchen, then sits down at the table.

—Herr Gruber ate a lot of chicken, says Rosa.

—Chicken? says Inga. I haven't had chicken for years.

The evening stretches on. Inga retires to her room to write some letters. Rosa, not knowing what else to do, continues with the food preparations by candlelight, wincing at her mother's sneezes. A storm is gently brewing above Berlin, clouds are gathering in dark masses beyond the reach of the city lights. Rosa wonders if Herr Gruber has children. Time wears on and soon the food is ready, but Rosa, not wanting to disturb her mother, busies herself with setting the table, and cleaning again the floor, the sink, the surfaces, reorganising the kitchen cupboards; and all the while her mind is churning, trying desperately to come up with a solution to the problem of where in Berlin they can live.

Finally the list of chores runs out. Just as Rosa is about to knock on her mother's door, she hears a lorry stopping in front of the tenements and people jumping out, and the lorry moving away again. Her heart quickens, and she strains her ears into the silence, telling herself that surely it is nothing. A door slams downstairs, in the courtyard. Rosa takes a step forward, then back again. Is that – yes, footsteps in the stairwell, she is sure of it. Inga has not emerged from her bedroom; she must be out of earshot. And now the footsteps are ascending the stairs, slowly, deliberately, floor by floor, getting louder, closer to their apartment, finally coming to a halt directly outside their door.

There is the sound of a man's voice, quiet yet unmistakable, a man's voice. Then there is a knock at the door, not a thump but a fluttering tap. Rosa does not move, and the person knocks again. She hears movement coming from her mother's bedroom – finally Inga has heard what's going on. Knowing she has no choice, Rosa crosses to the door and, heart pounding, releases the lock and swings it slowly open, staring through the doorway into the gloom, trying to make out the figures that are standing outside.

—Who is it, she says, who is there?

The doorway gradually lights up as Inga approaches from her bedroom with a candle. There, standing awkwardly at the top of the stairs, are two waif-like figures with pinched cheeks and shaven heads; the younger one is stooping slightly, the older one standing erect; they have no hats, no jackets and no overcoats, just shirtsleeves and over-sized trousers. The candlelight laps softly against them.

—Otto! gasps Inga. Heinrich!

For a moment there is a pause while they look at each other, speech-less, unable to breathe or think. Then Inga rushes to the doorway and helps the two men inside; they gaze around the apartment as if for the first time, their shaven heads like crustaceans in the half-light. The family embraces, stony-faced and tearful, without speaking, for many minutes. Then Rosa takes the candle, hurries to her bedroom and comes back with some blankets, for they both look so cold. How greatly they have changed in just two weeks! She raises the candle to see them better, puts blankets over their shoulders and embraces them again. A smell of rotten wood and sweat slips from the folds of their clothes, their eyes are dark and empty, their fingers blackened, their lips cast into crust and cracked. Papa laughs for the first time; his voice is dry and thin yet the melody is the same, and Heinrich smiles, his lips stretching a familiar shape across reduced cheeks, and then Rosa knows for sure that it is them, it is undeniably them, these are indeed her father and brother, finally she has them back, after so many sleepless nights, so many days fearing the worst, the family is together again. Inga goes to find Hedi, brings her from her bedroom to greet the homecomers, at first she is scared but then she recognises them, runs to her papa, he attempts to sweep her into the air but is only able to lift her to waist height, he puts her down, kneels to embrace her, and so does Heinrich; and from then on, for a long while, Hedi clings to Papa's grimy trousers without letting go. As night sets in overhead, and turbulent clouds mass in phalanxes across the black sky, the family gets used to each other again, and a little happiness arises, and the candlelit apartment shines like a pinprick in the darkness.

4

Rosa, luckily, in her exuberance earlier in the evening, cooked more food than she, Inga and Hedi could possibly have eaten; but it has turned out for the best, and the family sits round the damaged table, and Rosa serves, and there is just enough to go round. Upon seeing the food, a single expression comes over the faces of Papa and Heinrich: the lines smooth from their skin, their eyes open like infants' freshly to the world, then close again as the warm savoury scents drift into their nostrils. Then, while Heinrich remains in a stupor, Papa hunches over his plate, eats furiously, guarding his prize with his forearm, flushed with effort, devouring mouthful after mouthful, feverishly; it is only when Inga touches him on the elbow that he looks up and, as if awaking from a dream, corrects his posture and clears his throat and makes a visible effort to recall the notion of etiquette. Hedi is wordless, open-mouthed, and Rosa stares at her plate, not eating despite her gnawing hunger. Heinrich is still sitting with his eyes closed; then he lowers his head and begins to spoon food into his mouth, rapidly, mechanically, seemingly unaware of anything around him, mouthful after mouthful at a persistent pace, pausing only to drink glasses of water, obsessively, as if eating were a job to be done as rapidly and efficiently as possible.

—Don't rush, says Inga, you will make yourself sick.

Heinrich does not reply. The crown of his shaven head, bent over the table, is silvery with bristles in the gloom; as he eats his left hand runs over it repeatedly as if checking for cracks, the sound is loud and scraping.

—Papa, says Rosa, what . . .

Klein looks up at his daughter sharply, the power of his eyes accentuated by his awful baldness.

—Do not ask me, Püppchen, he says hoarsely. To discuss it is off-limits. If Heinrich or I were to breathe one word about it, one single word, we would be taken back immediately and that would be the end. None of us would survive even one more week there, none of us.

There is a silence filled by the noise of the pipes, the barely audible sound of traffic passing across the city and the scraping of Heinrich's hand over his head.

—The main thing, says Klein, is that we have been released. We are together again.

He continues to eat, slower this time, his head erect yet inclined in a way that Rosa has never seen before.

—I was convinced you would be kept there for a month at least, says Inga softly.

—I am ashamed, says Klein in a quiet voice.

Nobody moves, nobody responds; even Heinrich looks up from his plate and stares at his father.

—I am ashamed, repeats Klein louder.

—Liebling, says Inga, perhaps this is a conversation for later . . .

—No, says her husband, it is a conversation for now.

He raises his gaze and looks at each member of his family in turn, scanning their faces, reading them, his face cast with shadows, amber from the candle. Then he gets unsteadily to his feet, crosses to the drawer and takes out his pipe and tobacco; he packs and lights the pipe, facing the wall, then returns to the table, breathing smoke in front of sad eyes, holding his pipe like a delicate thing, his customary confidence absent.

—Until this morning we had no hope, he whispers, drawing his family to him. We were in the Appelplatz, lined up as usual for roll-call. Among the officers was somebody different, a man in a different uniform. He singled out Heinrich, he singled out me. We were told that we were to be released, that we were to leave Deutschland as soon as we can. We were given a medical examination, no sign of overt maltreatment was found, our clothes were returned to us . . . mein Gott I am ashamed.

Pipe smoke leaks gently from his nose and the room is filled with the pungent aroma of tobacco.

—There is no reason to be ashamed, says Inga.

—The man who released us was Krützfeld, says her husband bluntly. There is a pause.

—Krützfeld, he repeats louder. Krützfeld released us. Krützfeld looked us in the eyes, and released us, Krützfeld gave us back our freedom, such as it is. Krützfeld granted us our lives. And I was ashamed. And now, sitting here, I am ashamed. I am ashamed, I am ashamed.

There is another pause, then Klein lays his pipe gently on the table and continues to eat. Taking the signal, the other members of the family turn back to their plates, their eyes downcast, any hope of conversation impossible. Rosa cannot eat, yet she is unavoidably hungry; she cuts her food, moves it from one side of the plate to the other, tasting the occasional morsel.

—And something else, says Klein.

—Perhaps later, Liebling, says Inga anxiously.

—I have been wrong all these years, he says bitterly, picking up his pipe again. I have been wrong about everything. Inga, we must emigrate. We must leave Deutschland, for it has left us. This land for which my blood was spilt in the war, for which my father and his father before him lived and breathed and loved, has betrayed us, made us prisoners in our own city, homeless in our own homes, lifeless in our own lives, inhabiting shells like snails. We must leave Deutschland, children, do you hear? We must leave this accursed country with its blackened face and broken promises. Never again shall I be a German, and never again a Prussian. Never again. It finishes today, this hour, this minute, here, at this table, today.

He bows his head, his face falls into shadow, and his pipe gradually and quietly goes out. Rosa gets to her feet and gathers up the plates, stacks them and deposits them in the sink; Inga kisses her husband gently on his head, then, sneezing, takes Hedi to her bedroom and begins to warm the water for the men, and to prepare their bedclothes. Heinrich goes to his room and can be heard moving gingerly about, opening and closing the wardrobe and drawers. Klein continues to sit at the table, rubbing a finger in little circles upon its surface, saying nothing. Rosa crosses the kitchen, stands behind him, places a hand on his shoulder; he turns in his chair, pulls her to him, embraces her tightly, tightly, as if he never will let go, his shoulders shuddering with heavy, violent sobs.

5

For several days the men do nothing but sleep, waking occasionally to devour some food, and then slipping again into oblivion, as if the waking world is nothing but an inconvenience. Night after night Rosa is awoken by her father's shouts, hears her mother calming him, filtering soothing words into his sleep. By day, he will only be roused from his lethargy by news of embassies, consulates, quotas and visas; Rosa and Inga keep up their feverish pursuit of emigration, buckling under a mounting sense of despair as door after door is closed to them, glimmer after glimmer is extinguished, and again and again they find themselves back at the beginning with nothing to show for their efforts. Klein daily swears that tomorrow he will go back to work, start making enquiries in the Gemeinde regarding passage abroad, but tomorrow comes and he finds that he cannot lift his bony head from the pillow. Heinrich receives regular visits from Jizchak and Edith, who have received word of his release; they arrive after nightfall, spend time with him talking in his room, only to emerge closing the door quietly behind them, motioning that Heinrich has fallen asleep.

The threat of eviction hangs over Inga and Rosa secretly, they discuss it in whispers, not wanting to worry the men; Rosa makes enquiries amongst friends to find another apartment, but it seems that nobody can help. They decide to write to Herr Gruber proposing to increase the rent by ten per cent if he allows them to stay and along with the letter they leave on his doorstep half a chicken, even though the food supply is diminishing rapidly. A reply arrives with surprising swiftness: Christmas is approaching, and in the spirit of the season Gruber will accept an increase of twenty-five per cent, and not a pfennig less, to be reconsidered in the new year. They accept Gruber's offer via another letter, presented on his doorstep beside a bowl of asparagus in white sauce.

After a time, the men gradually begin to regain their strength, to stay awake, to talk, to weave themselves back into the fabric of life. Heinrich's hair sprouts in a thick black fur, but Klein's scalp has become raw and infected, tufts appearing but nothing more; he rubs vinegar every night onto the skin, the infection is subdued, not dispelled.

And then, finally, Heinrich gathers enough energy to leave the apartment. He attends a Makkabi meeting, returns exhausted but jubilant, enthused anew about Palestine, saying that he will study farming to be part of the Chalutz. The next day Klein finds the strength to get up, starts to walk around the apartment in his dressing gown, putting things in order; miraculously he finds his gold watch just where he left it, in the top drawer of his bedside cabinet, he fastens it to his wrist, it is looser than before but makes him feel civilised. He asks why Hedi and Rosa have not been going to school, and it is decided that Hedi should return to school but not Rosa, who should instead help with the laundry and the housekeeping and the search for emigration. The next day Klein goes back to work; Inga isn't convinced of his health but he insists he must go, he will take Hedi to school on the way. He starts to look like his old self again, standing by the door in his greatcoat and spats, trilby concealing his patchy head, his moustache waxed and natty again, his battered briefcase by his side.

In the evening he returns, his eyes deeply bloodshot, saying, the whole Gemeinde is in a frenzy of emigration, half of my pupils have vanished, and more are leaving all the time, and many of the teachers too; in the staff room that's all everybody is talking about, they were surprised to see me as it happens, they had assumed that we had emigrated already. Everyone is trying to get out, Inga, everyone, and how much closer to emigration are we? And Inga looks at him in a strained sort of way, not wanting to say that her every waking moment has been dedicated to emigration ever since he was interned, holding herself back from pointing out that she has been arguing in its favour for years; Liebling, she says, God willing.

The New Year comes and goes, and nobody seems to notice. Days and weeks tumble by in a rush, in a whirlwind of consulates, embassies, waiting rooms and queues; Heinrich joins his sister and mother in the effort, and Klein takes time off work; some days see the entire family queuing at different embassies, apart from Hedi of course, who sits in a dusty classroom amongst a diminishing group of children, watching her teacher with a bewildered apathy. Now everything is visas, in the morning the conversation is dominated by them, and all day is spent in their pursuit; in the evening, again, visas are on the lips of every member of the household, exit visas, entry visas, transit visas, documents, this piece of paperwork and that, passports and tickets, approvals and stamps, Mexico and Shanghai and the Dominican Republic, Cuba and the British Crown Colony of Northern Rhodesia and Guatemala, where, rumour has it, Jews may be admitted so long as they do not engage in business. All night they dream of visas, emigration wraps seamlessly around their lives; every moment, day and night, they are queuing and begging and pleading, exhausted, frustrated, despondent, despairing, yet what else can possibly be done? Truly there is no alternative; everywhere Jews are clamouring for the same thing, for a lifeline, for a visa.

At around this time it so happens that one afternoon Klein is late to collect Hedi from school. As Hedi waits in the Gymnasium with Frau Ostreicher, all alone in the big echoing hall, she is anxious for her papa to arrive, because she wants to tell him something. She waits and waits, it is almost unbearable, and Frau Ostreicher says, what's biting you, you are never normally as jumpy as this, and Hedi replies, I just want to see my papa and go home, and Frau Ostreicher replies, I want to go home too, believe me. And they wait and wait until finally Klein arrives, out of breath and apologising repeatedly, and he loses hold of his briefcase and it crashes to the Gymnasium floor, and he has to gather all the papers up in any order and stuff them back in, flustered; Frau Ostreicher gives him a disapproving glance as he guides Hedi out of the Gymnasium and towards the streets, looking left and right for signs of danger and leading her into the shadows. As soon as they are out of earshot and she has her papa alone, Hedi tells him the secret immediately, in a loud whisper. Papa, Hana Grün is going to see the king of England tomorrow, with other children who are not from our school, they are going on trains. Klein, whose instincts have been heightened by his time in Sachsenhausen, turns to Hedi very seriously and says, who told you this secret? And Hedi replies, Hana Grün told me herself, when we were telling secrets. And Klein thinks for a while, and replies, thank you for telling me, meine kleine. Now, how is your mathematics coming along? Later that evening, Inga, exhausted by another day spent in embassy waiting rooms, says, Liebling, the child is just being fanciful, but Klein replies, let's wait and see if Hana Grün is seen again at school. Then we'll know.

So it is that three days later, still plagued by a crushing exhaustion, Klein finds himself in the east of the city, standing outside an ochre-coloured building with crumbling masonry, in which, on the third floor, is the modest apartment of Familie Grün. This is a sad building, thinks Klein as he scans the cluster of doorbells, it reminds him of a monastery. He raises his hand and presses the doorbell; he cannot hear a sound, so he presses again, and still nothing. He walks backwards into the street and looks up. The curtains twitch. Klein sighs in frustration and returns to the door, presses again the mute doorbell. Finally a dim light fills the hall, he hears the sound of footsteps, and a figure appears on the other side of the door, visible through the frosted glass.

—Who is it? comes a woman's voice.

—My name is Doktor Otto Klein. My daughter goes to school with Hana.

—What do you want?

—Just a little of your time, if you please.

There is the sound of bolts scraping back and the door opens a crack. A man's voice can be heard calling from upstairs, who is at the door, and the woman calls back, just a parent from Hana's school. Then she turns to Klein and peers at him suspiciously. She is middle-aged perhaps, and wears a black headscarf tight round her hair. Her face looks pale, fresh, as sad as the building.

—What do you want? she says again.

—It's about Hana, says Klein.

—Oh?

—I have heard that she travelled secretly to England.

Frau Grün looks startled and tries to close the door, but Klein presses his elbow into the opening.

—Please, he whispers, I just need a little information. Did you arrange it yourself or through an organisation? Are you going to follow her to England? How can I—

—It is preposterous, says Frau Grün, my daughter is visiting relatives in Hamburg.

Klein pauses but does not remove his elbow from the door.

—She has gone by herself all the way to Hamburg, he says, at the age of seven?

—Please, Herr Klein, says Frau Grün, let me close the door and leave us in peace.

Klein removes his hat and thrusts his face, his raw-skinned head, into the doorway.

—Look at me, he whispers, look. They did this to me at Sachsenhausen, do you hear? Sachsenhausen. If you have information you must share it with me. Freedom is for everybody, not just your daughter.

Frau Grün's face crumples in a strange way. There is a long pause. Finally the door opens wider, spilling a rectangle of light onto the pavement. Klein straightens his jacket and puts on his hat.

—Come in, says Frau Grün, quietly.

Klein follows her up a narrow staircase that smells faintly of herrings, into a cramped apartment. The Grün family is religious; dominating the room is a sideboard upon which stands a silver candelabra and a portrait of a bearded sage. Several chairs face the sideboard like a shrine, and the room is given a yellowish glow by a low-hanging lamp.

A man in a skullcap and shirtsleeves enters the room, a surprised expression on his face; Klein shakes him by the hand.

—This is Herr Doktor Klein, says the woman, coming back into the room, he won't be staying long.

—A pleasure, says the man confusedly, my name is Haim Grün.

Before Klein can sit down, the woman hands him a piece of foolscap.

—This is the address of the Jewish Refuge Committee, she says. It is in the west of the city. You should speak to somebody called Norbert Wollheim. She whispers the name as if afraid of the evil eye.

—So it is official, says Klein, folding the paper into his pocket. Can a whole family apply?

—No, replies Frau Grün tersely, England will only accept children, and you need a sponsor as well.

—Yes, but how many children can you send? asks Klein, his voice sounding loud in his ears.

—We didn't ask, says Frau Grün, we had only one.

There is a silence so deep that Klein can hear his watch ticking on his wrist. It is almost a religious silence.

—There will be more transports? he asks.

—Please, Herr Klein, my wife has given you the information, says Herr Grün, now leave us in peace.

—Of course, says Klein, thank you.

He backs awkwardly to the door and makes his way down the herring-smelling stairs. Above he can hear Herr and Frau Grün talking, the woman's voice staccato and distressed, her husband's voice soothing. He takes the piece of foolscap from his pocket and checks that it is legible. Then, feeling somehow as if the world has changed around him, Klein leaves the sad ochre building and steps out into the street, breathing the cold air deep. The world looks strange somehow, it feels different with this piece of foolscap in his pocket with its scribbled address. He is filled with the sense that his life, and the lives of his family, are about to change irreversibly. Part of him wishes to tear the paper up, let the pieces flutter away into the dark Berlin air, forget it had ever existed. Yet at the same time he wishes to protect this most fragile of notes, for those few lines may truly contain the elusive promise of freedom, the glimmer of light for which he and his family have been searching so desperately. No time like the present, he thinks; glancing anxiously over his shoulder, and clutching his hand to his breast pocket, he fights off his tiredness and makes his way westwards across the city.

By the time he arrives at the address the streets are shrouded in darkness. There is nothing to indicate that this is the headquarters of the Jewish Refugee Committee; it does not even appear to be an official building. The curtains have been drawn for the night but a glow can be seen in several of the windows. He finds the correct doorbell and rings; immediately the lights in the windows go out. Just as he is about to press the bell again, a key turns in the lock and the door is eased open. Nothing can be seen of the person behind the door.

—What is your business?

—I wish to speak to Herr Norbert Wollheim.

—What is your business?

—It is private and personal.

—You can tell me. I am in his confidence.

Klein hesitates and the door begins to close.

—Wait, he says, I wish to register my children for the transports to England.

—I'm sorry, we cannot help you.

—Why not?

—Please, sir. We cannot help you.

The door starts to close again and Klein darts his knee into it, followed by his elbow; but this person, whoever he is, is not as gentle as Frau Grün and attempts to force him out. He scuffles to keep the door open, baring his teeth like a dog and shaking his hat from his head; it bounces onto the road.

—Look at me, he says urgently, they did this to me at Sachsenhausen. Just look.

—I can see, comes the voice, but you are not the only one to have been to Sachsenhausen. Many people have been to Sachsenhausen. We cannot help everyone. We cannot help you.

—Then who can you help? If not me, then who?

—We cannot help you. There are procedures.

—Procedures? What procedures? Tell me what they are, I will follow the procedures.

—We cannot help you.

Klein, realising that he may be struggling for his children's very survival, refuses to remove his elbow. The door begins to bite into his flesh.

—I will not leave. You may break my arm but I will not leave. You will have to kill me. Tell me about the transports.

—We know nothing about any transports.

—You know nothing?

—There is no such thing.

—Then I am sure you will have no objection to my telling the whole community about it? And passing around your address?

The person in the darkness stops struggling but does not release the pressure on the door. Klein stands there panting, his arm and leg trapped in the doorway, trying to catch his breath. Finally, the door opens wider, just enough for a single man to slip inside. Klein picks up his hat from the road, straightens his jacket and steps into the darkness, massaging his bruised arm with his surgeon's fingers.

The room is in complete darkness: not even outlines can be seen. Outside, the stars are obscured by a thick layer of cloud. The windows of the apartment are still broken, still boarded up; the room is in complete darkness, not even outlines can be seen.

Klein rolls over in bed with a groaning sound, trapping the blankets under him. Inga fights to pull them back, her legs have been suddenly exposed to the impenetrable cold.

—This is unbearable, whispers Klein.

—You were so confident earlier. What happened? Inga replies.

—This is unbearable, he repeats.

—Don't you think we have made the right decision?

—I wasn't aware we had arrived at a decision.

—Only one child should be sent at a time you said, says Inga.

—Indeed.

—Then it must be Heinrich first, or Rosa. From England they will be able to get us a visa.

—Heinrich is nineteen, he is too old, says Klein, you know that.

—Well, then. It must be Rosa. Not Hedi.

—This is unbearable. I cannot bear it.

—Don't say that, you're making it worse.

The night is a wall of silence.

—Ach, I cannot sleep, says Klein.

—I cannot either, says Inga.

—Rosa should stay here, she can help with getting visas, help with the laundry. Hedi is so little, her whole life lies ahead. She will adapt better to a new country and new parents. Perhaps we should send her after all.

—But she is so young to be away from her mama and papa.

—I know. Ach, what a decision, nobody should make such a decision.

—I think, says Inga, if Rosa were to go we can send Hedi later. Rosa will be there to look after her until we arrive.

—Perhaps.

—And once Rosa's there, she might find someone there to employ us. She might get us a visa.

—You make it sound so rational, but nothing is certain, whispers Klein. We might not get a visa, there could be a war, the transports could stop, we could be trapped. The children could be imprisoned at the border.

—Liebling, please. Talking like that doesn't help.

—This is unbearable.

There is the sound of blankets being pushed aside and an upheaval on the bed as Klein gets to his feet.

—Where are you going? says Inga.

—Water, to get water.

There is the sound of the door opening and closing as he leaves the room, followed by fumbling and clinking in the kitchen; then the scrape of a match as he lights a candle. Inga turns over and presses her face into the pillow.

—Papa?

—Rosa, what are you doing awake?

—I cannot sleep.

Rosa enters the kitchen, a blanket round her shoulders, and sits opposite her father. He passes her a glass of water across the table.

—What time is it? asks Rosa.

—It is . . . twenty-four minutes past the hour.

—Which hour?

—Three.

—I have not slept a wink.

—Nor have I.

From the darkness the soft flap of bare feet on floorboards can be heard, then Inga appears in the doorway.

—Mama?

—I'm afraid so. May I join you?

—I might have a glass of something, says Klein, rising from his chair. I think there is a little brandy left. Will anybody join me?

The question was not intended for an answer, and none is forthcoming.

—I have been thinking, says Rosa, perhaps we can make some kind of cutlery out of wood. Heinrich and I could do it. We still have some pieces left from the bookshelves.

—That is a possibility, says Inga, we can look into it tomorrow.

—What the Reich wants with our cutlery is a mystery to me, says Rosa.

—The madness of these decrees will never end, says Klein from beside the drinks cabinet, we have not a scrap of silver left and nor does any Jew. We shall have to eat with our fingers, or directly from the plate, like pigs.

He sits down again at the table and sips, wincing, from the glowing glass of ginger-coloured liquid. Inga takes a deep breath.

—Liebling, she says, perhaps we should speak to Rosa now?

—Very well, says her husband resignedly.

Inga turns to her daughter, and as their eyes meet Rosa feels unsettled.

—My darling, says Inga, there is something I think we should discuss. Your father and I were undecided about when to mention it to you. But you are fifteen, and old enough. Perhaps we were meant to discuss it tonight.

Rosa rubs her eyes and draws her blanket tighter around her shoulders.

—What is it? she says.

—We have managed to get a special visa for England, says Inga.

Rosa's eyes widen in disbelief but she does not reply; from the expression on her mother's face it is clear that there is more to be said.

—However, Inga continues, we only have one, and it is only for a child, not an adult. One child, under the age of eighteen. We will apply for another of these visas as soon as we can, but for the moment there is only one.

Rosa looks from her mother to her father and back again. They both start to speak at once, and then fall silent.

—Heinrich cannot go, says Rosa.

—No, her father replies, and nor can we. Only you or Hedi. We have decided it would be best if you went first and settled in, and Hedi goes to join you in a few months.

—Where would we live?

—In London, he says, with the Kremers. My cousin Gerald. We've been writing, and he's happy to have you. Do you remember him?

—When will you be coming? Rosa asks.

Inga glances briefly at her husband.

—We have no arrangements, she admits, yet. But if you are in England, you will be able to find somebody there to employ us as domestic staff. Then we can get a work visa and join you in London.

—What if I cannot find anybody?

—You will, says Inga, her face illuminated and pale.

—What if I do not wish to go? says Rosa suddenly.

—What do you mean? says Inga.

—I can choose, can I not?

—Well, of course.

—How long have you been planning this? says Rosa.

—Perhaps a month.

—A month? And you were not going to tell me?

—Pfui, we are telling you now, says Inga.

Klein drains his brandy.

—Let's all keep calm, he says.

—It is difficult to be calm, says Rosa, when one is not being treated as an adult.

There is a tense silence.

—I am brave enough to stay with you, says Rosa at last, I am not afraid.

—This isn't about bravery, darling, says Inga.

—I go to the embassies the same as you. I do the customers' laundry, says Rosa. I should not be forced out of the family.

—Nobody is forcing you out, says Inga, please, Rosa.

—I am being forced. I do not want to leave.

—If you don't want to go, Püppchen—

—Don't call me that.

—If you don't want to go, says Klein, we may reconsider.

—You will reconsider, says Rosa.

—The Kremers will make wonderful foster parents, says Inga.

—Foster parents? So now I am being fostered?

—Oh, Rosa, you know what I mean. They are referred to as foster parents by the Jewish Refugee Committee. I didn't mean you're actually being fostered.

—I don't need parents, says Rosa, if my parents don't need me.

She gets up from the table, gathers her blanket and hurries out. Her parents, carrying the candle, go after her into her bedroom.

—Stop following me, says Rosa.

—We want you to listen, says Inga. It's just not true to suggest that we want to send you away.

Inga sits beside Rosa on the bed but Klein remains standing, his raw tufty head casting a round shadow behind him.

—This plan is the best one we have, he says, the only one in fact. Believe me, the last thing we want is to send you away. You are our daughter, the most precious thing in the world. But with things as they are . . .

—Anyway, says Inga, if you're truly not happy you don't have to go. We can send Hedi instead. It's just that it makes more sense to send you so that you can try to get us visas.

—Very well, says Rosa, her face burning. I'm sorry.

—Darling, says Inga, touching Rosa's cheek, we may get a visa for the whole family soon, anyway, for Chile or Shanghai. We mustn't lose hope.

—When do I leave?

—In March. So you've got a little time. You can think about it.

—I shall be unable to think about anything else.

7

Rosa breathes deeply, smelling the cotton pillow, feeling it against her cheeks, her forehead; air filters through the weave of the fabric into her body, filling her lungs with the familiar scent of home. It is daytime but the room is dark, her back is divided by a slit of light coming from a crack in the board on the window. She is tired and her fingers are sore from the laundry; she kicks her feet a few times against the mattress and lies still again. Soon she must get up and continue with the housework, but for a few short minutes she can lie here, doing nothing, alone. There are only a few days left now, yet it's as if time is standing still. She will be glad to leave this hellish city, and when it is all over she will be glad to come back and become once again a normal German girl. And then, she supposes, she will have to go back to her books. She should like to study nursing, she has always wanted to be a nurse, or maybe she will even qualify as a doctor. And she will get married, to whom she does not yet know, she can see him in silhouette but his face is hidden; he is tall and slim, with very black hair, yes, and the sort of hands that are equally at home tilling the land and cradling the face of a lover; and he will get on well with Papa, they will smoke together and drink Schnaps, and he will play handball with Heinrich, and take Hedi on outings to the cinema and buy her ice cream. And they will have four children, two of each. Is she really going to leave Berlin? What will happen if the SS catch her at the border? What if she cannot get visas for her family? No, don't think of it. What will the Kremers be like? All these questions and not an answer in sight, she has no choice but to wait and see; she cannot believe the end will truly come.

After a time Rosa's mind begins to clear and she feels exhausted. The sound of cooking can be heard, and the smell of vegetable soup slips into the room, vegetable soup until Berta comes again. Rosa rolls over and sits up against the wall, her cheek creased with red, looking at the crack of light at the edge of the board over the window; she cannot help but feel a pang of jealousy, for Heinrich is not leaving, and nor is Hedi, they are staying here with Mama and Papa, and they will continue, as a family, without her; as time goes by they will have a life together that Rosa will not share, and their letters will surely reduce over time. She will become the distant aunt, the lonely grey-haired old spinster living in the British Isles where everybody wears brown and drinks tea. Perhaps she should have refused to go.

—Rosa? May I come in?

So deeply has Rosa been involved in her thoughts that she has not heard the knock. She gathers her thoughts and opens her bedroom door.

—I've brought a candle. It is always dark in your room, says Heinrich.

He enters the room and sits beside her, the candlelight picking out a corona of hair on his head, half grown and matted like a bear's.

—How are you holding up?

—All right, says Rosa, not long to go now.

—Have you started packing?

—I've got ages really. And we are only allowed one suitcase.

—I am sorry I can't come with you. What an adventure, don't you think? I've always wanted to go to England, although of course I will be going to Palestine in the end.

—Yes, it will be an adventure.

—I can't wait to join you in England. I'm sure it won't be long.

—I will do my very best to get you all a visa. I hope I can do it.

—It cannot be that difficult when you are actually in England yourself.

—I hope not.

Heinrich reaches into his jacket and pulls out a rectangular object wrapped in a rag.

—Here, I have something for you. To take to England.

Rosa accepts the gift and peels the rag away. In her hands, in an embossed silver frame, is a photograph. For the first time in a long while, she smiles.

—When was this taken?

—Years ago, in Wiesbaden. See, you look about eight maybe. And look at Hedi, she's tiny, can't be more than a few months old.

—Look at Papa, he's so funny with his trousers tucked in his socks all the way to the knee.

—Yes, his hiking style.

—I wonder why I haven't seen this before?

—I stumbled across it after my room was destroyed. It must have been at the back of a cupboard somewhere, but it was lying in the corner completely unscathed.

—I hope it doesn't break in my suitcase.

—I've wrapped it in a rag, and you can wrap it in a jumper or something as well.

—Judah, thank you.

117

Heinrich puts the candle down on the floor, and they embrace; then he relaxes his grip but his sister continues to hold him for a few moments; then she lets go.

—Keep your spirits up, says Heinrich, within months we will all be safe.

There is something within the melody of his voice, something unusual, a dissonant chain of notes that act against the meaning of his words. Rosa looks up at her brother, into his eyes, and sees – perhaps she's imagining it – a lingering presence of doubt.

8

Rosa will always remember: in the few short days leading up to her departure, Papa took her on frequent walks through the Grunewald on the outskirts of Berlin. It wasn't safe, but nowhere was at the time, and there were usually few people in the woods, which made things a little easier. The sun fell gently upon the weave of Papa's jacket as she followed him up the hill overlooking the city. He was a brisk walker, it was difficult for his daughter to keep pace, but he made no allowances; it wasn't that he was being unkind, it was simply that he didn't notice her struggling, he was too engrossed in the conversation, this had always been his way, why should things be different now? He climbed the hill with great gangly strides, his ankles flashing as his trouser legs rode up, stride by stride, talking over his shoulder as Rosa bobbed in his wake.

When they got to the brow of the hill he sat down, rather out of breath, waited for the girl to catch up and removed his hat, placing it on the grass beside him, leaving his poor infected head exposed like a thumb, feathery wisps of hair and patches of bare white skin; his bald-ness made a mockery of his proud bearing, and his moustache, still waxed and smooth as ever, looked absurd, the tail pinned on the donkey. Rosa lay on her back and drew her knees up against the sky, the sky grey as her skirt; Papa sat for a few minutes gazing down at Berlin, a defiant smile playing over his lips, his bald head higher than the highest point in the city: look, Deutschland, what you have done to me, raise your eyes to my hatless head, O Berlin, and be ashamed.

And they talked, and a comfortable discussion developed, a conver-sation of which silence was a friend, that neither of them wanted to conclude, for although they did not mention it they were both aware with every breath that Rosa was leaving. Papa had a medicine bottle full of brandy which he sipped from time to time, a poor replacement for the Weiße mit Schuss that he used to enjoy at the end of his hikes in happier times, the white beer with that lovely squirt of raspberry served in a bulbous stemmed glass on a little circle of paper as he lounged in his favourite seat in the Alpengrund restaurant, looking out at the forest clearing. This memory was vivid as he propped himself up uncomfortably on his elbows, tilted the brown bottle and sipped, wincing with each swallow, and gazed blankly over the city, imprisoned beneath the steely sky. The breeze was strong, not blustery as such, but strong, and Rosa's curls fluttered off to the west, into the grass, the brown mingling with the green, the colours barely discernible in the dusky afternoon light. She was concerned about tangles and gathered her hair under her shoulder, it kept flapping out, Mama was cutting it at home by that time with those great kitchen scissors, a clumsy instrument but she made a good job of it, she had a sharp eye for fashion even then.

And they sat, and the conversation meandered here and there, and Papa's words were full of advice: always be strong, Püppchen, and always make us proud, very soon we will be together again, I am sure you will manage to get us passage to England. Make yourself useful when living with the Kremers, remember they are doing us a great kindness, they didn't have to take you in, you know, so we owe them a debt of gratitude. And what better use for all those English lessons we have given you? Now, your mother and I have been thinking; although until recently we have not brought you up with any sense of religious conviction, we should like to request that when the time comes, please give your own sons a bar mitzvah – will you promise me this, Püppchen? Speaking of which, my daughter, before your trip to England there are a few things I would like to tell you about how babies are made – so, Mama told you already? What a relief. Yes, Papa, I *am* fifteen.

16 March 1939, Berlin

I

The broad avenue that leads to the Bahnhof Friedrichstraße is all but deserted, its tramlines glimmering like eels in the darkness. The city slumbers. Three people are making their way along the pavement in the direction of the station, in and out of the light from the incandescent streetlamps, as wary as street-dogs. They link arms as if the figure in the middle might collapse.

—This suitcase is heavy, are you sure you will be able to carry it once we've left you? asks Klein.

—Yes, Papa, I can manage, Rosa replies, surprised at the strength of her voice.

—I shall try the Brazilian Embassy tomorrow, Klein says into the bitter air.

—Yes, Liebling, that's a good idea, replies his wife. And I will try Argentina.

A tense silence falls as they make their way with inevitable steps towards the railway station, step by step towards the station, the doorway to the rest of the world. This is the moment they all thought would never arrive, yet now it is occurring, it is happening so fast, like a dream.

The three figures walk on along the pavement through the darkness, and now they can see the lights of the thick-walled, red-bricked Bahnhof. Rosa's upper arm is uncomfortable, she squirms but stops herself; under her father's fingers, beneath the sleeve of her woollen coat, under her cardigan sleeve and the sleeve of her very best blouse, is Papa's gold watch, clamped around her bicep so tightly that it pinches the skin. Although Rosa cannot hear the familiar whisper of the second hand, she knows it is measuring out the seconds exactly – she can visualise it perfectly, the tiny needle moving precisely from point to point to point, continuing unremittingly, regardless.

Rosa's suitcase is tied with one of Heinrich's belts like a quid of tobacco. She glances across at it intermittently, watches it bumping against her father's knees. She is amazed it has not split and spewed its contents all over the pavement by now; she and Inga both had to sit on it before Papa could get the buckles to close, and now it is straining and bulging like a fat man's fist. It was packed, not once, or twice even, but many times, packed and repacked, with only her finest things, her best frock, or Shabbat frock as Inga calls it these days, which she hasn't worn for many months, her warmest jumper, her favourite books and Inga's cashmere shawl, which may be a little worn and frayed, but is nevertheless of a wonderful quality and retains the warmth like nothing on earth. And Heinrich's photograph from years before, taken in carefree Wiesbaden, each child is allowed one photograph; and Hedi's dolly Gigi, wrapped in a pillowcase to keep it hidden, her favourite toy, with the crack along her face caked with UHU, offered to her sister by way of goodbye, and also to keep it safe.

Inga had to unpack the suitcase, fit in the doll and put everything back again, shaking out clothes with a professional flourish, refolding various items, all freshly laundered and scented with the Grunewald lavender that she picked last summer; maybe this jumper would be better at the bottom, let's lay the socks out flat and line the case with them, here inside your shoes there is a little space, if only you were allowed two suitcases! Then Papa put down his glass of brandy and helped to close the case, Inga and Rosa sitting on it, side by side, while Papa reached behind their ankles and strained with the buckles, trying to point out the comedy in the situation; it was not until Heinrich joined the struggle that the suitcase was finally fastened. The only clothes that were not infused with the scent of Inga's lavender were the ones Rosa was wearing, which smelled vividly of newness, of material which has been cut freshly from a roll. That smell belonged to old Berlin, the Berlin of several years ago, and it seemed incongruous, but Inga wanted her daughter to arrive in England looking her very best, to have the best possible start with her new family, for first impressions last.

Now they are almost at the ugly pillared entrance of the station, and little groups of parents and children can be seen moving silently around the concourse, standing in pale-faced clusters, bleached yellow by the incandescent lights. The Kleins join them, each family contained within its own bell jar. Most of the children are younger than Rosa – there are a pair of twin girls in identical black felt coats and berets, an assortment of boys of various levels of scruffiness, some girls of various heights and, there, a woman holding a baby bundled up in a blanket, nothing to be seen but a small sleeping face.

"Rosa is unable to recall saying goodbye to Heinrich; she must have said goodbye to him at the apartment, but try as she might she is not be able to remember exactly – ah, memories, memories, already they are becoming important, it is strange what the memory does, the tricks it pulls, the games it plays, its priorities are all skewed, but she cannot remember, in her mind when she tries to remember there is only a blank space. Hedi, however, she vividly recalls giving up her doll, no don't think of it, her little morbid face with those liquid eyes, her only crime to be born at that particular time, in that particular place, her young unhappy life."

—Ladies and gentlemen, please listen. You cannot go to the platform. The police will not allow it. You will have to say goodbye in the waiting room. Follow me if you please.

The astute-looking man checks that he has been understood then steps off the chair and carries it across the concourse, the small crowd of parents and children ambling in his wake. Klein and Inga grip Rosa's biceps, the gold wristwatch on her arm pinches, and they manoeuvre to the waiting room as a unit. The door is closed. The waiting room is boxy, stuffy, smells of disinfectant, someone coughs. The walls are painted black to shoulder height and grey above, light bulbs dangle from the ceiling collared with green cones. No one removes their coat. A group of youth leaders register the children on clipboards and tag them and their luggage with labels.

Rosa looks from her mother to her father and back again. Papa is standing silently, pale and distracted, Mama is saying something about how they will see each other again soon, just as soon as they can get passage to England – or Argentina or Brazil, thinks Rosa, you might be going there, mightn't you, if you get your way at the embassies tomorrow; and many of the children here are Hedi's age, some younger, yet Hedi is not being sent away. The twins are wailing and it is putting everyone on edge; their mother is kneeling, trying to comfort them, crying herself now. It is difficult even to think clearly. Rosa's throat feels blocked like a tube of bamboo, she is surprised she is still breathing, she does not know how the air is getting in. A youth leader with a clipboard comes over, his fingers stained with cobalt ink, yes, Rosa is on the list. Papa hands over Rosa's passport and he checks that it has been stamped with the word 'Staatenlose' – 'stateless' – and the letter 'J', and that 'Sara' has been inserted as a middle name as is required by the Reich for Jewish girls; then he places it in his folder and moves on to the next person. Rosa is surprised to be processed so easily, surprised that this isn't just a game, some kind of practical joke, a stunt pulled by someone somewhere for some reason. She receives her tags, feels somewhat foolish being labelled like a parcel; it's not so bad for the little ones. Inga helps her tie one tag round the handle of her suitcase and loops the other over her head, a number printed on a piece of cardboard, hanging round her neck from a shoelace.

The mood has been subdued, but suddenly it begins to change. There is the sound of laughter from a corner, and some confusion regarding a little girl who does not appear on the list; at the same time a small boy in the centre of the room begins to howl, burrowing into his mother's skirts and twisting round and round. Now Rosa looks at her parents again: she is finding it difficult to focus and the watch on her bicep is pinching uncomfortably. Papa is fiddling with her suitcase, tightening the belt, his hat slips as he bends over and he has to keep pushing it back on his head, exposing his tufty scalp, it is like a comedy in a way, Mama is saying something, her face is red, she must be hot, perhaps she should remove her scarf, it is a little warm in here, Rosa didn't think she felt the heat so much, if only those twins would stop wailing, their shrieks are quite piercing, she is finding it hard to swallow, and the watch on her bicep is actually giving her pain. The astute-looking man gets up on his chair again and says:

—Now it's your last goodbye. The guides will take over and they will accompany the children to the train. Please don't come to the platform because it only causes trouble for us.

The constriction in Rosa's throat builds to an almost unbearable degree. Inga is terribly red now, and she is trying to smile and say something, but her face is creasing in a way that Rosa has never seen before, from somewhere she produces a handkerchief, then replaces it in her pocket and smiles an awful smile, she has become so thin, Mama you are so thin, now Papa is standing back from the suitcase acting as if he feels a genuine sense of accomplishment, he says, Püppchen, if this suitcase does not survive your adventure to England I will eat my brush, maybe we will meet again before you even manage to open it, and he smiles too, another awful smile, then he says, don't spit out of the window, it will come back in your face, and smiles again. Rosa does not want to go, it is all happening too quickly, everything unravelling before her eyes, she can smell Papa's cologne, she realises she has never smelt it before, not really, not properly, never paid it much attention, and she looks at her parents, she has never seen them before, not properly, she must remember every detail of their faces, imprint them in her mind, the way her mother touches her cheek, with that kind of insouciant affection, it is part of her, that gesture, part of the whole experience of her, a throwaway caress, yet filled with an everyday kind of love, it seems strange under these circumstances, now Rosa's eyes are itching and she does not want to go, Papa carries her suitcase to the door, then can go no further, Rosa must go alone. He puts down the suitcase, takes her shoulders and turns her gently towards him, puts his hands on her head, closes his eyes, says a blessing, the last blessing, his hands rest on her hair in the familiar way, and he whispers be strong, meine Püppchen, be strong; and then Mama does the same, murmuring her prayer silently, then her trembling hands slip away. Rosa must carry her suitcase herself, she heaves it up, walks through the doorway, looks back one final time: Papa and Mama are standing arm in arm, they are waving, but their masks have fallen away, they look hopeless, and that is the worst thing of all; Rosa turns her back and they are gone. She has seen them for the last time.

As she walks towards the platform, Rosa can't feel her feet. She remembers Mama saying once that angels have no feet, they simply glide along without them, and that is how she feels, it is a surprise that her feet are carrying her along as normal. A youth leader helps her to board, she places her hand on the cool metal side of the train, feels its rivets beneath her fingers, sees the oblong letters DEUTSCHE REICHSBAHN, then the youth leader directs her along a cramped corridor into one of the compartments, heaves her suitcase into the air and stows it on the rope luggage rack overhead, it must be the heaviest suitcase on the whole train, the rack bulges like a fishing net under the weight, the youth leader groans as he lifts it, the same sound that Papa makes as he removes his coat and hat at the end of a day; Rosa glides over to a seat as if nothing unusual were occurring, and she raises the window using the little leather stub, rests her elbows on the sill and looks out; the night air is cool on her face, she wants to catch another glimpse of her parents but they are hidden away in that room, only a few metres away after all.

Suddenly she is overwhelmed by a desire to write to her parents, to tell them how she has been feeling these last few days, to confess everything, for she now feels that they truly love her. But her pencils are packed deep in the bowels of her suitcase and Papa has secured it so tightly she is afraid to open it, and – oh, her compartment is full now, all children, little girls, quite young, one or two a bit older, and great clouds of steam are spurting up past the window, this train does not seem mobile at all, seems more like a house, and there's the shout, Alles einsteigen! Alles einsteigen, can this train really move, it seems too heavy, like a house, look at all that steam, it's as if it is surrounded by fog, and somewhere those twins are still howling, their cries can be heard above the noise of the engine, who knows how they got them on the train, but here they are, sitting side by side and wailing in an identical fashion, the train must be about to depart, these are the last few seconds—

Just as the cramped train begins to tug and groan, the carriage door opens and something is slid in. The door slams, and Rosa cranes out of the window. A slight figure hurries away along the platform and disappears in a cloud of steam. The train pulls painfully away.

Rosa and the other children sit in silence as the train picks up speed and the distance from their parents widens. Along the narrow corridor the silhouette of a rectangular object can be seen next to the train door, moving from side to side as the carriage jolts over the tracks. Dim lights and telegraph poles judder by in the darkness.

After a time Rosa gets to her feet, leaves the compartment and walks unsteadily down the corridor towards the object. When she gets near enough she stops. There in the shadows sits a wicker basket filled with blankets, and in the middle is the motionless face of a baby. Rosa puts her hand gently on the child's chest and detects a gentle movement, he must be in a deep sleep. Then her fingers brush a hard object – she withdraws a bottle filled with milk that has been tucked inside the blankets. She looks around. No youth leaders can be seen anywhere. The carriage is crammed with little girls, all peering out of their compartments, their tags swaying from side to side to the rhythm of the train, their hollow eyes fixed blankly upon her.

2

The door is firmly closed and none of the parents attempt to leave, they are doomed to remain in this adult domain, an empty Hameln suddenly devoid of children. Klein clears his throat. There is no Rosa, no fat suitcase, only nothingness. We will see her soon, Inga. We will all join her soon. Inga's face is motionless, her eyes fixed on the door of the waiting room. The minutes pass and then there is the sound of a train's whistle, that familiar sound beloved of children. Then the noise of steam and the speeding-up rhythm of a train's engines, they're leaving, they're leaving, they're leaving, finally fading to silence.

Eighteen months later, a few miles away, at the Grunewald goods station, most of these parents will be boarding freight trains bound for the east. But for now all they can do is leave the waiting room, pass through the concourse and make their way home.

3

The train is, for the most part, normal enough, headed by a great black engine with its eagle-and-Hakenkreuz insignia, spurting steam into the cold blackness of the German night; its occupants are largely businessmen returning from the city, their spongy overcoats smelling of alcohol and cigarette smoke, their hatted heads nodding to their chests, dreaming vaguely of home, or dwelling upon the various issues that concern them, swaying in a single wave as the train shudders rhythmically forwards. So much for the first few carriages. Yet the last carriages, dimly lit like the rest, windows soapy with reflections like the rest, smelling of steam and carpets like the rest, are full of dark-eyed, still sitting children, their tags swaying with the motion of the train, looking at the fifteen-year-old girl standing in the narrow corridor, a wicker basket awkwardly in her arms, practically a grown-up yet wearing a tag like the rest of them, occasional shadows falling upon her shoulders then passing, falling then passing, as buildings slip past outside.

—Where are we going, Fräulein? asks one of the black-coated twins as Rosa enters the compartment, the basket in her arms. The other is still crying.

—Don't you know? responds Rosa, casting her eyes around the carriage for a space to place the basket. We're going to England.

—When will we get there, Fräulein? asks the girl again. She can't be more than seven or eight, about Hedi's age.

—We will arrive when we arrive.

The girl falls silent and continues to watch Rosa. Gradually her sister stops crying.

Rosa moves her to another seat and shifts a few children along. Then she places the basket on the empty seat and crouches on the carpet beside it.

—Is that a baby? says a girl in a scratchy-looking woollen skirt, several sizes too big. Her palms are pressed together between her knees.

—Yes, says Rosa looking in vain for a youth leader. It's a baby.

—Can I give him a cuddle?

—Can't you see he's asleep?

The girl gives Rosa a cheeky grin. Her skin is very white.

The train judders on and the children, in subdued tones, begin to talk. Rosa checks that no one is watching and adjusts the watch on her bicep. She recalls seeing a couple of girls of her own age in one of the compartments that she passed earlier; she picks up the basket and makes her way down the dim corridor, holding on to the brass handrail for support, trying not to bump the basket against the polished wood panelling on either side.

We're leaving, we're leaving, we're leaving.

The door of the compartment is closed, and curtains are drawn across the window. Rosa hesitates, then knocks and enters.

—Hello, she says.

This compartment, like all the others, is full of children, amongst whom sit the two older girls wearing the long skirts and sleeves of the Orthodox.

—Is that your baby? one of them asks. She has blonde hair in two Heidi-style plaits, and a blouse with a wide white collar.

—No, replies Rosa.

—So why have you got it then?

The baby moves, tilting his head upwards and moving it from side to side. Two tiny hands appear and flail against the sides of the basket. Then a cry can be heard, small and breathless like the mewing of a cat.

—Have you seen a youth leader anywhere? asks Rosa.

—It's hungry, says the blonde girl. I can tell.

—How do you know? says Rosa.

—She has a baby brother, that's how, responds the other girl. She is swarthy with meditative black eyes, and her arms are firmly folded across her chest.

—I think he's tired, not hungry, says Rosa, losing her balance slightly as the train lurches on. And I've got a baby sister.

—How can it be tired? It's just been asleep, says the blonde girl. Rosa flushes. The black-eyed girl gives the barest hint of a smile. The blonde girl speaks again:

—You'd better give the baby some food, since you're looking after it. Look, it's going all red in the face.

—Shall I pick him up? asks Rosa.

—I suppose so, says the blonde girl. What do you think, Britta?

The black-eyed girl nods, her arms still folded.

—Pick it up. Then sit down. What's your name, anyway?

—Rosa.

—I'm Gusti. And this is Britta.

Rosa sets the basket on the seat, takes the baby carefully under the arms and draws him out. He arches his back and kicks his legs, crying relentlessly, gasping for breath. One of the blankets unravels and drops to the floor; Gusti tuts and tucks it back round the baby.

—You've got to support its head, she says.

—It's not an *it*, it's a *he*, says Rosa, defensively.

—How do you know it's a he?

—I don't know, I just know.

—What's his name, then?

—How should I know?

—Well whatever his name is, if he cries for much longer he's going to be sick.

—I think I shall feed him, suggests Rosa. Would you please pass me the bottle? It's in the basket.

Gusti complies and sits down next to Rosa, who takes the bottle and aims it cautiously at the baby's mouth, jolting to the rhythm of the train.

—Not like that. You need to tip it up or else nothing will come out, says Gusti.

—If only the train wasn't bumping so much, says Rosa.

—Do you want me to do it?

—No, I can manage.

Suddenly the teat slips in and the baby begins to suck ferociously, making little distressed noises in the back of his throat.

—There, that's better, isn't it? says Rosa. That's much better. There.

—Keep it covered up, it'll get cold, says Gusti.

Suddenly the baby begins to cough violently.

—Take the bottle out, says Gusti. It's choking.

Rosa removes the bottle so sharply that she almost drops it.

—You need to wind it. Here, let me. Gusti takes the baby from Rosa's arms, puts him over her shoulder and starts to pat his back.

—Be careful, says Rosa, you might hit his head on the window.

—I know what I'm doing, says Gusti.

There is a loud burp and the baby seems to settle. Gusti hands the baby back to Rosa and he is immediately sick. Britta, once again, from within her solemn black eyes, almost smiles, adjusting the tag around her neck. Rosa dabs her skirt anxiously with the baby's blanket and picks up the bottle again. The baby sucks ferociously.

—Careful, says Gusti, you'd better make sure you've enough left for later.

—What do you mean? says Rosa.

—She means, says Britta, that it'll be hours and hours before we get to England. You mustn't use up all the milk.

Rosa removes the bottle with a pop and holds it up to the dim light, the milk inside dancing to the movement of the train.

—There's not very much left, says Gusti. It's a good eater.

—Perhaps you can dilute it, says Britta.

The baby sucks his tongue for a while, dribble bubbling between his lips; then his lower lip protrudes, his face crumples and he begins to cry.

—It's still hungry, says Gusti.

—Yes I know, says Rosa, but you told me to stop feeding him.

—You have to hold him to the side and jig him up and down, says Britta, chipping in. That's the only way. I've seen people do it before.

—Like this? asks Rosa.

—Not quite, says Britta. Let me.

Britta takes the baby from Rosa and begins to rock and bounce him to and fro. Almost immediately, the baby stops crying.

—That's right, says Gusti, very good.

The train cuts noisily through the moonless night and it feels as though they will never arrive. Several of the children doze, and the others retreat into themselves. The baby falls asleep in Britta's arms, and she places him back in the basket. The clank and grumble of the train has a hypnotic effect and Rosa's mind begins to cloud over; she rubs her bicep absent-mindedly, falls into a fitful sleep.

We're leaving, we're leaving, we're leaving.

4

—I say, are you all right?

Rosa is woken by Gusti moving to the seat opposite where a round-faced girl is sitting, staring vacantly into space; the girl does not respond, does not acknowledge Gusti's presence. She is sitting on her hands, staring straight ahead, lips clamped into a crease, eyes two blank buttons. She might be four or five.

—Are you all right? Gusti asks again. There is no answer, no movement, no response.

—Your nose is running. Gusti pulls a wrinkled handkerchief from her pocket and applies it to the girl's face.

—Is there a problem here? comes a male voice. Rosa looks up to see the astute-looking man from the station leaning against the dark wood panelling, swaying from side to side with the movement of the train; his hair is swept neatly back and his dark, almost oriental eyes regard the world with certainty. I thought there were no youth leaders on board, she thinks, thought we had left them all in Berlin – thank goodness. She feels strangely comforted and, despite herself, imagines him slipping a golden ring onto her finger and sweeping her into his arms.

Gusti motions towards the round-faced girl. The man enters the compartment and crouches in front of her.

—I say, little one, are you not feeling well?

There is no response. He checks the girl's tag against a list on his clip-board.

—How long has she been motionless like this? he asks Gusti.

—Ever since we left Berlin, Herr Wollheim.

—She is a quiet girl, says Britta unexpectedly. I know her. Agnes Pfeifenkopf.

—I see, says the man. Perhaps kleine Agnes is tired.

He lifts the child gently in his arms; the girl flops against him, expressionless. Then he hoists her onto the rope luggage rack, cushioning her with bags and suitcases, laying her there as if in a hammock. The little girl turns onto her side, burying her face in the crook of her elbow. Wollheim clears his throat, walks into the corridor and turns to address the children.

—Now listen everybody, girls, please.

Heads appear from compartments and a nervous ripple goes through the carriage.

—We are approaching the border at Bentheim. In approximately one hour we will leave Deutschland and enter Holland. But there is one thing I must tell you: the customs officers have been replaced by SS guards. So please be compliant, stay in your seats and do whatever they say.

Wollheim walks along the corridor, holding on to the handrail, peering into the compartments, showing smiles to the tired children, and Rosa feels a kind of strength coming from him; she knows she should tell him about the baby but for some reason remains silent. He catches her eye, and her heart makes a small palpitation – then he walks through to the boys' carriage.

Night gives way to a thick grey dawn that closes upon the train as it noses its way towards Holland, spurting white steam into the air as if there were nothing to hide. Rosa massages her bicep and rests back in the seat, allowing her mind to drift. Then, out of the corner of her eye, she notices a movement; she opens her eyes to see the little twins struggling down the bumpy corridor towards her compartment, one leading the other by the hand. She sits woozily up.

—What are you doing here? Speak up, now.

—May we please sit next to you, Fräulein?

—Certainly not, there isn't room. Everyone must stay in her own place. Back to your seats at once.

The leading twin looks at her steadily, neither accepting nor resisting her order. The one behind rubs her eyes with a balled-up dimpled fist. Then, without a word, they turn and make their way laboriously back down the corridor.

—That was mean, says Gusti. She is sitting by the window twisting one of her plaits, her fingers dimly reflected in the glass.

—No it wasn't, says Rosa. We must stay in our seats, that's the rule.

Gusti shrugs and gets to her feet. She slides past Rosa into the corridor and makes her way down the carriage. Rosa cranes her neck and sees her entering the twins' compartment.

Gradually the train begins to slow, and the jolts become more spaced out, as if the engine is falling asleep. Lights appear outside: illuminated buildings, warehouses, factories, strings of streetlamps forming erratic lines across the landscape, which is flatter than that of Berlin. A jigsaw of fields can be seen stretching out across the plains, emerging as the grey light grows. Rosa tucks the baby's basket as far as possible under the seat, concealing it from view in anticipation of the search. A silence falls inside the carriage, more profound than before, and the children who were sleeping start to awake.

—Rosa! comes a sharp whisper. She jumps – this is the first time that anyone has used her name since they left Berlin. She looks over to see Britta leaning towards her, an expression of alarm on her face.

—Up there. We'd better lift her down.

She follows Britta's pointing finger and is surprised to see the round-faced girl still lying in the rope luggage rack, her head still nuzzling the crook of her elbow. She gets to her feet and climbs onto the seat; Britta scrambles up beside her, holding the luggage rack; together they manage to drag the little girl awkwardly into their arms and sit her on one of the seats. She rubs her eyes and looks around, silently, before resuming her vacant stare. The two older girls take their seats once again just as the train draws into the station; they smooth their dresses and hair, and Rosa pushes the wristwatch firmly up her arm.

She looks out of the window, through her own reflection, watching as Bentheim station rumbles into view, wrought iron and concrete appearing and disappearing in clouds of steam. Finally the train comes to a halt. Doors are swung noisily open and passengers disembark from the front carriages, turning their collars up and swarming towards the exit. Rosa sees a man in a beige greatcoat and homburg hat walking drunkenly, leaning on a cane. And she sees SS officers striding along the platform as if immune to the cold, passing documents brusquely back and forth, patent peaks crowning their chiselled features, clouds jumping from their mouths as they speak.

—Don't look, hisses Gusti, keep your face away from the window.

Rosa continues to look, watching the SS officers, the passengers, the platform, the scene – this is the border, and along that track, through that mist, lies Holland.

Herr Wollheim steps off the train and approaches the group of SS officers. He is hidden by a cloud of steam and then is visible; he hangs back until one of the officers calls him over, then approaches, head bowed, and hands some papers over. The SS are all several inches taller than him, more erect, more vital, one of them claps him hard on the back, causing him to drop his clipboard on the platform; the others laugh and light cigarettes as the Jude picks up the clipboard and smooths the papers on it. After a few more minutes of conversation Wollheim does a little awkward bow and hurries back to the train.

Rosa looks into the basket on the floor beside her – the baby is beginning to wake up, moving his head from side to side and stretching his arms. She reaches down and gently pats his chest, and the baby's hands grip her cold fingers; she glances up to see Gusti watching her silently, her hands not moving from her knees. Rosa rocks the basket and eventually, with a sigh, the baby falls asleep again, his arms flopping limply to either side. Rosa tucks the blanket tighter, avoiding Gusti's gaze, and pushes it deeper under the seat.

Hushed voices can be heard outside and, after a short while, Herr Wollheim comes back into the carriage, a little out of breath.

—Girls, please listen, he announces down the corridor. We are almost out of Deutschland. All that remains is for the SS to check you are on their list and search your belongings. I have had to allow them to take one child from each carriage away for questioning. So please . . . comply with whatever they want and we will be on our way shortly.

Once again he glances into the compartments, showing a smile to the children, and disappears. Rosa looks out of the window. On the platform, two SS officers are sucking the last flickers of life out of their cigarettes – they grind them under their heels, grab the train's handrail and swing onto the carriage without using the steps. The train seems to drop under their weight, and a deathly silence falls upon the children.

Loud voices suddenly fill the corridor, and the sound of confident footsteps. Then the same command can be heard repeatedly: Name! Name! Name! The children's responses cannot be heard. The voices come closer, and nobody dares move. Rosa's bicep is itching furiously, and it takes all of her willpower not to reach up to the contraband wristwatch. Britta has unfolded her arms, and they are by her sides, stiffly, her fingers gripping the seat; everyone in the compartment is staring down at the floor.

A man in a black uniform strides in. He has taken off his cap and holds it awkwardly under his arm; Rosa can see the inside as he ticks off names on his list, it is plushly lined and looks comfortable. The polished silver badge, in the shape of a skull, winks from the hatband in the gloom. She sneaks a glance at his face: he is surprisingly young, about Heinrich's age, and looks quite incongruous in his stiff uniform. There is something bookish about him, he could pass for a science student, a physicist perhaps, carrying out his duties in earnest. Just a man in a uniform, a boy really, no reason to be afraid, a boy like Heinrich, like any other.

—Name?

—Wolf, Hanna.

—Name?

—Holtzapfel, Ursula.

—Name?

The round-faced girl stares into space, making no response, her button-eyes blank and dull.

—Name? the SS officer demands again. Britta speaks up.

—Please, Herr Soldat, her name is Agnes Pfeifenkopf.

—She can speak for herself.

—Please, Herr Soldat, she is too scared.

—So. What kind of a name is Pfeifenkopf?

—It's her name, Herr Soldat. I don't know.

The officer scans through his list, shrugs and continues.

—Name?

—Schwarz, Britta.

—Name?

—Klein, Rosa.

—Gut.

He glances at his watch and looks round the carriage, scrutinising each detail: the luggage bulging in the rope racks above, the twin rows of children sitting solemnly on their high-backed benches, their cardboard tags hanging round their necks. Rosa spreads her skirt across the seat, letting it hang and conceal more of the baby's basket. He swivels on his feet – there is not much room for manoeuvre between the children's knees – and his gaze finally settles on Britta, perhaps because she has spoken up.

—Komm doch mal mit, he says, without smiling.

—Ich?

—Komm mit.

Britta gets to her feet obediently, her arms still stiffly by her sides, and shuffles over to him. He motions silently to the luggage racks; Britta clambers onto the seat, stretches up to reach her suitcase; she overbalances and has to step heavily down. The officer blows out his cheeks short-temperedly, reaches up and grabs her suitcase by the handle, but he underestimates the weight and the suitcase topples to the floor, striking the knees of several of the girls. He curses; the suitcase has split open and he stuffs the clothes back in before shutting it clumsily and gathering it up in his arms. One of the smaller girls starts to cry, and he silences her with a glare. There is a moment of stillness in which shouts can be heard from the other compartments, Name! Name! Name! Then the SS officer nudges Britta out of the door, prods her along the corridor and disappears out of sight.

Nobody in the compartment dares to breathe, and they keep their eyes fixed on the floor, listening to the shouts from the other compartments, the sound of things being dragged violently along the corridor; from time to time SS men stride past, setting the door of their compartment rattling like a loose tooth.

There is a noise from under the seat – a fumbling sound followed by a high-pitched yelp. Rosa glances nervously at the door and slips her hand into the basket, patting the baby on the chest. There is another yelp, then another, then the beginnings of a cry. The children fix their eyes harder on the floor as Rosa drops to her knees and pulls the basket out a little. Boots thump past in the corridor outside, and the children can hear an argument beginning amongst the SS further along the carriage. She feels in the basket for the bottle and slips it into the baby's mouth. The crying stops immediately and is replaced by a guzzling noise. After a few minutes there is the sound of sucking air, and Rosa takes out the bottle. It is empty, but the baby has fallen quiet. She presses the basket back beneath the seat.

Eventually things begin to die down. Out of the window Rosa can see a pile of suitcases and bags lying open on the platform, surrounded by a group of SS officers. Rosa watches as they snatch up articles of clothing carefully folded by many mothers, tubes of toothpaste, shoes and hairbrushes and belts, scrutinise them for contraband and toss them back into the suitcases, exchanging jokes and passing around cigarettes. There is no sign of Britta or any of the children who have been taken away. One of the SS men glances up and catches Rosa's eye – she sits back and looks at the floor again, forcing herself to be still. The wrist-watch begins to sting her arm, itching as if it were made of sandpaper.

The children sit like this for a long time. We're leaving, we're leaving, we're leaving. Then, finally, they hear luggage being dragged back onto the carriages and the nervous steps of children reboarding the train. The door opens, and Britta appears, her arms folded tightly across her chest, her black eyes downcast. There is no sign of her suitcase. She enters the compartment and sits down without looking at anybody, and without leaning back in her seat.

More time passes and suddenly, Alles einsteigen! Alles einsteigen, could it be that the train is moving, yes certainly it is moving, tugging and groaning, pulling out of the station, leaving this accursed platform, leaving this accursed country. Rosa turns her face full to the window and looks back; the SS men are milling about and talking amongst themselves, the platform slides by and then disappears from view, the train's whistle sings a note into the half-light, then there is nothing but flat landscape, covered in mist, punctuated by the occasional illumi-nated building or thread of lamps from the nearby villages.

As the train rushes into Holland there is a noise from the adjoining carriage. Rosa runs to the compartment door and looks out; the corridor is full of poked-out heads gazing towards the next carriage from which can be heard a cacophony of shouts and screams. The noise gets louder, and Rosa can see silhouettes of people moving violently around; then the door bursts open and all at once the carriage is full of boys, little boys, big boys, all shapes and sizes, singing and dancing, punching the air, bursting into the girls' compartments and grabbing them by the hands, hugging, laughing, hollering, dancing. Suddenly she feels a rushing sensation, as if a dark weight is fading from around her, and all at once she feels free, she is alive! She is caught up in a whirl-wind of children, intoxicated with jubilation. Beaming smiles are every-where, there is the sound of many songs being sung at once, some in Hebrew – in Hebrew, bold and loud! Rosa does not know the words but she sings along, la la la, finds herself arm in arm with Gusti doing a kind of jig, then Gusti starts singing Am Yisrael chai, and Rosa learnt this one from Mama, and she joins in with all her heart, Am Yisrael chai! The People of Israel live! Od avinu chai! Our forefathers live on! A boy appears and grabs her hands, and they spin along the corridor in a whirlwind of excitement, colliding with other children and the walls of the corridor, goodbye, Berlin, good riddance! Farewell! Farewell! Farewell!

The train, a joyous cylinder of frenetic activity, slips along the track flanked by an expanse of fields turning yellow and pink as the sun starts to rise. After a time the girls collapse back in their seats, giggling and exhausted, while Zionist songs can still be heard from the boys' carriage. As Rosa settles into her seat she catches eyes with Britta and asks, softly, are you all right? Britta nods and looks out of the window; she is still sitting erect, her back not touching the seat, her hands folded tightly across her chest.

Rosa gazes out of the window at the vastness of the countryside. Suddenly she remembers the baby and reaches under her seat for the basket – but it is not there.

—Oh, don't worry, says Gusti, noticing her expression, Herr Wollheim came in and we gave the baby to him.

—Who said you could do that? says Rosa sharply.

—Nobody, says Gusti. But you wouldn't have got it off the train anyway.

Rosa is suddenly enraged, furious with Gusti, with Wollheim, with herself. She bites her tongue and stares fixedly out of the window; then, as the minutes pass and the sun rises, her thoughts disperse into a dreamless sleep.

We're leaving, we're leaving, we're leaving.

As the train draws into the station on the Dutch side of the border the children become subdued once more, gazing apprehensively at the window. Rosa untangles the shoelaces round her neck and lays the tag flat on her chest. As the train comes to a standstill at the platform a hand appears and knocks on the dew-spotted glass; a plump female face hangs in the dawn light, nestling in a fur scarf and hat, gesturing for her to open it. Rosa grips the leather stub and slides the window down – the woman clucks in Dutch and passes her a steaming metal mug. Rosa, perplexed, accepts it; a smell fills the air, an old aroma, from a distant time, soothing, bitter-sweet; it takes Rosa a few seconds to fix a name to the smell, but when she does so she can barely believe it. Cocoa.

The woman on the platform is joined by some others and, smiling and honking like a group of good-natured geese, they dispense the cocoa from a huge cauldron as naturally as if they had drawn it from the river. Rosa helps them distribute the mugs, taking care not to catch Gusti's eye, for she still cannot forgive her. Finally they hand Rosa a bulging paper bag, pat her cheek and lug the cauldron away, chuckling to each other good-naturedly.

Rosa heaves the window closed, opens the bag and dips into it: a handful of miniature slices of bread emerge, dried-out little crackers, golden and crispy: Dutch Zwieback. She bites into one, leans back against the seat and closes her eyes again, allowing the bag to gape open on her lap, feeling little hungry hands plunging into it and hearing the children giggle at the crunch. Gusti remains seated, looking out of the window.

There is a noise at the door, and Wollheim enters the carriage holding the baby. Rosa gets to her feet and reaches out but he holds the baby out of reach, asks her where it came from, what she knows about it. Gusti is still gazing out of the window. Rosa stumbles over her words and can only watch, mute, as Wollheim strides urgently out of the compartment and down the carriage, taking the baby with him.

As the train pulls heavily out of the station en route to the port, and the sun brightens and the mist disperses, Rosa's mind begins to drift to Papa, Mama, Heinrich and Hedi, asleep in their beds in Berlin behind boarded-up windows as she heads towards the freedom of England. How she wishes they could be here. At that moment a weight begins to settle in her heart, an irrational weight that can be neither explained nor reasoned away, a heaviness that comes and goes as it pleases, impossible to control. She cannot give to this weight a name, dares not identify it for what it is: a deep-seated, life-denying guilt.

It is this same weight that hangs in her heart as she pushes her suitcase into her cabin and shuts the door behind her. The same heaviness prevents her from stretching out on the heavenly bed with the clean cotton sheets; the same guilt stops her from smiling at the steward who comes to serve her tea, odd tea with milk in that she drinks only for the heat. And yet, what keeps her awake as the ship ploughs its way through the chilly waves of the North Sea, apart from the cold and the sea-sickness, apart from thoughts of the baby and her family, apart from the guilt even, is a feeling of dislocation, as if she has been cut off, somehow, from herself.

17 March 1939, London

I

As the ferry foghorn blares overhead, Rosa rests on the railing and looks into the mist. At first she can see nothing; then a quay emerges, teeming with life, followed by England itself. Her first impression is of an over-crowded, bustling city in browns and blacks and greys, smelling of coal and oil, covered in cloud, where people have white, knobby faces and terrible teeth, seem to be smiling for no reason at all, and speak in voices that come from the belly. She walks down the gangplank, single file, with all the other children, as if on a factory conveyor belt, each with a single suitcase and a number round the neck. Carefully she steps, holding the handrail, somebody checks her number again, England is nothing like she expected, she thought it would be more stately, somehow, more refined, filled with people like the king and queen, who conducted themselves with an air of nobility, not these gangs of scruffy-looking men with cloth caps and potato noses, not these urchins darting round corners and down alleyways, not these women sitting idly in doorways in the middle of the day.

The sky hangs brown over the children's heads like the lid of a shoebox. Rosa is caught up in a whirl of busyness and bustle, followed by a period of waiting, followed by more busyness, and throughout she speaks not a word to anyone, least of all to Gusti. Soon, numbed by an endless stream of checks of her passport and her number, and dazed by lack of sleep, Rosa slips into a blankness, allowing herself to be herded from one queue to another, along pavement after pavement, into a railway station.

Then there is a period of rest, collapsed on the seat of an English train, among foreign colours, smells and words, packed in with other disoriented children. Rosa finds her head lolling; it hits the window a few times then comes to rest upon it, the vibrations of the engine erode her thoughts and the whipping telegraph poles outside the window lull her to sleep. And then she is awake again, trying to rub her eyes, lugging her suitcase with both hands, struggling down the aisle and out of the train, the younger children are noisy, they seem so cheerful, somehow, the little ones; and there is Wollheim – the baby is nowhere to be seen – what is he saying, something about Liverpool Street, better just wait and see. Then forward along the platform, causing a disruption to the English people streaming by alongside, and there are soldiers dotted about, different from the ones in Germany, scruffier, more cheerful, quite silly-looking. How busy everything is, Rosa thinks, England seems to exist in a perpetual state of chaos!

The children settle down in a corner amid occasional clouds of steam, and there follows an endless period of waiting. One of the black-coated twins falls instantly asleep, the other looks worriedly about. Wollheim is the only one who does not seem to be tired, patrolling the perimeter of the group of children, speaking occasionally to a policeman wearing an impressive swooping cape and a cone-shaped helmet topped with silver. Rosa sits on her suitcase and stands again, then, exhausted by the commotion around her, sits down and cups her chin in her hands. This station is so different from the ones in Berlin; it is strange that if one turns in any direction and keeps going, eventually one will arrive in a place where people speak a different language, and have different buildings, and different air and food. The whole world is one country. If she were to travel east at a precise trajectory, eventually she would end up back in Berlin with her parents, she would be home in a matter of days.

The wait is interminable, and Liverpool Street station slides around her like a dream. Hundreds of feet overhead is a spectacular web of girders curving into interlocking domes, and the air is filled with coal dust. Then, two by two, the adults start to arrive, they speak to Wollheim, locate the children they are fostering and lead them away. The little ones seem to be going first. Rosa, with a start, thinks about Herr and Frau Kremer for the first time; what will they look like? How will she recognise them? Will Herr Kremer look like Papa? They are cousins – she thinks Papa said they are cousins. Do they have children of their own? Papa wasn't sure, he hasn't seen them for years, and they haven't been in touch. Situations like these tend to bring families together, meine Püppchen, he had told her, as well as tear them apart; I am sure they are very nice, a little religious for our taste, but that's neither here nor there, they are willing to take you in and that's all that counts, it will only be a temporary arrangement, just for a matter of weeks or months until we are able to join you.

But now the Kremers are late, many of the children have been collected already. Perhaps they have changed their minds, perhaps they have decided not to come. Perhaps she will be sent back to Berlin.

Finally, after a long and troublesome journey, the conductor bellows, Liverpool Street station, the tram judders to a halt, and Gerald and Mimi Kremer are caught up in the bustle of passengers disembarking.

—Well, shouts Gerald, this is it.

—I don't doubt it, says Mimi.

—We're late, we'd best hurry, says Gerald.

—Go on then, lead the way, says Mimi.

They pass through the row of stone plinths at the entrance, wind their way through banks of taxis and enter the station proper. Immediately they are confronted by the morning crowds; they pause for a moment, a black film of coal dust settling gently on their shoulders.

—I wouldn't want to be in London, says Mimi, if there's a war.

—I've told you, says Gerald distractedly, if war breaks out I'll shift us all out to Harry's place in Norfolk quick smart. I've made the preparations already. Now where are those refugees?

He raises himself to his toes, jutting his chin in the air and swivelling his head left and right above the seething crowds. The strap of his gas mask box slips from his shoulder to his elbow; he hitches it back up, automatically.

—We're really rather late, he says, looking at his watch. Can't see the children anywhere.

—Maybe we've missed them, says Mimi.

—Don't be daft. They're not going anywhere, are they? says Gerald and pushes his way into the crowd, trailing his wife from his arm.

—There they are, says Gerald, over there.

They break free of the crowd and make their way towards a corner of the concourse where a group of exhausted-looking children can be seen sitting on their suitcases, dozing at strange angles, tags round their necks.

—I hope our little girl's still there, says Gerald. Where's the man in charge, can you see him?

—Afraid not, dear, says Mimi.

Gerald leads his wife past the children, picking his way round ankles and luggage, waving to catch the attention of Wollheim, who is standing beside the group of children, his gaunt face incongruous in the London crowds. Rosa, sitting on her suitcase at the back, watches the Kremers closely.

—Are you in charge? says Gerald, out of breath.

—You could say so, says Wollheim in accented English. You are here to collect a child?

—Yes indeed, says Gerald.

—Very good. Names please?

—Gerald and Mimi Kremer, how do you do.

—Thank you, says Wollheim. Now let's see: Kremer.

He runs his finger down the list of names on his clipboard.

—Chaos, this station, isn't it, says Gerald. Like *The Last Train from Madrid* only without the guns. Did you see that picture?

—No, says Wollheim, I didn't.

There is an awkward pause. Gerald looks into Wollheim's face and is taken aback; the man's skin is stretched like a drum over his skull, his forehead is etched with lines and his eyes burn with deprivation.

—Are you ill, old boy? says Gerald, failing to disguise his concern.

—I'm fine, Wollheim replies. A little tired. We've been travelling all night.

—How are the conditions in Germany? I have heard that things are not so good.

—Rabbi Baeck says the hour of German Jewry has come to an end.

—You're going to stay in England, surely?

—I must return or they'll stop the transports for the children.

Gerald, acutely aware of his own freedom, coughs and clears his throat. There is a pause while both men search for a place to rest their eyes. Mimi picks at her embroidered gas mask case.

—Ah so, says Wollheim suddenly, number 126, Klein. You will find her over there somewhere, wearing the number. At least I hope she is wearing the number. Some of the children have taken their tags off. That's children, no?

The Kremers look over at the group of children but are unable to see a 126. Wollheim rummages in a briefcase.

—In this envelope, he says, are the necessary documents, her passport and so on. Sign here, if you please.

—Of course.

—Many thanks to you both. He who saves one life saves the world in time. I wish you the very best of luck.

—Thank you kindly, says Gerald. Before you go, please think of yourself also. If there's anything we can do . . .

—Naturally.

Wollheim hands over the envelope of documents, shakes Gerald by the hand, raises his hat to Mimi, then turns to greet another couple. Gerald and Mimi walk over to the children.

—The poor sod, says Gerald, to be stuck in Germany like that.

—For a moment I thought you were going to adopt him as well, says Mimi. How about this pretty little thing over here? What's your number, dear?

The round-faced girl makes no response. Mimi rummages in her pocket for a bag of barley sugar and offers one, but the girl does not acknowledge it.

—Not very friendly, are you, dear? says Mimi, putting the bag back in her pocket. How about your little friend here? she says. And what number are you?

The children fall silent as Mimi and Gerald approach, regarding them with unblinking eyes or turning their gaze to the floor. Some of them make an effort to smile – don't, Gerald wants to say, we're here for one girl and one girl only, we can't possibly take any more of you in, we have a family of our own to think about. Suddenly he can look into their eyes no longer, it is as if they are scrutinising his soul for the shadows that lie upon it.

Rosa, at the back, near the wall, looks away. It's not them, she thinks, it can't be them, those people are looking for a little one. I really have been forgotten – I really will be sent back to Berlin. Her head is heavy, she sits on the ground, rests her head on the suitcase, allowing her eyes to close.

After a while Gerald and Mimi have gone the length and breadth of the group and checked the tags of all the girls who look the right age; still 126 is nowhere to be found. They stand at the corner of the concourse, watching as more and more children are led away. Gerald puts his hands on his hips and arches his back.

—Hard work this, he says, rummaging in his pockets for a cigarette.

—Somebody has probably taken her by mistake, says Mimi. Or perhaps she has removed her tag.

—Your guess is as good as mine, replies her husband. Let's have one more try and then I'll go and consult the man in charge again. Where's he gone, anyway?

—Talking to that policeman.

—Yes, I see.

Gerald lights his cigarette, pushes his hat back, blows smoke from his nose and looks pensively around. There is a pause.

—Hello, says Mimi. Can you see that one over there? The one in the middle?

Gerald follows her finger to an older girl slumped over her suitcase at the back of the group, with tightly curling hair and crescent-shaped eyes at once innocent and distrustful, bold and afraid; around her neck hangs the number 126.

—It was 126, wasn't it? says Mimi.

—It's probably a mistake, says Gerald, sucking deeply on his cigarette. I'll go and talk to her. Let's hope she speaks some English.

—There's no point, dear, says Mimi, that girl's fifteen if she's a day. You'd better consult the man in charge again.

—Might as well have a go, says Gerald. It won't do any harm.

He picks his way through the cluster of children; the girl regards him silently and he clears his throat.

—Number 126? he says, hesitantly. She gets hurriedly to her feet.

—Yes, she says in heavily accented English. Is me.

—You're not called Klein, are you? asks Gerald.

—Klein? Yes, is me.

—Your name is Klein?

—Yes.

—Rosa Klein?

—Yes.

—Who are your parents?

—I beg your pardon?

—Your parents? Father and mother?

—Ah, so. Yes. Klein, Otto und Inga.

—Well I'll be . . . wait there a moment.

Gerald weaves his way back to his wife, sucking tensely on his cigarette.

—Well? says Mimi, glancing doubtfully in the direction of the girl.

—Her name is Klein, says Gerald. And her first name is Rosa. And her parents are Otto and Inga.

—Are you sure? That can't be right.

Struck by a sudden brainwave, Gerald opens the envelope Wollheim gave him; among the documents is a passport showing a picture of a curly-haired girl of around fifteen.

—That's settled, then, he says. It's her.

—No it's not, says Mimi. We agreed to take an eight-year-old. I'm not taking a girl of that age into my house. Her little sister could be on the train, did you ask her that? That older one could be going somewhere else.

—There can't be two sisters by the same name, says Gerald. We are collecting a Rosa.

—Perhaps we could swap her. Oh, where is the man in charge when you need him?

—There's nothing for it.

Gerald adjusts his gas mask box on his shoulder and makes his way once more through the refugee children.

—Rosa Klein, correct? he says.

—Yes, the girl replies.

—We were expecting someone a little younger.

Rosa looks blank.

—Are there any other Kleins here? Do you have a sister?

—A sister yes I have.

—How old is she?

—She is eight, says Rosa, concentrating hard.

—That's the one. What is her name?

—Her name is Hedi.

—Ah, Hedi. And she is here?

—In Germany.

—No more Kleins here? No sisters?

—Only me.

—And your parents are Otto and Inga?

—Father and Mother.

—Right. Gerald sighs, draws on his cigarette, then extinguishes it on the ground with the toe of his shoe.

—Very well. This is your suitcase? Come with me.

He carries Rosa's suitcase towards his wife, who is standing with an expression of incredulity on her face.

—This is Mrs Kremer, says Gerald. Be polite, Mimi, come on. And I am Mr Kremer. Sorry, I don't shake women's hands. It's the religion, you see. Nothing personal.

Rosa lowers her hand, baffled.

—Perhaps you should call us Aunt Mimi and Uncle Gerald, says Gerald.

Mimi, thin-lipped, rolls her eyes. Gerald opens Rosa's passport.

—There are two names here, he says, Rosa and Sara. Which one is it?

—Jewish girl Sara, says the girl, Jewish boy Israel.

—Sorry? says Gerald.

—*It's the law*, says Rosa, speaking in German. *In Deutschland they gave all Jewish girls the name Sara and all boys the name Israel.*

—I'm sorry, love, says Gerald. You're in England now. A bissel Yiddish but that's about all you'll get.

—Rosa looks like the official name to me, says Mimi tersely.

—Very well, Rosa it is then, says Gerald breezily. Let's get you home, Rosa.

145

—Get her home? says Mimi.

—What are we going to do, send her back to Berlin? Gerald replies.

—I don't give a hoot, says Mimi. I need a fifteen-year-old girl like I need a hole in the head. Where's the man in charge?

—Give it a rest, says Gerald sharply. I gave Otto and Inga my word and I'm not going back on it. Now come along. I'll hear no more about it.

—I would never have agreed if I'd known, says Mimi subversively.

Gerald ignores her, heaves Rosa's suitcase onto his thigh the way her father had done the day before and staggers towards the exit.

—What've you got in here, rocks? he says.

—I beg your pardon? says Rosa.

—More fine clothes I shouldn't wonder, says Mimi. Well dressed for a refugee, aren't you, dear?

3

They walk out of the station onto Bishopsgate and wait at a tram stop in the heavy London cold. Gerald tries to catch his breath and lights another cigarette.

—So, Rosa, he says, did you have a good journey?

—I beg your pardon? says Rosa.

—Her English isn't up to much, says Mimi, looking aimlessly across the street.

—We go home now, Rosa, yes? says Gerald in a loud voice.

—Yes, says Rosa.

—Looks like rain, says Mimi, and hugs her fur collar tighter.

They settle into an uncomfortable silence. Gerald watches Rosa gazing glassy-eyed and tries to imagine how the grimy splendour of Bishopsgate must look to her; not as glamorous as it used to be, things are getting harder, people aren't spending as much as they were, especially not on furs if recent business is anything to go by. And here they are with another mouth to feed. He clenches his cigarette between his lips and pulls himself together.

—It'll be grand, says Gerald, having a guest in the house.

—Don't know why I agreed to it in the first place, says Mimi.

—Why don't you just give over, says Gerald, blowing a double jet of smoke from his nose. I've taken the day off work, you know.

—It was your idea.

—Well we couldn't very well refuse, could we? There's going to be a war, we've got to do our bit.

—Yes, but what if we have to evacuate?

—What about it?

—The cottage up in Norfolk isn't very large, you know.

—We'll only have her for a while, says Gerald. Until her parents come over.

—I jolly well hope so, says Mimi testily. It simply won't do to have her for long.

She glances at Rosa, who sends a faltering smile back. There is a pause. Gerald finishes his cigarette and stubs it out on a sandbag.

—I hope the workshop is running without me, he says, you can't take your eyes off those boys for a second or they'll slack off, and they've got a consignment of mink arriving this afternoon. Maybe when we've settled the girl in, I'll pop down to Petticoat Lane.

A graceful-lined car trundles past making a clanking noise, driven by a man wrapped in a greatcoat, hat and scarf .

—Carburettor, that noise, says Gerald, or the clutch.

—When's that tram going to put in an appearance then? says Mimi.

—Here you go, says Gerald. Number forty-nine. See that, Rosa? Four, nine. Forty-nine.

—Can you read that from here? says Mimi. Perhaps I need spectacles.

—It's this pea-souper, says Gerald.

The tram lumbers to the stop and comes to a halt, its pole crackling on the overhead wire; it is red and tall, a double-decker, with an open platform at the back where the conductor is standing like a policeman. Gerald gestures for Rosa to get on, and she climbs carefully aboard, receiving disapproving glances from hurrying Londoners. Gerald helps Mimi onto the tram then climbs on himself, lugging the suitcase and puffing.

Having stowed the suitcase on the lower deck, they clamber up the spiral staircase and sit at the front, like elephant riders. A scruffy-looking boy on the pavement glances up and gives them a cheery wave as their heads appear in the sooty windows above the advertising banner for Whitbread's Ale & Stout. The upper deck of the tram is thick with cigarette smoke and the windows are steamed up with cold.

—Here you are, says Gerald, front row seats.

—Yes, says Rosa uncertainly.

—Grand view of London, he says, don't you think?

—Yes, says Rosa again.

—Come on, Gerald, she hasn't got a clue, says Mimi.

Gerald buries his chin in his black fur collar, rubs the window absent-mindedly with his sleeve and lights another cigarette. The three of them sit in silence as drizzle begins to fall outside; drops slip down the window in irregular trails, joining and splitting into pools and globes; the buildings are hazy in the smog. Rosa gazes continuously around as if in a dream, baffled by the newness of every detail of the city, trying to make out words on advertisements. Mimi pulls her foxtail muffler tighter round her neck and slides her hands under her armpits, for it is terribly cold. When the conductor arrives, she jumps.

—That's threepence each if you please, he says. Mild today, isn't it?

The tram jolts to a stop – the conductor looks at the mirror in the stairwell, sees that there is nobody on the platform and stamps on the floor, signalling the driver below to move off. Then he drops Gerald's coins jangling into his leather pouch, tears off the tickets, clips them with his ticket-punch and hands them over, tweaking the peak of his cap.

—There you are, squire, he says. Mild today, isn't it?

—Yes, says Gerald, shivering, mild. Thank you very much.

—What do you think of it all then, guv?

—I'm sorry?

—Got to stop old Hitler's gallop, I reckon. I was in the last one, me.

—Oh . . . yes.

—No question to my mind, says the conductor. I'll be staying put in London town even if it's gas. Incendiaries are worse anyhow, he says, turning his back and making his way on sea-legs down the aisle.

At the top of Bishopsgate they pass the goods yard, outside which a knot of hats are milling: trilbies, homburgs, army caps, fur hats, all moving about in patterns on the pavement, interweaving with bicycles, newspaper vendors, policemen, tramps. A panicked-looking man can be seen using a telephone in a police box; Rosa cranes her neck until he is out of sight. As they move away from the heart of the city the atmosphere is less frantic, people pass like ghosts in and out of the smog. Gerald blows cigarette smoke against the window.

—Colman's starch, he says, we could use some of that. And it comes in a cardboard box.

—I do hope this girl is not going to be trouble, says Mimi as they trundle onto Stoke Newington High Street.

—Don't be daft, Gerald responds.

—We've got to consider what's best for Samuel.

—Samuel's all right. The boy's all right.

—No, Gerald, he is not. I fancy he might be soft on that Cailingold girl.

—Esther Cailingold? Honestly, Mimi, she's out of his league. Anyway, the boy's eighteen already.

—And when did you last see him in synagogue?

Gerald rubs his eyes and smooths his fur collar.

—It's a risk, dear, says Mimi.

—Heaven preserve us, mumbles Gerald, rolling his eyes and pulling a newspaper out of his pocket.

As the tram trundles onto the Kingsland Road, Rosa begins to think how she will describe Herr and Frau Kremer when she writes her first letter to her parents: Frau Kremer is a little like an owl, and her husband, with his patchy beard, resembles a goat, and is not in the least like Papa; the Kremers may be religious but they also look worldly, and can seem abrupt at times; they are not affectionate, but then Papa had warned her of the English temperament, and in truth she is glad to be left alone. The thought of home makes the pain start again, and the heaviness immediately returns; she pushes her hands into her coat pockets and gazes listlessly out of the window at a cloud of pigeons rising from behind the post office into the dirty-looking sky. After a while she finds herself watching the conductor as he nips busily up and down the stairs, clamping coins in the coin-tester to check for counterfeits, calling out stop names, pulling bell-cords, talking about it all, stamping on the floor. People embark and disembark, talking, smoking, hurrying, waiting, lost in worlds of their own. The tram presses through the smog like a scarlet bathtub, like a boat. Rosa feels as if she has been travelling forever, as if she has no past and will have no future, but will remain in this crimson English tram indefinitely.

Then, as the tram rolls deeper into Hackney, Gerald, as if awakening from a dream, gets unsteadily to his feet, pulls the bell-cord and climbs down the stairs followed by Mimi and Rosa; the tram stops and they step out onto the pavement. The drizzle has passed, and an ominous layer of coal smoke hangs in the sky. Gerald beckons to Rosa and walks off down the street, lurching and puffing under the weight of her suitcase. A gang of workmen in cloth caps are erecting some trolleybus wires overhead, sharing rough jokes and spitting on the ground; Rosa flinches from them instinctively and is surprised that Gerald and Mimi do not. The workmen's gas masks are piled up beside them on the pavement; it is striking how neat the pile is, for workmen.

—'Jews back to Palestine', mutters Gerald, motioning vaguely towards the words scrawled on the sooty wall of the convent on the corner of Heathland Road.

—Oh, haven't they cleaned that off yet? says Mimi.

—I'd be the first to go to Palestine, says Gerald, if I could.

—If there's a war you won't be going anywhere, says Mimi.

—If there is a war, Gerald replies, the boy will be off and you'll be in a frenzy.

Finally they arrive at a white, square house surrounded by a hedge of little round leaves overlapping each other in uniform contentedness; the hedge is penetrated by way of a miniature gate, the point of which Rosa fails to understand. Gerald and Mimi enter, touching the mezuzah on the doorpost and kissing their fingers. To Rosa, the whole building seems wholly inelegant, a building for passing days and nights, nothing more.

—Mind the steps, says Mimi, they're icy.

—Yes, Rosa replies. She takes a deep breath, clenches her fists and goes inside.

4

—Where's the little German girl? asks Samuel, walking into the dining room and adjusting his collar.

—On her way, says Gerald. But I must tell you, she is actually fifteen.

—Fifteen?

Samuel warms his hands at the coal fire then takes his seat at the dinner table, the tips of his fingers reflecting in the mahogany.

—Where's she going to sleep? he says.

Before Gerald can reply, a hush falls upon the family as Rosa enters the dining room, her hands clasped in front of her, taking everything in. Savoury smells fill the air, the table is laden with food. Herr Kremer sits at the head of the table directly beneath a heavy-looking brass light that, if it were to fall, would land in the exact centre of his homburg hat, which he is wearing indoors. To her right she sees an aged man with a pointed skullcap, his bleached beard covering his chest like a mat; to her left a boy of around Heinrich's age with the lanky strength of a giraffe, Brylcreemed black hair and eyes like cocoa. And there is Frau Kremer, stirring a tureen of soup; she has replaced her hat with a headscarf, little locks of hair peep from under it like confectionery. The appearance of the dining room is Jewish yet English, and very alien: contrasting floral patterns provide a backdrop for ornaments, symmetry, a wind-up gramophone, framed pictures of Hebrew calligraphy, brown paintings of men with beards, faded lace cushion covers, row upon row of gleaming leather-bound Hebrew books; everything is cold and stuffy at once.

—Here you are, says Gerald, do come and join us. Allow me to introduce to you my father-in-law Zeidi, and my son Samuel.

The old man grimaces from his chair, and the Brylcreemed boy gets to his feet and bows his head; Rosa extends her hand, and for a moment it hangs in the air; Samuel grasps it and shakes it, a little violently, and returns, red-faced, to his seat. Mimi says:

—We don't do that, Samuel.

—Honestly, Samuel replies, it's only a handshake.

—I'll speak to the boy later, says Gerald in a low voice.

Mimi turns back to the soup. Rosa, unable to understand, smiles again, shrugs and takes her seat, her head is heavy and her eyes itch, yet she is overwhelmed by the array of food that she sees before her, like a vision of paradise. In the centre is a basket overflowing with rolls and slices of bread, white bread that looks almost like cake. Beside it is a fluffy salmon mousse sitting cold and delicious in a bowl, garnished with a sprig of parsley; and then there is a carrot salad, a potato salad, a dish of boiled eggs, chopped liver, pickled herring, a cluster of white gefilte fish balls crowned with individual slices of carrot and, on the sideboard, a real bottle of wine.

—You must be hungry, says Gerald, taking note of her expression.

—I beg your pardon? says Rosa.

—Food, says Gerald, for you.

—Ah so, says Rosa, food.

—Her English isn't up to much, says Samuel. I'll tutor her until I get mobilised.

—No you won't, says Mimi, serving the soup.

—Honestly, says Samuel, it's only tutoring.

—It's a slippery slope, says Mimi.

—Oh, says Gerald, I've got a gift for you, Rosa.

He reaches underneath his chair and brings out a package wrapped in brown paper.

—What's all this about? says Mimi.

—A present, says Gerald, make her feel at home and all that.

Rosa accepts the package and places it on the table beside her plate. Then she bends her head and inhales the wet scent of the soup that Mimi has placed in front of her.

—Aren't you going to open it? says Samuel.

—They have different ways in Germany, says Mimi.

—Nonsense, says Gerald, open it. Go on, open it. It's all right.

Rosa takes the package in her fingers and carefully removes the wrapping paper, folding it and placing it to one side before giving the present her full attention.

—She's very neat, isn't she, says Mimi.

—What a super present, says Samuel, a dictionary. Do you know how to use it, Rosa?

Rosa looks at Samuel blankly, not comprehending.

—It's easy. You just look up the word you want here, in alphabetical order, and then the translation is presented alongside.

—I think the girl will know how to use a dictionary, says Gerald.

—They might not have them in Germany, says Samuel.

—Don't be silly, says Mimi. Mind out of the way, you'll have the soup over.

Rosa gets to her feet, pushes her chair in, enacts a stiff little bow and says:

—I beg your pardon.

—Call of nature, dear? says Mimi.

—I beg your pardon, says Rosa, and hurries from the room.

—Could be the crossing, says Gerald, the Channel is jolly choppy this time of year.

—Ech hob dir in drerd, says the old man malevolently, glowering from under his eyebrows.

—Sha now, Zeidi, drink your soup, says Mimi. Drink up, everybody.

—Ver derharget, mutters Zeidi.

After a few minutes Rosa comes back into the room, takes her seat once more and begins to eat, closing her eyes, allowing the heat of the soup to fill her mouth like the essence of life itself, swallowing hard, forcing the soup past the knot in her throat.

—I say, your eyes are rather red, says Samuel.

—She can't understand, you'll have to speak slower, says Gerald.

—Your eyes, Samuel mimes with his hands.

—Sorry, says Rosa, sorry.

—No, don't . . . don't apologise, says Samuel.

The family continues with their meal and the conversation drifts along familiar lines: Chamberlain and Eden, Stamford Hill and Hendon, the likelihood of mobilisation, evacuation to Norfolk. Rosa sinks into a somnambulant state, peering at her reflection in the polished mahogany table, looking out of the window at the sooty garden with its bedraggled Alexandra roses. She finds herself wondering what would happen if the brass light really did come crashing down on Herr Kremer's head, considering whether it would be impolite to take another gefilte fish, wondering at the floral wallpaper. Then, suddenly, she thinks of home, of Berlin, of her family, of what sort of lunch they must be having, their current supplies were running low yesterday; and she wonders about her bedroom with its boarded-up windows, which is probably full of laundry by now, and her bed is probably stripped bare, Papa may have even got rid of it altogether to make more space; the knot in her throat closes like a fist and her eyes blur with water. She folds her napkin beside her plate, gets to her feet and pushes in her chair.

—I beg your pardon, she says.

—Lavatory again? asks Mimi.

Rosa hurries from the room.

5

Downstairs, moonlight is slanting through the dappled glass in the front door and illuminating a shelf of ceramic ornaments. In the drawing room Gerald is sitting in an armchair, his skullcap tipped forward onto his forehead, scratching his neck with one hand, leafing gently through a volume of the Talmud with the other, his lips moving silently as he follows the ancient Aramaic. Opposite him sits Zeidi, his head tipped back and his beard bristling horizontally. In the dimly lit kitchen Mimi opens the crockery cupboard and removes a pile of plates, examining each in turn before replacing them; no fault can be found with Rosa's washing up. She takes a handkerchief from her sleeve and wipes her eyes, then opens the cupboard that holds the glasses.

There is a sound on the stairs. Gerald looks up from his Talmud sharply; his skullcap tumbles from his head and lands with a soft thud on the pages of his tome. He peers into the gloom of the hall, leaning forward in his chair. There is a creak – then another. There is no doubt about it, someone is coming down the stairs. He sits up straight and stares into the darkness. A figure appears; it is Rosa, stealing down the stairs. From the kitchen the quiet sound of clinking glass can be heard, together with the occasional sigh. Gerald is about to call out, but something makes him stop. Rosa's silhouette pads silently along the hall until she reaches the front door. She touches the handle, allows her fingers to rest there for a moment; then she reaches up to the hatstand and straightens her coat. Finally she makes sure her shoes are lined up neatly, creeps back along the hall and disappears up the stairs to bed.

Samuel is lying under the blankets, surrounded by quiet darkness, thinking apprehensively about the army. He has never been one to shrink from an adventure, but part of him hopes he won't have to go. An icy glaze of frost is building up on the window above his bed, the frozen condensation of his breath. As his mind drifts, somewhere deep down in his heart, beneath the blankets, jumpers, pyjama jacket and vest, something is beginning to stir. His father thinks that part of the reason he wants to join the army is so that he can later be of use in Palestine, and his mother is under the impression that he still attends synagogue. From the outside, generally speaking, he looks the same, nothing is different. Inside, however, is where the big changes, the seismic shifts, have been occurring ever since the family moved to North London, even before. The East End had been getting claustrophobic, suffocating even, and for years Samuel longed, on a deep and unspoken level, to be free from the shtetl squalor of the Whitechapel Road and Cable Street, where people spoke Yiddish, Polish and Russian, and rubbish rose in great steaming piles on the cobbles in the summer, and families of six lived in two rooms, and everyone believed, against all the odds, that wealth and fame lay just around the corner, the cobbler, the butcher, the schneider, everyone. And when the family moved north a few years ago it was as if a universe had suddenly been opened; he was released into a wider world, getting a secular education at Tottenham Grammar, moving every day within gentile society, and like a silent rabbit he stopped and stared at gentile life and gentile girls, the gentile theatre and the gentile pictures, gentile pubs and gentile books, and in the evenings, in his bedroom, could not help but recall the story that Rabbi Grossberg once told him about a Jewish man who was about to have extra-marital relations, and whose tzitzis rose up miraculously and lashed him repeatedly in the face. Samuel's mind wanders, images of the German girl mingling with thoughts of his upcoming mobilisation, until, after a time, he falls asleep.

On the other side of his bedroom wall, on a table, dimly lit in the light of a floral-shaded lamp, stands the Klein family photograph. The glass has been cracked in Rosa's suitcase, and now a jagged line passes from left to right, splitting each of the figures in two. Next to the photograph is Hedi's doll, sitting slumped against the bedpost like a commuter. On the floor Rosa is crouching over her suitcase, slitting the lining with a butter knife. Carefully, one by one, she slides out a series of banknotes, English pounds which her father had inserted the night before she left. She gathers them into a modest pile and counts them. Then she takes the photograph from the bedside table, removes the frame and slips the notes behind the photograph. She places it back on the bedside table and tucks herself into bed.

For a long while she lies open-eyed and freezing, tensing her jaw to keep her teeth from chattering. Between her legs is a hot water bottle that Samuel gave her before she went to bed. She was slightly taken aback at first – in Germany hot water bottles are only used by invalid old women – but she accepted it anyway and now she is grateful for this slippery lozenge of heat. She traces her fingers up her sleeve until she touches the wristwatch on her bicep. With trembling fingers she prises open the lever; there is a click and it rattles down her arm, coming to rest in the crook of her elbow. She threads the wristwatch out of the blankets and holds it up to her ear. It is still ticking as if nothing has happened, as if it is still in Berlin. Slowly she loops it over her other wrist, pushing it halfway up the forearm where it rests quite comfortably. Then she lies still.

Rosa is glad for the privacy of her bed, having spent much of the day in the lavatory, wiping her face and blowing her nose on that horrible shiny toilet paper. She is spent, exhausted, wishes she could sleep. The heaviness descends, and her throat begins to knot again. She slides the hot water bottle from under the blankets and places it on the icy linoleum beside the bed. For hours it radiates its heat wantonly into the unfeeling air while she lies cold and unblinking in the gloom.

18 March 1939, London

I

The following morning, Rosa awakes to find that yesterday's freeze has been replaced by an early spring brightness which strikes her as particularly English. As she steps out into the street, holding her dictionary, she feels vulnerable; she could get lost in minutes and be unable to read the street signs, or ask for directions. She stands on the pavement outside the gate, the round-leaved hedge shoulder-high behind her, and looks left and right, trying to commit to memory her immediate surroundings: the telegraph pole with its little metal plaque, the wine-coloured curtains in the house opposite, the odd wooden fences, the trees with translucent foliage.

She begins to walk, dictionary in hand. This may be the first time that German shoes have struck this particular pavement, the first time even that a German person has walked along this road. Not a single aspect of the street bears the remotest resemblance to Berlin; there are no tenements stretching into the air, no half-pyramid stacks of stone steps, no lines of stucco along the buildings, no wooden double doors leading into courtyards, no advertising pillars displaying political slogans. Here, instead, there are individual houses with porches and hedges, gates and fences, front gardens and notices about dogs. The smells are different too; the brassy fug of Berlin has been replaced by the scent of hedges and tea, and a coal soot that leaves a bitter film at the back of the throat.

Rosa walks uncertainly to the end of the road and turns left. The streets are dull and quiet, here and there people stand aimlessly on corners; in the distance, a single barrage balloon drifts like a ripening raincloud. As she walks the streets become busier, people are staring at her, she fights the urge to hurry away, head for a shadowy alley, she carries on as normal, she does not want to get lost. London is truly nothing like she imagined, it is dirty and dilapidated, people seem to take very little pride in their appearance, and things look miniature somehow, rather humorous, the little gardens and trams and policemen, though nothing is miniature at all, of course, and nothing is humorous either. She wonders if her family, in Berlin, had enough food for breakfast this morning; there will be more to go round without her. By now Papa will be walking Hedi to school, and Mama will be doing the laundry, there were many orders to be done yesterday and she hasn't got Rosa to help her. Heinrich will be off to an embassy somewhere, and Papa will join him later probably, that is a comforting thought, in a way, they are all struggling together, separated by a sea but engaged in the same efforts. And here are two men sitting on a bench, gas mask boxes on their laps, she thinks they are Jews – but so confident! Talking loudly and smoking, their legs stretched out almost into the centre of the pavement, and they seem to be quite well off, they have felt collars and silky hats, and their beards are trim; yes, she is sure they are Jews, ah, one of them has removed his hat to scratch his head, there is the telltale skullcap, she was right. Compose yourself now, Rosa, this is no time to be shy, go forward, forward—

—I beg your pardon?

—Yes?

She fumbles with her dictionary. Tucked inside the front cover is a sheet of Berlin foolscap upon which her father's narrow-looped hand-writing is inscribed in uniform rows.

—I apologise to inconvenience you, she reads, using Papa's intonation, but may I beg some minutes to speak?

The men look up, their eyes glinting beneath the brims of their hats. They murmur to each other, then to her, but she cannot understand what they are saying. One of them tips his hat back on his head, he is holding a silver-topped cane which he rests upon heavily; they suck their cigarettes.

—I am a Jewish girl coming from Berlin, Rosa continues, and my family is currently requiring a work permit and a visa also, for the United Kingdom. For any household they will be very hard-working and obedient, any type of work they will engage, as a cook or gardener or butler or maid or bottle-washer, in a city or a town, a village or a farm, they do not need much money, enough for surviving only, or even no money at all, just a little food and somewhere to live.

The men's faces, under the brims of their hats, wear grave expressions when Rosa, having finished her speech, looks up. One drops his cigarette on the pavement and extinguishes it with the tip of his cane, the other adjusts his felt collar and begins to speak. Rosa tries to catch what he says but can make out barely a single word; she looks at him at a loss, then opens her dictionary, vaguely turning the pages. The man reaches over and plucks her sheet of foolscap from her fingers, suddenly in his hand gleams a fountain pen, he writes something diagonally across the back of the foolscap and returns it to her.

Rosa looks at what he has written: it is a sketch of an envelope, then an arrow, then the words Baron de Rothschild, Waddesdon Manor, Buckinghamshire. She looks at the man again, who is miming the act of writing, scribbling zigzags in the air, jabbing a finger at the address.

—Letter here? says Rosa.

—Yes, he replies, letter here. Baron de Rothschild.

Suddenly there is a roaring sound, and a scarlet tram draws up clattering to the kerb. The men are on their feet, they raise their hats to Rosa in a formal sort of way and board the tram, gripping the pole and swinging themselves up. Overhead wires crackle, and the tram lumbers heavily away.

Rosa walks on, heaviness building in her heart, imagining Heinrich and Mama and Papa standing in never-ending queues; she will write to this Baron when she gets back to the Kremers', she will use her dictionary and stay awake all night if she has to, translating word by word, or perhaps somebody will help her, the Kremer boy perhaps, Samuel. But for now the search must continue.

After a while the streets grow an increasingly affluent air. Large houses with bay windows and elaborate entrances stand on either side, and there are motorcars parked in the road. Rosa walks slowly past house after house, scrutinising them from a distance, looking for a sign of Jewishness – ah, here is a house painted a gleaming white, and the door is smart, and there is a highly polished silver mezuzah fixed prominently to the doorpost; come on, this place is as good as any, the richer they are the better, and this is no time for cowardice, there is no choice but to go on, and what is the worst that could happen?

Birdsong hangs like fog in the grey air, and Rosa's heels thud on the clean stone as she makes her way along the path and up the stairs. In the shadow of the stone porch, set into the wall, there is a ring of stone, in the centre of which, like a brass bullet, is a button; Rosa presses it and is surprised by the sound, like a fire engine's bell; she can feel herself blushing even though the door is closed, perhaps there is nobody at home; then, without warning, the door opens to reveal a fresh-faced maid in a black-and-white uniform. Rosa thinks of a penguin and feels her blushes deepen.

—I beg your pardon, hello, she says, clutching her dictionary to her chest and enacting a little bow.

—Yes? comes the terse reply.

Rosa opens and closes her mouth, unsure of what to say, not knowing if it would be appropriate to address her speech to a maid. But she has no choice. She opens the dictionary and reads from the sheet of foolscap:

—I apologise to inconvenience you, but may I beg some minutes to speak?

Without a word the maid disappears into the house, leaving Rosa on the doorstep with the birdsong. She wants to flee, but the maid has left the door ajar, which compels her to stay, and anyway she cannot flee, for there is nowhere to flee to, and what if the people in the house turn out to be the ones who will rescue her family? Then, if she flees, she will have betrayed her family, through her cowardice, and the opportunity will have been wasted, never to come again. Yes, from this moment on, every second she spends fleeing, or reading, or eating, or lying in bed, or laughing even, that may have been the very moment when, some-where, if she had been applying herself to the search for visas and work permits, without cowardice or laziness, she would have met with success, someone would have said yes, I will employ your parents, I will offer them visas, work permits, freedom.

There is the sound of footsteps, and the door opens wider. A handsome woman with perfectly straight grey hair stands framed in the doorway.

—Hello, she says in a lipsticked voice.

Rosa clears her throat, bows again and focuses on the veins of blue ink threading from left to right across her piece of foolscap.

—I am a Jewish girl coming from Berlin, she reads, and my family is currently requiring a work permit and a visa also, for the United Kingdom. For any household they will be very hard-working and obedient, any type of work they will engage, as a cook or gardener or butler or maid or bottle-washer, in a city or a town, a village or a farm, they do not need much money, enough for surviving only, or even no money at all, just a little food and somewhere to live.

The woman looks at her coolly. Just a moment, she says, and reaches behind the door for her purse. She flicks open the catch, removes a pound note and hands it to Rosa, saying something she does not understand. Then the door closes. Rosa stands on the doorstep for a moment, the bird-song loud in her ears. The strange, oversized note lies in her hands, the grainy paper against her palm, the eyes of the monarch regarding her disparagingly. Blood rushes to her face. She wasn't asking for money, like some common beggar! She won't have it. She raises the pound note to the gleaming letterbox and slides it halfway in, it remains there like a tongue, she is about to push it through but then she pauses; slowly she removes it, inch by papery inch, and then the flap snaps back. She folds the money carefully and puts it in her pocket. Then, her face red and her head bowed with shame, she walks back along the path and onto the pavement.

For the rest of the day Rosa continues to knock on doors and stop Jewish people in the street. The sun arcs gradually across the sky, shadows shortening to the west, then lengthening towards the east. The heaviness in her heart increases yet she presses on, from house to house, from person to person, ringing and knocking, repeating her speech, being turned away, on occasion, with sympathy. She does not eat or drink all day, she has not brought anything with her. In the late afternoon she has to sit on the wall of a front garden, her coat hanging on either side of her legs to the pavement, recovering her strength, for she is beginning to feel quite light-headed. As dusk begins to fall, despite her desire to carry on, despite the possibility that behind the next front door may lie her family's salvation, she finds her way back to the Kremers' house, as she had promised, in time for tea. Yet she vows to continue tomorrow, and the next day, for as long as it takes, until she finds that single house, that single person, who will help her to rescue her family.

2

—Not bad at all, says Samuel, just let me make a few adjustments. Oh, I can't cross out your words, it needs to be neat. Don't worry, I shall write it out again. It won't take a minute.

The sages have taught that one should not make the slightest physical contact with somebody of the opposite sex. Samuel reaches across the desk and plucks the pen from Rosa's hand, quickly, as if picking a flower, then lays out a fresh sheet of foolscap. Rosa, at first, does not know what he is doing, but then, as he begins to copy out, very carefully, her letter, making adjustments here and there, she understands and is overwhelmed with relief. Finally someone is helping her, after a day of continuous rejection.

His brow furrows as he writes, and he runs a hand over his Brylcreemed hair, smoothing the errant locks. Rosa finds herself looking at his face, at every detail – the aquiline nose, the high cheekbones, the small mouth that, when smiling, lends his face a handsome charm, the cocoa-coloured eyes that regard the world head on. And she watches his hand as he writes, the long, powerful fingers guiding the pen in zigzagging movements, the flesh on the end of his forefinger pressing against the barrel, flushing and draining as pressure is applied and released, deep blue liquid forming angles and loops upon his command. It is different, a man's hand from a woman's, his hand from mine, it is constructed for a different purpose, it is an instrument for gripping, for tearing, for building things and fighting enemies and protecting the ones that he loves.

The nib scratches loudly, somehow calling Rosa's attention to the fact that she is tired. Nobody spoke to her at supper, of course, how could they, yet the stew was so satisfying that she didn't mind, she just concentrated on eating, filling her soul with mouthful after mouthful of sustenance. Afterwards she did the washing up, at Frau Kremer's request, while the char mopped the floor around her ankles; then she went straight to her room to compose the letter to Baron de Rothschild, taking the script that her father had written her in Berlin, that she has been using all day, that she almost knows by heart already, and building in a salutation, expository sentences, an introduction, translating word after word using the dictionary. For a while she toiled at her desk by the yellowish light of a lamp, wrapped in her mother's cashmere shawl, smelling the dying scent of Berlin, her shadow still and steady against the floral wallpaper, the curtains muffling the sound of the windows creaking in their frames, a carriage clock ticking gently to itself on the mantelpiece.

When there was a knock on the door, she jumped; it was Samuel, he had filled the hot water bottle for her, she accepted it gratefully, and he said something, he seemed to be asking what she was doing, she showed him the letter, and using signs he volunteered to help. And now he sits, brow creased with concentration, strong fingers guiding the pen, forming neat, slanting letters with high, narrow loops, stroking from time to time the shining black shell of his hair.

—There, he says at last, that should do it.

He slides the letter across the desk, and Rosa looks at it out of politeness, for she cannot understand a word.

—Good, she says, good.

He addresses the envelope for her, slips the letter inside and seals it.

—I hope it works, he says, placing the envelope on the desk, I really do. Gosh, it's cold, isn't it? I thought spring had come today.

He rubs his hands together; his palms make the sound of the sea.

—Do you know the word 'friend', says Samuel, 'friend'?

—Friend, yes, says Rosa, Freund.

—A friend of mine, says Samuel deliberately, from school, has a motorcycle. I've been helping him fix it up. Do you know the word 'motorcycle'?

He picks up the pen and, on a scrap of paper, sketches a crude semblance. Rosa's face shows a sudden understanding.

—Ah so, she says, Motorrad. Motorcycle.

—Yes, says Samuel, a Coventry Eagle Pullman, jolly good one too. Green as a toad. Understand?

There is the sound of a doorbell downstairs.

—I can ride, says Samuel, miming the twist of a throttle, yes?

—Yes, says Rosa.

He smiles charmingly and, despite everything, Rosa feels a smile slipping across her lips in return.

—Do you want to go for a ride with me?

—I beg your pardon?

—We can go for a quick spin. It's a two-seater and everything. What do you say? I've only got it until tomorrow.

—Now?

—Yes, now. What do you say? It'll cheer you up.

—No, no, thank you.

—What do you mean, no?

Rosa thinks for a moment, trying to recall her English lessons from a dusty Berlin classroom, all of which seem so remote.

—I apologise to inconvenience you, she says finally. I must write my letter to parents.

—Oh, I see. Well, you can get on with that afterwards, can't you? I'll help you with it. It's only eight o'clock.

There is a knock on the door, and it swings open to reveal Mimi Kremer, wearing a navy headscarf, a long cotton housecoat over her clothes and an expression of disapproval on her face.

—Samuel, she exclaims, what do you think you're doing?

—I'm helping Rosa write a letter to Baron de Rothschild.

—I don't care if you're writing to His Majesty himself, you're to keep your distance from the girl, do you hear? I've told you till I'm blue in the face.

Samuel starts to explain but his mother cuts him short.

—Look, she says, suddenly exhausted, go downstairs. That Cailingold girl is here to see you. I've told you to keep your distance from her as well. I've half a mind to turn her away. The shame of it.

—Esther? says Samuel, surprised.

—That's the one, says his mother, there seems to be no end to the number of young women my son is cavorting with.

Samuel slips from the room and his footsteps cascade down the stairs. The sages have taught that a man and a woman should never be left together in seclusion; what possibilities they must see in people to infer such danger! Or, believing in the danger, how often must they consider the possibilities! Without looking at Rosa, Mimi goes after him.

Rosa sits for a minute in silence, then gathers up the shawl and hot water bottle and lies on her back on the bed; turning her head to the side, she feels cool cotton against her cheek. Her feet ache all the way up to the knee from today's walking. In a moment she must sit at the desk and write a letter to her parents, but what to write? That the journey from Deutschland was lovely, that England is delightful, that the Kremers are wonderful and she is very happy here, that she had been knocking on doors and the English are very nice, and she is sure she will find them an employer soon? Ah, tomorrow she must give herself longer, get up earlier, walk faster, hurry straight to the place where she finished the day before and continue from that point onwards systematically, not stopping until she finds the unknown person who needs to be found. She will continue every day; even if she is struck down with a dreadful illness she will go on—

There is another knock, the door opens partially, and Mimi's head appears.

—May I come in? she says.

—Yes, says Rosa.

Mimi sits beside her on the bed, setting the mattress springs groaning. She is holding a piece of paper.

—Here, she says, I have drawn you up a list. These columns are for Monday, Tuesday, Wednesday and so forth. And here's what you need to be doing. Kitchen, that's floors, surfaces and washing up, then there's laundry, and ironing, dusting, and so on and so forth. The char will show you how to do it all before she leaves, and so forth.

—Work? says Rosa.

—Indeed, Mimi replies. Paying your way, as it were. Singing for your supper. Perhaps there are certain advantages to your not being eight years old.

—But I need to get visas for family.

—Of course you do, says Mimi, there'll be enough weekends for that. Mustn't go over the top, must we? The char will be expecting you downstairs in the scullery at half past seven tomorrow morning.

She heaves herself from the bed and crosses to the mantelpiece where she demonstrates half past seven on the carriage clock. Rosa is suddenly overwhelmed with an irrational anger which she struggles to contain.

—I do not clean in daytime, she says, I clean in evening.

—In the evening?

—I get visa in daytime. I clean in evening.

Mimi thinks for a moment, reading Rosa's face.

—It's most unconventional, she says hesitantly. I suppose we could try it and see how we go. But I still want you in the scullery at half past seven tomorrow morning. So the char can show you the ropes and so forth.

Giving her an odd sort of look, Mimi leaves the room. For several minutes Rosa doesn't move, allowing her heart to settle, her rage to sink into a less venomous depression. This house is claustrophobic, all the rooms too small and cluttered, as if the walls are slanted over her, and the light is dingy, and it is cold; she wants to open the window and leap out, tread the air, float, or fly, disappear into the darkness.

Suddenly there is a noise outside. She walks to the window, fists away the glaze of condensation, looks out: Samuel is sitting astride a great grasshopper-shaped machine, revving the engine with aggressive screws of the throttle, pulling goggles down over his face; clouds of exhaust are flurrying into the air behind him, the headlamp is sweeping a funnel of light across the road. A girl appears, bundled up in a coat with a scarf round her head, and mounts the motorcycle as well. The wine-coloured curtains part in the house opposite and heads appear in silhouette. Samuel fires the engine and lurches off precariously down the street and into the night.

Rosa turns away from the window and sits down at her desk. The lamp is buzzing softly. Suddenly she crumples up Mimi's timetable and throws it violently against the wall. She takes out a new sheet of foolscap and places it in front of her, then removes the lid of her pen. For a long time she sits looking at the blank paper in the lamplight, pen poised but unmoving, as the carriage clock ticks and the temperature drops, trying to write, trying to think, trying to find a way to begin the letter to her parents. Eventually she lets out a long sigh, picks up the balled-up timetable from the floor, smooths it out and places it on the desk beside her.

3

Samuel, holding a sheet of Rosa's English exercises with his comments and suggestions written in red ink, taps on her bedroom door. He suspects that she might not be there – in all probability she has already left for another relentless day on the streets – but knocks anyway.

—Rosa, he says, you're not in there, are you?

As expected, there is no response. To his surprise the door gives way, swings partially open, Rosa cannot have closed it properly when she left. He pauses. A column of light spills from the door onto the landing, he can see the edge of her bed. The house is quiet, nobody is here apart from Zeidi, who is asleep. Father has gone to his workshop at Petticoat Lane, Mother has gone shopping, and Samuel has been left at home to receive the Anderson shelter, the delivery of which, according to the council, is due this afternoon. He knows he should close the door, slip the sheet of paper underneath it, and go about his business; but curiosity is growing within him, he has allowed it to brew for too long, he can no longer resist.

He pushes the door softly, it swings wider with a sigh, revealing Rosa's room, laying it bare. The curtains are open, the April sunshine rests in a rectangle across the bed, and dust particles turn gently in the air. He leans across the threshold, peering surreptitiously around – Rosa has given the room a different scent, not quite perfume, nor sweet feminine breath, nor freshly laundered underwear, but related to all of these; undeniably the scent of a girl. Our sages tell us that men of independent means should engage in sexual intercourse with their wife every day, workmen twice a week, donkey drivers weekly, camel drivers monthly and sailors every six months. He places one foot inside the room, then the other. Get out, he thinks, forget about this room, this scent, this bed. He hesitates, then creeps further inside and closes the door behind him.

Now he is sealed in her room; should anybody find him, should Mother come home early and find him, he would have no excuse. He should leave now, before it's too late. He gazes at the bed, the blankets have been tucked in so tightly that there is not a single crease, like a fabric-covered brick. Yet in the pillow there is an indentation. He kneels beside the bed and places his hand gently in the hollow; it is the shape of Rosa's head, he is sure of it, or even her face perhaps. He bends carefully over and lowers his own cheek gently onto the pillow, feeling the indentation against his cheek. A single hair lies on the cotton, curling like the flimsiest of springs, its tip raised an inch or two above the fabric, flicking occasionally in a barely discernible breeze. Samuel watches it for a moment, feeling connected to Rosa in the most intimate way. Then he rests back on his heels on the linoleum.

All is still. He has gone too far, this is inexcusable, already he has sinned terribly. The faint sounds from the street, the occasional call of a blackbird, snatch of conversation, thrum of a tram, seem to be passing quiet judgement against him; the faded linoleum is hard and unforgiving beneath his knees, and his breath tickles his upper lip. He passes his hand over his comb-furrowed hair and picks up the photograph from the bedside table. Jolly strange, those Germans, so serious and formal, a family standing to attention for the camera, look at how the father has his socks pulled up to the knee, oh look at Rosa, doesn't she look funny, much younger, and her unruly curls are really rather comical. If she'd been living in London then, he's sure they would have been friends. He replaces the photograph, thinks for a moment, then, following an instinct, peers into the shadows under the bed. There, nestling against one of the legs against the wall, is a small painted box, a cigar box or a jewellery case. He should leave now, he's done enough. He reaches under and slides it out, then pauses for a moment. His intentions are not malign, he simply wants to get to know Rosa, everything about her, and in real life he cannot even attempt a conversation without his mother interfering, or an insurmountable language barrier coming up between them, or a crippling shyness on Rosa's part – or his own – putting paid to any hope of a relationship. He waits for a sign from God, some indication that he is sinning, some threat of retribution; nothing comes. He opens the lid.

The first thing that catches his eye is the glint of a golden watch. He peers closely with a synagogue awe, not daring to lay a finger on it, admiring the elegant face, the embossed numbers, the heavy strap. The only other object in the box is an envelope with postage stamps bearing the image of Mr Hitler. He stretches out his finger and touches it; the contours of the face undulate beneath his fingertip, he draws his hand away. The guilt is beginning to clutch him; he tries to shut the box and walk away, but something prevents him, as if he is possessed. He watches his hand sliding the envelope from the box, opening it, removing two letters; they are written in German, both in elegant fountain pen, on tissue-thin, well-thumbed paper. So this is what Rosa reads, this is her true self. He watches himself sit at the desk, heart pounding, spread out the letters. Occasional words jump out at him: England, Kremer, Berlin. Rosa's dictionary lies on the desk; he opens it, the spine makes a creaking sound and then a crack. He is sitting in her room, at her desk, in her chair, using her dictionary, exactly as she does night after night; this is her exact view of the window, the wall, the desk. His

German is atrocious, of course, practically non-existent, but his curiosity is burning, his desire to really know this German girl, to learn her innermost thoughts, and those of her family. He still expects, somehow, a sign from God, something to tell him to stop; when still nothing comes he continues, surrounded by the silence of an empty house, looking up word after word in the dictionary, piecing together sentences, deriving meanings, line after line, as the rectangle of light slips imperceptibly eastwards.

6. April 1939
Mein liebes Püppchen,

What a surprise to see a letter from England in the postbox, with all its funny stamps! I can see your English is improving already, how useful those lessons were that we gave you. It does indeed sound strange that the Kremers have a lavatory in a separate room from the bathroom, but these, perhaps, are the ways of the English.

Mama, Heinrich and Hedi all send their love to you. Heinrich wishes me to tell you that he has become a leader in his youth group, and we are all very proud of him. Your mother has been cooking some particularly delicious food of late, even with the limited resources available, what a clever and wonderful woman she is. Hedi is missing you very much and says that as soon as she is big enough she wants to learn to ride a bicycle like you. We are all, of course, pursuing visas as much as we can, but things here are as difficult as ever. I do hope your searches will prove fruitful, it must be a lot easier in England, everything must be I suppose.

Now for one of Papa's tales. A boy that I teach at school, a little lad by the name of Pfeifenkopf, developed a gigantic boil on the side of his nose last week. Being a surgeon I was elected to deal with the situation. Every day I gave the boy a little brandy and advised him to rub it on the boil. And within four days it had completely vanished! So you see the healing powers of brandy.

The Kremers sound like very kind and capable people. Do be sure to make yourself useful around the house, be polite and tidy up any mess you happen to make. Don't forget that they are showing you great kindness in giving you a home, and always be grateful and obedient. Be sure to study hard, a facility with English will stand you in good stead for the future. Your mother wishes me to say that although the situation here in Berlin is not the easiest, we are spurred on by the thought that you at least are well and happy and it will surely not be long until we see you again. We have no doubt that you will be able to find someone to offer us a visa very soon. Please do your very best – we are counting on you. Be strong, mein Püppchen, be strong! Until then we are sending you lots of love.

With an abundance of hugs and kisses,
Papa (also Mama, Heinrich and Hedi)

The letter is unremarkable, not even that private really, Samuel is sure that Rosa would have happily let him read it, he hasn't done anything wrong. As he puts it to one side, something in the other letter catches his eye: his own name, shining like a beacon from halfway down the page. Immediately he turns to it – if he features in a letter, he should be entitled to read it, should he not? It is a shorter note, and signed by her brother Heinrich:

Rosa:

Well done for arriving safely in England. I'm sorry to hear that Mimi and Gerald are so awkward to get along with, I suppose all you can do is remember that they are your benefactors and be as cordial as possible (England does sound strange – why on earth do they feel compelled to paint everything scarlet?). I am glad that you feel a certain kinship for Samuel, I have never met him personally but Papa says he is a decent enough boy. Perhaps he can be a big brother to you whilst I am still here – if you don't fall in love, of course!

Write back soon.
Heinrich

As Samuel puts the crackling paper down and looks out of Rosa's window, a strange feeling grows inside him, a feeling that he normally associates with the tiny glasses of whisky that are provided by the synagogue at bar mitzvahs and circumcisions. The letter has profoundly changed things; suddenly he has a window into Rosa's life, without the shutters and curtains and filters that normally lie between one person and another, and he has found, lying there already, an image of himself.

He folds the letters and replaces them beneath the golden watch, then slides the box back under the bed into exactly the place where he found it. As he does so a deeper, more serious thought rises to the surface of his mind. Even when translating so laboriously, even when focused on adjectives and synonyms and conjunctions, the desperation of Rosa's family was palpable; he, sitting in Rosa's room, by her window, has, to some extent, received the transmission of her parents' desperation; and he should share the responsibility for rescuing them.

Samuel gets to his feet, turns towards the door, catches sight of the wardrobe. We are told in Genesis that Adam and Eve, being perfectly innocent, did not wear clothes until after eating from the Tree of Knowledge, when they used fig leaves to cover their shame. There is a ring on the doorbell. He pauses then leaves the room, frustrated on the one hand, yet at the same time relieved that something has arisen to give him a reprieve from himself. As soon as he is outside on the landing and the door is shut safely behind him, he feels a wave of self-disgust. O Lord, I have sinned, I don't know what came over me; I do not know what punishment awaits, but I repent, here and now, and swear that I shall never do it again.

He opens the door to a rough-looking man in a cloth cap. Behind him, in the middle of the road, engine running, is a lorry from which neighbours are unloading curved sheets of corrugated iron. Ah, the Anderson shelter, he had completely forgotten. He walks through the warm spring sunlight to the lorry. As he unloads a shelter and carries it in, despite his lingering self-disgust and promises to God, his mind remains on the first floor, in the bedroom next door to his, by the desk where the German girl reads and writes letters to her family, and by the bed, where she sleeps – or attempts to – each night.

4

—Now, says Samuel softly, I shall do the talking. Try to follow if you can, and I shall explain later whatever you can't understand.

—I should not talk? says Rosa.

—That's right, Samuel replies, but you can say 'shouldn't', remember? Shouldn't. Not 'should not'.

—Shouldn't, she repeats.

—That's the one. There, you're getting the hang of it.

They are sitting in an echoing chamber fuggy with heat; summer is making its approach, and the windows, being covered already in galvanised iron, cannot open, making the building even warmer than it is outside. The room has the twilight atmosphere of blocked sunlight. Paintings line the walls, an elaborate chandelier hangs many feet above them, and Rosa, wearing her very best clothes, feels incongruous.

—It is warm, she whispers.

—Indeed, Samuel replies, but you can say 'it's', you know.

—It's warm.

—Too right.

They continue to wait in silence, their gas mask boxes on their laps. Harried-looking officials hurry past with overstuffed folders under their arms, mopping their brows with handkerchiefs, their shoes clacking and squeaking on the polished floor; somebody behind them is smoking a pipe.

—Thank you for helping me, says Rosa nervously.

—Not at all, says Samuel, it's my pleasure, whatever Mother and Father might say. It's useless reasoning with them, wouldn't you agree?

Some way off there is the bang of a double door and the regular clack of heels approaching. Then from a corridor emerges a short man with wire-rimmed glasses and a pronounced double chin. He makes his way over to where they are sitting.

—Rosa Klein? he says in a librarian's tones.

—Yes, says Rosa.

—This way, if you please.

The corridor is long, so long that the ceiling, walls and floor meet in a single point far into the distance; the man is walking quickly and they struggle to keep up. Samuel tries to show a reassuring smile to Rosa but she is staring straight ahead, her face a mask of determination.

Finally they are shown into an office with a carpet so thick that their feet sink into it like snow. The man disappears, the door closes, and a voice floats from behind a mahogany desk:

—Sam Kremer?

—Yes indeed, says Samuel, and this is my friend Rosa Klein.

—Welcome to the Home Office. My name is Addison. Yes, yes, take a seat. Warm, isn't it? I can almost feel the malaria coming on.

They sit down, and Samuel clears his throat. At first not much can be seen on the other side of the desk on account of the cigarette smoke that swirls in great blue sheets at head height; but then the fug clears slightly, and there appears a bald man with a moustache curling up at the corners, a dishevelled collar and hooded eyes; his desk is weighed down with masses of folders, stacks of paper tied with string and an overflowing marble ashtray.

—So, says Addison, I am informed that you go to school with John.

Samuel clears his throat again.

—Your son and I are fellow cricketers, he says. John is an accomplished bowler.

—Forgive me, but I was under the impression that you were together at Winchester.

—I'm afraid not, sir.

—From which school do you hail? says Addison.

—Tottenham, sir. Tottenham Grammar.

—A grammar school boy, says Addison, rolling the words in his mouth.

He sits back in his chair and slides a cigarette case between two piles of paperwork towards them. Neither Samuel or Rosa moves to receive it.

—Speak, says Addison, looking at his watch.

Samuel glances at Rosa and begins.

—I am here on behalf of Rosa. She is a refugee from Germany, a Jew.

—Cat got your tongue, my dear? says Addison, looking at Rosa.

—Her English, while improving, is not yet adequate, says Samuel.

—I see, Addison replies in a circumspect tone of voice.

—Both of her parents, as well as her brother and sister, are trapped in Germany.

—Rotten luck. Thus you wish to bring them to our green and pleasant land, says Addison.

—In a manner of speaking.

—And you have sufficient funds collected to support them once they arrive?

—A small sum might be raised.

—They have valid passports?

—The Germans won't give them one without a British visa.

—You're not suggesting that we issue a visa without a valid passport? says Addison.

Samuel searches his mind for a reply.

—My dear chap, says Addison, we can't go around issuing visas willy-nilly. The applicant must at the very least be in possession of a passport. It really is the minimum.

—But it's an impossible situation, says Samuel, feeling his neck flushing, they'll only be issued a passport if you give them a visa.

—I do understand, comes the reply, but your friend's family must play by the same rules as everybody else. You're a cricketing man, I'm sure you understand.

Samuel is speechless. Addison draws on his cigarette.

—If you want my advice, he says, find them an employer. If they had a work permit, that would make all the difference. Gainful employment, old chap, that's the thing.

—We're trying that, says Samuel, we're doing our very best.

—Good show, says Addison.

Redness is spreading into Samuel's face like a cloud at sunset. Rosa leans forward.

—Please, she says, we need help. My father, my brother, in prison. Berlin is not safe for us. We are one small family. England must have room for one small family.

—Gainful employment, says Addison, that's what His Majesty is looking for. Many people believe that there is a war coming, you know. We can't be taking in scroungers.

—Quite, says Samuel, and they have no intention of scrounging. They are hard-working, honest people. But we need to get them out now. If war is declared, the borders will be closed and they will be unable to escape.

—I appreciate that, says Addison, but if you are unable to present me with a passport or a work permit, my hands are tied.

He gets to his feet, signalling the end of the meeting. Samuel and Rosa rise and, in turn, shake him by the hand; Samuel's face is bright red and Rosa's is startlingly pale. They leave the office, close the door and make their way back down the corridor.

—That cad, says Samuel almost at a run, that absolute prize-winning cad.

Rosa hurries after him, trying to catch up, her thoughts racing: how long must this nightmare go on for? How difficult can it be to find somewhere for a middle-aged couple, their son and daughter? The world is vast, there are hundreds of countries, billions of people, yet not enough space just for a surgeon and his wife, and their son and daughter. And Baron de Rothschild has not even replied to her letter, perhaps she should write to him again, how humiliating, this entire process is degrading, and exhaustion is beginning to take its toll, knocking on doors all day, housekeeping in the evenings, English study at night, it is grinding her into the ground. If only she could sink underground for a hundred years and sleep.

They walk through the baking streets and descend into the bowels of the earth. They do not speak as they wait on the platform in the smoky subterranean gloom; it is not until they take their seats on the scarlet train, and it picks up speed and clatters noisily northwards, that Samuel breaks the silence.

—I was convinced that Addison would help. John swore blind that he would.

Rosa does not seem to hear him. The train clatters towards a tunnel, the lights flicker on and off, and the passengers jolt in their seats, in unison.

—I will write again for Baron de Rothschild, says Rosa.

—'To' Baron de Rothschild.

—I beg your pardon?

—'To' Baron de Rothschild. Not 'for' him, 'to' him. Remember?

Rosa's head nods to the rhythm of the train, there is nothing but solid blackness outside. Her reflection glimmers in the window, how old she looks, like a different person, nothing like how she imagines she would appear. As the blackness deepens and the reflection becomes more vivid, a hollow-eyed doppelgänger stares back at her, shuddering morbidly, hunched and small in the seat. It begins to change, becomes younger, sheds months, years, and in the space behind appear Mama and Papa, hands resting affectionately on her shoulders, the Wiesbaden hills extending behind them; on either side are Heinrich and Hedi, both smiling broadly, frozen in time, the wind catching their clothes. Look at herself, her younger self, with unruly curls and crescent-shaped eyes, enfolded in the centre of the scene! She is in the very bosom of her family, encased by her parents like a nut, innocent, and loved, her life filled with school, bicycles, birthdays.

—We'll put an advert in the *Jewish Chronicle*, says Samuel.

—What?

—The newspaper, you know? We'll put an advert in, I've seen them before, hard-working German couple seeks employment as butler and cook, that sort of thing.

Rosa squints at him in the flickering light of the train.

—I'm sorry, she says, I don't understand. I don't understand.

Samuel looks away, trying to think of a way to explain, but when he looks back Rosa's hands are over her face. He touches her arm, gently, but she does not look up. Our sages teach us that all physical contact with the opposite sex is forbidden. He slips his arm round her shoulder and she bows towards him very slightly, her body stiff and unyielding, suppressing with all her strength the sobs that every night stab incessantly into her pillow. Our sages have ruled that even accepting a handshake, even when there is no sexual motivation, is forbidden. Samuel places his hand over hers, and for the remainder of the journey they sit like this, Samuel watching their reflection in the window, his heart beating hard in his chest; they look small, dwarfed by the juddering train, two young people on train seats, divided by language, divided by culture, yet somehow united against the opaque blackness that surrounds them.

5

20. June 1939
Meine liebe Rosa,

Thank you for another lovely letter. We are glad that your English is improving and that the Kremers are treating you well. It is a great comfort to us that you are safe and happy, and we look forward every day to hearing from you. How overjoyed we are when we find your letters in the postbox!

Meanwhile the situation is bleak here. But we refuse to give up hope. Thankfully Papa's position as a schoolteacher is still secure, but for how much longer? Everybody is saying that war is coming, and the doors of the world are closed to us. Please try as hard as you can to get somebody to help us. We will do anything, cleaning, cooking, gardening. If war breaks out while we are still in Germany, we will be trapped. Every night I pray long and hard that we will be able to come to England soon. This is the only hope we have left, as all other avenues are now exhausted. I think that the only thing I pray for harder is the well-being of a certain English German girl! Papa, of course, has never been inclined towards religion but on occasion he prays as well.

Now all there is left to say is that we are sending you lots and lots of love from across the sea. We think about you always. Your letters are a shaft of light during these black times. Do everything you can to get us passage to England, we are desperate and have no other hope left. Be brave, my dear, and be strong, and remember that our love is always with you.

With endless love, hugs and kisses,
Your Mama

Rosa folds the thin paper and replaces it in the envelope. She is sitting on her bed in a short-sleeved summer dress, with a beret at an angle on her head, ready to leave the house; she had been on her way out when she saw the letter on the mat. A blaze of sunshine fills her bedroom, and a bumblebee bats against the window. She weighs the envelope in her hands, feeling the desperation with which her mother posted it, but today tears do not fill her eyes; instead her face is set in an expression of steely determination, for today will be the day, she will make sure of it, she will simply not accept another rejection. She glances at the carriage clock on the mantelpiece – she must go, or according to Samuel's timetable she will miss her train. She drops to her knees and feels under the bed for the painted box.

Samuel is in his bedroom, lying on his back on the bed, looking at the shadows moving on the ceiling. One of his hands hangs over the side of the mattress, holding between its fingers a flimsy piece of paper, a telegram which he received this morning. When he came down for breakfast it was waiting for him on his plate, Mother had restrained herself from reading it, it is important to give her son his privacy, or that's what Gerald says at least. Samuel took it upstairs to his bedroom immediately, where he sat on his bed, just as Rosa was sitting on hers on the other side of the wall; and just as Rosa was reading her mother's letter, he opened the envelope and read the brief lines of the telegram. For a long time he had known that this day would come and he'd been looking forward to it, in a way, fantasising about it even; but now that it has happened, it is somewhat different. Feeling strange, unsettled, he lies back on his bed, letting his hand hang over the side, and fixes his eyes on the ceiling; this is where he remains.

He hears the footsteps in Rosa's room, then on the landing, then a knock at the door, he does not reply immediately, he feels somehow distant, as if he has already left. Another knock.

—Yes? he calls at last.

—May I come in?

—Please do.

Rosa opens the door, dressed to go out, that dress looks lovely, ah yes, she is catching the train this morning, that's right.

—You'd better hurry, says Samuel, you'll be late.

—My box, says Rosa in a tense voice, have you seen?

—A box? What kind of box?

—Small, she says, like this. Inside it is my letters.

Samuel's heart jumps.

—Haven't seen it, he says casually. Have you looked downstairs?

Without a word Rosa closes the door and rushes down the stairs, her mother's letter still in her hand. Where could it be? How can it have vanished from her room like that, she is always so careful to leave it beneath the bed, in exactly the same place – it is simply inconceivable that she has misplaced it, yet she must have done, for it is not there, certainly not there.

—What's biting you? says Gerald, walking into the sitting room.

—My box, says Rosa looking up from the sofa where she has been searching under the cushions, have you seen?

—What kind of box?

—A small box, like this. For my letters.

—Afraid not, dear.

Rosa turns back to the sofa, pulling the cushions onto the floor; finding nothing she puts them hurriedly back and begins to search in the cupboards.

Upstairs, a block of summer light falls from the window onto the landing. A foot steps into it, leaving a long shadow, and then a whole person, and Samuel stands in the light on the landing, half of his body illuminated, the other half cast into shadow, quietly closing Rosa's bedroom door. He can hear her searching, dashing frantically from one room to the next.

—Where did you last see it? he calls over the banister.

—In my bedroom, Rosa replies from the kitchen.

—Why not look there again? You might have missed it.

—Upstairs no, says Rosa. I looked.

—You'll be late for your train, says Samuel.

Rosa looks at him fiercely.

—I know.

—Suit yourself.

He disappears into his bedroom and closes the door. Without a word Rosa stalks back up the stairs to her room. She drops to her knees and, in despair, looks once more under the bed; there, pushed slightly further back than usual, and half obscured by the leg of the bed, is the painted box. She scrabbles for it, pulls it out, checks the contents, yes, everything is still there, the letters, the watch, she closes it again, presses it to her forehead, eyes closed; then, breathing a deep sigh, places the letter from her mother inside. She holds the box delicately in her hands for a few moments. Then she places the contents of the box carefully in her bag; she will find a more secure hiding place upon her return.

As Rosa hurries onto the landing, Samuel happens to be leaving his room. He catches her eye and almost gives way to a tidal wave of self-loathing, almost confesses that he has been reading her letters, almost throws himself at her feet; but he does not. His heart is beating fast and for an instant he considers telling her about the telegram, but again something prevents him. Rosa smiles, nods a farewell, hurries down the stairs and out of the house, finally on her way to the railway station. Today will be the day, today she is determined, and nothing in the world will stop her.

6

Several hours later, after a tortuous train journey, Rosa finds herself walking along a perfectly straight driveway the colour of gold. To her left and right lie immaculate lawns and flowerbeds, and carefully culti-vated trees, all alive with a bounty of colour; on the horizon there stands a fairytale castle with turrets and pillars, and row upon row of windows, topped by a languidly flapping flag. Her feet are heavy, and she is breathless with nerves; an impulse to flee overwhelms her, she thinks of her family, walks on.

After a time she steps into the lilac shadow of the castle. When seen close up it appears vast and deserted, like a museum, and she can hear the dry noise of the flag flapping high up on the roof. She rests her foot, in a shoe polished for the occasion, on the lowest step and pauses; then gathers her courage and climbs the steps until she is standing in front of the imposing front door, flanked by pillars and topped by an ornate lintel. Glassy lawns sweep out like great fields behind her, and her hair trembles in the breeze.

She winces, having rung the bell too hard; it resounds like the peal of a cathedral bell, echoing many times off surfaces of marble, glass and silver. A grand silence returns, interrupted only by the occasional bird-call. She waits anxiously on the cool stone steps, adjusting her dress and her beret.

She is about to ring again when, without warning, the door swings smoothly open and she is regarded by a coiffed butler.

—Yes? he says deliberately.

—Please I must to speak to Baron de Rothschild.

—Do you have an appointment?

—I beg your pardon?

—An appointment, madam. Do you have one?

—I wrote to him a letter. My name is Rosa Klein.

There is a pause while the butler sweeps his eyes across her, noting every detail.

—I must to see Baron de Rothschild, says Rosa boldly, I must to see him today.

—If you'd like to wait, says the butler, we shall see.

She is directed to sit on a red-upholstered chair before the butler vanishes, leaving her waiting like a pedlar, breathless with nerves, tracing the veins on the marble floor. It is surprisingly cold in the castle and she presses her palms between her knees.

—Miss Klein?

A strong voice, with an accent, not completely English, French perhaps. Rosa looks up to see a tall, slightly dishevelled-looking man with a large, blunt face and a monocle. As she gets to her feet and shakes his hand, the monocle falls from his eye and dangles on his chest.

—Follow me, he says in a resonant baritone. Rosa follows him up a set of shallow stairs into a womb-like study filled with the breath of old books, the voices of long-dead generations and the richness of oil paintings, chandeliers and dark wooden furniture. The man scrapes at the fire with a poker, replacing his monocle as he does so.

—Please I must to speak with Baron de Rothschild, says Rosa.

—I'm the baron, says the baron casually, can't you tell?

With some difficulty he replaces the poker in a brass frame, brushes off his hands and takes a seat behind a desk, gesturing Rosa to sit down. Then he lights a pipe.

—In March I wrote to you a letter, says Rosa.

—I've been abroad. Only just got back.

—I beg your pardon?

—Abroad, you know. The Continent?

—Sorry, my English is not good, says Rosa.

—My German is appalling, replies the baron, but I'll have a bash. *I've been abroad.*

—*Ah, you speak German?*

—*A little.*

This is the first time Rosa has been able to speak German since her arrival, and the baron's German sounds excellent. She starts to talk, hesitantly at first, but then the words come spilling out, about her family, about Sachsenhausen, about the transport, about the Kremers and how she has been trying to find somebody to offer her family employment; she tells him how she knocks on doors, but there is so much housework to be done, and she is getting very tired, but she must carry on, all she needs is a work permit, a visa and a sponsor, and please, Baron de Rothschild, can you help?

The baron, brow wrinkled, places his pipe on the table and steeples his fingers. Then he makes some notes on a pad of paper with a heavy-looking pen.

—*There's a realistic possibility of war*, he says. *I have twenty-six children from Germany living at the Cedars already. They came here on transports like you.*

—*Please*, says Rosa.

He puts down his pen and looks at her intently.

—*What does your father do?* he asks.

—*He is a surgeon.*

—*Will a surgeon work on a chicken farm?* he asks.

Rosa's heart jumps.

—*He will work anywhere, he will do anything*, she says.

—*And your mother? Your brother?*

—*Of course, anything.*

He gets to his feet, towering to the ceiling, and his monocle falls from his eye, dangling on his chest; Rosa, a little dazed, gets to her feet as well.

—*I shall visit the notary straight away*, he says, puffing on his pipe, *and have them draw up a work permit.*

Rosa stumbles and has to support herself on her chair; the baron steps round the desk and takes her arm.

—*Come now*, he says, *I shall get you a glass of water and then you may accompany me.*

—*No*, says Rosa, *no water. Let us go now.*

The baron smiles and a dappled light plays across his face.

—*Very well*, he says, breathing strings of smoke from his nose, *I'll get my hat.*

7

24. July 1939
Meine liebe Rosa,

Thank you so much for your letter. We are so very heartened by your news about the wonderful Baron de Rothschild. Will we be living in London, near you? What jobs will we have? How about

Heinrich? Please write as many details as you can in your next letter, even small details that might seem irrelevant. We are very anxious to find out as much as possible.

As it happens, we have some news of our own. This morning we received notification that Hedi has been accepted onto a transport. Could it be that our bad luck is lifting at last? The Kremers were reluctant, quite understandably, to take in another child, but they have agreed to look after her until we arrive, which after all may only be a few days. Needless to say, we are sure that you will look after Hedi very well indeed and prevent her from burdening the Kremers. Hedi will be so happy to see you!

Wonderful, wonderful news! We will be together again soon! Please do write and explain all the details of Herr Rothschild's offer.

With so much love and kisses,
Mama (also Papa, Heinrich and Hedi)

Rosa folds the letter again and replaces it in the envelope; then she tucks it back into the pocket of her skirt and looks up at the August sky, cobalt blue, not a cloud in sight. On the arms of the deckchair her fingers are still, and her body relaxes in the red-and-white striped canvas; the narrow garden cradles her like a bijou, flowers tumble everywhere, even atop the Anderson shelter, which has a wig of hyacinths on its roof. She can hear the neighbours having a conversation about the threat of war; by now she can understand the gist, but even if she couldn't the subject would be obvious, it's all anyone talks about these days. In the distance rows of barrage balloons hang heavily, and from inside the house comes the sound of a crackling wireless, as the valves warm up it becomes more audible, again the war, the likelihood of war. The policemen wear uncomfortable-looking tin helmets now, and piles of sandbags have appeared on the main roads, nestling against the walls; yesterday in the street Rosa saw a man with a sandwich board advertising for ARP volunteers, he was wearing a gas mask and looking very frightening indeed. Her fingers tense and grip the arms of the deckchair. Hedi will arrive in just a few days, and her parents a week later, if war does not break out first; then they will be safe at Waddesdon Manor. Just a few more minutes and she will go back inside, continue with the housework, the floor still needs to be mopped.

Inside, Mimi and Gerald are not listening to the wireless. They are sitting in the drawing room, and the wireless is muttering to itself in the corner, but they are not listening.

—I've got the wind up, says Mimi, I don't mind telling you.

—Honestly, Gerald replies, you had the same jitters over Czechoslovakia last September. Perhaps it's an annual event, your jitters.

—That was different. There's a war coming now, everyone says so. And this time Samuel will be all caught up.

—Nonsense, says Gerald. It's all just a lot of old sabre-rattling.

—I know, I know. But with Samuel going off, it's all a bit much. I shall sew blackout curtains for the dining room at least. Maybe for the other rooms also.

—Dear, I've told you. If war does break out we'll be moving to Harry's place in Norfolk quick smart.

—And the Germans won't bomb Norfolk?

—We're already doomed with all these electric torches you keep buying at Boots.

—They're going up in price, Gerald, they've gone from sixpence to one and ninepence. The batteries will be rationed, and the globes.

—There's only so many electric torches a man can take, says Gerald. And blackout material. And tinned potatoes. And hot water bottles.

—Hot water bottles fell into short supply last time round, I'll have you know. And tins are important, Gerald. They are resistant to the damp and the gas.

—The gas!

There is a pause. The wireless crackles on in the background, and the floorboards creak beneath Samuel's feet upstairs.

—I hope Samuel will be all right, says Mimi.

—It's good for a man, the army. He'll be able to pull his weight when he gets to Palestine. And it's best to get Rosa off his radar, you said so yourself.

—Yes, but the army? I don't like it, I just don't like it. Perhaps I should go up and help him pack.

—For goodness' sake, just let him alone. He'll be down in his own time to say goodbye.

Samuel's silhouette approaches the window, and suddenly Rosa, in the garden, can see him clearly. He is wearing his uniform, army cap at an angle, how different he looks – he hauls the window up and leans out, the curtains flapping in the breeze beside him. Pressing a finger to his lips, he swings one foot over the windowsill; Rosa sits upright in the deckchair, what is he doing, he might fall; he swings the other leg over and clambers down the drainpipe to the ground. His cap falls from his head, he snatches it up and dodges behind the shed. Rosa gets to her feet and, as casually as she can, walks over to join him. They are out of sight, but they do not have long.

—What are you doing? says Rosa, you could hurt.

—Nonsense, Samuel replies, grinning broadly, I've done it hundreds of times before. Just wanted to say goodbye.

—When you are going?

—A few minutes.

They regard each other silently for a moment, Rosa searching amongst her limited palette of words, Samuel wishing he had prepared something to say.

—I'll have two weeks' leave in November, says Samuel at last, then it's Crimbo.

Rosa squints up at him. He laughs awkwardly.

—Sorry, I forget. Christmas.

There is a pause.

—Thank you, says Rosa solemnly, for all you have helped me.

—Not at all, Samuel replies. When is your family coming?

—My sister in some days, says Rosa, then my parents a week later.

—By the time I'm home on leave, you'll be mistress of Waddesdon Manor.

—I will write to you a letter.

—Just say 'I'll write'.

—I'll write.

—Just the job.

Neither of them intends to reach out, but suddenly they are in embrace; the rough weave of Samuel's uniform is against Rosa's cheek, she can smell the newness of the material, feel the rise and fall of his chest; Samuel cups one hand on her hair, the other he lays on the small of her back, he thinks he can feel her breasts against him, her curls are soft on his face. And then, without either of them knowing who brought the embrace to an end, there is space between them, only a few feet but it is the beginning, and Samuel is looking left and right to check the coast is clear; he shins up the drainpipe and climbs back into his bedroom.

Rosa walks quickly into the house in search of the mop, trying to give herself something to do. She does not know if Samuel's departure compounds her sadness or alleviates it, for he will be back, most certainly, in November, she will be able to travel to London from Waddesdon to meet him away from the watchful eye of Aunt Mimi. And Hedi will be here soon, as well as her parents, so it has turned out that parting is only temporary, and the long days of absence will be telescoped into the moment of reunion, enhancing its bitter-sweet pleasure, its joy.

She dunks the head of the mop into the water and slaps it onto the linoleum, skidding it back and forth, back and forth. She hears Samuel descending the stairs with laboured steps, he must be carrying a heavy load, she hears Mimi and Gerald going to meet him at the bottom of the stairs. Still holding the mop she sees Samuel standing in the creamy morning light from the frosted front door, tall and impressive in his uniform, a shapeless kitbag over his shoulder, his black hair forming little sleek waves from underneath his army cap; his mother is saying something, her arms are about his neck, and his father is shaking him by the hand, they are exchanging words, he smiles, wipes his eyes on his sleeve – and now his uniform is no longer new, it has been soiled with his tears, the first hint of the suffering of war, the suffering of parting. He looks up and sees Rosa standing in the doorway, winks and tries to muster a grin, his parents do not notice; Rosa smiles and lowers her gaze. When she raises her eyes the door is open and he is gone.

8

Summer burns on, sandbags multiply in the streets, and London is pervaded by a suppressed sense of excitement. In the days following Samuel's departure the house becomes darker, quieter, emptier. It seems bigger somehow, also, stuffy, filled with artefacts. Gerald continues with his life as normal, going to Petticoat Lane each day, returning home in time for tea, smoking endless cigarettes; Mimi becomes obsessed with stockpiling, stacking the cupboards full of butter substitutes, vacuum-packed coffee and boxes of batteries, and purchasing multiple frocks; in the evenings she writes letters to her son. Neither of them takes much notice of Rosa, but it doesn't matter, because soon her family will be here.

On 2nd September, in the evening, after Gerald concludes the sabbath with the blessings over the wine and the candle and the spices, Rosa decides to bake bread. It is not a chore listed on Mimi's rota but Hedi is arriving tomorrow and it would be lovely to welcome her with some home-cooked bread in the German style. Rosa remembers that when she herself arrived almost six months ago – has it truly been six months? – she was shocked by English bread, traumatised even, it was like eating cake, with a solid panel of butter sitting smoothly on the top like icing. As she submerges her hands in a bowl of wholemeal flour, light brown dust that sifts softly through her fingers like sand and rises into the air in gentle clouds, muffling the electric light, she tries to forget that Danzig has fallen, Warsaw is being bombed, Gdynia has been evacuated and the Poles are retaliating; she suppresses any recollection of people in the streets with rolls of black paper over their shoulders, and trams and buses running only with headlights. No, there is no reason to panic. Even though the evacuation is now in full force, many people still believe that war will be averted, and she counts herself amongst their number, she has to. She bakes, and as she kneads the dough she thinks through, once again, the preparations for Hedi's arrival. Her bed has been pushed against the wall to make room for Hedi's, and half of her wardrobe has been cleared, as well as half of her chest of drawers; as a finishing touch she has placed Hedi's dolly, Gigi, in the bed, under the blankets, for her to discover as a surprise.

That night there is a storm, and Rosa does not sleep. Downstairs, as the rain sprays against the window, and thunder rolls across London like a curse, her bread remains in the oven, cooling in the darkness as the night wears gradually on. Lightning flings itself into the heavens, and the rain lashes down in wicked sheets; she cannot help but imagine that the noise of the storm is, in reality, the sound of the fighting over Poland, which must be taking place this very moment. In her bedroom a leak develops, she finds a bucket and sits by the window, curtains open, lights off, listening to the hollow clang of the drops in the bucket. A solitary motorcar rumbles by outside, water streaming down its windows, headlights dimmed.

She closes the curtains, sits at her desk and turns on the electric lamp. It is late but she does not feel tired. She takes out a sheet of foolscap and her dictionary, and removes the cap of her pen. For over an hour she sits and writes, not to her parents but to Samuel, painstakingly, translating word after word. Everything was easier before Samuel left, he gave a certain colour to life, an energy, and she misses it now that she is alone with Mimi and Gerald in this dark old relic of a house. She imagines him now at his army base in Aldershot, sleeping in a steel-framed bed with a single khaki blanket, rifle by his side; that is how she pictures it, at least, and she has nothing to contradict the image. Perhaps he is in charge of a tank, or a machine gun, surely he is responsible for some sort of heavy machinery. Her eyelids grow heavy and she finds herself thinking about the evacuation: yesterday she witnessed the chaos as she passed the railway station, and now the images float vividly back, the stony-faced husbands, the children clustering in smeared train windows, the women in headscarves carrying coats, the old ladies dragging suitcases, asking, where are all the porters? The harassed-looking volunteers wearing armbands, seeming to make no difference at all.

Now sleep has pulled her under, her head nods and she snaps awake, focus Rosa, there is a blot on the letter now, where is the blotting paper, there, as good as new, where was she; she writes a little more but then an old man is saying he'd be no use in a war at his age, and a cluster of naval reservists, middle-aged veterans of the last war, are tramping morbidly along a train platform smoking cigarettes – she shakes her head and bites her lip, she has dropped her pen, she picks it up, do not give in, focus, but the images are incessant, perhaps if she rests her head here just for a minute, gathers her strength, just for a minute – a group of lads in ill-fitting uniforms are hurrying to the platforms, stumbling under the weight of their kitbags, a crowd of schoolchildren are gathering round the clock tower with blankets and bags, mackintoshes and wellingtons and toys, there is so much luggage it's a wonder anyone keeps track of anything at all, there are piles of bags everywhere, like castles, like islands; the blackness rises up. Within minutes she is slumped over her desk, in the dim glow of the lamp, asleep.

9

Rosa awakes, somehow, in her bed, fully clothed, but she has no idea how she got there, no recollection; her last memory is of writing at her desk. Her sleep was deep but disturbed, filled with nightmares that fragment as she tries to recall them, leaving behind nothing but an uncomfortable sensation in her body. She struggles to her feet, she is still wearing yesterday's clothes, she crosses to the window and parts the curtains. Last night's storm has blown itself out leaving the streets wet and glaring; the sun is white and relentless, and a half-rainbow slants across the sky. She squints around the room, sees the carriage clock, blinks and looks again; it is true, it is eleven o'clock. She glances back out of the window, the sun is unbearable and her head hurts, why hasn't someone woken her up? Surely Mimi and Gerald would have wondered what had become of her, but they didn't come to check on her, they decided to let her sleep.

She splashes some water on her face and makes her way downstairs, today is the day that Hedi arrives, though not until this afternoon. The noise of the wireless can be heard, it is incessant these days. Inside the house it is dark, like a clam's shell, the shadows are blacker due to the brightness of the sun, its relentless whiteness. She is thirsty. She goes into the kitchen, drinks a glass of water, then another, perhaps she is coming down with something, but she does not feel ill as such, it's just that her head hurts, and she has a dull thud in her stomach. Aunt Mimi must be in the drawing room, let's go and see.

Rosa enters the drawing room and is surprised to see not just Mimi but also Gerald sitting in the twin armchairs, upright, their faces grave; she begins to speak but they gesture to her to be quiet, to sit down, to listen. The thud in her stomach intensifies, and she sits on the sofa, trying to understand the fuzzy voice on the wireless; something out of the ordinary must be happening, she tells herself that she does not know what it is.

The voice is slow and morose, with weighty pauses.

—This morning the British ambassador in Berlin handed the German government a final note stating that unless we heard from them by eleven o'clock that they were prepared at once to withdraw their troops from Poland, a state of war would exist between us. I have to tell you now that no such undertaking has been received, and that consequently this country is at war with Germany.

There is more, but Rosa does not hear it, and nor, it seems, do Mimi and Gerald; Mimi's head is in her hands and Gerald, although still sitting upright, eyes wide open, has turned extremely pale. Mimi says a single word, Samuel, and Gerald mumbles, I'd better ring Harry, but he doesn't move; they sit motionless, all three of them, until the end of the national anthem. Mimi goes into the garden to look for aeroplanes overhead, and the air-raid siren sounds, and Gerald says that no aeroplane could possibly fly over from Germany so quickly, he thinks it must be a test, but they shutter the windows anyway and file down to the cellar, in silence, putting on their gas masks and adjusting the straps; the storm inside Rosa grows, the realisation slowly reveals itself, the truth of what has happened. They sit in silence in the chilly dampness of the cellar listening to each other breathing.

At this very moment, in Berlin, at the Friedrichstraße Bahnhof, a train is at a platform. It is stationary, having been delayed for many hours, and clouds of steam billow around it. Alongside the train two officers of the SS stride in the direction of the engine, their legs cutting through the steam, boots falling loudly on the concrete, black uniforms flashing past the windows of the carriages; as they pass, the children in the carriages look up in alarm, they should have been on their way hours and hours ago, the delays have been endless, all this waiting in the train is agonising. Between two older girls is Hedi, wearing the number 273 round her neck, it dangles almost to her knees, she is sitting quietly, she does not dare to move; the SS officers have arrived at the front of the train, they are speaking to the driver who is leaning out of the engine. War has been declared, they are saying, the borders have been closed, this train is forbidden to leave.

The children will be bundled out of the train. Soon the door to the waiting room will open, and the parents will watch, open-mouthed, as their children are returned to them, their children whom they have just said goodbye to for ever, returning impossibly, what sort of blessing is this? Klein will take Hedi in his arms, and Inga will fall to the ground, fainting at the sight of her second daughter with her little suitcase whom she thought she would never see again. The news will spread throughout the room that war has been declared, a cacophony of sounds will fill the air, cries, and gasps, and conversation, and shouts; afterwards, when it has died down, a procession of parents and children will leave the waiting room, will make their way round the edge of the concourse, out of the Bahnhof and, looking over their shoulders, back onto the streets of Berlin.

Rosa, in England, in London, in the basement, gazes straight ahead, she cannot see anything, cannot move, for finally the realisation is making itself known to her. The worst has happened, the iron door has closed, the shutters have come down; all her efforts to get her family out of Germany have failed.

PART TWO

19 June 1941, Norfolk

I

Could, would. Couldn't, wouldn't. She could have done more, she should have. She would have done more, but – she should have. Memories fading like an old photograph in the sun, like this old photograph from Wiesbaden, which she keeps out of the sun, which fades still. Have to, had to, she had to do more, she didn't. She had to do more, she couldn't. She would have done more, she couldn't. She had to do more. What's happening to them? To her? A steel shutter down, a family cut in two. It shouldn't be like this, didn't have to. She had to do more, she didn't. She could have done more, couldn't she? She could. She didn't. Memories are useless, they have ended, and she could have done more.

Rosa's consciousness breaks the surface, leaving her weighed down by the familiar heaviness, trying to capture her thoughts as she opens her sleep-thickened eyes to the quiet of another Norfolk morning. Little lines of light lie upon the slanting walls of the cottage, the oak-beamed ceiling, the sagging floor; when she was first evacuated she had been astounded by these thick irregular walls, these bowed floors and bulging ceilings, which were unlike anything she had ever experienced in London, and of course Berlin. But familiarity has dulled her sense of wonder, replacing it first with a deep boredom and then, as the fingers of wartime deprivation began to close, despondency.

Thump-thump: her two bare feet land on the gnarled floorboards as she slips out of the net of sheets, crosses the room and, dressing-gowned, listens at the door without opening it: it sounds as though nobody is about, ah yes, Gerald and Mimi are off to a meeting with the Ladies' Hospitality Committee about a canteen for Jewish servicemen in Norfolk. She allows her dressing gown to fall to the floor in a curved concertina then raises her arms towards the ceiling, stretching her fingers as high as they can go, and lets out a long, open note that falls into the cottage like snow falling into the ocean. Her heaviness lifts slightly, or rather is partitioned into a secret place. Today hard work lies ahead, but at least it isn't housework; she will be out working in the fields, contributing to the war effort. She looks at her watch, late already, she doesn't have time for breakfast, she will snatch a piece of bread on her way out. She begins to dress: tough dungarees, thick cotton blouse, scratchy woollen socks, a pair of Samuel's wellington boots which she has stuffed with hay to make them fit, a jumper just in case, and finally her beret, tilted to the right as fashion dictates, to keep her hair in place when riding at speed. Then downstairs for some bread and butter.

Rosa hurries into the brick-floored parlour, cuts herself a slice of bread and spreads it thinly with a scrape of butter from her four-ounce ration. She fills a bottle with barley water and turns to leave, but is surprised to see Samuel leaning casually on the doorpost. His black hair is unruly, unBrylcreemed; his shirt is untucked, untidy; the morning light catches his cheekbones and forehead, emphasising his sharply cut features; his shirt parts halfway down to reveal a wrinkled swathe of bandage; he is pale.

—What are you doing out of bed? says Rosa.

—Where are you rushing off to in my wellies? he replies lazily, regarding her with languid eyes, and why are you wearing that hat?

—To help with sugar beet.

—Don't leave me all alone again, says Samuel, I can't play Solo all day by myself, you know. No pun intended. God, it's so boring convalescing.

He pronounces the word with exaggerated consonants and Rosa has to smile. As she does so, her heaviness sinks out of sight like a sea creature submerging, biding its time for the next attack.

—Convalescing is always boring, she says, it's supposed to be like this.

—The boredom's worse than the shrapnel wound, Samuel replies sorrowfully. Let me come with you. I could do with a breath of air.

—Come with me? says Rosa, pushing past him. You're telling a joke? You're not allowed to ride a bicycle even. Aunt Mimi would have me crucified.

—She wouldn't find out if we're back before seven. And I can ride a bicycle, I'm a lot stronger than I was. The infection's passing, Doctor Ashfield said, and that's been the worst of it. Come on, I'd rather ache for a few days than die of boredom at home.

—If Aunt Mimi found out, says Rosa doubtfully.

—I assure you, they're not coming back until seven. I've got my barbiturates, they're magical. I won't help with the harvest, I'll just sit under a tree and convalesce, what do you say?

—Very well. But I warn you, I'm late, I will ride fast.

—Actually I can't ride a bicycle, says Samuel, following her into the hall, doctor's orders. I'd better sit on your handlebars.

—Don't be flipping, says Rosa.

—Flippant, says Samuel. I'm not being flippant. Why don't you ever take me seriously?

It certainly is a glorious day. A yellow wall of light greets them as they leave the cottage, fading into an eyewateringly bright blue sky. The world is vivid, every object so distinct that the hedgerows, the leaves, the blackbirds, look weightless. This is the England, thinks Rosa, that she will remember when she is back in Germany, that she will describe to her family when the war is over and they go for walks in the Grunewald. The erratic buzz of a bee draws circles round her head as she mounts her bicycle, swinging her knees over the low crossbar, and helps Samuel onto the handlebars. Then she pedals off down the lane, gaining momentum with every downward plunge, her gas mask box swinging against her hip. Samuel whoops with delight as they bounce past a row of ivy-clad trees, and Rosa's heaviness is buried so deeply that it is almost imperceptible.

Rosa likes English bicycles. If there is one thing that she never tires of, it is riding this graceful machine with its narrow tyres, slim wheels and gently curving handlebars, especially in fine weather. The bicycle, of course, does not belong to her but to Aunt Mimi, who allows her to use it strictly for errands or the war effort. Compared to riding the squat, thick-tyred machine she used to own back in Berlin, now she is the picture of elegance, perched straight-backed atop the saddle like a concert pianist, the wind fanning the eyelashes that line her crescent-shaped eyes. Samuel is rather less dignified in appearance, the soles of his feet flapping in the air, his hands grasping awkwardly the handlebars, his hair tangling in the breeze – yet his face is the picture of joy. At the front of the bicycle, between his legs, an empty cocoa tin with shielded slits has been fitted over the headlamp for after the blackout; it rattles and clangs with the bumps in the road. As the hedgerows on either side blur smooth with speed and the telegraph poles slip by he begins to sing, louder than decorum would normally permit, causing the sparrows flitting in the hedgerows to fly up into the air as they approach: when they sound the last All Clear, how happy my darling we'll be, when they turn up the lights and those dark gloomy nights will be only a memory! Rosa laughs, tells Samuel to shut up, pokes him in the ribs, pedals faster.

—Sorry, dear, says Samuel, it's just that there's nothing like freedom for a soldier like me, nothing like freedom for me!

—What song is that?

—I don't know, I invented it.

—Invented?

—Yes, you know, made up.

—Made up?

They trundle over a stone bridge, turn left at the pill-box and join the main thoroughfare, rattling past lazy-looking farmers sitting in horse-drawn carts and groups of young farm hands with roughly woven shirts and caps. Rosa's oversized wellingtons seem to be fixed to the pedals, clamping them between rubbery heel and sole. In the distance a truck comes into view in a cloud of dust, an unusual sight these days. Rosa freewheels to the grass bank as it roars past and Samuel almost falls off – they catch a glimpse of wiry-looking soldiers in khaki uniforms, sitting sullenly, equipment rattling. The dust cloud disperses and Rosa, being late, picks up the pace again, negotiating the potholes and bumps in the road. Samuel begins to sing once more, his voice jogging with the bounce of the bicycle, the cocoa tin rattling maniacally on the headlight as the tyres bounce in and out of the furrows.

—What are those red flowers called again? asks Rosa, gesturing towards the patches of scarlet at the roadside.

—Poppies, says Samuel. I may be a Londoner but even I know that.

—Poppies, Rosa repeats, poppies.

Yes, Mama, they have these lovely red flowers called poppies growing wild in the hedgerows, and more greenery than you could possibly imagine; we must go to England on holiday, really we must.

2

Sugar beet, sugar beet, sugar beet: it has been nothing but sugar beet, every Saturday since Christmas for Rosa and the motley collection of schoolboys, off-duty troops, local volunteers and Land Girls she works with. Rosa admires the Land Girls, how she wishes she could join them, or better still the nursing corps, for what she really wants to do is train to be a nurse, she has harboured this ambition ever since she was a child, perhaps inspired by Papa; but she is a few months away from being old enough yet for any of this, and Mimi and Gerald have expressed the opinion that nursing has a brutalising effect on young women and will not let her pursue such a career. It was hard enough to persuade them to let her train as a First Aid volunteer, and the classes were only once a fortnight, and they were most reluctant to allow her to join the sugar beet harvest too; Rosa suspects that the housework might have something to do with it.

After some hours of toil the fatigue sets in, and the lines of labourers become straggly and uneven. Rosa's back is sore and she tries to find another way of stooping that uses a different set of muscles. The sun is getting hotter, or so it seems, and a film of sweat lies on her forehead like glass. She glances over to the oak tree where Samuel is sitting in the shade convalescing; he is whittling a stick with a penknife and doesn't notice her gaze. She bends again, lifting the leathery white bulbs of sugar beet and dropping them into the sack that she drags behind her; then she wipes her brow, puts her hands on her hips and stretches backwards, tilting her chin up to the cloudless sky, you are only supposed to stretch on the hour but she can't go on any longer. She drags her jumper over her head, ties it round her waist and unbuttons the collar of her blouse, trying to prevent herself from glancing at Samuel again. The smooth sun falls on her face for another few seconds, then she picks up the sack and reaches for another sugar beet. As she does so she catches the eye of the ruddy-faced lad in front; he pauses, beet-hook in hand, frozen for a moment in the act of decapitating another vegetable. Beads of sweat are stippling his fore-head, dark patches have spread around his armpits, and his chest rises and falls with effort. He grins and cocks his head, then brings the beet-hook down, severing the cluster of leaves at the head of the vegetable with a clack. Then he tosses the sugar beet lightly towards her, grins again, and turns away to reach into the fresh furrows overturned by the tractor. She feels herself flush and bends to pick up the vegetable.

Oh, mademoiselle from Armentières, parlez-vous, someone sings. There are laughs and squeals from the girls. Oh, mademoiselle from Armentières, parlez-vous. More laughs, and a shout from the farmer to pipe down. She'll do it for wine, she'll do it for rum, and sometimes for chocolate or chewing gum, hinky-dinky, parlez-vous. Put a sock in it, Charlie, someone says, there're ladies here you know. More laughter ensues, and somebody throws a sugar beet. The farmer stops the tractor, leaving the engine chugging beneath him, and turns to face the workers behind. Will you lot stop larking about, he shouts. Come on, mate, says a schoolboy, chewing something. It's time for our break now, anyway, ain't it? It's not your break till I say so, you cheeky little blighter, says the farmer. Hang on, lads, says a soldier who has unbuttoned his shirt, here comes the grub.

A cheer goes up from the workers as a group of farm women come into view laden with baskets of bread and a keg of fresh cider. Within minutes everyone has settled down under the shade of Samuel's oak tree, and in the translucent light cider is poured, bread is cut into tough little chunks, and people massage their aching limbs. The farmer sits glumly on his tractor, nursing a mug of tea and eating bacon sandwiches from a wax paper parcel. Rosa sloshes some cider into two tin mugs, sits on her jumper next to Samuel and hands one to him. They both drink long from the cool liquid, which is fresh, thick and dusky, and has specks of apple floating in it. Immediately Rosa feels light-headed, and Samuel does too, a little. Someone is singing Mademoiselle from Armentières again, and a group of schoolboys are lying around a bouncy-looking Land Girl, making her laugh and throwing handfuls of grass into her hair. Two girls are practising kisses on each other's arms. Suddenly Rosa looks up to see the ruddy-faced lad standing over her, silhouetted against pure blueness.

—Mind if I sit down? he asks, his voice stretched by the Norfolk tongue.

—Please yourself, says Rosa with forced nonchalance, and reaches for another hunk of bread.

—Don't mind if I do, says the boy, sitting down. My name's Roddy, what's yours?

—Rosie, says Rosa reluctantly, and this is Samuel.

—Charmed, I'm sure. You've got a funny accent, lass. Not a Hun spy, are we? Better watch me careless talk.

—Don't be stupid, says Samuel, she's Polish. And your own accent isn't exactly college-and-peerage either.

—All right, bruiser, settle down, says Roddy, taking another swig of cider, the sun glinting off the edge of his tin mug. Can't be too careful these days. Keep mum she's not so dumb and all that. Pass the bread, love.

—There's none left here, says Samuel defensively. You'll have to look in that basket.

—I was addressing the foreign lady not the posh town-boy, says Roddy, locking his dull eyes on Samuel. What right have you to be drinking our cider, anyway? I've had my eye on you, lazing about in the sun while the rest of us work our arses off.

—He was wounded in France, says Rosa boldly, his wound is making for him pain.

The boy sniffs.

—Making for him pain? That's rich, he says. Don't look too bad to me. What did you do, leave the cork out your Molotov cocktail?

—The doctor wants for him to rest, says Rosa, flushing. Can't you see the bandage?

But Roddy has lost interest; he turns away and makes a grab for the bread basket.

Just then there is a thunder of engines, and a cluster of black silhouettes appear in the sky. Everyone gets to their feet. The silhouettes bank and swoop, then the sound of machine-gun fire spatters through the blueness. Cheering breaks out among the boys. One plane cuts away and dives low over the fields before disappearing over the horizon. Smoke springs up from another; it corkscrews off to the west before nose-diving into a distant field with a thud. A cloud of smoke rises gently into the unmoving air.

—That was one of theirs, shouts Roddy.

—No it wasn't, says Samuel quietly, but the celebrations are already under way.

The remaining planes bank and disappear.

—Right then, shouts the farmer, twisting round in his tractor seat, that's enough lying around. Back to work the lot of you. There's a war on in case you hadn't noticed.

Roddy lumbers to his feet, drains his mug and directs a wink at Rosa.

—It's you and me in the field again, he says. You'll be a bit nicer this time, won't you?

—Come on, says Samuel, drawing Rosa behind the tree, those lot really are the limit. Damned locals. Let's scarper. They won't miss you for one afternoon, won't even notice probably.

—I can't, says Rosa guiltily.

—Come on, Samuel replies, waving away her doubts like insects. Let's get your bicycle and go for an adventure.

—God.

—Nobody believes in God. Come on.

They thread their way furtively past the farm women who are gathering up the mugs and baskets, and trot down the other side of the bank in the sunshine. Samuel notices Rosa's anxious expression.

—Relax, he says, everybody deserves a day off once in a while, otherwise we're as bad as the Germans. Come on.

They hurry along the fence at the edge of the field, Samuel's shoes skidding in the dry mud, their gas masks bumping on their backs.

—Hold on, says Rosa, I'm leaving behind my jumper.

—Never mind, says Samuel, throwing his face back to face the sun and breaking into a hobbling run, never mind, never mind, never mind!

All at once Rosa feels liberated, weightless, as if she might float away over the treetops and disappear into the sky. She stumbles, grabs Samuel's shirt-tails and starts to giggle – Samuel begins to laugh as well, and the two of them run as best they can until they reach the bicycle.

—Must stop laughing, says Samuel, it's agony for my wound.

He perches on the handlebars as Rosa strains to get the bicycle moving, pressing on the pedals with all her weight; finally the bicycle gathers momentum and she steers past the farmhouse, past a group of chickens that scatter noisily in the yard, through the open stile and out onto the track, where they laugh again into the shimmering air.

—Stop laughing, please, stop laughing, says Samuel, his black hair streaming in the wind, you'll be the absolute death of me.

—Where are we going? says Rosa.

—I don't know, how about Cromer?

—Cromer?

—Yes, Cromer. A warm, still seaside nest. That's Swinburne.

—Why there?

—It would be fun. We could go crab fishing. And it sounds like Kremer.

—All right, says Rosa, the sensation of freedom returning, which way to go?

—How am I supposed to know, says Samuel, shouting above the wind. Anyway, all roads lead to Cromer, don't you know.

They ride on for a while until the bicycle slides smoothly round a bend in the path and joins the coastal road. Samuel calls to passers-by, asking them directions; a spunky-looking soldier assures them they are on the right track. Rosa pedals on and on, and the fields spread out around them, mile after flat mile, dotted with hamlets and poppies and villages; in the distance planes are still darting above the earth in dogfights.

—I can't believe I am running away, laughs Rosa as they speed on in the direction of Cromer, this is your fault. They'll be having my guts for starters.

—Garters, not starters, shouts Samuel over his shoulder. It's not easy for me either, I'll have you know, these handlebars are hurting my arse.

As they travel on, Rosa begins to worry about her conversation with that man, Roddy; she must be more careful, her accent may give her away, she wouldn't want a policeman knocking on the door and taking her away as an enemy alien, not now.

3

Eventually they arrive in Cromer, a Victorian seaside resort with bluff-turreted hotels and a pier jutting into the sea. They dismount and walk through the sandbagged streets, Rosa wheeling the bicycle by her side, Samuel massaging his behind. Bomb-blasts can be seen more frequently as they near the centre; a gang of men are working on ladders to repair a gaping roof, seagulls circling above their heads; people queue patiently at salvage sales; the front of the post office has been blasted, and the church looks in a sorry state.

—This is fun, says Samuel. I haven't had this much fun in ages.

—Your wound is making for you pain? asks Rosa.

—Look, says Samuel, the Regal. Let's go to the pictures. Oh, they're showing *Foreign Correspondent*. That's the countryside for you, always behind the times. I'll pay.

—You mustn't. Too much money for you. Crab fishing is fine.

—I want to. Think of it as an early birthday present. How old are you going to be?

—Eighteen.

—Exactly. Far too young. Now let's join the queue. If it stretches past Woolworth's we'll never get in.

Samuel pays one and sixpence for the balcony, and they settle down in the springy velvet seats. They sit through the B picture, then the Pathé news, then finally the main feature starts: blasting horn section, swelling strings, dramatic images of a wind-swept Holland. Rosa and Samuel sit together in the dark womb of the cinema, clutching the arms of their seats as the picture opens with a gruesome murder. They cringe as the assassin plunges off the tower of Westminster Cathedral, gasp as a U-boat shells a British plane, and look on in wonderment as Jones proposes to Carol in the midst of a raging storm; the German soldiers on the screen appear comical, with stiff uniforms and funny accents. Rosa's mind wanders, her heaviness seeps to the surface, and she finds herself thinking of her family. Since war broke out she has received only intermittent letters via the Red Cross, with sentences and even paragraphs blacked out by the censor; in the latest her parents indicated that they may be moving, they do not yet have their new address but will forward it as soon as they can; these letters, blunted by the censor, only reinforce the sense that her family are images from a hazy past, unconnected to her life, now, in England.

By the time Samuel and Rosa emerge blinking from the cinema, borne along in a crowd of off-duty troops, Rosa's heaviness has sunk back into a subterranean level of her mind; Cromer looks golden and beautiful, and it feels good to be with Samuel, doing something, for once, for fun.

—Why don't we go for a stroll along the pier, says Samuel. I'll buy some buns from that bakery and then we'll— hang on, we'd better be back by seven or Mother and Father will know we've been out.

—Yes, never mind the pier, Rosa replies.

—Very well, but you can't be expected to pedal on an empty stomach, says Samuel, and disappears into the bakery.

Rosa hangs her gas mask box over her shoulder and prepares herself for the long ride home. Then she sits astride the bicycle, the late afternoon bustle of Cromer milling dreamily about her. As the sun slants into her eyes she feels a sense of warmth inside, as if the light is finally filtering through to her core, thawing the ice, dispelling the heaviness a little. Sitting back on the saddle, she looks up at the empty Norfolk skies. Did she really grow up in Berlin? It has only been two years, yet it all seems so distant. How much has she missed, how many family conversations and family arguments and meals and stories? And what horrors are her family experiencing now, this moment, as she tastes this happiness with Samuel? Ah, she has forgotten even how to remember them! Every night she has cried until she is numb, yearned for them until they have been reduced to myths, gazed at the photograph for so long that it doesn't mean anything any more; her memories have dislocated themselves from the real people, eclipsed them. It is only during her dreams that Papa, Mama, Heinrich and Hedi truly come back to her, but these days when she sleeps she simply slips into oblivion. And yet, at the same time, her life is only half lived in England, she is not letting herself settle, she is passing the time until the end of the war when she can start living her life again, when these few years will be nothing but a brief, unpleasant interruption.

The buns, when they come, are delicious. They eat by the side of the road, ignoring the disapproving glances from passers-by, then remount the bicycle and set off. Before long they are out of the town; the trees thin as they join the coastal road, and they catch glimpses of the sea as they clank along, cocoa tin rattling between Samuel's legs. Rosa pedals on, and the lighthouse looms into view, proudly prodding the air, blotched with camouflage for the duration.

—Golly, I'm thirsty, calls Samuel over his shoulder.

—Oh, says Rosa, I have a bottle of barley water.

—You're joking, shouts Samuel into the wind, why ever didn't you mention it? Steer up that track, there are some cliffs there, we can have a rest overlooking the sea.

—We must get back, says Rosa hesitantly.

—Don't worry, says Samuel, it will only take a minute.

The track turns into a gravel path as they approach the ridge, and Rosa is forced to dismount. Together they walk the bicycle up to the barren cliffs and stand silhouetted against the vast Norfolk sky, gulls honking overhead, their hair and clothes whipping off to the east, the cliffs punctuated at intervals by gun batteries. The great grey sea stretches out in a boundless circle in front of them, rippling like a flag and grinding its bones against the barbed wire on the shore far below. Samuel lies down in the tough grass; Rosa puts the bicycle on its side, finds the bottle of barley water and lies down beside him, stretching her arms above her head and breathing the sea air deep into her lungs, trying to quell her racing heart. Fresh wind rustles the grass all around.

—I say, thanks for the drink, says Samuel, and also riding all this way. It must be jolly tiring.

—That's my pleasure, Rosa replies.

—I can take over the riding if you like.

—The doctor would not be pleased if you splat.

—Split, says Samuel, not splat.

As they share the barley water, the sound of distant engines can be heard; they look up to see a large blunt-nosed plane approaching over the ocean, surrounded by a group of smaller ones, the size of wasps. The planes bank, cut into the sky and disappear. A gull flaps lazily by.

—Did you see that? says Rosa.

—Bomber, says Samuel tersely. Don't worry, we'll get him in this light.

—Do you think it is safe here? says Rosa.

—Don't worry, Samuel replies, that lot were miles away. Much farther than it looks.

They sit in silence for a while. His name is Samuel, Mama, I think you will like him, he has been like a brother to me; he fought in France, you know, and was wounded terribly, and it got infected but he fought it off, and he helped so much with trying to get you passage to England, and one day we were lying on the grass on the cliffs in Norfolk, these beautiful cliffs overlooking the ocean, and—

—Good picture, wasn't it, says Samuel dreamily. Their shoulders are touching as they lie in the tickly grass. Rosa tells herself to move her arm away.

—Yes, says Rosa, lovely windmills. I do love the Dutchmen.

—When have you ever met a Dutchman? asks Samuel, chuckling.

Rosa thinks for a moment.

—A few years ago, she says tentatively.

—What do you mean?

—When I was coming on the train from Germany. We stopped in Holland. There were on the platform some Dutch women giving to us cocoa and the crackers. For years the cocoa we hadn't tasted.

—I'm somewhat partial to cocoa myself, says Samuel.

There is a pause. The breeze drifts in from the sea, mingling with the warmth of the sun on their skin; the ocean whispers roughly to itself far below them.

—What's Germany like? says Samuel. I mean what's it really like?

—I don't know. As a child it was very nice.

—Do you think of your family much? You never mention them.

—I do, says Rosa, all the time.

—Do you know where they are?

—Not really.

She manages to roll onto her side, bunching her hair under her to prevent it from stringing in the wind; she is facing Samuel now, and their hearts quicken.

—It's a funny thing, war, says Samuel.

—Funny?

—Yes, funny. You know, strange.

—Do you think it will one day end? says Rosa.

—I bleeding well hope so. Shame the Frogs couldn't hold their own, though. He stops and groans softly.

—Does your wound make for you pain? says Rosa.

—Sometimes.

—No, I mean now.

—A little. Hang on, my barbiturates.

He twists his body to the side, fumbles in his pocket and administers himself a dose. Then he turns back to Rosa, his hair springing upwards towards the heavens in the breeze.

—I am a little afraid of your wounds, says Rosa.

—I'm a little afraid of yours, Samuel replies.

He takes her hand and places it softly on his stomach. She can feel the bandage beneath her fingers.

—Does that make for you pain? she says.

—It's fine, says Samuel.

Our sages recommend maintaining a distance of at least four cubits from members of the opposite sex; there were one or two girls during his time in the army, French girls, but nothing remotely like this.

—Have you ever been kissed before? says Samuel, pushing his words through a barrier of nervousness.

Rosa shakes her head, suddenly tingling all over her body. Samuel cups his hands round her neck and draws her lips to his. They kiss under the sky, amongst the wild grass on top of the lofty cliffs, with the noise of the ocean beating the shore below. Samuel's body slowly slips towards hers, and the bicycle wheel ticks round quietly in the breeze.

—I'm sorry, says Rosa, pulling suddenly away, I don't know, I am trembling.

—I know, says Samuel, very well. Let's just hold hands.

—I can't.

There is a pause, and a light breeze fills the space between them.

—You mustn't love me, says Rosa at last. I won't be here for long.

—What do you mean?

—After the war has ended I will be with my parents again.

Samuel thinks for a moment.

—Well, I jolly well look forward to meeting them.

Rosa gives Samuel a startled look – then looks back up at the sky. Silence falls, and time passes, and her emotions fold one over the other inside. Suddenly her life in Germany is more than just a dream. Her family are more than just fantasies. They are people who one day might stand in the same room as Samuel, Papa could shake him by the hand, and Mama could kiss his cheek, and Heinrich could teach him handball, and Hedi could sit on his knee; and her life in England is more than a temporary episode where nothing she does can have a lasting result. As she lies there quietly beneath the vast Norfolk sky, her family become real again, and a fresh pain grows in her heart, and she turns to look at Samuel and feels an overwhelming love for him; and all at once she feels rooted in England.

4

When Mimi and Gerald are next out for the day, Rosa sneaks back from the fields to be with Samuel. They make themselves a jug of lemonade. For a while they sit in the pair of armchairs that belong to Mimi and Gerald, but it soon becomes clear that they are play-acting adults, and they feel uncomfortable, and exposed, as if at any moment the secret of their love might be discovered, even though neither of them has mentioned it since Cromer.

So they go upstairs, carrying their glasses, and decide to sit in Samuel's bedroom, where it is brightest and there is the most space. Rosa sits by the window, and Samuel lies on the bed on account of his wound – the infection is coming back, and worsening; Doctor Ashfield is considering changing the medication. The aroma of freshly cut grass is carried in upon the breeze through the window, and Rosa breathes it deeply. Her nerves cause her to laugh at everything Samuel says, even when it is not meant to be funny. Suddenly Samuel seems so far away there on the bed, the distance between them is unbearable. Here is a person who knows her intimately and loves her nevertheless, and his love tempers the pain of her family's absence, and it feels somehow disjointed to have a physical separation from the person to whom she is closest. So she crosses to his bed, and he takes her hand and draws her closer, and they kiss with trembling lips, the bitter lemon is still on his tongue, and everything falls away, all barriers and hesitancies and awareness of themselves; and in a fog of mouths and skin and slipping fingers they become absorbed, and the pleasure is such that it is indistinguishable from pain, like water that is so hot it could be cold; but they rein themselves in before the full sexual act has occurred and then it is over, and the feverishness evaporates and they lie quietly for a while, until the ravens of guilt land heavily upon them.

5

By the autumn, things have changed. The branches of the apple tree click against Rosa's window, the curtain above her bed moves slightly in a draught, and outside the call of birds can be heard. Her eyelids flutter in the light and she groans into her pillow; her chest tightens. She rolls her head to the side and squints at the clock, well at least I managed to get two hours, that's the most sleep I've had for days, in a single stretch at least. It is cold and she feels suddenly nauseous, she looks around at the room's age-mellowed contours as if they will somehow soothe her – is she imagining it, or are the gentle dips and curves moving slowly, pulsing like an organic thing? She closes her eyes again.

Rosa does not want to move from her bed, she wants to stay in bed forever, she wants to die there. She knows that she must swing her legs out into the cold and stand, feel the rough wooden floorboards under her feet, make her way downstairs and start the housework. But she does not move, lying exhaustedly on her back, her mind prickling with anxiety. Her hand falls over the side of the mattress, the fingers brushing the gnarled floorboards and coming to rest inches from where, in the shadows beneath the bed, there sits her painted wooden box, inside which is the following hurried note:

19. August 1941
Meine liebe Rosa,

So far we are still together, and as it turns out still in Berlin. We thought we were being relocated, but it turned out to be a false alarm. Many people are being relocated to the east, the rumour is to Poland. We don't know how long it will be before we are also relocated. I am sorry we cannot write more. We hope you are happy and will see you again once this is all over.

With all my love,
Mama (also Papa, Heinrich and Hedi)

There is a knock at the door.
—Rosa? Come on now, says Mimi.
—I am just getting up, Rosa replies weakly.
—You're ill, aren't you, says Mimi impatiently, her voice muffled by the wood.
—Not at all, says Rosa, I'm just a little tired.
—I can't wait any longer. We have to go to synagogue or we'll miss the service. Don't forget, the kitchen requires a thorough clean, and the shabbos lunch needs preparing.
—Yes, Aunt Mimi, says Rosa, in a moment I shall be down.
—Samuel's wound is hurting him horribly this morning. The infection has set in, and he hasn't the strength to accompany us. He's to stay in bed, and you mustn't bother him. Do you hear?
—Yes, Aunt Mimi.
Mimi, on the other side of the door, rubs her knuckles anxiously but is unsure of what else to say; after a time she retreats downstairs and stands before the mirror in the hall, where she puts the finishing touches to her hat: she has pinned it at a forty-five-degree angle in the style of the Duchess of Kent, and although lacking a feather it matches perfectly her flowing beige overcoat with its glittering brooch and foxtail muffler. In the shadows beneath her skirts can be seen two stout brown shoes, lying on the

floorboards like Brazil nuts, and in the folds of her overcoat, dangling from her shoulder, nestles her embroidered gas mask bag. When her husband emerges from the kitchen, Mimi makes the final adjustments to her outfit and turns to face him, hoping for a compliment.

—Well don't just stand there, says Gerald, opening the front door and putting on his homburg.

—Oh dear, maybe I should stay, says Mimi. It does worry me to leave them alone.

—Nonsense, says Gerald abruptly, it's Shabbos Shuvah, Reverend Fabritz is making a special sermon. Now come along, Harry'll be waiting.

As they leave the cottage Gerald reaches up to the mezuzah on the doorpost, kisses his fingers, then makes his way past the hedge and down the lane. In two days' time it will be Yom Kippur, when the judgement will be sealed for the coming year – how many will pass from the earth and how many will be created, who will rest and who will wander, who will be impoverished and who will be enriched, who will be degraded and who will be exalted – yes, just two days left to overturn the evil decrees, and now he's late for synagogue. What's more he'll be making Harry late too, and if he leaves without them they'll miss the service altogether. The weather is colder than it looks; a dusting of frost clings to the hedgerows, the sky stretches out crisp and blue above, and rubbery brown leaves lie in clumps along the lane.

—Harry'll have gone by now, mutters Gerald.

—No he won't, says Mimi, he'll wait five minutes.

—What I wouldn't give for a cigarette now.

—Not on shabbos, says Mimi, out of breath.

—Oh, give over, replies Gerald. Just said I fancied one, that's all.

They approach the bridge, gas masks bobbling, and Harry is waiting dutifully for them, blowing into his hands. He doesn't mention the fact that they're late. They wish him good shabbos, climb into his contraption – a home-made light weight motorcar with bars for your feet – and make themselves as comfortable as possible. Gerald's face is grim and overcast; Mimi knows from experience that when her husband falls silent it is best not to disturb him until his mood has blown itself out. The autumn countryside flicks past outside, heads turn as they phut by, three Jews in a home-made contraption, quite a sight for Norfolk even in the topsy-turvy days of wartime.

As soon as the front door slams, Rosa breathes a deep sigh and walks out onto the landing, huddled in her dressing gown. She puts her head to one side and listens. The cottage is completely quiet. A little furtively, she makes her way along the corridor and listens at Samuel's door. There is nothing but silence within, textured by the quiet rustle of the breeze.

—Samuel, she whispers, are you awake? Samuel?

No answer. She walks back along the sloping floorboards and down the stairs, but when she gets to the kitchen she stops; an overpowering odour of cholent stew, special for shabbos, hangs heavily in the air. Her stomach contorts, then opens violently. She is just able to make it to the back door, can't get to the outhouse in time, not even to the rubbish pile; when the vomit gulps forth it is into the vegetable patch, Gerald's victory garden.

Eventually the spasms cease and she sits back on the grass, gasping in the frosty air. Shielding her eyes against the sun, she looks up at the undulating flint wall of the cottage. There is no movement in Samuel's window. She wonders if he heard her being sick, wonders if he is even there at all. Chintz curtains hang in his window like tongues, lapping gently in the draught. She lowers her head, and for the first time that morning water builds up in her eyes as a cluster of sycamore seeds blow clumsily past her.

6

—Samuel?

—Yes?

Finally an answer. Rosa tries the handle but it does not move.

—Your parents have gone to synagogue, she says.

There is a pause, then the sound of movement inside the room, then the door is unlocked and flung open. Samuel stands in the doorway, framed by brightness, his shirt and hair unkempt, his eyes red-rimmed and dark. Immediately they fall into embrace, Samuel pushing his lips against Rosa's curls and swaying slightly, Rosa pressing her forehead against his chest. Their hair mingles, the black and the brown; for a while they do not speak.

—Do you have pain today? asks Rosa after a time.

—I'm managing all right.

—Your wound is getting worse.

—Seems that way. It's the infection. I've taken up praying again.

—But you don't believe in the God.

—I need all the help I can get.

—You're joking.

—Might be.

Samuel walks back into his room and collapses onto the bed. Rosa sits down next to him on the creaking mattress, the breeze cooling her neck. The blankets are twisted and she smooths them absent-mindedly.

—How's your sickness? says Samuel.

—Still the same, Rosa replies.

He tries to roll over.

—Ah, bugger it.

—Pain?

—Just a twinge.

—Where are your barbiturates? says Rosa.

—Run out, Samuel replies. Doctor Ashfield's bringing some more on Monday.

—Monday? But that is a long time. Can he not come sooner?

—Apparently not.

—Samuel, you mustn't be too proud. You need barbiturates. Maybe the doctor can come tonight.

Samuel kisses Rosa's hand, gets awkwardly to his feet and crosses to the bookshelf. He scans the spines as if seeking a volume, but makes no move to pluck one from the shelf.

—It's the Aseres Yemei Teshuvah, he says over his shoulder, the Ten Days of Repentance. That means we've two days left until Yom Kippur, when the final judgement will be sealed.

Rosa walks over to him and lays her palms lightly on his chest.

—I just wish we could have done it properly, he continues, you know, got married and everything. I hate feeling ashamed, and I hate you feeling ashamed.

They stand for a few moments, holding each other close, the ancient floorboards creaking beneath their feet. Rosa is reminded of how his bedroom used to appear to her – so intimidating – and the bed so private, so alien.

—It is worse for me. I have betrayed your parents, says Rosa. I don't deserve to live here any more.

—Of course you do.

—My own parents, says Rosa, if they knew . . .

—Look, we'll get married. After the war, your parents will be over-joyed. You'll see. And my parents will be all right too, once they get used to the idea. Once we are married and respectable.

—Then why don't you tell them? says Rosa. If you wait much longer it will only make things worse.

—I'll tell them after Yom Kippur, Samuel replies. I promise.

He pauses, rubbing the bridge of his nose between thumb and fore-finger.

—The main thing is, he says, that we love each other. It will be splendid. I will make sure it will be splendid. It will be grand.

He flinches again, then sits down heavily on the bed. The mattress creaks, and he groans.

—Pain again? says Rosa.

—The old cut's been giving me gip, says Samuel, his voice somewhat restricted. I think I must have been overdoing it. And this infection is irrepressible. Just when the doctor thinks it's easing off . . .

—Lie down and I'll bring you tea, says Rosa, helping him into bed.

—Oh, don't, says Samuel. I can't take any more of that dandelion and burdock swill.

—From this week's ration I have a pinch of tea still, says Rosa. You can have that.

—You're very kind, says Samuel, pressing his face into the pillow. And my ointment's in the bathroom, if you wouldn't mind. That might help a bit.

—Of course, says Rosa. I shan't be long.

—I love you, says Samuel suddenly.

Rosa stops and turns towards him. His dark eyes are burning with an intensity she hasn't seen before. Sycamore seeds rise and fall in the breeze outside, tapping softly against the window.

—I love you also, she says.

7

At last everything is ready for the shabbos meal, the goblet for the prayer over the wine, the bread under its traditional cover, the thin soup, the cholent stew made with vegetables from the victory garden, the apple compote for pudding, made from the rough-skinned apples from the orchard. They haven't had meat since the start of the war, to get kosher meat in north Norfolk is impossible; they tend to swap their bacon coupons for fish, but if the fishmonger is out of stock nothing can be done. Rosa sets to work cleaning the kitchen and putting out the cutlery.

After a time Gerald and Mimi return, and the family take their places at the table. To some extent Samuel's ointment has worked, the pain is still there but he's feeling a little better. Gerald conducts the rituals over the wine and the bread, and then they settle down to eat. Rosa takes a deep breath, holds it and goes into the kitchen to fetch the tureen of soup; she brings it into the dining room, places it on the side and tries to serve without inhaling its aroma. As she stirs with the ladle, and the kreplach dumplings bob and sink in the cloudy liquid, she begins to feel queasy again.

—I'm sorry, she says, and hurries out of the back door and into the outhouse.

—Call of nature, says Gerald.

—She's unwell by the looks of things, says Mimi.

—Not to worry, I'll take over, says Samuel, getting up to serve the soup.

—You sit down, says Mimi, you're an invalid.

After a few minutes Rosa comes back into the room; the atmosphere is tense and her soup is no longer steaming. She takes her place, closes her eyes, swallows hard, forcing the soup down. As the meal wears on, Rosa is dimly aware of a conversation over whether or not the man in the post office is Jewish, he's not Jewish, well he looks Jewish, but his wife's as Caucasian as they come, maybe he has some Jewish blood in him somewhere along the line, come on, there's more Jewishness in my little finger than in the whole of East Anglia. Rosa sinks into a somnambulant state, tapping the table absently with her fingernails, looking out of the window at the garden where grass can be seen swaying on top of the Anderson shelter, outlined against the apple trees. The movement makes her queasy, and she averts her eyes. At a nod from Mimi she clears up the soup bowls, avoiding Samuel's gaze, and goes through to the kitchen to serve the cholent, steeling herself as best she can against the smell. But it is no use.

—The girl's dashed to the outhouse again, says Gerald.

—She must be jolly ill, says Mimi. I knew she was ill when I woke her this morning.

—I'll serve the cholent, says Samuel.

—You'll do nothing of the sort, says Mimi. I've told you before, you're an invalid.

—Someone had better go and see if she's all right, says Gerald.

—Don't let's disturb her, says Samuel. It'll be an upset stomach I shouldn't wonder.

Mimi gives her son a strange look as she gets up from her seat to serve; the family eat in silence until eventually Rosa returns.

—Rosa, my dear, says Gerald, are you unwell?

—There is maybe something bad with my stomach.

—Shall we call a doctor? asks Gerald.

—That won't be necessary, says Samuel.

—Are you sure it's your stomach, Rosa, says Mimi, or is the smell of the food making you sick?

Rosa and Samuel exchange glances, and Mimi raises her eyebrows.

—Is there something you would like to tell us, Rosa? she says quietly.

There is a pause that seems to last forever. Gerald peers up from his cholent, fork poised in the air, small droplets tumbling from the prongs and rejoining the stew in the bowl. Rosa looks silently at Mimi, and Samuel studies the table.

—Yes, says Rosa finally, I think maybe there is something we need to tell.

—We? repeats Mimi.

—Yes, we, says Rosa, me and Samuel.

Samuel still does not look up from the table; from his neck a scarlet smudge is beginning to creep across his face.

—Well, what is it? Samuel? Tell me, says Mimi, gripping a napkin tight between her fingers.

—I think . . . no, I don't think, I know . . . that is . . . says Samuel.

—I am sick because I am going to have a baby, says Rosa finally.

There is a tense silence.

—A baby, exclaims Gerald at last, a baby? When?

—Knew it, says Mimi quietly.

—I'm sorry, says Rosa, her voice wavering.

Gerald gets up from his seat, walks across to the window, unfolds and refolds the bread cloth, returns to his chair and sits down, rubbing his beard roughly.

—Oh, this takes the biscuit, he says at last. What an absolute disgrace. We've taken you into our house, given you a roof over your head, and this is how you repay us, with I don't know what, with nothing but lewdness and immorality. Otto and Inga we were doing a favour, they are fine people. But you . . . how shameful, he says, shaking his head.

—I can't believe it, whispers Mimi.

—Dare I ask the identity of the lucky father? says Gerald.

Rosa takes a deep breath but no words will come. She gestures towards Samuel and looks down at the tablecloth.

There is another stunned silence, more profound than before. Mimi and Gerald's eyes fix on their son, who by now has gone completely red.

—My son, tell me this is not true, says Gerald. She's lying. Tell me she's lying.

—I'm not, says Rosa. We're getting married.

—Silence, Gerald retorts. When I wish to address this wanton girl I shall do so.

—Keep quiet, Rosa, says Mimi, don't make a scene.

—A scene? splutters Gerald. I think we have a scene already, do we not? He turns to Samuel again.

—I want to hear it from you, Samuel, my son, he says. Be honest now. True or false?

Another solid silence stretches out second by second.

—Samuel . . . says Rosa.

—Will you shut up! shouts Gerald, hitting the table with his palm. A glass, upended by the blow, smashes on the floor.

—Calm down, dear, says Mimi, we'd do better dealing with this calmly.

—How can I calm down when two days before Yom Kippur my son stands accused of fathering a bastard? says Gerald. He removes his hat and passes his hand over his face. Samuel, tell me it is not true. Tell me she's lying.

Samuel raises his eyes and looks his father full in the face.

—Father, he says, it's true. I'm sorry. But it isn't just . . . we are in love. We wish to marry. I'm sorry.

Gerald stares at his son, his lips struggling to settle. Samuel lowers his eyes again.

—Have you forgotten who you are, my son? says Gerald at last.

Samuel does not reply.

—I am sorry, says Rosa again.

—You keep your mouth shut, you dirty shikse! shouts Gerald.

Rosa reacts as if she has been hit by an electric charge and buries her face in her hands.

—I wish to converse with my wife in private, says Gerald, his voice repressed and hoarse, at a shabbos table free from impurity. Go upstairs, both of you, to your rooms. To your own rooms, yes? And if you talk to each other, if I hear so much as a single word, I will throw you both out of the house and you shall never come back, by God's name I swear it. Go on, what are you waiting for? Go on.

Like chastened children Rosa and Samuel get to their feet, their chairs scraping loudly on the floor, and leave the room. Rosa follows Samuel up the stairs; when they get to the landing she tries to catch his eye, but his gaze is downcast. He enters his room and shuts the door behind him. Rosa goes into hers, closes the door and lies on the bed, pressing her face into the pillow.

8

It is almost an hour before her sobs subside and Rosa lifts her head. The shadows have lengthened on the wall, and the light has grown yellow; through the floorboards, Gerald and Mimi can still be heard in discussion. She raises herself awkwardly to a sitting position, creases fanning out around her in the blankets, and cleans her face with a handkerchief. Her face is swollen and flushed, her eyes are bloodshot, yet the pain itself has not changed; the notion of feeling better after a good cry, which seemed such wisdom when she was a child, has over these past few years become absurd. She gets to her feet, tidies her clothes and her hair, tries to regain some composure. Then she crosses to the window, heaves at the sash and plunges her face into the cold air. The orchard lies beneath her, and beyond that a range of stubbly flats stretches towards the sea and the horizon. She rests her hands on the outside wall, feeling the cool, craggy flint beneath her palms, seeking to be stabilised by its ancientness and solidity. Inside she can feel the baby moving, or is it her imagination, after all she is not even slightly rounded yet, but she can certainly feel something; overwhelmed by a desire to protect it, she cups her hands over her belly. She peers left, along the wall, towards Samuel's window, willing him to open it, to look out, to see her. She waits, but he does not come.

After a time, she wraps her mother's cashmere shawl round her shoulders and sits in the wooden chair, watching the elderly sycamore beating its head against the breeze, moving on its root. There is the dry call of a rook, and then a cloud of them appear; black socks buffeted by the wind, they settle on the telegraph wires stretched between the poles along the lane beyond the hedgerow. Rosa's emotions have settled now, she feels numb and thick-headed from all the crying, heavy with shame, mired in a bovine docility. Yet as time passes, and her head is cleared by looking out into the brilliant freshness of the autumn sky, her thoughts begin to churn again. She has been in here for a long time without any food or water, confined to her room like a child, she could just go downstairs, nothing is stopping her; but how can she disobey Gerald and Mimi when her freedom, her very existence, rests on their charity? Ah, perhaps this imprisonment is a good thing, at least if she is shut away in her bedroom there is nobody to witness her degradation; she can stay here, in her room, in the gathering darkness, like an insect. Samuel has not dared to leave his room either; he, who has faced the German guns, fought, nearly died for his country, is afraid to confront his parents, ashamed.

Time passes, and the sun draws rosy hues from the horizon. The baby in her belly stops moving, lies still. She tries to write to her parents, but each time no words will come; then she decides to write to Heinrich and finds herself pouring out her feelings in a letter so long that the postage would be more than she can afford. For almost an hour she writes as the sun curves gently across the sky and shadows turn on their apex. Finally she seals the envelope and places it in her painted box. Then, listlessly, she sits in the chair by the window, looking out across the orchard into the vast expanse of the sky, listening to the occasional sounds of Mimi and Gerald going about their lives downstairs. From time to time she thinks she hears the creak of floorboards in Samuel's room, the shame of it all, the shame – this heaviness will never leave her, she knows it, and what a way to bring a baby into the world.

By nightfall nobody has entered her room, nobody has even come upstairs, and Rosa is starting to feel hungry. She gets to her feet and draws the blackout curtains; the starless night of the countryside is oppressive to her. The room is plunged into darkness; she lights a paraffin lamp. She is numb and stiff from the prolonged period of sitting, and her head feels congested and heavy; she gets to her feet, paces the room, sits down again, gets up, goes to the bed, lies down.

An hour later there are footsteps on the stairs. Rosa sits upright but instead of a knock, something is left outside her room. She waits until all is still, then tentatively opens the door – there in the shadows, on a plate, is a husk of bread with a scrape of butter and a glass of water. Despite herself she picks them up, and before re-entering her room pauses in front of Samuel's bedroom door, willing it to open. As if by magic there is a scuffling sound and the door creaks ajar; Samuel appears, his hair in disarray, his shirt-tails hanging over his thighs and his eyes blotched with red. He stoops to collect his bread and butter, and for a moment Rosa catches his eye – how to describe his expression? Broken, or perhaps breaking, as if each muscle in his face is straining to separate from the rest. Yet in his eyes Rosa thinks she can detect a burning defiance. Without a word Samuel goes back into his room and closes the door, leaving her on the landing in the gloom.

That night Rosa cannot sleep. Rain whips across the cottage, and she lies in bed in the darkness, listening to the sound of distant cannons rumbling over the Norfolk flats. A charge is running through her body, pressing her eyes open and her mind awake. The rain lashes the window like salt, the darkness is a living entity, moving and shifting before her eyes. From time to time sleep attempts to drag her under, but then she is snapped awake again, the electricity in her body combating the sleep as if it were a virus. The carriage clock counts off the hours at a painstaking pace, the house creaks and groans to itself as it ages, and the night gradually passes.

By morning the storm has blown itself out, leaving the world cold and new. Rosa wants to go outside, but still she does not leave her bedroom. Gerald and Mimi will surely call them down today, they can't leave them up here forever. Another husk of bread and butter is deposited outside her door at breakfast time, and when she collects it Samuel is nowhere to be seen. She eats it slowly, with discipline, one bite every half-hour, staring aimlessly out of the window, and the morning trickles away. At lunchtime another husk is delivered, and this time Rosa devours it without hesitation, even though it will not make a difference to her hunger, it will probably make things worse.

Time passes, and the afternoon is threatened by another evening, and the despair of another sleepless night begins to make its descent; Rosa thinks, if nobody has come within the hour, I am going downstairs. There can be nothing worse than this interminable wait, and it is cruel to be left with so little food.

9

Samuel is lying on his bed, his arms wrapped around his bandaged midriff, trying to block out the pain. Our sages tell us that honouring one's father and mother is equivalent to all the other commandments. Since being confined to his room he has thought about the situation myriad times, his anger at being treated like a child, his humiliation, wishing that the clock could be turned back, the frustration and anxiety and distress; the same thoughts have been following each other relentlessly like an awful merry-go-round, but now the ointment has run out, his infected wound has started to throb, the pain has become searing, and he can think of nothing else. And God blessed them, saying, be fruitful, and multiply, and fill the waters in the seas, and let fowl multiply in the earth, and there was evening, and there was morning, the fifth day. Strange to think there is a German, somewhere, who dropped the particular bomb that created the shrapnel that is causing this pain. If Samuel were to meet him, would he rejoice? He might be dead by now. Samuel does not know how he will get through another night, he certainly cannot sleep in this state, and the doctor is not due until tomorrow morning. He can feel with vividness every detail of his rotting wound, every contour and seam and ridge, and when he moves he feels it twist within him, a crease in his side, hardened and sharp.

There is a noise – somebody coming up the stairs, someone outside his door. There is a knock.

—Yes? he says, surprised at the weakness of his voice.

The door opens and his mother enters. She stands still for a moment, gazing at her son; then she sits on the bed and takes his hand.

—You look in a frightful state, she says.

—Are you surprised?

—Where are your barbiturates?

—Run out.

—I'll send for the doctor immediately.

—He is coming tomorrow.

—You don't look as if you can wait until tomorrow. Anyway it's Yom Kippur tomorrow. Father's gone to synagogue already, for Kol Nidre, but I stayed behind to keep an eye on you. Why didn't you tell me you're in so much pain?

—Have you forgotten? We were banished to our rooms.

—Yes, but we didn't realise you were in such a state, says Mimi. You should have come down. You should have told us.

—You should have jolly well checked. You know my wound's playing up, and Rosa's pregnant. You shouldn't have left us languishing in our rooms like a couple of prisoners. I almost came downstairs several times, you know, but each time I thought better of it. I decided to let you have your way. It was stupid to leave us for so long. Stupid and cruel.

There is a pause. Mimi adjusts her headscarf and clears her throat.

—Your father is extremely upset, she says. He can't think straight. He's carrying on about the workhouse at West Beckham.

—The workhouse?

—Yes, he's on about sending Rosa there. Says she should give the baby to someone who wants it. What with the war, and spending so much time in Norfolk, his business has been deteriorating, Samuel. Unless God performs a miracle, we'll be struggling to make ends meet by the end of the month. We cannot afford to pay for a wedding, and certainly not another mouth to feed. There's a war on, Samuel.

—I won't stand for it. I'd rather die than see Rosa sent to the workhouse.

Samuel winces, clutches his bandage and rolls away from his mother; a bitter silence hangs in the air. Then Mimi speaks again, in a softer tone this time.

—You're supposed to ask for forgiveness before Yom Kippur, she says, before the judgement is sealed.

—I've said I'm sorry, says Samuel. I don't know what more you want.

—That's not what I mean, says Mimi. I've been thinking about things myself, I've been praying. And I've realised something. This entire situation, it's my fault.

—What do you mean? says Samuel.

—Oh, it's my fault, it's all my fault, she says, sighing. Ever since Rosa arrived in our house I've done nothing but come between you. I've tried to stop you growing fond of one another, I've been terrified that you would fall in love and stoop to immorality. As it turns out, all I've done is drive you secretly into each other's arms. Here's me galloping about like a bull in a china shop, and I've ended up causing precisely what I was afraid of. That's the reason we left the East End, to get away from those old-fashioned ways of thinking. We could see you were being suffocated, that's why we sent you to Tottenham Grammar. But I've gone and ruined it all.

There is a pause while she adjusts her headscarf again and dabs her eyes.

—The irony is, she continues, Rosa has turned out to be a wonderful girl. She is diligent, loyal, kind . . . she would have been perfect for you, Samuel, if I'd given it a thought. But now my meddling has caused you to make an almighty mess of things.

—I take full responsibility, says Samuel.

—You're young, says Mimi. I know what it's like to be young. And you've been suffering with your wound, and Rosa has been suffering with her parents trapped in Germany. I should have known better. I should have been a better mother, I should have kept my nose out of your affairs, I should have been more tolerant of Rosa. I drove you to it. I'm to blame.

She dabs her eyes again.

—Will you forgive me, she says, will you ever be able to forgive me?

Samuel raises himself on his elbows, and Mimi takes him in her arms, rubbing his back the way she used to when he was a child.

—You and Rosa still have your future ahead of you, she says into his shoulder, when the war's over you could still get married, have children and be happy. If only it wasn't for this small obstacle.

—That's one way of putting it.

—I'm going to find a way round it for you, she says, don't you worry. I'll make everything all right.

—What about Father?

—Don't worry about Father. I know how to deal with him. She pulls herself together and gets to her feet.

—First things first, she says, your barbiturates. We can't have you lying here in pain all evening. I'll send for Doctor Ashfield straight away. And while he's at it, I'll have him examine Rosa too. There are procedures that doctors carry out when girls fall pregnant.

Samuel looks up at her from his bed, still feeling like a child. His mother is looking at him knowingly.

—Procedures? he says.

—Yes, procedures. You know, pregnancy procedures. Ladies' matters. Samuel nods.

—I love you, my darling, says Mimi. Everything will be all right.

The door closes and her footsteps descend the stairs. Samuel turns onto his back, gasping with pain, and presses the heels of his hands over his eyes.

10

Rosa lies on her back in her bed, watching a funnel of shadow flicker on the ceiling. Several times she has walked to the door, laid her hand upon the handle, but each time something has stopped her; for a while now she has been lying in bed, anticipation building inside her, anticipation for she knows not what.

And then a new sound can be heard downstairs, a male voice alternating with Mimi's, one that Rosa does not recognise. Her sense of anticipation becomes almost unbearable, she is sure that this man has something to do with her, she tries to dismiss the thought, tells herself she is being paranoid; she feels sick to her stomach and thinks she can feel the baby moving, side to side, crouching, curling up protectively like a hedgehog. She rests her hands on her belly, and her breathing is short; individual words, sentences, snatches of conversation float up from below, Mimi is mentioning tea, the man is declining, they are discussing the weather and the war, nothing out of the ordinary, apart from the fact that this is a Sunday evening, and it is the night of Yom Kippur, and by no means a normal time to entertain.

Now the man's voice has left the hall and is sliding along beneath the floorboards towards the stairs. He and Mimi are in earnest discussion but their tones are hushed now, nothing can be made out. Now footfalls on the stairs, four feet like an animal, like a horse, a pantomime horse climbing the stairs, the front half talking to the behind in whispers, suppressed whispers, the sound of a gas mask box tapping against the wall, the floorboards creaking, and now they have arrived on the landing, they are almost outside her door, they are outside her door, will they knock, no, they pass by, it is Samuel's room they are after. The sound of them knocking, of the door opening.

—Samuel? comes Mimi's voice. Doctor Ashfield is here.

—Come in, says Samuel.

—Ah Samuel, says the doctor, I came immediately when I heard. The wound is playing up, is it?

The door closes and the voices become muffled. Something doesn't seem right. Rosa has never liked Doctor Ashfield, his striking ugliness, the eyes that seem to have been pressed too high into the forehead, creating a wrinkled, overhanging brow tufted with black eyebrows, the lumpen and shapeless nose, and the sallow cheeks which flap like sails as the over-full lips twist around their words. He is a hairy man, and his voice sounds hairy too, as if his larynx is lined with fur; it is a gruff yet smooth voice, a lilting, persuasive voice, a voice in which even the sincerest of sentiments sound false.

The conversation continues in Samuel's room. What is happening, what was Mimi discussing with Samuel earlier, what is the doctor doing? Rosa's sense of anticipation grows into anxiety, nervousness, nausea, she tries to pull herself together, she knows she is being paranoid. The funnel of shadow on the ceiling darkens as night draws in; she gets to her feet, stands for a moment, closes the curtains. Then she lights the paraffin lamp.

After a time Mimi and the doctor can be heard leaving Samuel's room, bidding him good night and coming along the landing. There are whispers outside her room, followed by a knock at the door. She pauses, unsure whether her ears have deceived her; there is another knock.

—Yes? she says.

—Only me, comes Mimi's voice, may I come in?

Her voice is cheerful, sing-song, and something does not seem right, after all Rosa has been isolated for more than a day; perhaps Mimi is labouring under a façade of politeness, keeping up appearances for the doctor.

—Come in, says Rosa.

The door opens and Mimi enters the room, smiling awkwardly. She turns to Doctor Ashfield who is standing like a shadow behind her.

—If you wouldn't mind just waiting outside for a moment, she says, there is a comfy chair just over there. I shan't be long.

—Certainly, comes the doctor's fur-lined voice. I shall be here when you need me.

Mimi closes the door behind her, and a quietude settles in the room.

—Rosa, she says, I am sorry we have left you in here so long. Uncle Gerald is very upset. He's gone to synagogue now, but he's very upset.

Rosa does not reply.

—Shall we sit down? says Mimi, gesturing towards the bed.

They sit on the bed side by side, as if on a train, and Rosa is struck by the absurdity of the scene.

—Why is the doctor here? she says.

Mimi clears her throat.

—I sent for him to examine Samuel, he's been in terrible pain. The doctor has prescribed him some stronger medicine. I thought you could do with a once-over at the same time, she says.

—I could do with some food, says Rosa.

—Of course, Mimi replies, I will get you something nice in a moment. But first I want to say one or two things.

She pauses, smoothing her skirt and gathering her thoughts.

—As you know, she begins, Gerald and I have welcomed you whole-heartedly into our family. We have given you a roof over your head and food in your belly for two and a half years. And might I say, during that period you have been a pleasure to live with, an absolute pleasure.

Rosa glances up at her but cannot make out Mimi's expression: she is silhouetted against the glow of the paraffin lamp.

—We have been thinking long and hard, Mimi continues, and we can see that you and Samuel are certainly fond of one another. This may just be an immature infatuation, of course, but it may also be something more serious.

She adjusts her headscarf, compulsively.

—Now, she says, I know that in the past I have not been best pleased with the idea of you and Samuel becoming close. But I think I was wrong about that. There's nothing objectionable about you two getting to know each other, especially as you are nearly eighteen years of age.

And there is nothing objectionable about your getting married, either, in principle. In fact I think it is a good idea. I think you might have a long and happy future together.

Rosa, struggling to understand where this is leading, does not speak.

—The problem, of course, Mimi continues, is that you and Samuel have embarked upon starting a family a little too soon. If you were married already, and Samuel was earning money, and you could support yourselves, it would be wonderful. But you have to understand, Rosa, that Gerald's business has been suffering from the shortages. We are struggling with money, and we can't afford a wedding, or another mouth to feed. Can you understand that?

—I'm sorry, says Rosa.

—Once the war is over, says Mimi, and your family are free and Gerald's business has picked up, we will happily make you a lovely wedding with a proper chupah, and a dinner, and a band, and brides-maids, and everything a girl could want. At the moment, however, things are a little difficult.

—I understand, says Rosa hesitantly, feeling that she understands nothing.

—So what I have in mind, says Mimi, is this. First of all Doctor Ashfield carries out a little procedure. Then we can all start again. You and Samuel can go out together once a week, just the two of you, to a tearoom or something, so long as you are back by blackout. And then, after the war, if you are still fond of one another, you can marry. Your futures will still be ahead of you, Rosa, and they will be wonderful.

—I don't understand, says Rosa, a procedure?

—Yes, yes, says Mimi, I shall explain. Now, biologically speaking, dear, you don't have a baby inside you as such. It is more like a cluster of cells, like a little bit of yoghurt or something. With the right training, certain doctors can flush it out.

—Flush it out? My baby?

—Not your baby, dear. The cluster of cells.

—Cluster of cells?

—Indeed. I have just been speaking to Samuel. He wants a proper future with you, he doesn't want life to be a struggle. He wants to do things properly.

—Samuel wants to marry me. We want to have the baby.

—Of course he does, dear, says Mimi. And you can do that, in your own good time, after the procedure. The procedure will make everything all right, it will give you back your future, it will give you all the time you need.

You must understand, Gerald and I cannot afford to support both of you and a newborn. We have supported you for over two years without a single word of complaint, we have given you everything that we give ourselves, welcomed you into our family, despite the financial drain. You're not a selfish girl, we know that. So now you must do something for us.

—I want to speak to Samuel.

—He's sleeping now, says Mimi, Doctor Ashfield had to give him sleeping pills. The poor boy was in terrible pain. But he's all right now, he's asleep.

Rosa turns away, her mind spinning.

—Shall I tell you a secret, dear? says Mimi.

Rosa turns back to her.

—When I was a girl, I had one of these procedures myself. Looking back, it was the best decision I ever made.

Mimi gets to her feet and opens the door.

—Doctor? she calls. Ready for you now.

Doctor Ashfield enters the room, looking uncomfortable and glancing around. He removes his jacket, rolls up his sleeves, squats over his leather Gladstone bag and opens the catch with a clack.

—All present and correct, he says in his resonant voice, let's get it over with. Mrs Kremer, we will be requiring a bowl of hot water and some towels, if you please.

—But of course, doctor, there is some water heating on the stove, says Mimi and disappears downstairs.

—Now Miss Klein, says the doctor, regarding her with the chimpanzee eyes set high in his forehead, if you would just lie on the bed.

Rosa, sitting, does not move. The doctor is still squatting.

—So far as I am aware, says the doctor, rummaging in his bag, you have a condition that needs to be remedied?

—I am pregnant, says Rosa.

—Ah, says the doctor and winces.

Footsteps can be heard on the stairs, and then Mimi appears balancing a steaming bowl of water and some towels.

—Here we are, she says, was there anything else?

—Yes, says Rosa, getting to her feet. I have not agreed to anything. What is this hot water, these towels? What is all this?

Doctor Ashfield, from his crouching position, looks up sharply at Mimi; the chain of his pocket watch gleams in the light of the paraffin lamp.

—I thought everything was going to be smooth, he says, I can't be getting involved in anything messy.

—Rosa, as we discussed, says Mimi impatiently, this procedure is the very best way forward. This is for your own benefit—

—I wish to speak to Samuel. I wish to speak to him. Does he know what is going on? Have you discussed it with him?

Samuel, in his room, hears voices from across the landing, raised voices, Rosa's voice among them. He is dizzy, woozy from the barbiturates, and having trouble marshalling his thoughts. He gets to his feet, leaves the room and walks out onto the landing, his feet as heavy as in a nightmare, his mouth terribly dry. He turns the handle of Rosa's door and it swings open; in the copper light of the lamp, as if in an oil painting, he sees Rosa sitting on the bed, his mother standing over her and Doctor Ashfield squatting on the floor, looking over his shoulder at the intruder, half obscured by a coil of steam rising from a bowl of water. Samuel squints, shakes his head, trying to clear it.

—Samuel, says Rosa, at last.

—My dear boy, says Mimi, what are you doing out of bed? The doctor said that you must rest.

—I thought I heard something, says Samuel, thick-tongued. What is going on here?

Doctor Ashfield, exasperated, gets to his feet.

—This is a medical procedure, he says. I can't be having all these interruptions. What are you doing out of bed?

—Ah, says Samuel, yes. Ladies' matters. Sorry to interrupt. Carry on.

—You knew about it, says Rosa, you knew?

—Go back to bed, says the doctor, you look as if you're about to pass out. And so you should, given the medication you've taken.

Samuel takes a step back, suddenly the cottage is spinning, Rosa is saying something – he is aware, on the edge of his mind, that she is saying something – he thinks she is addressing him, but he cannot be sure; his eyes are drooping, his mother is taking him by the arm, ushering him from the room, and she is speaking, and there is movement, and then it is dark, and he is in bed, sinking into the mattress, being tucked up like a boy. The covers are being drawn up round his ears, he feels light-headed and disoriented, as if he is floating, and it is not altogether unpleasant, just a procedure, a procedure for pregnant women, ladies' matters, the voices are fading, his bed is spinning, he falls asleep.

Mimi comes back into the room, smoothing her skirt.

—There now, she says, let's get on with it.

—Wait, says Rosa, just wait. I need some time to think. Leave me alone for a moment. Please.

The doctor looks at Mimi, then consults his pocket watch and replaces it in his waistcoat.

—I'm not feeling very confident about this, he says. If it gets messy it could be rather compromising.

—Come now, Mimi replies, she just needs to gather her thoughts, that's all. Why don't we go outside and settle up in advance, I've got the money in my handbag.

They leave the room, closing the door behind them. Rosa paces to the window and back again several times, then sits down heavily on the bed. She is trembling and her face feels hot and shiny, like steel. Dumbfounded, she tries to gather her thoughts. He has betrayed her. Samuel has betrayed her. He knew all about the procedure, he knew; he agreed it behind her back, without consulting her, and then he walked out, leaving her alone, refusing to come back, refusing to talk about it; he has betrayed her. Now what can she do? She must decide, she has only minutes to decide. Papa would tell her to be strong, she must be strong, but how? Should she run away? Where could she go, what would happen to the baby? And what if Samuel is right, what if Mimi is right? They didn't ask for this child, they didn't intend to have it, and it would put a strain on the Kremers, and Mimi did promise that after the war they can marry, and have children, and that would be perfect – ah, perhaps wishing to keep the baby is weak, perhaps she is giving in to her emotions, not thinking clearly. Mimi had this procedure herself, after all, perhaps everyone has it, perhaps it is common in England, perhaps it isn't so bad. A cluster of cells, a cluster of cells. Would it really be strong to— should she run away? No question, she couldn't survive. She has no money, nowhere to live, no family or friends, she would be done for.

Rosa turns to her parents, she can almost see them sitting beside her, Papa with his pipe, serious yet calm, and Mama holding her hand, stroking it with her thumb the way she used to, what are they saying, what are they saying? I cannot hear, thinks Rosa, your words are too faint, I cannot hear your advice. Speak louder, Papa, can you not? Mama, speak louder, I cannot hear. I need to know what you are saying, I need your advice. What should I do, Papa, Mama? Tell me, what should I do?

The door opens and Mimi enters with the steaming bowl of water, followed by a twitchy-looking Doctor Ashfield.

—There now, says Mimi, are you ready, dear? I had to take more water from the stove, the first lot had cooled already. So no messing about now, do you hear?

—Did you really have this procedure yourself, says Rosa, when you were a girl?

Mimi glances awkwardly at the doctor.

—Indeed, she says. Best thing I've ever done.

Doctor Ashfield arranges his jacket carefully on the wooden chair and begins rummaging in his Gladstone bag again. Rosa catches sight of a range of wicked-looking implements, like teeth in the jaws of a whale; the doctor spreads a rubber sheet on the floor and begins arranging his equipment, an orange tube, some medicine bottles. Rosa cannot watch.

—Very well, says Mimi, I'll leave you to it. Let me know if you require anything further, doctor, yes? I'll be downstairs.

With that she leaves the room, closing the door firmly behind her. Doctor Ashfield turns to Rosa, his cheeks creasing around his fleshy lips as he attempts to smile.

—Now, Miss Klein, he says, let's get this over with before I change my mind. There's a war on, you know, money is scarce. Lie down if you please.

Rosa hesitates.

—Lie down, Miss Klein, says the doctor sharply. I haven't got all night. I'm a medical man and I've a job to do.

Rosa does not move. The doctor makes an exasperated noise.

—Good God, he exclaims, you'd better lie down now or I'll jolly well pack up and go home. Then you'll be in trouble.

He takes her by the arm, steers her to the bed, sits her down and swings her legs up onto the mattress. Her heart is racing, she tells herself to resist, but this man is a doctor, and he is taking control, and she is rooted to the spot; she wants to challenge him but no words will come. He crouches once more over his instruments. Perhaps it is a feeling of duty, perhaps it is nothing more than fear; perhaps she is buckling to his air of authority, perhaps she has come to the end of her strength. Trembling, she presses her head into the pillow and does not move. The funnel of shadow has spread across the ceiling, seeping into the corners, no longer a funnel but an opaque rectangle of darkness. She closes her eyes.

II

Another morning breaks. The sun rises upon the village of Northrepps, and in the bedroom window of an ancient, flint cottage a white face looks out, motionlessly watching the dawn. It is Yom Kippur, the Day of Atonement, or as Gerald likes to call it, at-one-ment; he will spend the day in prayer, fasting, not drinking water even, praying for a favourable judgement for the forthcoming year. Mimi, too, will fast, though she will not go to synagogue Samuel and Rosa need to be looked after, she cannot leave them. At the moment, however, as the sun lifts its bloody head inch by inch above the ocean, everyone in the house is in slumber, everyone apart from the white face at the window, looking out at the sun, the distant sea.

Rosa has been awake ever since the barbiturates wore off. In her abdomen there is a hot pain, like a piece of coal embedded, and its malicious heat spreads down through her thighs, her legs and into her feet. She gazes out of the window, in her hands is a folded note, in her mind are images of the baby from the train, and the baby that she might have had, she would have had, if only she had not been so stupid as to mistake weakness for strength. Last night was a mistake, she knew it as soon as she regained consciousness, and now it cannot be undone; a single moment is all it takes to start a life, and a single moment to undo it. She might have been under pressure, unable to think, and Samuel might have betrayed her, and Mimi might have been persuading her, but ultimately she knows it was her weakness that was to blame. Yes, her weakness, but not any more; for she has vowed never again to give in, she has vowed from now on to be strong. She turns the note over in her fingers, resisting the urge to read it again. Painfully she raises herself from her chair and pads quietly around the room, dressing; then, with some effort, she drags her old suitcase from the top of the wardrobe, dusts it off silently and packs. It does not take long, she does not have many possessions; soon the suitcase is filled.

Nothing can be heard save the sound of draughts, the creak of beams. Rosa drops to her knees and feels under the bed, draws out her painted box, looks inside; yes, here are the letters, here is the doll, the watch, all present. She tucks it into the suitcase and fumbles with the buckles, fastening them tightly. Then, wincing from the pain, she takes a final dry-eyed glance around the room and creeps onto the landing.

The shadows are deep and orange, falling fuzzily into each other, and heavy breathing can be heard from Gerald and Mimi's room. Rosa creeps to Samuel's door, crouches and slips the note underneath – there, it is gone, she can no longer change it. She makes her way silently downstairs.

In the hall she puts on her coat and hat quietly, then buckles her shoes, puts her gas mask over her shoulder, opens the door and steps out. The air is cold and foul with the remnants of night. She slips along the path and searches in the privet hedge for the bicycle; it takes only seconds to strap the suitcase onto the rack, she is surprised at how snugly it fits. She pauses, looks back one last time at the lopsided flint cottage looming behind her like an apparition. The windows are dark apart from the one in the sitting room, which despite the blackout glows with a flickering candlelight. She swings her legs gingerly over the bar, wincing as coils of pain unravel around her pelvis and down her legs, and steers the bicycle through the garden gate and out onto the lane.

Slowly she pedals, rotation by painful rotation. The pain becomes excruciating but just when she can pedal no more she reaches the hill, and the bicycle picks up speed of its own accord. She knows that soon she will have to abandon the bicycle, it is too agonising, she will have to walk somehow; but for now she guides the machine down the hill, her coat flapping behind her. The world becomes a blur as she races through the autumn countryside, the cold air causing tears to spring from her eyes, streak sideways across her face and disappear in her fluttering curls. I'm leaving, I'm leaving, I'm leaving. Her mind fills with visions of Samuel, sitting on the handlebars of her bicycle, kissing her in the fields, on the cliffs, in the woods, tenderly cradling her head in his arms, reassuring her; and then, with that cruel insouciant face, betraying her.

A long journey lies ahead of her to Gunton, especially weighed down by the suitcase. The hill steepens, and as she cuts through the dawn the dynamo heats up, the headlight glows inside the cocoa tin and a hazy row of slits appear, shuddering on the ground in front of the bicycle. The pain throbs with each jolt, and Rosa fixes her mind on her destination, Gunton railway station. Soon she will be leaving Samuel behind, leaving the Kremers behind, leaving the countryside behind, and never coming back. I'm leaving, I'm leaving, I'm leaving. Yes, soon she will be stepping off the train, pushing through the crowds; her German shoes will again be beating the hard pavements of London.

25 November 1941, Brentwood, Essex

This place is like a maze, thinks Rosa nervously, not a house but a maze, and here she is dragging her suitcase along this endless corridor, with every step it is growing heavier, and this parcel under her arm is not exactly light either, and it is a little painful to carry heavy objects, it has been weeks but she can't have fully healed. Her shoes make a strange thudding noise on the thinly carpeted floorboards, the thuds echo off the walls, resound off the fire hoses coiled on drums, the posters displaying evacuation procedures, and rise up to the ceiling, where they settle around the lights with their blackout shades, where they fade. Here, it is one of these rooms on the left. Not this one, and not this one, perhaps it is the next; yes, here it is, a nondescript door like all the others, welcome to Merrymeade, welcome home.

Merrymeade House is a large country house in Essex, built in 1921 on the twin principles of sturdiness and symmetry, with a servants' wing, voluminous attics and extensive grounds. It is the elegant family dwelling of Mrs Horne Payne no longer; since the beginning of the war the house has been commandeered as a training centre, packed to the rafters with new sets of students every seven weeks; now, two years later, it is beginning to show signs of significant wear and tear. As Rosa stands outside her room, her hand resting on the door handle, thirty-four other girls of the new set are settling in, unpacking suitcases, changing into uniforms, freshening up over washstands, tidying their hair; at last she is not alone.

Rosa is looking forward to her new life. Her first days in London were filled with nothing but darkness, day and night, staying in a moribund B & B in Russell Square, shutting her ears against the arguing couple next door, crying herself to sleep in the cold as her body slowly healed, thinking again and again of Samuel, wishing he were here, glad that he is not, thinking she loves him, thinking she does not, struggling with the guilt of the baby that might have been, rereading the letters from her parents, walking the streets of London looking for work, staring at the bomb sites, the salvage sales, the rubble. As soon as she arrived in the city she wrote to Heinrich, confiding in him about the true circumstances surrounding her move and notifying him of her new, temporary address; after a very short time she received his reply, astounded at the speed of delivery – the Red Cross usually took months to process the post – and upon finishing the letter she knew exactly what she must do.

Rosa:

I am terribly sorry and absolutely incensed to hear about how Samuel has treated you (how wrong we were about him: he sounds like a first class rogue, and if I were there I would waste no time in breaking his nose for you). My advice would be to forget all about that weasel, put it behind you and take control of things, start your life again. Despite the temptation, which may be strong at times, never contact him; never waste even a single tear on him. And even if one day he were to come begging to you on bleeding knees, never, ever forgive him.

Stay strong and write soon.
Heinrich

When Rosa finished the letter, she raised her eyes to the cracked B & B ceiling and let out a sigh of determination, a sigh of certainty and strength; she remembered her vow to be strong, to never again give in, and her courage began to flow back; no longer would weakness bind her. So she steeled herself, put on her best clothes, which by now were rather tatty, and visited the Central Office for Refugees at Bloomsbury House to ask for assistance in realising her ambition.

Now, before entering, Rosa rests her ear against the door of her new bedroom. Not a sound comes from within. She tries the handle and it swings open. A narrow room is revealed, perfectly symmetrical, as if a mirror has been installed along the centre: two beds are in identical positions on opposite sides, and beside each there is a cabinet, a wardrobe and a small chest of drawers. She is unsure which bed to take until she looks closer and sees some personal effects on one of the cabinets, and a red-and-white sleeve protruding from beneath one of the pillows. She heaves her suitcase and parcel onto the other bed and sits down beside them, catching her breath. The bedroom smells of polished wood and dust; the window looks out onto the cricket ground, smooth as the sea, and the fragrance of the last few chrysanthemums slips in upon the draught. Rosa is glad to be out of the city, London is different now, compared to how she remembered it; the bombs have made it bleak, shot through with a defiant resignation. She opens her suitcase and begins to unpack her clothes into the wardrobe, it doesn't take long, she will not need most of them anyway, and in her underwear drawer she stashes her painted box. Then she turns her attention to the parcel, which cost twenty pounds, which used up all the money she had left after paying for the B & B. And the salary will only be eighteen pounds a year, seems ridiculous really, board and lodging is included of course, but now she has not a shilling to her name, not a single farthing. She unties the prickly string, peels back the brown paper; on top are several dense-looking textbooks, and underneath is a pile of uniforms which she sewed herself, based on an unlikely-looking sketch and set of instructions. They do not look as bad as she had thought; heavy smocks in a lavender check with puffed shoulders and detachable sleeves, white aprons with shoulder straps. She had been advised to use a dressmaker but couldn't afford it, and she had an aptitude for sewing anyway, she had been taught by her mother as a child. The accessories she had to purchase from Debenhams; the starched collars to be wrapped round the neck like pieces of tape and fastened with studs, the double-breasted caped coat, the cloak, the woollen gloves, the straw hat for outdoors in the summer. She separates the items, brushes them down, hangs them, leaves a full uniform out to put on. The smock fits nicely, she looks in the mirror to affix her cap, which was provided upon arrival – and then the look is complete. She feels different, official, as if she finally belongs to something. At this stage, of course, it is nothing but an illusion, after all she knows nothing but basic First Aid, yet the uniform is an indication that she has crossed a boundary, if only by a single inch; and it is an expression of what she, in four years' time, might achieve.

She picks up the sleeves, two tubes of tough white cotton with a configuration of brass buttons and slits at the end. The idea is that they should be attached to the shoulder of the smock, but she has been having some trouble getting the buttons to fit through the slits. Of course, she thinks as she slips one onto her arm, before the four years are up the war will end, and her family will be freed, and she will be on her way back to Germany; I might be able to transfer my training to Berlin, in fact, so long as my spoken German has not deserted me completely. These buttons, how fiddly – she clicks her tongue in frustration, she cannot seem to get the sleeve to fasten properly to the smock, she slides the sleeve off her arm, holds it up to the light, squinting.

Bloomsbury House had been very sympathetic when Rosa arrived asking for help; they had made enquiries on her behalf, ascertained that interviews were held every Tuesday at two o'clock, and all one had to do was turn up, dressed for interview, and join the queue. But her clothes, by now, were hardly smart, and in some cases were practically in tatters, so, swallowing her pride, she wrote to Baron de Rothschild explaining her predicament and asking, politely, for assistance. His response was swift; several days later a Daimler drew up and produced a dapper and waspish governess with instructions to take her shopping. Taken aback, Rosa was driven into town, nervous of touching even the door handles; the governess took her to Selfridges and kitted her out with an expensive suit in navy, and a pair of spotless white gloves. Then Rosa was deposited back at her B & B, and left with a jewellery case containing a string of pearls, a personal gift from the baron. Rosa, in a daze, accepted the present, watched the motorcar roar away into the distance.

The door opens without a knock; Rosa turns to see a hearty-looking girl with hysterical eyes and thick blonde hair stopping in her tracks and covering her hand with her mouth. She too is wearing a nurse's smock, with angular creases indicating that it has only recently been unfolded – but there the similarity with Rosa's uniform ends. The girl's skirts are practically floor-length, her collar so huge that it braces her chin, and her pockets nothing but minute patches, big enough only for a key or a single pen; her dressmaker clearly had a rather different interpretation of the uniform sketch than Rosa.

—Oh, I beg your pardon, says the girl.

—Not at all, says Rosa.

—We must be sharing a room. I'm Betty Robinson.

—Rosie Clark, says Rosa.

They shake hands.

—Where's your trunk? says Betty. They're supposed to be outside ready for taking to the attics.

—I don't have a trunk, I have a suitcase, says Rosa.

—Goodness. Have you managed to work out these darned sleeves yet? I haven't.

Betty juts out her bare elbows like a chicken.

—Afraid not, says Rosa, I am myself struggling with them.

—I say, you're not English, are you? says Betty.

—Dutch, says Rosa seamlessly.

—I say, Holland. That's awfully exciting, says Betty and giggles. I'm only from Croydon.

—Croydon?

—Yes, you know. Croydon.

There is a silence and Rosa clicks her tongue again in frustration as once more the button of the sleeve eludes her.

—Do you want a hand with those sleeves? says Betty. Perhaps it's easier with somebody else.

—I'm all right.

—Nonsense, says Betty maternally, let's see.

They move to the window for light, but the wintry sky has turned the colour of porridge, and there is little illumination to be had; Betty struggles with Rosa's sleeve.

—Goodness, says Betty, your uniform is rather different from mine. Do you think that's all right? I look like a nun next to you.

—I don't know, says Rosa. I suppose that we shall find out soon enough.

—I'm a Methodist, says Betty, my father is an organ blower. What are you?

—Well, nothing really.

—I'm used to sharing a bedroom, says Betty, I've got three sisters and a brother. How old are you?

—Eighteen, says Rosa.

—I'd have thought you were a lot older.

Betty persists doggedly with the sleeve and Rosa cannot help but warm towards this homely girl, so young, so unspoilt by the darkness of the world; something in her heart is beginning to stir, something she thought was long dead. After weeks in purgatory, watching her savings slip through her fingers at the dismal B & B, waiting for her womb to stop hurting, lying on stained sheets in the communal air-raid shelter while the couple from the next room fumbled in the corner, finally she has something to hold on to, something substantial that she can put between her and the Kremers in Norfolk, something that can protect her from the events of the past; the days with the Kremers are over.

—There, says Betty. Hallelujah.

The interview had been at once terrifying and exhilarating. Rosa, awkward in her new suit, self-conscious in her white gloves, uncomfortable in her pearls, took the underground to Whitechapel and walked from there to the London Hospital, a vast square building stained black with soot, with a huge round clock set like the unwinking eye of a Cyclops below the point of the roof. Dwarfed, she climbed the stone steps, past the row of four squat pillars and into the entrance hall. She managed to stop a passing nurse to ask directions and was looked up and down quite shamelessly before being directed to Matron's office; there she immediately encountered the queue of prospective candidates, all girls, all wearing identical navy suits and white gloves. She stood amongst the throng, indistinguishable, and was suddenly flooded with a sense of relief, an ecstatic sensation of belonging. But as she watched the other girls chatting easily amongst themselves in clipped tones, her sense of isolation gradually returned; she might look the same as the others, but that, in reality, was window-dressing. She was a German girl in England, and a Jew, her experiences set her aside in a way that nobody could ever understand; none of these girls had ever left England probably, and certainly none of them had been through what she had in Norfolk. Not wanting to upset what little equilibrium she had before the interview had even begun, she took care not to catch anybody's eye, gazing instead out of the grille-covered windows at the endless range of interlocking roofs, overhung by a cloud of smog through which blunt-nosed barrage balloons lethargically drifted.

Finally she arrived at the front of the queue. By this time she was nervous, her breath was short, her palms were clammy beneath the white gloves; for a moment she considered running, but she steeled herself, set her chin and sought to quell her anxiety, for she had vowed to be strong now and she would not give up without a fight. The black door was so highly polished that she could see her reflection in the paintwork, a reflection she did not recognise at first. A sign hanging above the lintel read, *Matron's Office Please Walk In*; should she obey the sign or wait to be called? What had the others done?

—Why don't you go in? came a voice from behind her.

Rosa turned to see a ginger-haired girl regarding her intently.

—Do you think so?

—That's what it says up there.

Rosa touched the handle but applied no pressure.

—Go on, said the ginger girl.

She took a breath and opened the door. The room was large with several desks arranged in formation; behind each desk was a lady in a dark-coloured uniform, a stiff white cap perched like a seagull on the uppermost point of her head, from which lace streamers hung down her back. They all stopped what they were doing and looked at Rosa.

—I'm here for an interview, said Rosa awkwardly. It says walk in.

—Don't be ridiculous, nurse, wait outside.

Rosa shut the door, mortified, and forced herself to stand firm, gluing her shoes to the turquoise floor and clenching her hands by her sides. You idiot, she thought, you idiot, now you'll certainly be done for. What could have possessed me—

—What did they say? said the ginger-haired girl.

—We're to wait, said Rosa bitterly, without turning around.

The girl made an inaudible response. As Rosa waited for another few minutes, trying to compose herself, preparing to salvage the interview as best she could, berating herself inside, something suddenly occurred to her, something that gave her, despite the calamity, a sense of hope: the lady had called her 'nurse'.

A few minutes later the door opened and Rosa was beckoned in, ushered past the rows of desks, ladies and typewriters, and shown into the inner sanctum of the hospital – the nucleus, the kernel – Matron's personal office.

Matron Alexander was taller and more slender than Rosa had imagined, and somewhat less intimidating. Her uniform was unassuming: a navy smock with a single line of domed buttons down the centre, a white cap and a plain-looking brooch on the right breast. For a moment Rosa was reminded of the final scenes of *The Wizard of Oz*, where the fire-breathing monster was revealed to be a normal-looking gentleman, but the thought was dispelled when Matron spoke; her voice was like a sabre. She took a note from the top of a pile, laid it symmetrically in front of her and scanned it, lifting a pair of pince-nez to her eyes.

—So, she said, you're the one.

—I beg your pardon? said Rosa.

—Baron de Rothschild has spoken highly of you.

—Thank you, Matron.

There was a pause while Matron studied her closely.

—Why do you want to be a nurse, Miss Klein? she said abruptly.

—I wish to find peace, Rosa replied instinctively.

Matron looked at her strangely.

—Find peace? she replied. That's the first time I've received that particular answer.

—My father is a surgeon, Rosa compensated.

—A medical family, said Matron, very good.

—And I did some First Aid training in Norfolk.

—Ah, Norfolk, said Matron, a healthy country girl. I appreciate the value of the healthy country girl. Miss Nightingale would have approved.

—Thank you, Matron, said Rosa.

—Full of thanks, Miss Klein. Gratitude becomes a girl in our line of work.

—Thank you, Matron.

Another pause.

—I do feel that the surname 'Klein' . . . not to put too fine a point on it . . . how about Clark?

—Clark?

—Yes. Rosie Clark. Matron leaned forward over her desk, peering at Rosa's hair.

—Take down your hair, if you please, Miss Clark, she said.

Rosa fumbled at her hair and allowed it to fall freely.

—You do realise that we cannot accept any nurse with short hair?

—My hair is not short, said Rosa boldly, it is curly.

Matron reached up and pulled at a lock of Rosa's hair; it extended, then bounced back. Crisply and efficiently she parted it in the middle, drew it back from the ears and wrapped it into a bun on the top of Rosa's head.

—What say you, said Matron, will the cap fit?

—I think it will, please, Matron.

—Very well.

Rosa's hair was released and fell about her face; she moved it aside, pushing it back and tucking it behind her ears. Matron reached under her desk and presented a brown paper parcel tied with prickly string.

—Here you are, Nurse Clark, she said, congratulations.

Head spinning, Rosa accepted the parcel.

—Thank you, Matron.

—In there you will find your uniform material and textbooks. You must pay one of the assistant matrons for it – twenty pounds. Now go away and have your uniform made, and report to Merrymeade in two weeks' time. An assistant matron will give you the details.

—Thank you, Matron.

Matron leant closer.

—Fall at Merrymeade, she breathed, and there will be no second chances.

—Very well, Matron.

—That will be all.

Nineteen miles from Matron's office, in Essex, in Brentwood, in a cavernous dining room on the ground floor of Merrymeade, with unlit candelabras and huge windows covered in blackout drapes, supper is held. Several of the girls have not managed to affix their sleeves; they are not reprimanded, not yet at least. Everyone's uniform is slightly different; within days, however, they will be knocked into shape, all skirts will fall eight inches from the ground, and all puffed shoulders will be of the correct height and angle, and each cap will fit snugly around the bun, and every nurse will look indistinguishable from the others, in sartorial terms at least. Amid the cold, the fear of air raids and a tangible claustrophobia, rows of girls eat Oxo-boiled vegetables grudgingly yielded by the Merrymeade garden, slices of mackerel and powdered eggs, which are chewy, sticky, yellow in colour, the consistency of semolina, served scrambled for the main course, and later on reappearing in the guise of a pudding. They sit at long tables, eat from polished plates, try not to drop food on their aprons, whisper to each other nervously; Rosa and Betty sit together, participating occasionally in a conversation concerning prior experience of First Aid, led by the ginger-haired girl, whose name is Maureen and who claims to have dealt with a dead body while she was a junior with the St John Ambulance service in Southwark. Oh dear, mumbles Betty, do you think there will be dead bodies, and she raises another forkful of mackerel to her mouth; this comment is enough to catch Maureen's attention.

—You've got a magnificent bosom, she whispers, you're halfway to being a Sister already.

—Hardly, says Betty uncertainly.

Suppressed giggles ripple across the table and then fall silent as a lady materialises from the shadows, broad, erect and poised; she is wearing a dusky blue Sister's uniform and a white frilly cap, from which two long tails of lace hang down her back like strips of flypaper. She sails past on patrol, regarding the girls with a stony look, then settles back in her chair at the head of the table.

—You, whispers Maureen, what's your name?

—Rosie Clark, says Rosa.

—I remember you from interview. You were the one who entered the office before being called.

—And you were the one who thought it would be a good idea, says Rosa.

There is a quiet titter and Maureen frowns.

—Can I have your bread, if you're not eating it? she says.

—I am eating it, says Rosa, or I'm going to.

Maureen makes a face.

—You're not English, are you? she says suddenly.

—She's Dutch, says Betty defensively.

—Clark doesn't sound very Dutch to me, says Maureen.

—My Dutch name is Klein, says Rosa, reddening.

—Oh, says Maureen brightly, the thin red Klein.

There is another laugh amongst some of the girls, and Rosa's blushes deepen.

—I rather fancy there's a whiff of the Hun about you, says Maureen slowly.

—Don't be stupid, says Betty.

—Don't you be stupid, says Maureen, you've only known each other for five minutes.

Suddenly another voice breaks in.

—Well, I think she's rather exotic.

They turn to identify the speaker: an older girl, a silver 'S' brooch identifying her as a staff probationer, slender and beautiful, with flaxen hair and an elegant bearing. Nobody knows why she is here; she looks as if she will be involved in their training.

—Did you say you were from Holland? she says to Rosa.

—Yes, Amsterdam, Rosa replies.

—I know Amsterdam, says the staff probationer, very picturesque. Take no notice of that girl there. Jealousy is a terrible affliction, especially in those of limited faculties.

Maureen turns white and looks down at her plate.

—My father used to go to Holland frequently, the older nurse continues. He's with the War Office. Very good people, the Dutch. I'm Lottie Barnes, by the way.

—Rosie Clark.

—A pleasure. Lottie leans towards Rosa conspiratorially.

—I say, she says, we're having a little do tonight in my room. Some of the medical students are coming over, and there are bound to be several men. How about it? They'd love to hear your tales of Holland, I'm sure. You can come too, if you like, she says to Betty.

There is a hush while all the girls strain to hear Rosa's response. Betty makes a little squeal of anticipation.

—Thank you, says Rosa nervously, but tonight I must write a letter to my parents. I'm long overdue . . .

—Of course, says the staff probationer, silly me. Your parents must be still in Holland. You must be frightfully brave.

—I'm sorry . . .

—Not at all, says Lottie, there's always a next time, is there not? Lots of people will be dying to meet you once word gets round. I think it's all terribly exciting.

She smiles and turns back to her food, and a burble of conversation gradually returns. Betty glances across the table and shows Maureen a broad smile.

—Betty, says Rosa, would you like to share my bread roll?

—Don't mind if I do, says Betty.

After supper the girls return to their rooms to finish their unpacking; lectures begin tomorrow, and an air of apprehension is palpable. Some of them declare that they intend to spend the evening swotting up, though the subject is anyone's guess; Maureen, having recovered a degree of confidence, is telling people not to bother, she has had a cursory glance through the textbooks and the syllabus looks rather elementary. Half an hour before lights out cocoa is made available in a huge pot in the corridor; they ladle it into metal mugs and return with the bounty to their rooms. It is cold; they put on extra pairs of socks and huddle in blankets, blowing into their hands and warming them on the cocoa. Betty puts on a pair of oversized gentleman's pyjamas and paces up and down, cradling her mug of cocoa, thinking of what to write to her parents. Rosa lies on her bed with a pad of paper, composing her letter with a stubby pencil, since pen and ink is forbidden in bed and the room does not contain a writing desk. For the first time in many weeks she finds the words coming; they flow from the pencil in spindly grey loops and spread, line by line, down the paper, describing the London Hospital, Merrymeade, her new life, and the minutes slip by unnoticed. Finally she folds the letter crisply and slips it into an envelope; it is only then that she becomes aware of her surroundings, looks up. The room has grown very dim, the blackout curtains are drawn, and the only light is coming from the oil lamp at her bedside, she must have written through lights out. Betty can just be made out in the gloom, lying on her side on her bed, seemingly asleep; from somewhere far along the corridor outside, a hushed conversation is faintly audible.

Rosa places the envelope on her bedside cabinet and is starting to undress when a tiny sob comes from Betty's side of the room. Or was it a noise made in sleep? Rosa unbuttons her sleeves, carefully, straining her ears into the darkness – another sob, followed by a sharp intake of breath.

—Betty, she whispers, are you all right?

Betty rolls onto her back, her hands over her eyes.

—I'm sorry, Rosie, she says in an uncontrolled voice, I'm sorry.

Rosa crosses to her bed and sits down; the mattress is hard, it gives barely at all.

—What's the matter? asks Rosa. What's wrong?

—I'm sorry, says Betty, I shouldn't make a fuss, especially not to you, what with your family in Holland and everything.

—Are you homesick?

Betty nods tearfully.

—I know it's silly, she says, but I've never been away from home before. And I've a sweetheart in the Navy.

Rosa feels her chest tighten, but she takes Betty's hand and strokes it.

—Don't worry, she says, you'll see them all again soon. It will be as if you've never been away. Apart from all the heroic stories you'll have, of course.

Betty giggles through her tears.

—Separation, says Rosa, is only ever temporary. It's like a dream, as soon as you wake up you won't remember a thing. Everything will be as good as new, you'll be back with your sweetheart, and life will be fine.

Betty leans over to her cabinet and blows her nose on a handkerchief.

—Thank you, Rosie, she says. I'm sorry, you must think I'm a frightful bore.

—Not in the least, says Rosa, it's quite all right.

—Go on, says Betty, you get ready for bed. We're not supposed to have the light on.

—Good night, then, Betty, says Rosa.

—Good night.

Rosa changes into her nightgown, extinguishes the oil lamp and climbs into her icy bed. As soon as she closes her eyes Samuel appears, smiling against the backdrop of the sea, wind playing in his hair. She finds herself once again rifling through her memories, searching for a giveaway that she might have missed, some indication that he was nothing but a liar and a coward; and once again all she can find is a memory from when he first returned, wounded, from North Africa. Aunt Mimi had taken her to see him in his bedroom, her English was less than perfect at the time, she was shocked to see him so thin and pale, though deep within his eyes burned the fire of defiance that she has never known him to lose – never, that is, until the night when he betrayed her.

—Ah, Rosa, he said, how lovely to see you.

He spoke as if he had encountered an acquaintance in the street. Rosa expressed her condolences and her wishes for him to get better, and they talked for a while of insignificant things, he showed her the jagged barb of shrapnel that he kept by his bed wrapped in newspaper; they almost ran out of conversation. Then Mimi left the room, Rosa cannot recall where she went, but she remembers the earnestness with which Samuel leant over to clutch her wrist, and the delirium in his eyes.

—Rosa, listen. Do you know, I'm a new person, I'm seeing everything through new eyes, past, present and future. I swore to myself that if I pulled through, if I ever saw you again, I would apologise to you immediately, and now's the time to do it. I must confess: before I left for war, on several occasions, I went into your room and read your letters. Ah, now that you're in front of me, in the flesh . . . do you forgive me? You can't fathom the pressure. All my life I've been told that every moment I was being watched by God, my every move was being scrutinised. You would have thought that would make one behave better, but in reality it just drives everything underground. I mean, your life gets . . . you're torn between faith and doubt, you're worried that God will punish you, and that is what compels you to sin; you sin to challenge him, and if no punishment is brought upon your head, you sin and sin again, and the guilt builds up, but that only makes it worse, it's a compulsion. I wanted to be part of your life so terribly, but Mother was coming between us, the termites were thriving underground – you don't understand, Rosa, I can see that, but I read your letters and I am sorry, and this horrible wound is my punishment.

Ah, ah, the distractions of the day are gone and the nightly gallery starts, images appear in flashbulbs: the baby that might have been, her parents and brother and sister, all slipping into her mind like ghosts, illuminated with the vividness of memory by night. And then comes the main scene, played back in her head in minute detail, the colour of the shades on the lights, the roughness of the walls, how the suitcase was straining, how Papa leant over it trying to tighten the buckles, Mama's expression as she stroked her cheek, the noise of the train, the steam and the night, everything in the most vivid detail, bursting forth into her mind as if it had been looking for an opportunity to make itself known. She rolls onto her side and draws the blankets up to her chin, knowing that another sleepless night awaits.

2

Rosa's time in Merrymeade passes quickly. Days become a seamless blur of classrooms and textbooks, notes and report forms, dummy legs and bandages, with baths limited to one a week on account of the fragile drainage system, and barely enough time to sleep. By day Rosa is wholly preoccupied with Hygiene, Dietetics, Practical Nursing and Invalid Cookery; everything else is flushed out of her mind, all thoughts of the Kremers, even of her parents. By night she barely has the strength to drink her cocoa before falling into unconsciousness, and she does not notice when the twinges in her womb subside and she is healed.

Each day begins with the rising bell at quarter past six, followed by a cursory wash alongside Betty in their bedroom, using washstands which will be subject to inspection later – each day the rooms must be left surgically clean, with mattresses stripped, bedclothes folded and windows open. Breakfast is at seven o'clock, for which checked sleeves must be worn (they must wear checked sleeves for meals, white sleeves for administering medicine and speaking to doctors, and have bare arms for treatment. To address a doctor sleeveless is considered a heinous offence). Each meal requires a seat rotation so that they all have equal contact with Sister at the table's head. After breakfast there is an hour of housework, conducted at top speed against Sister's stopwatch. Following prayers, the lectures begin in the cold and gloomy attics, the bare floorboards of which become so easily filthy that they must be scrubbed daily. After lunch (in checked sleeves) there are more classes, culminating in Practical Nursing between five and seven o'clock, using Mrs Brown, the practice-dummy, who is condemned to forever wear a mackintosh, has been weighted to nine stone and whose skin is so slippery that all bandaging is doomed. Then supper; letter writing; study time; cocoa; bed."

So the weeks pass, allowing Rosa neither time nor space to dwell upon her family, or Samuel, and finally, like a distant country, examination day arrives. She rises at five o'clock for extra revision, for she refuses to fall at Merrymeade; in candlelight she sits on her bed, turning the pages of her textbook quietly to avoid waking Betty. After breakfast there is a final inspection of uniforms, and then the tests begin, written and oral, practical and theoretical, dragging on throughout the day. When, in the evening, there is the traditional address by Lord Knutsford, who christens Rosa's set the 'Speedy Susies' on account of the anecdotal evidence of a nurse who, in her eagerness, did not realise that a patient in a plaster jacket was lying face down and served his dinner squarely on his back, Rosa finds herself laughing with unusual abandon, and suddenly she knows in her heart that she has passed, but of course she cannot be sure. She goes to bed nervously, wakes up early and along with the other Speedy Susies spends the rest of the day preparing Merrymeade for the next set of students, scrubbing and cleaning and restocking; Betty writes a note containing examination tips and leaves it at the back of an underwear drawer. Finally, in the evening, Rosa is told, to her great relief, that she has passed, she has done it, the future is hers; at that moment something lifts from her shoulders, something so dark and heavy that she is left incredibly buoyant, as light as an angel. Tomorrow she will move to the London Hospital to commence her probationer's training; Betty has passed too.

The new probationers are driven by Green Line coach the nineteen miles into the scarred heart of the East End; a hush falls upon them as the sooty, sandbag-encircled London Hospital looms out of the smog like a mediaeval fortress. The nurses do not live in the hospital itself, but in four nurses' homes, which are connected to the hospital by enclosed iron bridges at the fourth floor. Rosa and Betty are both assigned to Cavell House, a large redbrick building with a spacious drawing room and sitting room, flower-print curtains and a smell of wood polish. No longer are they called upon to share a room, but are given their own study-bedrooms, next door to one another, each with a writing desk, an armchair and a window overlooking the nurses' garden, above which the charcoal London skyline hangs with a dystopian heaviness, and searchlights fan nightly for bombers, and barrage balloons pursue their dull, inanimate defence.

They are shown around the wards, which are cheerful enough, and homely; big coal fires burn at either end, blue check curtains hang beside every bed, the counterpanes are royal blue, and across the foot of all the beds are bright red blankets known as 'reds', which are exchanged for older 'night reds' in the evenings. A central lobby contains a coal-powered range for warming plates, an urn for boiling water, a medicine cupboard and a harmonium for accompanying daily prayers; annexed to this are the kitchen and the Sisters' sitting room, and each unit is connected to the rest of the hospital by arterial corridors with signs saying *Silence*.

The ward equipment is bewildering in its variety. In quick succession they are introduced to the Carbolic Stand for use with infectious patients, equipped with bowls of Lysol solution, cutlery and washing utensils; dressing-trolleys, firm pillows known as 'donkeys', an array of lotion bowls and porringers, each with a specific purpose, turpentine enema solutions and carbolics, white earthenware sputum mugs inscribed with THE LONDON HOSPITAL, enamel tooth mugs, rubber water pillows, toothed lice combs, four-fold wooden screens with bright red covers and china bedpans accompanied by white cloths with a maroon

243

trim, which must quite emphatically be used for no other purpose than to cover the patient's dignity. And they are shown the ledgers and paperwork, including the Head Book, containing a daily list of all the patients in the ward sorted into categories of Clean, Nits and Verminous, which must be signed by Sister each morning, and their own Record Book, in which their progress in training is dispassionately charted.

As a junior probationer, Rosa's day is spent mostly in the sinkroom, surrounded by racks of bedpans and bottles, brushes and scourers, and row upon row of porcelain pots inscribed S. & M.U. for Saved and Measured Urine. Hour after hour she works, feeling like a butcher in heavy rubbers, holding her breath while slopping out bedpans, trying not to retch, scrubbing them with antiseptic, stacking them ready to be returned to the wards. After bottlewashing she hurries to her room to scrub down, snatch a lunch and claim some extra study time before returning. Apart from Betty she does not make any friends, there is simply no time to socialise; even during the hallowed four o'clock tea break, rather than going to the sitting room with the other girls, she must go straight to her bedroom to consult her dictionary to revise the vocabulary from the morning's lecture.

Lottie invites her again to a do, but it is the evening before an exam and she cannot attend. The next day the rumour goes round that Sister discovered them and the people involved, including Lottie and two male medical students, were severely reprimanded by Matron and would have been dismissed had Lottie's father, who works with the War Office, not put in an emotional plea on their behalf; Rosa is relieved that she missed it after all.

The war grinds on; Rosa sees it through the lens of the wards, through conversations with patients, announcements made by Sister and the occasional newspaper headline. The Blitz has passed and Pearl Harbor has been bombed and the Americans have entered the war, and now it all seems to be happening far away, in a different world; in London war has become little more than a long haul of hardship, deprivation and blackouts, with no light to be seen at the end of the tunnel, and endless inconveniences, such as the compulsory leaving of one's children at nurseries to free up married women for the war effort, and the introduction of milkroundswomen and female road sweepers, which is widely taken as a prophesy of disaster.

One day, during morning bedpans, Lottie Barnes comes into the sinkroom unannounced. She is wearing the striped mauve smock and high-necked apron of the fully fledged staff nurse, and she has no business here in the domain of the junior probationers. Rosa is emptying a bedpan in great gobs into the sluice sink and looks up in surprise, almost drops it; self-consciously she smooths her rubbers, a pointless activity as her predicament is irremediable, there is nothing less dignified than being up to the elbows in brimming bedpans. The other probationers continue their tasks obliviously, facing in the opposite direction; Rosa is manning the sluice sink closest to the door, so she is the first to notice people coming and going. Lottie wrinkles her nose.

—Golly, she says, I'd forgotten how unpleasant it can be down here.

She takes a handkerchief from the pocket of her smock and places it over her nose, then backs towards the door and beckons with her hand. Rosa begins to remove her rubbers but Lottie gestures that it doesn't matter, that she should just get out of the sinkroom straight away so that they can have a proper conversation. Rosa steps into the corridor, keeping an eye out for Sister.

—I can't be long, she says, we're in the middle of it.

—I quite understand, says Lottie, you poor thing.

She chuckles, though not with derision but solidarity. Rosa smiles and shrugs, and Lottie laughs again. Her flaxen hair is gathered tightly under her nurse's cap, emphasising the length of her delicate neck, and as the light catches the angles of her cheekbones Rosa is struck afresh by her beauty and feels even more conscious of her rubbers and dirty hands. Lottie looks shiftily over each shoulder, leans across and speaks in a whisper, as if sharing a plot. Her breath is sweet and youthful.

—Look here, she says, we're having a do. Will you come?

—When is it? says Rosa.

—Tonight. Third floor, Alexandra House. Silly's room.

—Silly?

—Yes, Silly. Cecily Harrison, two doors down from mine. Her window's got a fire escape, might come in handy.

—A fire escape?

—Just joking.

—But how about Sister?

—Don't worry, says Lottie lightly, this time we've got reliable intelligence. They're having a meeting all evening. She glances again over her shoulder and gives Rosa a gentle nudge.

—Come on, she says, promise you'll come. You'll have a fabulous time, and the men are dying to meet you.

Rosa hesitates. She is sure that no other junior probationers have been invited.

—Very well, she says with a tingle of excitement, I'll come.

—Good-oh. That's splendid, says Lottie.

Without another word, she draws herself up and walks smoothly off along the corridor like a swan, glancing at the watch that hangs above her breast, a picture of the perfect nurse; she spots someone running, calls out Fire or haemorrhage? – the official reprimand – with a brazen stylishness. In the distance, the figure of Sister appears; Rosa slips back into the sinkroom, hurries back to her station and heaves at another brimming bedpan, the tingle of excitement shimmering up her spine, spreading through her body. She has never been to the staff nurse dormitories before – what Pro has? – and would be feeling rather daunted had she not been invited by Lottie Barnes herself, the highest princess of them all. A fresh uniform has just been returned from laundry, she will wear that, she was intending to leave it for next week but she mustn't look scruffy tonight. She has seen the medical men from afar but none of them have even noticed her, as a lowly junior probationer she would not even feature on their radars – until this evening, that is, when, as a guest of Lottie Barnes, she will ascend to the staff nurses' quarters and attend one of her infamous and celebrated dos.

The remainder of the day passes quickly. Rosa is put on folding duty in the lobby, surrounded by a bewildering variety of linen: tea cloths, medicine cloths, hand towels, roller towels, cloths for the bedpans, cloths for drying the tooth mugs. The task of lining up the labels proves more difficult than usual, her mind is distracted by the promise of the evening. By supper time she has still not finished the folding; she rushes through the final pile higgledy-piggledy, hoping that Sister will not inspect her work.

The room is cold and shadowy and Rosa sits next to Lottie on the bed, looking down into a dusky glass of black market sherry. She doesn't know what she had expected, but it was certainly nothing like this; the atmosphere is stilted and formal, and apart from her and Lottie there are only three people present: Silly – a sardonic-looking brunette with painted lips sipping from her sherry as if it were liquid gold – and two medical men standing at either end of the room, Roger Freebairn and Jeremy Capo-Bianco, exchanging witticisms through clouds of cigarette smoke.

—And then she said to the nurse, I distinctly told you to prick his boil, says Capo-Bianco, laughing through his moustache.

—You're drunk, says Freebairn.

—Chance, says Capo-Bianco, would be a fine thing.

To underscore his point he takes a gulp of sherry. There is a pause.

—So you're from Holland, eh? says Capo-Bianco. Relative of Queen Wilhelmina?

—Don't be an idiot, says Freebairn.

—She's from Amsterdam, says Lottie.

—Amsterdam, repeats Freebairn, how enchanting. I do admire the Dutch.

—Why, says Capo-Bianco, for getting overrun by Jerry?

—No, says Freebairn, for resisting.

—Rosie's being terribly brave, says Lottie, adding with an artistic flourish: her family are members of the Résistance.

—Indeed? says Freebairn, impressed. Vive la Hollande.

He drinks, without waiting for the salute to be returned. Rosa feels obligated to honour his toast; she raises her glass and sips, surprised by the fruity taste as the alcohol traces a hot line down her throat. She feels dizzy almost immediately.

—I went to Holland once, says Silly, before the war. We went bicycling. Lots of windmills.

Rosa glances at Freebairn who is regarding her admiringly, ignoring Silly and blowing smoke from his nose. Of the two men he is certainly the more palatable, but she cannot think of him as attractive; she cannot imagine thinking of anyone as attractive at the moment. She wishes that she hadn't pretended she was Dutch – if this conversation continues, in a short time she may be in a rather sticky situation.

—Did you go bicycling much? says Silly.

—A little, Rosa replies, though only on day-trips.

—Bicycling day-trips in Holland, says Freebairn, how romantic.

—Not really, says Rosa, it tends to be rather muddy.

Freebairn sucks on his cigarette and laughs uncertainly. Silly gets to her feet.

—Can I offer anybody a . . . she says, then stops mid-sentence and cocks her head.

—What's up? says Freebairn, looking more surprised than usual.

—Sssh, says Silly, I'm trying to listen.

—The thing about Holland, says Capo-Bianco, is the tulips.

—Be quiet, snaps Lottie, shut up.

From far away along the corridor the clack of heels can be heard.

—If I'm not very much mistaken . . . says Silly.

—I don't believe it, says Lottie, it's Sister.

—It can't be, says Freebairn, she's supposed to be in the meeting.

—She's bloody well here now, says Lottie, I'd recognise her footsteps anywhere. Action stations everyone.

The two men stub out their cigarettes, collect up the glasses and the sherry and hasten over to the window; evidently they have indeed planned an evacuation procedure involving the fire escape. Lottie takes Rosa by the hand and hurries her over to the wardrobe.

—Here, she says, get in quick.

They step inside, Lottie pulls the doors together but leaves a small chink of light through which they can see Capo-Bianco, giggling, following Freebairn out of the window; once he is safely out of sight the window is closed and the blackout curtains drawn. Lottie closes the wardrobe tight and pulls Rosa away from the door, burrowing deep into the hanging clothes, into the musty scent of uniforms and linen. The two girls stand together in the stifling darkness; Lottie is still holding Rosa's hand, and her other hand rests round her hip, calming her, it's all right, she whispers, just stay still. Lottie's breath is hot with alcohol and she presses her body against Rosa as the clothes close around them like a cocoon. Rosa bites her tongue, tries to quell her racing heart, forces herself to breathe quietly. The clack of heels approaches along the corridor and comes to a halt; there is a prim knock at the door.

—Who is it? calls Silly in a lazy voice, amazing Rosa with her panache.

—It's Sister, comes a shrill response, open the door immediately, Nurse Harrison.

From the darkness Rosa hears Silly crossing to the door, opening it; a muffled conversation ensues which, from the wardrobe, is unintelligible. Lottie pulls Rosa tighter, her breath is on her cheek, her breasts against her back; don't worry my darling, she whispers, just keep still, don't make a sound. Her lips brush Rosa's cheek, lightly; an odd sensation floods through Rosa's body as she stands stiff as a board in the darkness, Lottie's arms wrapped protectively around her, eyes staring into the blackness, ears straining for a hint of what is happening outside. She hears the door closing and movement inside the room, then the wardrobe doors are flung open and she squints against the light.

—Hurry, whispers Silly, grinning, it's all right for now but she'll be back.

They clamber out of the wardrobe and follow Silly over to the window. Lottie is giggling into her sleeve. Silly parts the blackout curtains and opens the window to the cold air.

—Here, she says, get going. Next time we'll be sure to invite Her Sisterness.

At this Lottie lets out a burst of laughter. Rosa swings her legs over the window ledge and drops down onto the wrought-iron fire escape, which clangs loudly in response to her heels. Ssssh, hisses Lottie, and giggles again; help me down, Rosie, help me, come on.

Rosa takes her by the elbow and supports her as she slips down onto the fire escape. Silly, in the window, throws them down their cloaks, shows them a quick thumbs-up and closes the blackout curtains. Outside it is cold; they draw their cloaks about their shoulders and look around. In the distance searchlights tilt against the clouds like lances, and there is barely a twinkle from the blacked-out city.

—Come on, says Lottie, I'm going to have hysterics.

—Let's take our shoes off, says Rosa, starting to feel light-headed.

—Good idea, Sergeant Clark, says Lottie.

She takes Rosa by the hand and they slip down the staircase, the wrought-iron freezing their stockinged feet, winding down the side of the building, floor after blacked-out floor. Suddenly Lottie laughs out loud; Rosa looks over and in the darkness can just make out that she is holding up a single shoe. My shoe, whispers Lottie, my shoe, I've dropped the bloody thing over the side. Without appreciating the futility of the action, they both lean on the railing and peer over into the blackness of space. Lottie starts to laugh again, Rosa tries to quieten her but then begins to giggle herself, and in a matter of seconds they are laughing uproariously into the night, supporting themselves against the railing of the fire escape, tears of laughter streaking down their cheeks and flicking into the night sky below them. Lottie moves towards Rosa and takes her by the hand, and Rosa, who despite the mirth is anxious to get back to the safety of her room, leads Lottie down the icy stairs.

Minutes later, having recovered somewhat, they clamber through the fire-exit door into a dimly lit corridor, their cloaks falling against their backs.

—Cavell's that way, whispers Lottie, you'd better get a move on. I'm off to find my shoe.

—Thank you, says Rosa, suppressing another giggle. I look forward to the next do with Her Sisterness.

Lottie leans over and kisses her, once, on the cheek, though the edge of her mouth strays over the corner of Rosa's lips; I'll be seeing you soon, she says, good luck, then she turns and disappears into the gloom. The odd sensation flows through Rosa's body again and she hurries along the corridor, up some stairs and out onto the enclosed iron bridge, the cool wind pressing her smock against her legs.

She reaches Cavell House without incident, creeps along the corridor to her own bedroom; finally she is safe. She kindles her oil lamp, changes into her nightgown and slides into bed, huddling against the late night chill, not wanting to extinguish the lamp, not wanting to sleep. The sheets are chilly and her body is filled with a tingling sensation, as if pure light were coursing through her veins. She takes out a pencil and paper and begins to write, imagining her family in the room with her, as if they are having a conversation. The words pour out from the scratchy tip of her pencil, introducing Lottie, describing the hospital, sketching her uniform and bedroom, offering them her life via this flimsy piece of paper. Eventually she signs her name, folds the letter into an envelope and places it in the painted box, ready for posting tomorrow.

Before lying back and going to sleep, for some reason she feels inspired to pray. She has never thought much about God, she has always been far too concerned with the everyday business of living, and even at her lowest points she has felt that a recourse to divine intervention would be an expression of failure. Yet now, in her new-found state of happiness, tempered but not dispelled by thinking about her parents and how they must be suffering, she finds herself making a request. Please God, she prays, protect my family and reunite us soon. It is a simple prayer, and a short one; she repeats it several times. Then she burrows back under the covers, extinguishes the oil lamp and closes her eyes. As a dark ocean of sleep wells up to meet her, and her body relinquishes its load of the day, she is unaware of an important fact: for the very first time since she ran away from Norfolk, she has fallen asleep without thinking of Samuel.

3

The seasons pass in a world of their own outside the hospital walls; war lumbers on in the distance, in the background, and life at the London is all-consuming. Rosa finds the role of the nurse coming more naturally to her; she begins to feel comfortable in the wards, with patients, with other nurses, even, gradually, with Sister. And as she sheds the chrysalis of Junior Pro and is awarded the silver brooch of the staff probationer, the news breaks of victory at El Alamein, and Africa falls to Monty, and the home stretch of the war seems to be in sight; few people believe that the war can now be lost, yet just as few dare predict how it might be won.

At three in the morning on Christmas Day 1942, the hospital is woken for carol singing, which commences in the wards with a rousing rendition of 'Christians Awake'; Rosa is impressed by the colourful paper shades on the lights, and the evergreens and balloons strung across the ceilings, and the Christmas scenes displayed on the tables, and the piles of Christmas stockings for the patients, and the traditional presentation of a bunch of violets to every nurse in the hospital. But 1943 wears on, and the mood in the city grows jaded. By night people have taken to roaming the streets during air raids to catch a view of the action, hampering the civil defence and putting themselves in danger; by day they huddle in scowling knots, grumbling about the rations, about the shortages, about the Jews. From the freezing womb of another winter 1944 is born, accompanied by the Luftwaffe who return with intense wrath to London under cover of darkness. The winter is exceptionally bitter, plagued by freezing fogs, and the days grow dark before their time. Rosa grips the side of the chilly enamel tub and raises herself from the water, leaning forward to the tap, trying to stop the infernal dripping, they are only allowed five inches as it is, and this is enforced by a tube of that height attached to the plughole, and her bath is currently five inches exactly, so this blasted drip must stop. Her fingers turn yellow and maroon as she applies pressure to the head of the tap, and then the drips stop and she lies back in the water. Sister made her promise that she will spend at least fifteen minutes in the bath, she has been working like a demon for weeks now without a break, even during teatime she does not join the other girls in the sitting room but continues to work in the wards, so she must rest, even if only for fifteen minutes, and what better way to do this than by soaking her aching limbs? She feels jumpy, unaccustomed to lying still, as if she is late for something, but she made a promise to Sister, and she has thirteen minutes left before she can get out and get back to work, and she knows that if she left the bath even one minute early Sister would know about it and make her do the whole procedure again.

On the wooden chair beside the basin her uniform hangs like a skin, the Staff Pro's silver 'S' glinting on the apron bib. Everything is different now, she thinks, even the uniforms have changed, there is less length in the skirt, less volume in the shoulders, the aprons are only to be worn in the wards, the capes have been exchanged for greatcoats, and Sister has to make do without the frilly streamers that used to hang down her back from her cap, or at least she must save them for special occasions. But most irritatingly of all, gone are the detachable sleeves which caused Rosa such distress when she first arrived! Gone, just like that, after she has finally grown used to them, and the new girls these days have had a lucky escape, from a sartorial point of view. Rosa avoids, whenever she can, the new girls, she dislikes the way they regard her, big dewy eyes and simpering grins; of course she understands that as a Staff Pro she will inevitably be impressive, but strangely, through no effort on her part, she has acquired a certain mystique-by-association, for as soon as Lottie left, Rosa was tacitly judged by the probationers to have inherited her status. This came about when, back in 1942, Lottie was caught by Matron outdoors after lights out. She claimed to be looking for her shoe in the hospital yard, but Matron considered this one infringement too many, and her parents were called, and she was transferred to a sector hospital closer to her home with the notion that her father might keep an eye on her. When news of this broke, and people realised that Rosa had been present at Lottie's do that very evening, in the eyes of the probationers, if not the staff nurses, her social status instantly skyrocketed. Rosa herself maintained an irregular correspondence with Lottie for several months until neither of them could remember whose turn it was to write, so neither of them did, and the brief relationship ended. It was several weeks before Rosa realised that she was being widely regarded as the heiress to Lottie's throne, and the more she tried to discourage this perception, keeping her affairs private and working diligently, the more her reputation grew. Then she received a letter that changed everything; she became rather withdrawn, and the old insomnia began to return, and she began to fill every minute of her spare time with extra shifts, surrendering herself to the regime of rules and procedures, scrubbing her hands with a block of soda every half-hour until they bled, replacing her identity with her uniform, becoming nothing but Probationer Clark, always on duty, always diligent, with chronic finger cramps and perpetually sore feet; this change was seen amongst the Junior Pros as a gesture of aloofness, and the more she drew away, the more she seemed to be revered.

Lying in the cooling bath trying to be still, the chilblains on her fingers stinging under the water, her nerves jangling with suppressed energy and still twelve minutes to go, Rosa remembers that letter. It was more of a postcard really, written in pencil, her mother's handwriting was barely recognisable, it was very brief, just a few lines, but those were enough to change Rosa's world, she remembers – no, don't think of it, there is no point in giving the mind free rein to dwell on whatever it pleases, she could make proper use of these few minutes to catalogue her tasks for the evening's shift, and then her efficiency will be enhanced; she might be forced to lie still in the bath, resting her body, but there can be no excuse for not disciplining her mind. Tonight: hot water bottles all round to mitigate the freezing temperatures, and Mr Everard's dressing will want changing; hopefully the bedpans, ashtrays and sputum mugs will have been emptied by the Juniors, but if not she will be required to pitch in. And the ventilators must be shut and the flowers taken out, then there is cocoa to be made before lights out, and Mrs Hopkins will need to be fed some more whites of egg before she goes to sleep, doubtless nobody will have thought to do that. And then – unless there is an air raid, for the Germans have been at it again with the bombs almost every night, Mr Churchill has declared that it's quite like old times, a 'little Blitz' – unless there is an air raid, she will go to bed for a few hours before the morning shift, when the usual routine will once again apply: pulling the blackout curtains away from the windows, morning bedpans, the brewing of Bovril, sweeping with tea leaves to settle the dust and refreshing the nibs in the pens on the inkstands, scrubbing and scouring with carbolic solution, fumigating and polishing and rinsing and wiping, emptying and changing and consoling and injecting, then the chime of the clock will throw everybody into a panic, then back to the bedrooms to collect notes and textbooks for the study period; then lunch, back to the wards, and so on.

Ten minutes to go, ten minutes. Rosa takes the grey-mapped pebble of soap and begins to wash, scrubbing her body vigorously and thoroughly, and she is distracted, her mind drops its guard, and immediately there it is:

Meine liebe Rosa,

Forgive me but I cannot write at length. We are being relocated tomorrow. I shall not be able to write again for a long time, and neither will you be able to write to us. Now we must say a very painful goodbye. We will love you always and are so proud of you, we will be with you always. You are in our thoughts, never forget us, please be strong, my darling.

All my love and prayers,
Mama

Ah, separation, in a way, is a simple thing, first there were five, then one was taken away, and then there were four, and the other one was elsewhere, that's all there is to it, a matter of mathematics, Rosa cannot seem to rouse any other emotion – apart from anger, for they sent her away when she wished to suffer with them, she did not wish to go, she did not ask to be the one to be saved, and now they will be unable to write for a long time, they declare their eternal love but she no longer feels as if she knows them even, and when they get back in touch they will barely recognise each other, she knows it, why should she be condemned to safety? Ah, her parents, so perfect in their absence, they sent her away to protect her, she understands that; they are saints, beyond reproach, virtuous and pure, unassailably untainted, especially when compared to her own stained and sinful life, blemished as it is with inadequacy, soiled with dirt and guilt.

No, don't think of it, don't think of it, there have been a few newspaper reports about Europe's Jews but this is wartime and such things are often distorted, and Mama sounded confident, she said she would not be able to write for a long time, and that implies that eventually she will write once again. The letter was painfully brief; she did not have time to write, well that might be true, but a little detail would have helped, it would not have taken long to suggest where they were going, and how long is long, and whether they are together still, and what is happening to the apartment, and when Rosa can expect to be contacted again. Don't think of it, tonight we shall need hot water bottles all round, and Mr Everard's dressing will need changing, Mrs Hopkins will need to be fed some whites of egg before she goes to sleep.

So Mama wants her to be strong, and she is strong now, she works hard and sleeps little and leaves no time for self-pity; she drives herself on. If only she had been stronger before – that night in the kitchen in Berlin she should have said no, Mama, I do not wish to go, I will stay with my family even if that means suffering, at least we shall suffer together; but she did not say it, she was weak. And she should have said no, Herr Wollheim, I do not wish you to take the baby from me, I have been caring for him ever since we left Berlin, he should not be absorbed into an orphanage or institution. And she should have said no, Samuel, I cannot love someone who has stooped so low as to read my private letters. And she should have said no, Aunt Mimi, I do not wish to undergo this procedure, whatever plan you and Samuel have concocted, I refuse to relinquish my baby; take your doctor and begone. And she shouldn't have left Samuel a note under his door, she should have been

254

bold, pushed her way in regardless of the early hour, you liar, she should have said, you told me we would marry and have the baby, you told me everything would be all right so long as we stay together, well, how flimsy your words have proved, may this sin be on your head forever. Yes, weakness, but now she is strong, and if she were to see Samuel again, if she were to visit the Kremers back in Norfolk with the intention of confronting them with her new-found strength, what would she say? Five minutes, five minutes more, then she can finally leave this bath and get back to work, and the water is practically at body temperature already and losing its heat fast, but one does not argue with Sister—

There it is: Moaning Minnie's lament, creeping up to a fever pitch, that solemn whine of the night, warning against hostile aircraft overhead. And now the guns sound, they can be heard in the distance like thunder, that didn't take long – and there, the giant heartbeat of the bombs, goodness but the enemy is almost at the gates, this new wave of intense raids has taken everyone by surprise, just when they thought the enemy were on their last legs; they may be worn down by years of hard work and meagre rations, but what choice is there but to get on with it? With three minutes yet to go Rosa pulls herself out of the bath, water falling from her body, she seizes a towel, dries hastily, reaches for her uniform; she may not be on duty for another half-hour but she knows she will be needed, the air raid is approaching fast and the wards must be prepared for casualties, the bedclothes must be folded ready to turn back, the dressing-trolleys must be fully loaded and equipped, the hot water bottles must be filled and placed in the beds, and everything must be rather especially to hand; by the sounds of things they do not have long.

She hurries into her bedroom and is reaching into the wardrobe for her apron when, from somewhere in the building, there is an echoing bang, followed by the sound of tinkling glass, and the floor beneath her feet trembles, and a rumble rolls and clanks inside the plumbing before disappearing into the silence. She hears hurried footsteps and stern orders, and somebody is blowing a whistle, and then the electric lights flicker, recover, then fizzle and fuse, and the gas goes out, and a darkness descends. In the blackness she feels her way to her bed, groping her way until the emergency lights flicker on. Then, adjusting her cap awkwardly, she hurries out of the room – not running, for even in emergencies nurses are forbidden to run – and walks swiftly along the corridor in the direction of the wards.

Her heart is beating hard, and fear is beginning to grip her from within, but this is a familiar feeling, and it makes her even more determined to head towards the heart of the danger. Her senses are heightening, she clenches her teeth, imagines herself to be like an automaton, emotionless, and this enables her to maintain control – she walks, does not run, towards the wards, past anxious First Aid volunteers and patients being pushed in beds, past blown-in doors and windows, round an uncoiled length of firefighting hose, heading in the direction of danger; something within her is welcoming this peril, for it is in these moments that she feels closest to her parents, finally experiencing a little of what they must be experiencing, and feels united with them, with their suffering. She has left her tin hat in the bedroom, she is wearing only her soft starched cap, if Sister sees her she will be sent back to get it, for it is dangerous to be in the wards during an air raid with nothing but a cap for protection. The fear mounts; Rosa thinks of her parents, hurries on.

When she arrives in the ward the emergency lights are on, sending an inadequate brassy light into the cavernous room, and nurses in tin helmets are hurrying to and fro with candles and lamps, bottles of carbolic solution, injection trays and blankets, and clinking dressing-trolleys. By the looks of things the patients have not yet begun to arrive. In the middle of the ward stands Sister, the strap on her tin hat tight under her chin, perfectly erect and poised, directing operations like a general on the Front. Rosa catches sight of her and is unsure what to do, she does not want to be sent back for her helmet, perhaps she should hide until Sister leaves the ward; then, as she is caught in a state of hesitation, there is a commotion outside. Everyone turns in the direction of the double doors as they burst open and the beam of a blackout torch swings upwards to illuminate a face; Rosa squints and recognises a dishevelled-looking Roger Freebairn, covered in soot, his hair unkempt, a stirrup pump in his hands.

—The roof's on fire, he calls, incendiaries. It's nothing to worry about but any assistance would be appreciated to avoid damage to the kitchens.

—I'll thank you not to trouble my nurses with histrionics, Mr Freebairn, says Sister sharply. Go on and extinguish the fires, you're doing us all a great disservice down here.

—I do apologise, Sister, says Freebairn, I had thought there were medical men present.

The doors clack and he is gone. Sister waves the nurses back to their duties; Rosa, however, with a growing sensation of being a spectator to her own actions, does an about-turn and hastens towards the door.

—Miss Clark, calls Sister, might I ask where you are going?

—To get my tin helmet, Rosa replies. I've left it in my bedroom.

—At the double, says Sister, we'll be needing you in the Receiving Room shortly. We can't afford all this shilly-shallying.

Rosa pushes through the double doors; Freebairn can just be seen up ahead.

—Mr Freebairn, she calls, wait a minute.

He stops and turns to face her.

—Rosie? he says. Rosie Clark?

—I've come to help you with the fire.

—I . . . well, are you sure? I mean, it's something of a man's job.

—It makes no difference to the fire to be extinguished by a man or a woman.

—Indeed, says Freebairn, if Sister can spare you, who am I to argue? Very well, follow me.

They hurry along the corridors in the half-light, weaving around the porters and patients who seem to materialise from the gloom. Finally Freebairn opens a squat metal door and leads Rosa up a staircase towards the roof; they cover their noses and mouths with handkerchiefs as smoke fills the stairwell.

—It's just you and me, calls Freebairn over his shoulder, everyone is busy in the wards.

They push their way into the night, steadying themselves against the stone wall round the edge of the roof. Rosa glances over the side: the rooftops of London stretch out for miles, fires are dotted erratically across the city and searchlights fence in the sky above. The freshness of the air is carrying the smoke upwards and it is less stifling up here than it was on the staircase. The roof slants upwards to their left as they skirt its perimeter, climbing behind the hulking hospital clock which stares like a single eye down at the Whitechapel Road. Rosa's legs feel weak and insubstantial as the wind whips her curls in the direction of the city.

—Here, says Freebairn, that's the worst of it.

Rosa turns the corner and sees lines of orange flame stretching haphazardly along the west side of the roof, lapping hungrily at the windows of the attic. She feels her heart quiver – suddenly she is back in Berlin, in the Scheunenviertel, peering from the window of a police car as Krützfeld strides towards the baying crowd, silhouetted against the burning synagogue; she shakes her head, remembers her parents and forces herself on. Freebairn clambers into an attic window and begins to pass her buckets of water and stirrup pumps.

—Do you know how to do this? he shouts above the noise of the fire, the wind.

—Of course, Rosa replies.

She plunges the stirrup pump into a bucket of water and heaves it towards the flames until the heat is almost unbearable. Then she sets it down, opens the valve and begins to pump, shielding her face, sending crystalline arcs of water into the flames. Now she is on top of the Rykestraße synagogue, pumping jets of water at the great stone star of David, fighting back the flames from the synagogue roof, she looks down to the street below, it is seething with a mob, she looks away, shields her face, pumps more water, her ears filled with chants of raus, raus, raus, Juden raus; she is bleached a vivid orange by the flames, and the black Berlin night stretches out around her.

Freebairn fetches some more buckets from the attic kitchens, and for several minutes they toil against the fire, smoke billowing around their heads, their eyes blurred and stinging from the smoke; at first the fire resists but then it begins to die; finally the flames vanish from the charred and sodden tiles of the roof, and it is over.

—Well done, says Freebairn, I think we've done it. The damage looks quite superficial. Jolly good show.

—I must return to the wards, says Rosa, somewhat dazed.

Freebairn smiles.

—You must be something of a chip off the old block, he says.

—What do you mean? says Rosa.

—Your parents are in the Dutch resistance, are they not?

—Ah, says Rosa, of course.

She turns, steadies herself against the perimeter wall and, leaving Freebairn with the stirrup pumps, makes her way around the roof and down the spiral staircase, disappointed at the ease with which the fires were extinguished.

4

—Miss Clark, says Sister, thank you for deigning to join us.

—I came as soon as I could, says Rosa.

—Might I ask the reason for the soot on your face?

—Soot? says Rosa, surprised that Sister can see it in the half-light, even under the shadow of her tin helmet, and even after she has washed.

Sister sighs.

—Report to the Receiving Room if you please, she says.

—Yes, Sister, says Rosa.

—And this time, Probationer Clark, do try to resist the temptation to take on the German army single-handedly.

—Of course, Sister, says Rosa.

—Carry on.

Rosa makes her way to the Receiving Room, tightening the strap on her tin helmet, sliding her hand across its dome. The casualties have started to arrive, prostrate on green wire stretchers, slung between dust-covered volunteers, carried cold and jolting into hospital. A row of them has already formed along the wall; women from the Voluntary Aid Detachment move among them, stooping to administer bandages and splints, blankets and hot water bottles. Junior Pros distribute cigarettes and cups of tea. Rosa scans the room for the staff nurse in charge – there, Cecily Harrison, she is standing at the end of the room directing the Red Cross nurses. Rosa picks her way over.

—Nurse Harrison? she says.

—Yes? says Cecily, turning towards her with an authoritative air.

—I've been sent from the Gloucester Ward to collect patients ready for transfer, says Rosa.

—And not before time. Is there only one of you?

—I'm afraid so.

—Well, when you get back tell your Sister to send us some more, says Cecily, there'll be carnage here before long.

She takes in the room with a sweep of her eyes.

—That patient there, she says, she's been lying there far too long. Get her installed and come back for the next.

Rosa makes her way over to the row of casualties and regards the patient who has been placed in her charge. A girl of not more than fifteen, with a pallid complexion, lies on her back, eyes closed, not moving; her hands are knotted in double fists by her sides and her hair lies in ropes on the stretcher, weaving amongst the wire frame like raffia. Her neck has been bandaged heavily, making her head look rather disembodied, and the bandages are stained a blackish scarlet. A sour smell fills Rosa's nostrils as she stoops over the patient. She looks down; the girl's skirt is darkened, sodden and foul. Rosa feels suddenly nauseous and looks away for a moment, then looks back. The patient has not moved, even her eyelashes no longer have the tiny vibrations of life. Rosa kneels beside her and presses two fingers onto the cool skin on the inside of her wrist; then she takes them away again, leaving a waxy indentation in the flesh, and places the fist carefully back in its place. She gets to her feet, reeling slightly.

—Probationer Clark, comes a voice from across the room, enough mucking about if you please. We're in for a busy night.

Rosa shudders and walks discreetly over to Cecily, who is surveying the ward with a critical eye.

—I'm afraid the patient is deceased, says Rosa. By the looks of things she has been for some time.

Cecily looks from Rosa to the dead girl and back again. Then she sighs.

—Bloody good start, she says. Look after the next patient along, nurse. And for heaven's sake cover her up with a sheet or something, it's just not dignified.

Rosa nods and looks around for a hospital sheet; there is not one to be seen, they are usually kept not in the Receiving Room but in the wards. Making a decision, she unties her apron and slips it over her head. Then, slowly, from the feet upwards, as if tucking the girl into bed, she slides the apron up over her body. The apron reaches the girl's neck, then moves over her chin, and now her mouth is obscured, and her nose, and now her eyes are gone, then her forehead and hair, and finally the apron lies undulating in peaks and hollows on the stretcher, the straps trailing onto the floor, and nothing can be seen of the girl but her feet, her hair, her knotted fists.

Rosa stands back as two Red Cross woman bustle past her to collect the stretcher; she closes her eyes for a moment, steadying herself, pushing her way through a growing nausea like a skiff cutting a course through a storm. Then, forcing herself to press on before she loses her momentum, she turns her attention to the next casualty in the line. This patient, a man this time, is clearly alive, breathing in great hungry gulps, and appears to be semi-conscious. His head is covered with a swathe of bandages through which a claret oval is spreading; an old shell-dressing has been applied to his face, bandaged round his head as if he has a toothache; his left arm is in a splint and bandaged from fingers to shoulder; the part of his face that is not covered by bandages is streaked and blackened with soot, and his lips are cracked and grey. Rosa searches for some notes but cannot find any, she asks the man his name but he mumbles something unintelligible. She finds a porter in the corridor and instructs him to assist her, they lift the wire stretcher, the patient groans. Rosa leads the way back to the Gloucester Ward where they transfer him into a bed, blackening instantly the sheets.

—Your name, what is your name? says Rosa, out of breath.

Again she cannot understand the reply. First things first, she thinks, that head dressing requires attention. She hauls the dressing-trolley over and draws the curtain round the bed, then finds an oil lamp and places it on the windowsill, illuminating the patient's bandage-swollen head. Streaks of light and shadow thread along the wrinkles of the bandage, and the scarlet oval is spreading visibly. The man is moaning, a thirsty noise that sounds like an expression of mild disappointment, and with his good arm he is clutching his side. Rosa puts on some sterile gloves and begins to cut the bandages away; there is the unpleasant crunch of scissor against fabric, and then the bandages fall open like a case, red and black on the inside, revealing patches of scarlet-stained gauze sticking to the wounds on the man's forehead and cheek. Patches of his hair have been blown away, revealing raw skin glinting in the light of the oil lamp, the colour of uncooked bacon. The man groans his groan of disappointment, and Rosa begins to clean his face, using a swab to wipe the soot away from his nose and cheeks, away from the areas of broken skin; then she peels away both gauzes, dropping the sodden material into a kidney dish, and cleans closer to the wounds. Part of the gauze has adhered to the skin; the man yelps as she pulls it away. He is groaning louder now, and jerking his head, Rosa tries to soothe him with calming words but it seems to make little difference; she turns away, searches on the dressing-trolley for the barbiturates, but none can be seen; she clicks her tongue in frustration, it is elementary practice to reset the dressing-trolleys in advance of an air raid, and this patient is clearly in desperate need. In the distance the guns continue their thumping into the sky, and a bang closer at hand rattles the windows and dressing-trolleys; everyone in the ward ducks instinctively, then carries on.

It is when Rosa turns back to the patient, and sees him from more of a distance, that it happens. His scorched eyelids open, revealing blood-shot eyes, and suddenly there is something familiar about him. His cheekbones are high and defined, his hair black and thick, his features confident, bold. With a gasp of recognition Rosa raises her hands to her mouth, and at that moment the patient begins to gurgle, his eyes open wide as if seeing an apparition, his lips draw back from his teeth.

—Rosa, he murmurs, Rosa?

She backs away from the bed and stumbles, and as she rights herself her hand automatically grips Samuel's leg. He sucks air through his teeth and winces; he tries to sit up but he is unable to raise himself from the bed.

—Rosa, he croaks, is that you? Is that you? Am I mad? Am I dead? Are you really there?

—Just lie back and close your eyes, says Rosa, grasping unconvincingly for her nurse's authority.

—It is you, says Samuel, it is you. Rosa, speak to me. Tell me it's you, tell me. Tell me you remember.

—You're delirious, says Rosa desperately, just lie back—

—I'm not delirious, I can see you. Are you not real?

—Lie back, Mr Kremer, please. Lie back and close your eyes.

Suddenly Samuel presses his head into the pillow and starts to moan, Rosa, Rosa, you must be real, you must. His words rise and merge into a howl, spittle flicks from his mouth, his arms thrash in the air, a lotion bowl is upset from the dressing-trolley and smashes on the floor. There is the sound of swift footsteps approaching, and suddenly the curtain is swept away from around the bed; there stands Sister, the dim light glinting off the rim of her tin helmet.

—Now that's quite enough, she says, show a little fortitude, for goodness' sake, or we shall waste no time putting you in a straitjacket.

Samuel stops for a moment and then resumes at a lower volume, wailing Rosa, Rosa, Rosa. Sister turns, her eyes flashing.

—Probationer Clark, she says, why have you told this patient your Christian name?

—I did not, stammers Rosa, he is an acquaintance. And he is delirious.

—Heavens above, where on earth is your apron?

Before Rosa can reply Samuel begins to moan, a wordless atavistic moan, and he suddenly goes very limp, panting hard and gazing in the direction of the darkened ceiling.

—Watch him, says Sister, I shall get some morphia if the cabinet is still intact.

She pushes through the curtains and there is the noise of her opening the lock on the cabinet; Rosa slips back into the shadows and watches Samuel wide-eyed. Finally Sister appears again. Without a word she administers the morphia with a syringe, impregnating the patient with a maximum dose; he sighs as it enters his bloodstream, twitches a little, closes his eyes.

Sister places the syringe on an injection tray. Then, in case of further outburst, she passes a blanket sideways across Samuel's bed, tucks it in and secures it tightly to the mattress using six-inch safety pins. Finally she straightens her back and tidies her apron.

—Well, she says, what do you have to say for yourself?

—I'm very sorry, Sister, says Rosa.

—Very well. Now get your apron on and clear up this blasted carnage. In all my years, I've never known a probationer to appear apronless in the wards. And for heaven's sake put the patient on a drip, he's badly burned. Where are his notes?

—I couldn't find them, Sister.

There is another bang outside followed by the tinkle of bottles on dressing-trolleys and the clatter of chart-boards being blown off the bed rails; everyone ducks apart from Sister, who does not flinch. Samuel is lying motionless, sweeping stains of blood smudged across the pillows, the sheets, the bedclothes; his eyes are closed tightly and his breathing is deep and laboured. Sister reaches into his shirt and withdraws a stained sheaf of notes.

—Look at the appalling state of these, she says, goodness gracious. Now let me see . . . yes, burn wounds mainly. He'll need a Bunyan bag on that arm, I should think, and clean dressings of course. Whoever put these bandages on has done a frightful job. Carry on, Probationer Clark.

—But Sister, says Rosa, I would rather be assigned elsewhere.

—You'll be assigned where I tell you, says Sister. For now you'll dress this man's wounds and then report back to the Receiving Room. Casualties are arriving thick and fast, you know.

With that Sister ghosts into the gloom, leaving Rosa alone again with the patient. She looks away, counts to ten, then turns slowly back to face Samuel, who is lying like a pharaoh in the golden half-light. Her heart is pounding, she breathes deeply to regain control, trying to remind herself that she is a nurse, in a ward, with a patient. But this is not an anonymous casualty, this is Samuel in front of her, prostrate and injured and brimming with morphia, what cruel turn of fate is this? For a brief, crazy moment she considers not treating him, leaving him to rot, for now he is at her mercy. But then she pulls herself together: he is a man, just a person, a patient like any other, with skin and muscles and lacerations and burns, treating his wounds is a scientific process, nothing more, she has dealt with wounds like these a hundred times before. She picks up the surgical scissors and starts to cut the bandages away from his arm, struggling to keep her hand steady and suppressing an impulse to weep.

21 February 1944, London

Samuel Kremer opens his eyes to a melancholy light and doesn't know where he is. He feels groggy; his head is in pain, heavy and swollen like a mushroom. He winces and tries to raise himself on his elbows, but only one of his arms will move, he finds himself thrusting backwards into a pillow, oh, I am in bed, this is not my bed, and that is not my ceiling, and why do I find it so difficult to move? He turns his head gingerly from one side to the other: his left arm is enclosed in a sort of cloudy plastic bag, and his right is hosting a long grey tube. Rows of steel-framed beds stretch out endlessly left and right, full of people, some of whom are moaning.

He closes his eyes and tries to think, piecing together fragments of memory: frantically working a stirrup pump, a burning roof somewhere in the East End, a tin hat with ARP printed across it, several sizes too big, he remembers having to keep pushing it back on his head; someone saying something about not being willing to risk his neck this time round, not with victory on the way.

Two girls dressed in uniforms walk briskly by, their lavender smocks and white aprons flapping in gentle triangles; both are carrying boxes of medicine bottles which clink together as they walk. They pass Samuel's feet, which are sticking out at the end of his bedclothes; he tries to call out but his voice remains stubbornly silent. It occurs to him that his bed is a carnival float and the girls are cheering him as he passes, throwing handfuls of flowers in the air. They disappear through the double doors, leaving him confused and alone and in pain. He lets his weighty head fall back, his headache is getting more intense by the moment, he closes his eyes, then opens them. The ceiling is lit by a dim light that soaks into the room from the soot-smeared windows, he can't tell if it is morning or evening. After a brief struggle he manages to withdraw his right hand and feel around his forehead: rough material, bandages, all round his head and under his chin as well. He looks at his left hand again – it is floating in a cloudy plastic tube, which on closer inspection appears to be full of liquid. Fine, he thinks, this is just fine, fine. His head is burning with a white heat, it is almost unbearable, and nobody seems to have noticed him, he is being left to rot. On the bedside cabinet his trousers are folded, he wonders who removed them; painfully he stretches over and rummages in the pockets until he finds his bottle of barbiturates; he swallows a dose and lies back to await the medication's sluggish embrace.

The doors to the ward swing open again and a rosy-faced girl appears, carrying an injection tray. She approaches his bed, places the tray on the dressing-trolley and draws the curtain round him.

—I'm Probationer Robinson, she says cheerily. How are you feeling this morning, Mr Kremer?

—Where am I? croaks Samuel, finally managing to force out a sound.

—The London.

—I know that, but where?

—The London Hospital, Mr Kremer. Gloucester Ward. Whitechapel, she says helpfully, as if to a child. You were brought in last night, during the air raid.

—What time is it? What's wrong with me?

—It is eight o'clock in the morning. You're suffering from some nasty burns and a wound to the head, shrapnel from a rocket gun shell. I'm told that your tin hat was split in the middle, imagine that!

—Those blasted rocket guns. What's this tube doing?

—That's a Bunyan bag, Mr Kremer. It contains Milton solution. For the burn, you understand, to stop it burning. You understand?

—Quite so.

—Your head must be a little sore, I imagine?

Samuel nods and groans. The nurse removes his chart-board from the bed rails and glances over it.

—Everything hurts, says Samuel, though I shouldn't grumble. And my feet are cold, frightful chilblains. I've taken a sleeping pill.

With efficient movements the nurse covers his feet with the blankets, then busies herself around his bed. She has a motherly manner and Samuel feels comforted. He thinks for a moment.

—I can't remember a damn thing, he says, groggily.

The nurse angles a syringe towards the ceiling and spurts liquid into the air.

—Here we are, Mr Kremer, she says, a little something to take the edge off.

Samuel turns his head to avoid sight of the needle and catches sight of a nurse walking briskly along the length of the ward, pushing a dressing-trolley. Something about her is familiar; he half-remembers something, a dream perhaps. He peers closer: curly hair bobs from under her starched white cap, her eyes look as if they have been designed to smile, but for a long time have been filled with other more sober expressions. She is very thin, everyone is thin these days but she is thinner than most; her apron is drawn tightly round her narrow waist, and she plucks at the shoulder of her smock as she walks. As she approaches Samuel's bed she turns her face away, and something in an inaccessible part of his mind awakens. He struggles to raise himself on his elbow, calls out, but then the vision is gone.

—Probationer Robinson, he says, who was that? The one pushing the trolley?

—Who? Oh, you mean Probationer Clark.

—Probationer Clark. Ah, I must be seeing things, I could have sworn it was Rosa Klein. It must be the medication, I'm seeing her everywhere.

Betty Robinson looks at him in surprise.

—Did you say Rosie Klein? she says.

—Indeed, says Samuel.

—Well now, there's a coincidence, says the nurse. How ever do you know her Dutch name?

Samuel tries to reply but the nurse's voice is beginning to fade into the distance as the barbiturates and the morphia take effect. For a moment he struggles against the tide. He is light-headed, his eyelids are leaden, the world has become soft, pliant and shimmering. Things do not seem particularly serious, in fact nothing seems to matter any more, and all he wants to do is to sleep, to fall into a velvety slumber for a very long time.

—Perhaps she can come and say hello, he mumbles, I'd appreciate that. When she has the time, you understand.

He does not hear Probationer Robinson's reply; within seconds he has fallen into unconsciousness.

2

Samuel awakes with a start. His head is throbbing with a dull pain, pulsing in time with his heartbeat. The smell of antiseptic is strong, the lofty ceiling is lit with a mid-morning sun, and subdued bustle is all around him. He tries to sit up, is restrained by his arm and falls back: Rosa. She is here. He cranes his neck and spies the rosy-faced nurse from earlier, he cannot remember her name.

—Please, he says, please.

The nurse comes over, balancing two bedpans on her hip, and scans his chart-board.

—Mr Kremer? she says.

—Have you spoken to Rosa yet? asks Samuel. Have you told her that I'm here?

—You're referring to Probationer Clark, I presume, the nurse replies primly.

—Yes, that's right, Probationer Clark. I must see her, she is a personal friend.

Betty leans over with a stony expression and drops her voice to a whisper.

—Probationer Clark has no interest in seeing you, she says.

—I need to see her.

—She doesn't want to see you.

—Look, nurse, just tell her I need to see her, only for a few minutes. Look at the state of me.

—She has no time for the likes of you.

Catching sight of Sister, the nurse straightens herself up and raises her voice to a sing-song.

—Now, Mr Kremer, you must lie back and rest. You're due another dose of morphia in half an hour, and then the doctor will be round to see you.

She glares at him meaningfully and walks away, holding herself erect, collecting another bedpan with a self-satisfied flourish. Samuel thumps the mattress in frustration with his good hand, sending a shock wave through the drip and earning himself a glare from Sister. Soon he will be able to get out of bed; Rosa might be avoiding him, she may hate him, but he will find her, and come hail or high water he will explain. He has been searching for her for years to no avail, and now that fate has delivered her to him, provided the opportunity to put things right, come what may he will clear his name. Reeling from the morphia and the sleeping pills, he says, my dear Rosa, will you forgive me? And he hears Rosa reply, of course I will, darling, I can see now that this has been nothing but a terrible misunderstanding, I love you now more than ever.

He closes his eyes. The pain is returning and the room begins to spin, he grips the bed with his good hand, tries to force it to be still, then abandons himself to the motion and finds it not altogether unpleasant. He remembers walking with Rosa along the cliffs, the sea a vast semicircle to their right, tough grasses stretching up past their ankles, the sun perfectly still overhead. Everything was perfect, the still summer day, the sea and the grass, the salt filling their hair with a coarse stickiness; the cliffs grew more shallow until they reached a point where they could scramble down to the beach, they lay down in the pebbles listening to the swell of the ocean as the waves swirled about the barbed wire and beach scaffolding, looking up at the camouflaged lighthouse far above. Gulls swooped in and out of view as Rosa rested her head on his shoulder and they lay there in perfect silence, illuminated, almost glowing in the sun, and his fingers were stroking her cheek. Later on that day, at home in the cottage before his parents came back, they engaged in the full sexual act for the first time. Rosa was nervous at first, and so was he, but passion took over, took them to a world in which strictures and laws and parents did not exist, only pure love and the desire to be one. And although they would make love again a few times after that, Samuel feels sure that it was that time, the very first, that Rosa conceived their child.

—The course of true love never did run smooth, comes a voice, do you know where that's from?

Samuel opens his eyes dizzily and looks over to the next bed. A pale-eyed, melancholy fellow is sitting in his pyjamas with his legs dangling over the side of the mattress, his sergeant-major's moustache twitching as he smokes a cigarette.

—I'm sorry, says Samuel groggily, are you addressing me?

—That quotation, says the man, where's it from? The course of true love never did run smooth.

—I don't know, says Samuel. John Donne?

—Bunkum. It's Shakespeare. Lysander to Hermia, *A Midsummer Night's Dream*.

Samuel blinks a few times to clear his head.

—What do they call you? says the man, blowing a cloud of smoke into the air.

—Call me? says Samuel.

—Yes, says the man, your name.

—Ah, it's Kremer.

—They call me Captain Farrow. Ex-RAF. I can see you've a Bunyan bag on that arm. That's an RAF technique, you know. You look like you've been knocked about a bit, Kremer.

—I'm all right, says Samuel, it's nothing serious. What are you in here for?

—Acute depression and hysteria, says Farrow, tried to drown myself on Aldgate.

—On Aldgate?

—I know, I know, there's no water on Aldgate. Apart from the Emergency Water Supply tank, if you must know. Seemed like a damn good idea at the time. I have a hundred times wished that one could resign life as an officer resigns a commission.

—Well put.

—Robert Burns, says Farrow, sucking on his cigarette, I'm surprised you didn't recognise it.

—My head hurts, says Samuel, more to himself than to Farrow.

—To die in order to avoid the pain of poverty, love, or anything that is disagreeable, is not the part of a brave man, but of a coward. I'm a coward, you see, Kremer.

—Everyone is a coward in his time, says Samuel.

—Where can you find it? says Farrow.

—Find what?

—That quotation.

—Which quotation?

—To die in order to avoid, et cetera.

—I'm afraid I don't particularly care.

—Aristotle.

Farrow smiles smugly, snorts into his moustache and presses his cigarette into an ashtray. Samuel turns away from those unnerving pale eyes and begins to wish the man had succeeded in the water tank.

—I have on my bedside table a notched candle by which to ration my nightly reading, says Farrow, coughing. I would recommend it.

—Indeed, says Samuel weakly.

—What are you after that nurse for, says Farrow, if you don't mind me asking.

—We're friends, says Samuel, from some time ago.

—Oh, I know all about that sort of thing. Seen a lot of that sort of thing in my time. Do you know the conclusion I have arrived at?

—I suppose you're going to tell me.

—Some of us think holding on makes us strong; but sometimes it is letting go.

—A quotation, I presume?

—Hermann Hesse. And he's a German.

—I thought he was Swiss.

—German by birth. And he attempted suicide.

—A kindred spirit.

—Do you know what I would do if I were you? Write her a note, a romantic note. Include some quotations from the greats. Come live with me and be my love, and we will some new pleasures prove, of golden sands, and crystal beaches, with silken lines and silver hooks . . .

—I don't think that would be appropriate.

—What do you mean, not appropriate? It's Donne.

—The fishing metaphor, it's not appropriate.

—Of course it is.

—Well, Mr Farrow, it's been a pleasure but if you'll excuse me, I've got some convalescing to do.

—Of course.

Samuel, his head hurting more than ever, turns his head away from Farrow and closes his eyes, wishing that he could get out of bed and draw the curtain for the sake of privacy. But perhaps the old nincompoop was right – perhaps a note would be a good idea. As soon as I get my arm out of this blasted bag—

—One more thing, Mr Kremer. Mr Kremer?

—What is it?

—'Three Pleas', by Henry Treece.

He clears his throat for recital, like a schoolboy.

—Mr Farrow, there is truly no need to recite any more poetry, says Samuel, but he is unable to stop him. Farrow intones:

> Stand by me, Death, lest these dark days
> Should hurt me more than I may know;
> I beg that if the wound grows sharp
> You take me when I ask to go.

He comes to a halt, clearly unable to remember the rest, and the verse lingers in the cold air.

—Thank you, Mr Farrow, for your insights, says Samuel.

—Not at all, old boy, says Farrow dreamily. Now I must get some rest. If you'll excuse me.

He salutes courteously and climbs back into bed.

3

It is several days before Samuel is relieved of the Bunyan bag and his arm is dressed and bandaged. Still Rosa is avoiding him, and if it weren't for Betty Robinson still sending him withering looks whenever she passes, he would be inclined to think that the entire episode was simply a figment of his imagination. Taking Mr Farrow's advice, he starts a letter to Rosa; he has no clue how he might deliver it to her but he decides, anyway, to compose it. Leaning awkwardly on the back of an injection tray he writes, crossing out, rephrasing, until the page is a mess of blotches and scribbles. But he perseveres, and finishes the letter, and gradually his health improves, and then the day comes when he is allowed to walk around the ward, leaning heavily on his drip-stand. Doctor Rowlands tells him that soon he will be transferred to a sector hospital – the window of opportunity, Samuel realises, is closing. As soon as he has enough strength, he vows to himself, he will escape into the labyrinth of the hospital, find Rosa and give her the letter himself.

One night, a few hours after darkness has fallen, there is another air raid. Moaning Minnie sounds at ten o'clock, but as ever there is little that can be done for the bed-bound patients. The usual procedure rumbles into action, and the wards are readied for fresh casualties: the centre lights are covered with the night's red shades, bedclothes are folded back, dressing-trolleys equipped, hot water bottles prepared and arranged in the beds. At half past ten the first bombs can be heard. Then the electricity fails and is replaced by the dim glow of lamps and candles and emergency lights. Samuel, lying in his bed next to Mr Farrow, watches the shadows play across the walls and ceiling, listens to the booms and rattles that echo into the night, some distant, others closer, one near enough to make the sooty windows vibrate. Ironically, Farrow lights a cigarette and his section of the ward becomes infused with smoke. Bide your time, Samuel thinks, bide your time until the chaos starts. He waits as the minutes creep by, his bandaged head propped up on a pile of pillows, reading through half-closed eyes the movement of the ward. The nurses are in the final stages of preparation, warming pans of Milton solution, the blue flames of the Primus stoves glowing in the half-light like deepwater fish. Sister patrols up and down the ward, hands clasped firmly behind her back, issuing curt orders from under her helmet. The emphasis is on attention to every last detail, and Samuel knows he must wait.

As the night wears on the gunfire and bombing become more intense. Samuel, torn up inside, lies on his back watching the windows rattle, hoping that the gummed strips that criss-cross them would be enough should the windows be blown in, watching the nurses hurry past with armfuls of equipment. He has a bad feeling, an instinctive sense of dread, which he tries to dismiss. High up towards the ceiling triangular wooden beams have been newly erected to reinforce the roof; it looks stable, they have done a good job, made the structure a good deal more resilient to enemy action, surely it would be madness to venture out on his mission, during an air raid, in his state; although his headache is manageable enough when lying down, he has to accept that apart from a single walk around the ward he has been lying in bed for days. What's more, he is still on a drip – surely it would be madness to wander around the hospital, pushing his drip-stand like a barrel organ, hoping to chance upon Rosa? He reaches over and takes his letter in his hand. He is due to be transferred soon, the doctor said, and if that were to happen he risks losing Rosa again, forever, after having come so close. It would be madness to lie here and do nothing.

Half an hour later, the first casualties arrive; there is a burned and blackened man who cannot bear the bedsheets to be lowered onto his skin, a young lad with both legs in makeshift splints who is taken straight to theatre and several people in states of unconsciousness, covered in white dust, looking like statues in the gloom. As the night wears on, more and more casualties are deposited in the beds from green wire stretchers which are then returned to the Receiving Room for another load; moans and cries begin to fill the air, and still Samuel waits.

Finally he sees his chance: there is a bang close at hand, everyone ducks, and a bucket of firefighting sand tumbles from its hook; a foggy sand haze rises into the air, there is the sound of screams and nurses' voices, and the endless pattering of footsteps. Now, thinks Samuel, do it now. Gingerly he raises himself on one elbow, holding his bandaged arm in front of him, and swings his legs over the side of the bed. He unbandages the drip, exposes the needle and plucks it from his vein like a bee-sting; fluid falls from the needle as it swings against the wall. He has to move now. The ward swims and he closes his eyes until it settles. Bombs are falling with irregular thuds, the floor is vibrating beneath his feet. Carefully he reaches down and laces his shoes. The movement causes his head to throb, he leans back on his good elbow and pauses. Then he gets shakily to his feet, shivers from the cold and pulls his heavy ARP greatcoat over his pyjamas – it feels heavier than he remembers, and the wool is cold to the touch. He feels in the pocket and his fingers brush against the smooth cylinder of his blackout torch, good, it's still there, bravo. He slides the letter carefully into his breast pocket; as he does so he catches eyes with the morbid-looking Mr Farrow who stubs out his cigarette and gives him the thumbs-up. Samuel slings his gas mask over his shoulder and makes his way stealthily along the ward, covering his face against the smell of disinfectant and smoke, past row after row of beds in which semi-conscious patients groan, until he reaches the double doors. He opens them a crack and peers furtively through – the corridor is deserted. The double doors swing together with a clack behind him.

—Nurse, calls a patient into the gloom, nurse?

Rosa stops in her tracks and squints through the greyness. She can just make out a middle-aged woman sitting bolt upright in bed, her hair gathered under a hairnet, her face ghostly in the gloom. She glances at her chart-board: Mrs Wilson.

—Yes, says Rosa, what is it?

—My bedpan needs changing, nurse.

Without a word Rosa puts down the bottle of carbolic solution she is carrying, pulls the curtain closed and squats beside the bed, biting her tongue in frustration. If only Sister had respected her judgement more! Rosa knows she does not need to rest, she was quite happy working on the First Aid post; she would rather be working hard amongst the blood and dirt than be stuck here in Currie, the women's convalescence ward, doing nothing but emptying bedpans and filling water pillows, especially during an air raid.

—I think hospital food might not agree with me, says Mrs Wilson, it's given me a touch of the runs.

Rosa glances at the chart-board on which is inscribed 'I' for meat, 'II' for fish, 'J&C' for jelly and custard, and 'Nil etc' for nil by mouth; Mrs Wilson has a circle around 'I'.

—I'll have you taken off meat, she says.

—Perhaps it was the turpentine enema, says Mrs Wilson, they didn't grease me up properly and it burned. I've the most terrible runs. I'm going every few minutes.

—Well don't go now, says Rosa a little tersely, not until I've replaced the bedpan.

—Would you mind furnishing me with a drink of water, says Mrs Wilson, once you've remedied the bedpan?

—Of course, says Rosa, anything else?

—No, no, that will be all.

The ceramic bedpan is not even half full. Rosa replaces the lid and remains kneeling on the floor for a moment, trying to muster the will to get up. The rattle and thud of the bombs and the guns can be heard spreading out across the city, and the wails of casualties echo from along the corridor, and here she is staring into a half-empty bedpan; somebody must be on the convalescent ward, of course, but why does it have to be her? Quite apart from the infuriating feeling of impotence, being stuck on a ward such as this leaves her with an unwelcome opportunity to think, and inevitably she thinks about Samuel. She has managed thus far to avoid him by getting reassigned mainly to the Crossman Ward, and this has suited her perfectly; not only is it located on the other side of the building, but as the resuscitation ward it also means a constant flow of action, enough to demand her full attention at all times, leaving her with not a single thought to herself. Daily she has checked with Betty Robinson: is he still there, has he not been transferred yet, well what are they waiting for? And daily Betty shakes her head and asks again about the nature of her relationship with Samuel. And daily Rosa refuses to discuss it.

—Will you be quick, dear, says Mrs Wilson, I'm afraid I shall want to go again.

—This bedpan is only half full, says Rosa, you've quite a way to go yet.

—It won't be half full by the time I'm finished, says Mrs Wilson.

Suddenly there is a whistle followed by a loud bang, and the floor trembles, and the emergency lights go out, and Rosa loses her balance and falls to the floor; she can hear Mrs Wilson calling into the darkness; after several seconds the emergency lights come buzzing on again, and Rosa sees that the bedpan has smashed under the bed, spilling the contents in a puddle that stretches all the way to the wall.

—Nurse, moans Mrs Wilson, I am in the most desperate state.

Rosa gets to her feet, exhales and provides her with another bedpan from the next bed; then she kneels again on the floor and proceeds to clear up the mess using handfuls of swabs from the dressing-trolley.

After several minutes the floor is clean. Rosa gets to her feet, stretching her back; a wave of tiredness breaks over her, and she shakes it off in a way that has become familiar. A new sound has joined the stuttering cacophony of the air raid: a steady, dull thud that pulsates the heart in its cage.

—Jolly good, says Mrs Wilson, a mobile gun crew.

—Sounds like it, Rosa replies.

Her senses sharpen – a chance to get out of the tedium of the Currie Ward has presented itself. She looks round and sees a movement close by, she calls into the gloom, Sister? Is that you? Sister materialises from the shadows instantly, imposing and contained, her tin helmet pushed back slightly from her face, wiping her hands on her apron.

—You called, Miss Clark? she says.

—I beg your pardon, Sister, but it sounds as if a gun crew is nearby.

—They are out on the Whitechapel Road, says Sister in omniscient tones. Well?

—It must be awfully hard work, says Rosa, out there with the guns. Don't you think they would like a cup of tea?

—I dare say they would, replies Sister drily.

—Matron said that we should offer the servicemen tea where appropriate. I would like to take them a tray of tea and cigarettes.

—Not one of your better ideas, Probationer Clark. The ward is never left, you know that.

—But I'm not doing anything here, Rosa replies boldly, apart from emptying bedpans and clearing up urine from the floor. The junior probationers can easily manage that.

—You should be thankful not to be in Crossman, replies the Sister a little snappishly. A high explosive came down in Middlesex Street, and the casualties are still coming in.

—Very well, send me back to Crossman, says Rosa, all I want is to be doing something worthwhile. I'm cooling my heels here.

—That's quite enough, says Sister. She cocks her head in a wily manner, taking stock of the situation; this is irregular but the girl hasn't done anything wrong, except for exhibiting a little wilfulness in the heat of the moment. Her voice softens.

—Very well then. But don't dally, do you hear? You can take that bedpan to the sinkroom on your way.

—Yes, Sister, thank you, says Rosa, and disappears into the shadows. The last things to vanish are the white apron-straps crossed across her back.

Mrs Wilson raises her hand.

—Sister, I beg your pardon, she says.

Sister turns towards her.

—Yes, she says, do you need something?

—I wasn't eavesdropping or anything, but I couldn't help but overhear your conversation. I'm not convinced that Probationer Clark should be risking her life for a cup of tea. My son Kenneth is an Air Raid Warden, you see, she adds, he's six foot one.

—You don't know Probationer Clark, Sister replies enigmatically, she has an uncanny thirst for this sort of thing. Now if you'll excuse me.

—But she's risking her neck, says Mrs Wilson.

—We all risk our necks these days, Mrs Wilson. Especially in the nursing profession.

Samuel's head is hurting, but not as much as he thought it would, his arm is stinging but not to an unbearable degree, and his mind feels strangely clear. He stumbles along the corridors, clinging to the walls and the shadows, avoiding the nurses and medical men, hoping against hope for a glimpse of Rosa as the noise of the air raid clatters on and orange light flashes through the smeared windows. He skids and almost falls on a flight of soapy stairs left half scrubbed by the night cleaners, but manages to right himself. As he walks the corridors get busier, and the floor is covered with a greasy black film; he must be approaching the front of the building. A noise grows, a blend of shouts, cries, screams, firm orders and soothing words, clinks of bottles and slams of doors and the trundling sound of wheels upon linoleum, the noise of the Home Front, echoing against the smooth walls and floors of the hospital. Samuel nears the entrance hall and finds himself plunged into bedlam. Everywhere there are people on stretchers, nurses in tin helmets carrying bowls and bandages, intense-looking doctors with stethoscopes, policemen and wardens and soot-covered women clutching their bags and weeping.

There – a nurse in a green greatcoat hurrying towards the exit, she is slight of frame like Rosa, and curls are springing from below her tin helmet. Samuel, heart quickening, calls Rosa, Rosa, just a minute, stumbles round a stretcher and plucks at the sleeve of her coat. The figure turns round: it is a Green Nurse, an emergency midwife, dressed for the street, case in her hand, gas mask over her shoulder, tin helmet on her head with LONDON HOSPITAL printed across it, ready to walk out through the air raid to deliver a baby.

—You haven't by any chance seen a probationer by the name of Clark? he asks.

The Green Nurse regards him blankly, exhaustion and confusion on her face, unsure what to make of this wild-eyed bandaged man in pyjamas and a greatcoat.

—There are hundreds of probationers, she says. Ask a night sister. You can find them in the wards with ribbon bows on the handles.

—Ribbon bows?

—Yes, ribbon bows mean that a night sister's there.

Suddenly Samuel glimpses another figure in a nurse's greatcoat navigating her way towards the main entrance, something balanced in her hands; this time the coat is not green but navy, and the curls are unmistakably Rosa's. He blinks; as quickly as she appeared, she is gone.

Dizzy and aching, he pushes his way through the crowds and finds himself at the top of the grimy steps at the front of the hospital, faced with the gaping entrance, gazing out into the night. In the street there is nothing but blackness; the sky is overcast with a thick fog, and the moonshine seeps dully down onto the city, onto the roofs with their missing tiles, the iron plates over the windows, the piles of sandbags, the cracked pavement. Splashes of light splutter on the horizon, silhouetting the barrage balloons, followed by the noise of explosions; searchlights sweep the clouds, and planes can everywhere be heard, but not seen. Was it really Rosa, or was his mind playing tricks on him? It could, after all, have been a Green Nurse, or nobody at all. What on earth would Rosa be doing venturing out at the height of an air raid? And even if it was Rosa, how can he find her now – which way did she turn, left or right? In an instant he makes up his mind; in a burst of insanity he decides to follow his instinct. He takes a breath, turns his lapels up high against his cheeks and plunges into the freezing smog.

4

Samuel stumbles along the Whitechapel Road, bandaged and freezing in the darkness, ignoring the pain in his arm, his head, placing his trust in his instincts, heading in the direction of Aldgate, towards Liverpool Street station. The blackout is total apart from a rectangle of light a little way ahead coming from the doorway of a pub; two figures stand unsteadily in the light until an Air Raid Warden approaches and the door is closed; then there is nothing but blackness. Samuel cups his blackout torch in his hand, allowing just enough light to spill between his fingers onto the pavement in front of him. Dotted about are mushrooms of rubble, spent shell cases and water mains gushing into the street; the flat drone of aircraft can be heard overhead, punctuated by the heavy thud of guns, and he begins to feel stupid, and vulnerable, without so much as a tin helmet for protection.

There – across the road, in the amber light of a fire, a slanting shadow slips across a wall. Samuel, heart punching in his chest, hurries over the road in pursuit, hoping against hope. He takes his fingers away from the mouth of the torch and allows the beam to illuminate the pavement in front of him – the shadow is moving up ahead, it could be Rosa, it could be the Green Nurse, it could be anyone really, or just a cat, or a trick of the light. An eerie quietude has fallen over the streets as a wave of bombers passes towards the north of the city, but Samuel knows that it will not be long before another squadron approaches, especially given the intensity of these raids. He slips his torch back into his pocket; the clouds have drifted away from the moon and, despite the smog, there is just enough light to see. He breaks into a jog, the impact of his feet on the pavement sending stinging waves of pain through his body, and suddenly he feels cripplingly thirsty; but it is Rosa up ahead, it has to be, and nothing, not his injuries, not the cold, not even the enemy, has the power to stop him now.

Balancing the tea tray Rosa hastens along the treacherous pavement. The mugs collide against each other as she walks, spilling tea onto the cigarettes, she really should turn back, the gun crew are nowhere to be seen, they must have moved on, the tea will be stone cold by now. But she cannot bring herself to return to the ward, to spend the remainder of the night in the company of bedpans and temperature charts and incontinent old ladies. A strange thrill is passing through her, a powerful sensation of freedom. She has not left the hospital building for weeks, months probably, in fact she cannot remember the last time she felt the winter breeze against her face, apart from when passing along the iron bridge from the nurses' homes to the hospital and back; and despite the bombers and the gunfire, and the knowledge that in the catacombs of the city below her millions of humans are cowering, a sense of peace seems to reign above ground. The city is hers, nobody is around, there might be Air Raid Wardens and gun crews and policemen, but they are lurking in the shadows and few and far between; yes, London is hers, for a few precious minutes, and the greater the distance between her and the hospital, the further she leaves Samuel behind. For a moment she imagines she is back in Berlin, passing through the deserted streets, for despite the fact that her family has been uprooted and flung asunder, and she speaks every day in English, and eats English food, and breathes English air, and even thinks in English these days; despite all this she is not English to the core, and never will be. She slows her pace and considers stopping, resting for a while on a wall, but it is perishingly cold and she has to keep moving. Across the street a rectangle of light catches her attention, two drunken figures are lolling in a pub doorway, for a moment she is struck by the crazy impulse to go in, order a drink; but then an ARP Warden approaches, tells the couple to stop volunteering themselves to Jerry as a target, and this brings Rosa down: what is she doing outside, in an air raid, by herself, with a tray of cold tea, when she should be back at hospital tending to the sick? Nursing is not about fulfilling one's own taste for adventure, it is about dedication to those in need. She is filled with shame and decides that she must go back. As she turns she sees, in the foggy street behind her, a silhouette approaching. Far off there is the boom of a high explosive; the figure approaches to within arm's reach and rummages in its pocket; then a blackout torch clicks on, dimly illuminating a pair of shoes on the pavement.

—Rosa, comes a breathless voice from the darkness, it is you. It is really you.

The yellow beam of the blackout torch swings upwards to spread a horrid light across a face half covered with bandages, deep black shadows sweeping up in triangles above the eyebrows.

—Friend or foe? says Rosa, alarmed.

—Put that light out! someone shouts from somewhere.

The torch is lowered and shines again on the shoes.

—Do not be afraid, Rosa. It is me. Samuel.

Rosa gasps and backs away, holding up the tea tray defensively.

—No, I refuse to believe it. Are you haunting me?

—You are haunting me.

—Where did you come from? Have you been following me?

—I wanted to give you a letter.

—I'll summon the police. After all this time, can't you just leave me alone?

—I just want to speak to you.

—You've been told I'm not interested, isn't that enough? What more must I do? And now you follow me into an air raid?

—Rosa, please. I need to explain. Just allow me five minutes.

—Five minutes is all it took to destroy our baby. If you continue to follow me I shall summon the police.

—You don't understand, says Samuel, it's not true.

Rosa turns and hurries off into the clinging mist, and as she does so the clouds knit in front of the moon and everything is shrouded in blackness. Samuel curses, shines his torch into the smog and hurries after her. His head is hurting, the dizziness has returned and the strength is draining from his limbs – why won't she stop, just for a moment, why won't she listen?

They weave their way along the Whitechapel Road, Samuel flicking on his blackout torch from time to time to illuminate the way ahead, struggling to keep her in sight, begging her to stop, to listen. In the eerie lull of the bombing, as a silence descends more profoundly than before, the subterranean level of the city awakens, and everywhere people creep from their shelters to make cups of tea. A solitary searchlight sways amongst the clouds, a lonely pillar of light, slicing past the barrage balloons that hang ominously in the sky, piercing the thickening smog. Piles of sandbags lie like rats against buildings; the air tastes sooty, like vinegar, like coal.

—Rosa, stop. I'm going to go mad, I swear it.

Suddenly Rosa stops and turns to face him.

—Go mad then, she says, go mad. I do not want to speak to you or listen to you or hear from you ever again, should I be condemned to live as long as God himself.

Without warning she steps sideways into the road and disappears. Samuel switches on his blackout torch, sweeps it through the mist and sees her on the other side of the road, silhouetted against an OXO advertisement. Suddenly something within him gives way. He turns the torch off, hurries across the street and grabs her roughly by the elbow.

—It wasn't me that made the decision to get rid of our baby, he says, it was you.

—Just leave me alone, cries Rosa, how can I get you to just leave me alone?

She tries to push his hand away but he holds fast to her sleeve.

—I shan't leave you alone, says Samuel, not until you listen to me.

Suddenly a distant screeching sound cuts through the sooty air, coming gradually closer. Samuel tries to pull Rosa to the ground, but she slips out of his grasp; he grabs at the empty air and his torch shoots from his hand, clunks onto the street and skitters into the gutter.

A silence falls, and for an eternity there is nothing but blackness. Samuel finds himself half sitting, half lying against a wall. He can't hear the noise of his breath, can't hear anything; he pulls himself numbly to his feet, he can feel nothing, as if he doesn't have a body, can hear nothing, see nothing, smell nothing. Gradually his vision returns – the night is illuminated by the sickly brightness of a fire that fills the buildings along the opposite side of the street and spills down into the road. He is coughing, his lungs are full of grime. A few feet away lies Rosa, on her side as if sleeping, coated in powdery dust, her tin hat beside her on the pavement, spinning on its dome; a blanket of broken glass lies across her, she still clutches the tea tray to her chest, although the teacups and cigarettes are nowhere to be seen. Samuel shuffles along the debris-strewn pavement and gathers her up like a doll. Shards of glass patter to the ground as he carries her through the rubble, staggering, coughing violently, unable to hear, to think; Rosa's greatcoat flaps beneath her as he walks, her head lolls limply backwards. Suddenly she raises her head and begins to moan, and Samuel tries to soothe her – to his surprise he can hear his own voice now, it is booming, filling his whole head, he can hear his own breathing as well. Rosa says something that he cannot hear, struggles out of his arms and drops to the pavement, stumbles, gets woozily to her feet and then falls to her knees. Samuel tries once again to pick her up, the feeling is returning to his limbs and his wounded arm is hurting, Rosa struggles away and manages to stand, steadying herself against a wall. A buzzing sound is beginning to fill Samuel's head, he pushes his fingers into his ears but it continues regardless.

—We must get to a shelter, he says, the underground is around here somewhere.

—Ich brauche keinen Luftschutz. Geht schon so, says Rosa, coughing a cloud of dust.

—You need a doctor, says Samuel, come on. You'll be safe with me.

Rosa continues to repeat geht schon so, geht schon so, geht schon so, I'm all right, I'm all right, as Samuel takes her by the elbow and steers her through the fog, through the milky rubble and dust, the shadows and the fumes, the rivers of water from burst pipes, the snowy drifts of glass, the split sandbags and cracked paving slabs and twists of metal that could have come from anywhere; the shattered moonscape of London's East End.

5

—You mean you never use the shelters? Even when you're off duty? whispers Samuel. His breath clouds in the air and his arms are clutched round his knees; it is so cold that he is glad of his bandages.

—I don't need to, replies Rosa, her whisper echoing against the tiled walls. She gathers her greatcoat against the chill. There is a reason that I am alive, she whispers, I don't know what it is. But if I die, I die. A lot of people are in far more danger than me.

—And they say the Jews are always the first ones in, says Samuel.

Her body stiffens but she makes no response. There is a silence. Samuel blows his nose, causing the man sleeping beside him to stir. He peers into his handkerchief; it is filled with an oily black deposit. He shivers, picks up Rosa's tin helmet and begins to rotate it in his hands. His ears are still ringing from the bomb blast.

—So finally I have the opportunity to explain, he says, leaning against the curved wall of the platform, his head haloed by the London Underground symbol.

—There is nothing to explain, whispers Rosa.

—I've written you a letter.

He rummages in his pockets but to no avail; the letter did not make it through the blast.

—Damned bombs, says Samuel, they're an absolute nuisance when it comes to keeping hold of things.

Rosa turns onto her side, presenting Samuel with her dust-covered back.

—Ironic, isn't it, he whispers, a nurse getting knocked off her feet within easy reach of her hospital. And this is where you first arrived, isn't it? When you came on the train from Germany? Liverpool Street?

Rosa does not respond. Samuel sighs and looks around him, spinning her helmet absent-mindedly in his hands as the bombers whirr through the thick night above, carrying their murderous load. The platform is murky with darkness, dense with slumbering Londoners, clustered together like field mice under blankets; it is like a communal bedroom, personal effects everywhere, hats and jackets hanging at all angles. Nearby a cloth-capped man is snoring loudly, stretched across a bicycle in a very uncomfortable-looking fashion. Somewhere along the platform a baby begins to cry as the bombs beat their irregular rhythm upon the earth above, and sheets of dust slip on occasion from the cracks in the tiles overhead. Who knows what would have happened to Rosa if he hadn't been there? Alone, she would surely have been done for; the bombardment above ground is gaining momentum if the racket is anything to go by. He looks over at her, she is still motionless, either asleep or pretending to be; her shoulders are tense, the muscles bunched together like a bag of walnuts.

—Are you awake? he whispers.

There is no response.

—I didn't know anything about the procedure, he says. Mother didn't tell me anything, you know.

Rosa remains silent.

—When I found out what Mother had done I was beside myself with rage, he goes on, almost to himself. I left home that day and haven't been back. I've been trying to find you ever since. My parents have made no effort to contact me, and I haven't even sent them a postcard. They could be dead for all I know.

There is a pause and then Rosa rolls over to face him.

—What? she whispers.

—I didn't know anything about the procedure, Samuel repeats.

—But you came into my bedroom, you saw what was going on. You saw it with your own eyes.

—I thought he was giving you a routine examination.

—But I called out to you, Samuel. I called out and you walked away. You can't deny that.

—I was away with the fairies. I didn't know if I was coming or going.

From along the platform somebody shushes, and immediately they both stop talking. Rosa turns away again, pulling the lapels of her great-coat over her face.

—You did hear me call out, she whispers, you should have known. You should have made it your business to know.

—Perhaps, whispers Samuel. And perhaps you should have stood up to Mother.

Suddenly, Rosa faces him.

—Don't you twist this back on me. I was just a guest in your house, not even a guest, your mother made me into her personal maid. I didn't have a hope, not once you betrayed me.

—I didn't betray you.

—You did betray me. I needed you, and you weren't there. You didn't have the backbone to stand up to your mother.

—Well then, nor did you.

—Very well, I admit it. I should have refused the procedure, I should have. Do you think I do not live with this guilt every day? Do you think there is a single night when I do not think of my weakness and suffer?

—You don't have all the suffering, you know. The baby was mine as much as yours, and so is the guilt.

—I've spent two years hating you, Samuel.

—I've spent two years loving you.

From along the platform there is another, more irritated shush. For the first time Rosa looks into Samuel's face, trying to read his emotions. Despite his bandages she sees instantly that the old tenderness has not died; it is still there, more intense perhaps now than it used to be, although covered with layers of suffering. Conflicting emotions rise within her, creeping from her stomach through her chest into her throat; she chokes and turns away again.

Samuel gets to his feet and picks his way along the platform, Rosa hears him go but does not move. The letter from Heinrich, which by now she knows by heart, slips uninvited into her mind: if one day he were to come begging to you on bleeding knees, never, ever forgive him. For years her family has been telling her to be strong – such a simple concept in the material world, but as a measure of the emotions how elusive! For so long she has resisted the tide of emotion, refusing to succumb to her weaknesses and fears, standing firm, doing her duty, carrying on; she has developed an impenetrable, armour-like shell that has frozen the world out, enabled her to withstand its pressures. Could it be that her hardness is not a sign of strength after all, but just another manifestation of weakness? Might the course of true strength be to lower her guard, to face the risks, to accept them? To accept him?

On the edge of the platform Samuel stands looking up at the curved ceiling of the tunnel, rubbing his bandaged head as if to alleviate his headache, absently reading the posters advertising Guinness and Austin

Reed. The war has brought endless confusion, and in the chaos, two years and four months ago, in a melting pot of selfishness, and duty, and fear, and love, another life dropped from the world. In times like these, does it matter? When millions are dying, does it matter? As the bombs continue to burst overhead, and the man with the cloth cap continues to snore across his bicycle, Samuel finds a feeling of peace settling inside him, as if his life makes a certain kind of sense now that he has finally put his case to Rosa. From this moment on he will be happy, somehow, to be alone. If she rejects him, if he never sees her again, if he ends up abandoned and lonely with not even his parents to turn to, he knows now that he will survive. He has followed Rosa through to the end, he has trusted his instincts and risked his life for her, and he has won the chance to tell her the truth of what happened two years ago in Norfolk; now their future is in her hands, and he is at peace with his conscience. How indifferent London can be, England can be, the planet can be, he thinks. Yet he can feel some of that indifference, finally, falling away from him, and as he turns round and makes his way back towards Rosa's slumbering form, he feels a new strength beginning to grow.

Rosa, hearing him approach, rolls achingly onto her back and opens her eyes.

—You're awake, says Samuel softly.

—Yes.

There is a pause.

—Have you heard from your parents since I last saw you? he says.

—They wrote to me saying that they would be unable to write for a long time, says Rosa.

—I see, says Samuel quietly.

Despite herself, Rosa finds that she is desperate to speak. She has not had the opportunity to talk to anyone about her family since she left Norfolk, and even after all this time there is nobody in existence who can understand her as deeply as Samuel.

—Sometimes I think I have forgotten them, she says, but then the memories come back with such strength that I expect them to walk through the door. Often I see reflections of them in the windows, but then I look and they have gone. I should be with them, not here. I should be suffering the same as them. I don't know even why I am alive. I am cursed with life.

—They know you are safe, and that must give them strength, says Samuel.

—I hope so, says Rosa, at least then I would have some use.

—They must be proud of your career as well.

—I am not qualified yet, but yes, they are proud. Especially Papa.

—So he should be. I think you might be doing more for them than you realise.

Rosa looks at Samuel and suddenly she feels alive, as if her shell has been dissolved and the breeze is touching her skin for the first time. The man in the cloth cap suddenly lets out a snore so loud that it produces murmurs of sleepy protest all around. Rosa cannot help but smile – Samuel notices her expression and feels suddenly a weight lifting.

—Come on, he says, we'll never get any sleep here.

—I'm too weak, says Rosa, I cannot even stand.

—Don't worry, says Samuel, I'll help.

Grabbing the sleeves of her greatcoat in cold-numbed fingers, he hauls her upright and supports her weight.

—Come on, he says, don't worry, I've got you.

He draws Rosa to him – she smells of antiseptic so strongly it is as if that is her natural scent – and they begin to shuffle in and out of groups of blanket-covered bodies, round suitcases and gas mask boxes, along the platform towards the exit. They make their slow way towards the stationary escalators, two dishevelled silhouettes without rhythm or coordination, stepping on each other's feet, their knees colliding again and again, a lumbering couple in the darkness. Now they are not smiling or laughing, not even looking at each other; Samuel is glancing around for a gap in the hundreds of slumbering bodies, and Rosa's eyes are closed, as if asleep, or about to faint, moving in time to the sporadic rhythm of his steps, allowing him to carry her in vague figure-of-eights around the station, supporting her on his bandaged arm as her greatcoat flaps gently against her ankles. She opens her eyes.

—Are we dancing? she whispers.

—Well, I've got two left feet, says Samuel, and there isn't any music. Hold on, there's a space just down there. This way.

He shuffles towards the escalator, aiming for a vacant lower step. All around them, throughout the tunnels and the escalators, people sleep, snore, scratch, like so many tramps. As they wind their way through legs and bags and slumbering faces, Rosa promises herself that from now on, during the air raids, she will start to use the shelters; for now she has feared enough.

They reach the escalator and sit down, exhausted, amongst the feet of the people on the steps above. A canvas bag lies on the end of the step,

Samuel reaches over to arrange it as a pillow for Rosa, she senses him moving towards her and raises her body to meet him; Samuel's trembling fingers cup her face, and Rosa's hand slips across the shoulders of his greatcoat. Their feelings are familiar yet different, more meaningful, grounded by suffering and at the same time more genuine for it. Rosa lowers her head onto Samuel's chest, she can feel him shivering beneath her forehead; she feels renewed, as if, in all the dark that surrounds them, she is emerging into the brightness; and she is filled with an absolute certainty.

—We can try again, says Samuel softly, I would like to try again.

—It's been a long time, says Rosa, we are different now.

—Yes, says Samuel, but nothing has changed. I still love you.

Rosa lifts her head, tears blurring her eyes, and attempts to reply.

—I've lost my family, and I've lost my baby, and I lost you, Samuel. I don't want to lose you again. I don't want to be alone.

—Don't, says Samuel, don't say it. You don't need to.

Rosa raises her mouth, and their lips meet once, lightly, and then again; they kiss, lifting their hands to each other's faces, tears mingling with soot on their cheeks and slipping between their fingers, cleaning white lines across their skin. As the bombs continue to fall overhead, and the guns pound shells into the sky, and the incendiaries whip vicious fires across the roofs, and twisted pieces of shrapnel tumble onto the city, in the tunnels under London millions of people sleep; yet Rosa and Samuel lie awake in each other's arms, awaiting the daybreak.

8 May 1945, London

I

The war in Europe is over. The streets of London are festive, crammed with so many people that, when seen from a vantage point at the top of a lamp-post, or on the back of a stone lion, or the roof of a bus, the impression is akin to millions of matches stacked side by side from building to building across every street, swarming round corners, coating every statue and vehicle and monument. Here is Nelson's Column, here the Houses of Parliament, here Buckingham Palace, here the Mall, and everywhere a jubilant mass of celebrating people forming bristling dunes around them. A constant fluttering motion sparkles on the surface of the crowd, everybody is waving something, flags, hats, handkerchiefs, hands. People are dancing in the fountains. The excitement is electric, more than electric, more visceral, more jubilant, triumphant, a celebration of human emotion that wells from millions of hearts in ecstatic quantities and manifests in movement, in laughter, in kissing, dancing and, above all, in sound. The noise is tremendous. The cheering is constant. Whistling, piping, singing, chanting, church bells pealing, laughing, laughing, laughing. Yet nowhere can there be seen a single glass of alcohol; the crowds are intoxicated by nothing other than the pure taste of freedom.

Rosa is sitting on the top of a lion, her hand raised above her head, holding a Union flag which slips and flutters in the breeze. She speaks over her shoulder to her fiancé:

—Is it three o'clock yet?

—Not yet, he replies, two more minutes.

And he cups his hand round her cheek and kisses her full on the mouth, an action which in any other circumstances would have invited disapproval, but today, for one day only, has become commonplace.

—I am so glad, he shouts above the noise of the crowd, I love you more than anything in the world. No more air raids, no more blackouts. Life begins again! Isn't it wonderful?

Rosa smiles but doesn't reply, and goes back to fluttering her flag; she knows she cannot leave, not yet, not until Mr Churchill's address, although she is desperate to get back to Whitechapel as soon as she can. Not that this isn't an excellent party and an excellent day, she feels it too, profoundly, and doesn't want to miss it; but she cannot deny that a part of her lies many miles away, across the sea, in Germany, and today that part of her is crying out louder than it ever has before, demanding that she act immediately.

Finally Big Ben chimes, and a hush falls upon the crowd; the clusters of loudspeakers nestling high on lamp-posts crackle, and all at once Mr Churchill's pugnacious voice bellows rousingly into the air: this is your victory! It is the victory of the cause of freedom in every land. In all our long history we have never seen a greater day than this, God bless you all. And then For he's a jolly good fellow, and Land of hope and glory, conducted by Mr Churchill himself, and more cheering, dancing, celebrating.

When the speech and songs and applause have ended, Rosa turns once again to her fiancé.

—I'm sorry, darling, I need to go home now, she says.

—Go home? Samuel replies. What ever for? The party has only just started.

—I know, she says, you stay and have a party to remember. But now the war has ended, there's something I need to do.

She slides over the black flank of the lion and slips down to the ground, showing him a reassuring smile. He appears concerned as he acknowledges her farewells with a half-smile of his own; now his is the sole face in the sea not to wear an expression of delight.

Yet going home is not as easy as Rosa had hoped. The crowds, in anticipation of Mr Churchill's procession along the Mall, are locked together as tightly as cement, and she is unable to push her way through until the Austin Cambridge finally appears, preceded by ceremonial guards on cantering horses; Churchill passes like Moses through the ocean, raising his hat and showing his scowl-smile to the cheering throng; and then the crowd-waters close behind him, hundreds of people run in his wake, waving their hats, chasing like children amid shouts of excitement and praise. Rosa makes her way to Piccadilly station, and from there home to the London.

The silence is magnified as she closes the door behind her and all sounds are muffled in the familiar quietude of Cavell House. The building is strangely deserted, she has never known it so quiet before; she is briefly struck by the impression that she has entered not her home but a museum. In an attempt to steady herself, rather than going straight upstairs she first makes her way to the kitchen to make herself a cup of tea – the home maids are all off duty, along with everybody else, for the celebrations. Then she makes her way upstairs to her cramped study-bedroom, sets the tea down on the writing desk, hangs her coat in her wardrobe then takes out a pen and paper, glad that everybody is out, as she needs to be alone – not only alone but also feeling alone – to write.

8. May 1945
Liebe Mama, lieber Papa, Heinrich and Hedi,

I don't know how to begin this letter. After six dark years there is at last hope that we shall be together once again. I can't tell you how I have longed for the war to end, and now that day has truly arrived and all I can think about is your welfare, and when we shall be reunited. I have so much to tell you, I don't know where to start. I am engaged to be married now, to a wonderful man by the name of Samuel Kremer (yes, the son of Gerald and Mimi), and I cannot wait to introduce him to you all. And I am less than a year away from qualifying as a nurse, a proper nurse, at the London Hospital, Papa will be so proud when he hears of it!

Please write soon and reassure me of your well-being. I have been worried out of my mind for years on end, and the only thing that has kept me going from one day to the next is the thought that one day we will be a family again. How wonderful it is that the day will be soon!

Mit lieben Grüßen,
Rosa

Surprised at the ease with which she has managed to write in German after all this time, she seals the envelope and addresses it to their apartment in Prenzlauer Berg. She knows that the chances of the letter finding its way to her parents are slim; but this is a day on which miracles have been allowed to occur, and despite the odds her heart is full of hope. Leaving her tea forgotten on the writing desk, she hurries downstairs and out into the street as if the slightest delay would cause the war to start again, her parents to be trapped and this precious opportunity to disappear as quickly as it arose.

It is not far to the letterbox on the Whitechapel Road; she allows the envelope to hang from her fingers inside the scarlet walls. The city, free from the shackles of blackout, is dusted with countless lights. A prayer comes into her mind, her prayer, please God, protect my family and reunite us soon. She releases the letter, and it tumbles down into the shadows. For a few moments she stands on the pavement before walking back to Cavell House, knowing that a new period of waiting has begun.

As she is fumbling with her keys outside the front door, there is the sound of somebody approaching. She turns to see Samuel emerging from the darkness, walking along the path towards her, his black hair ruffled and his shirt-tails untucked, dangling his hat by the brim, still exuberant from the party.

—Rosa, he says, it's you.

—What are you doing here? she replies, kissing him.

—I came to join you, says Samuel, to check that everything's all right.

—You should have stayed with everyone else. A war doesn't end every day, you know.

—The festivities will be going on all night and well into tomorrow, I shouldn't wonder, says Samuel. Can you believe it's over? It's finally over. We're living in the future.

Rosa opens the front door and steps into the hall.

—Why don't you come in? she says. At least we know that for once nobody is around and you won't need to sneak about like a burglar.

He follows her inside and attempts to toss his hat onto the banister, but it bounces off and falls to the ground; he swipes it up and perches it there, leaving it hanging like a scalp, a symbol of their temporary ownership of the house.

—Why did you run off? says Samuel. I followed you as soon as I could but the crowds were intolerable.

—Would you like a cup of tea? says Rosa.

—Yes please, says Samuel, I'm parched.

—I've been here, says Rosa, walking into the kitchen, writing to my family.

She puts the kettle on to boil and turns to Samuel, her face glowing with an unusual excitement.

—I can't wait for you to meet them, she says. You'll have to learn German, or they'll have to brush up on their English, or a bit of both. Hedi will be fourteen now, can you believe it? Fourteen. And Heinrich will be twenty-five. You'll love Papa, I'm sure of it.

The kettle whistles, and Rosa pours the water steaming into the teapot.

—Our first post-war cup of tea, says Samuel. I'm going to enjoy this.

—We could probably drink it in the sitting room, don't you think, says Rosa, now that the place is deserted? I've always wondered what it would be like to take tea with you in the sitting room. Perhaps we can play the piano. I don't think it's ever been used.

—I'm not sure, says Samuel. What if someone were to arrive unexpectedly? Let's go up to your room.

As they climb the stairs, Rosa removes Samuel's hat from the banister and takes it with them. They enter her bedroom, and she goes to shut the blackout curtains.

—You needn't do that, says Samuel, the war's over, remember?

—Ah, says Rosa, it's just such a habit. It feels criminal to let the lights blaze out like this.

She leaves the curtains open and sits beside him on the bed. He looks out of the window for inspiration, trying to find a way of phrasing what he wants to express; the hospital building hulks against the night sky, its windows alight like rectangular stars.

—We'll arrange for my family to come to London, says Rosa, we'll find them a little house somewhere nearby, and Mama will help look after our children, when we have them.

Samuel takes a breath.

—I'm certain that you will be reunited with your family, and very soon at that, he replies, but your parents have no known location. We must accept that there is a remote possibility . . .

His voice trails off and Rosa takes a sip of tea.

—Oh God, Samuel continues. What I'm trying to say is that I just can't help but feel that we should focus our thoughts on discovering their whereabouts rather than thinking about what we'll do when they get here. We don't want to build up a potential disappointment. I'm sorry, Rosa, this is sounding appalling even to me. I am sure they are alive, and I'm certain you will be together soon. I don't mean to dampen your spirits, I'm sorry.

—I don't know what you're saying, says Rosa.

—Indeed, says Samuel, getting to his feet and walking to the window, you're right. I'm sorry, let's talk about something else. Just look out there, no barrage balloons, no searchlights, just God's clear sky. After five and a half long years, amazing.

There is a pause while Rosa refills Samuel's cup from the teapot.

—Does it upset you when I speak about my parents? she says suddenly.

Samuel's profile is outlined against the glowing tapestry of the window.

—Upset me? he says. Why should it?

—Because I'm so keen to see them, and the end is in sight.

—So?

—In light of the situation with your own parents.

Samuel gives a barely perceptible flinch and turns back to the twinkling lights of London.

—That's completely different, he says. I've never missed Mother and Father, and I never shall. Not after what they did. I'll never miss them.

—They're still your parents.

—Yes, says Samuel, it's just . . . the only thing that troubles me is that they won't be present at our wedding. I know it's foolish, but I can't help it. One's parents are supposed to be there, aren't they?

—I'm sorry.

—Don't be, says Samuel stoically, I don't even want to talk about them.

Rosa goes to join him at the window, and they embrace, two silhouettes joining in the dazzling light.

2

In the months following the end of the war, Samuel finds a good use for his savings. If he's to get married to Rosa, and they are going to start a family together, he'll need to start earning some money. So he decides to take a step into the unknown, to shoulder the burden of risk, and put into action an idea for a business that had occurred to him when he looked into buying a motorcar several months ago. At the time he was regularly travelling by bus from his digs in Hendon to Whitechapel, to see Rosa; the buses and underground trains were reasonable, but he couldn't help but feel that the journey would be easier by motorcar, and it would enable him to take Rosa on day-trips as well. But when he looked into the purchase he found that there was an eighteen-month waiting list for new models and gave up on the idea; the next day, from the window of a bus, he noticed a derelict bomb site on the Finchley Road, and an idea started to form in his mind. Upon investigation he discovered that the plot of land was available for lease; he made other enquiries at various places, and put up advertisements, and in the January of 1946 he opened Kremer's Motors, a second-hand dealership selling Rileys, Austins, Morrises and MGs, all of which were popular vehicles, all of which he fixed up himself, and all of which attracted significant interest. He and Rosa met weekly, on Thursday evenings when she was off duty; she was surprised to learn of his new direction and somewhat bewildered when he arrived one week wearing a natty suit and driving a bright red 1935 Riley Kestrel Saloon, which he was going to sell the following day.

From the start business goes well for Samuel; demand is high, competition scarce. And Thursdays come, and Thursdays go, and he promises Rosa that he will buy a house as soon as they are married, a perfect house. As winter draws to a close and spring approaches, and he sells his twentieth motorcar, he feels that a celebration is in order. That Thursday he borrows a particularly special vehicle, a two-seater Midget from 1936, with elegant lines, a jet-black body and scarlet grille, and drives east across London to see Rosa; he is caught in a traffic jam on Aldgate on a scale unseen since before the war, a bottleneck has formed on account of the haycarts, he cleans the grease off his hands, unfolds a newspaper, takes a cursory glance then folds it up again, placing it in the pocket of his greatcoat and adjusting his hat. I miss the war, in a funny sort of way, he thinks, back then things were simpler, the papers reported victories, defeats, advances, retreats, numbers of wounded and killed, momentous events that were either good or bad, and we all had a purpose to life; these days things are more complicated.

He is tired, and would usually be looking forward to nothing more than supper, a spot of wireless and bed; but as the traffic clears and he guides the Midget nearer to Whitechapel, attracting looks of admiration from passers-by, Samuel is in high spirits, for in the breast pocket of his jacket lies a Manila envelope containing his surprise. Last week, a customer by the name of Tony Simons, while purchasing an old 1933 Morris Ten-Four, had mentioned in passing that he and his wife Ruth, for their honeymoon, had spent a wonderful weekend in Jersey, where there is no longer any rationing; and they had eaten butter and cream and steak to their hearts' content, and played skittles on the beach, and had a splendid time. So the following day Samuel purchased tickets of his own, made reservations at the Grand Hotel in Jersey and bought himself a set of skittles; now, as he parks the MG, steps onto the pavement, gathers his coat against the late winter cold and walks past the steps of the London, with the tickets in his pocket and a spring in his step, he is so excited to share the news with Rosa that, despite the tiredness, it takes all his willpower to prevent himself from breaking into a schoolboy's run.

On the corner of East Mount Street and Stepney Way, outside the dignified façade of the Edith Cavell House, Samuel waits, as usual, for Rosa. He is a little early, half an hour early to be precise, and finds it difficult to contain his exuberance; he looks up at Rosa's window, begging her to look out, see him and come down, but there is no movement inside; he attempts to distract himself by pacing up and down the frost-covered street, his breath blossoming into clouds above his head, but this only serves to agitate him further. Finally he can simply wait no longer. Without formulating a plan, he walks along the path to the front door of Cavell House and knocks, he doesn't ring, he knocks, furtively, hoping against hope that a friendly face will open it. As luck would have it, the door is opened by Betty Robinson who gapes at him agog and whispers, what on earth are you doing here? Samuel replies, I've simply got to see Rosa, I've a surprise for her; Betty gives him a knowing look and whispers, Rosie's in her room but don't blame me if you're caught; then she takes a few steps backwards, glances around surreptitiously and beckons him in. Samuel removes his hat, hurries past her into the antiseptic-smelling hall and dashes up the stairs, praying that he will not bump into the staff nurse, or even house sister, both of whom are confirmed dragons; then he tiptoes along the corridor and taps on Rosa's door, whispers, Rosa, it's me, open up, and is surprised when he does not receive a reply. He mustn't stay outside in the corridor, he's certain to be seen. Taking the Manila envelope out of his pocket, he tries the handle; it turns; he opens the door and peers round it, then slips into the bedroom. At first he doesn't see Rosa, she is so still.

—Rosa, he says softly, are you all right?

The dying winter light is filtering through the net curtains, illuminating a figure sitting straight-backed at her writing desk as if playing the piano, gazing blankly at her reflection in the mirror. Samuel calls her name again, and again she makes no answer; he approaches and puts his hands on her shoulders, and she slowly raises her head to look at his reflection in the glass.

—Whatever is the matter, he says, are you ill?

Rosa says nothing but continues to look at Samuel with eyes of indescribable sadness. He notices that she is clutching an envelope; he slides it from her fingers and holds it up to the light.

The envelope is addressed to Otto und Inga Klein, in Rosa's handwriting, postmarked yet unopened, still sealed. Samuel turns it over, and his heart misses a beat. Written on the back of the envelope, in squat black letters, are the words: *Deported Berlin–Auschwitz 12.01.1943.*

Samuel kneels on the floor next to Rosa, he can't think of anything to say. For a while, he cannot tell how long, she remains motionless as the long rays of sun fall through the window onto the dressing table, and the melody of a conversation can be heard outside. Then she speaks:

—It doesn't mean anything. It's not conclusive one way or the other. It may be a mistake. They may have gone elsewhere, or they may have escaped. Even if it is true, they would certainly have survived, many have. It doesn't mean anything.

—Yes, says Samuel unsteadily, you're right. Of course you're right.

—You would tell me, wouldn't you, if you thought it meant something?

—Of course. I agree with you, it's inconclusive.

Rosa falls silent and bows her head, weighing the letter in her hands. Then she gets to her feet, takes her painted box from her underwear drawer and places the envelope inside.

—I think, she says, I shall go back to Germany.

—Germany?

—Yes. It's the only way.

Samuel is about to reply but stops himself, swallows his words and says instead:

—Very well.

She sits back down at the writing desk and takes his hand.

—Will you come with me? she says.

Again Samuel swallows his words, preventing himself from mentioning his business, or Rosa's upcoming Hospital Finals, or the expense of airline travel, or the difficulties involved in travelling in Germany. Instead, he says:

—Of course.

Rosa notices, for the first time, the Manila envelope he is holding.

—What's that? she asks.

—This? Oh, nothing much, he replies.

—Yes it is, surely it's something. What is it?

—Well, now hardly seems the appropriate moment.

—Appropriate for what? Come on, tell me.

He passes her the envelope, and she opens it, curiously.

—Jersey.

—Yes, says Samuel, I thought we could go there for the weekend. Celebrate the sale of my twentieth motorcar. They haven't got rationing in Jersey, you know. We can have cream and butter and steak.

He is aware, even as he speaks, that his words are sounding hollow.

—Oh, that's terribly kind of you, says Rosa. Thank you so much. Do you think you will be able to get a refund?

—A refund?

—Yes, for these tickets.

—Why should I need to get a refund?

—Because we shall be in Germany.

—Are you planning to go so soon?

—As soon as possible.

—And how are you going to pay for it?

—I don't know. I have a little money.

—You have fifteen pounds' savings, which will hardly get you very far.

Rosa looks at herself in the mirror and then turns back to Samuel.

—Germany is three times the price of Jersey, says Samuel abruptly. And you've got your Hospital Finals coming up, which you'll need to swot up for. Don't you think you should wait a little? The authorities might be able to help.

—The authorities?

—They might provide some information.

Rosa gets to her feet again, paces to the door and back.

—I need to do something now, she says, I can't just sit around in London waiting for some authorities to grind into action.

—I appreciate that, but perhaps Bloomsbury House—

—Look, if you won't come with me I shall go alone. I'll find a way somehow.

—I never said I wouldn't come with you.

—That's what you implied.

There is a silence, and they avoid each other's eyes. Then both of them speak at the same time; Rosa says, it doesn't mean anything, and Samuel says, we don't have to go out tonight. Then there is silence again.

—The letter was here when I got back from the afternoon shift, says Rosa, sitting down.

—Were there any other details?

—Nothing.

—No mention of your brother and sister?

—I don't know, mumbles Rosa.

—Sorry?

—I don't know, she snaps. Please Samuel, I don't need an interrogation now. Let's just leave it for the moment, all right? We're supposed to go out, let's go out.

—I'm not sure we should, says Samuel, I think you need some time alone.

—Samuel, I'm fine. I'm happy to go out, one can't spend one's entire life moping.

—There will be other evenings, says Samuel. I can see I'm only making matters worse.

—You're not, of course you're not. I'm happy to go out.

He crosses the room and kisses her on the cheek.

—Please don't be angry with me, says Rosa.

—I'm not angry, says Samuel, don't worry.

He leaves the room, hurries down the stairs and strides out of Cavell House, ignoring the open mouths and wide eyes of the nurses emerging from the sitting room. Outside it is raining, a sort of floating rain that creates a soaking, indelible mist, and leathery leaves adhere to the pavement. Why does he always make a mess of things? Several schoolboys have gathered on the pavement admiring his Midget, and he finds that he does not have the heart to approach; despite the rain he continues to walk as a smog descends around him. Grey-specked liquid slides across the brim of his hat, the rain is getting heavier now, the hiss of it continuous, solid sheets of water instead of mist, his trousers are clinging to his legs, there is no longer any reason to avoid the puddles, and still he walks on, walks on. After a time he happens to pass the Blind Beggar, it is glowing like whisky in the fog; a quick drink before heading home might be just the thing. He climbs the rain-shined steps that were blasted half off in the war, then stops, hand resting on the door with its ugly Victorian glass, stained the colour of tea. Through the window he can see a cluster of overcoats and hats, hunched together conspiratorially on hatstands; he can hear the sound of laughter within, smell the cigarette smoke, the pipe smoke. The glass is tough under his fingers, somehow it must have withstood the bomb that damaged the steps, little lines of rain jerk at angles across its surface; Samuel, water slipping down the back of his greatcoat, pushes open the door and steps inside, grateful for the sweet fug that instantly enfolds him. He hangs up his coat and hat, approaches the bar, orders a pint and scans the room for a table, taking a cigarette case out of his pocket and lighting up; as he does so, he finds himself thinking about the logistics of travelling to Germany with Rosa.

—Kremer's Motors.

—It's me, Rosa.

—Oh, hello.

—Samuel, I . . . I'm sorry.

—Whatever for?

—I don't want to push you away. I don't want to lose you. It must be terrible being engaged to me. You're going to call off our engagement. I quite understand.

—Whatever gave you such an idea?

—But you stormed off last night. I've been thinking about it all day.

—I didn't storm off.

—We were supposed to go out.

—You'd just had a bit of a shock.

—I can't stop worrying, Samuel.

—I know, it's difficult. I wish there was more I could do.

—You needn't come with me to Germany.

—Perhaps we should talk about this face to face?

—Anyway, I'm sorry.

—I'm sorry too, Samuel replies. I always seem to make a mess of things.

There is a pause.

—I received a letter this morning, says Rosa, from the Central Office for Refugees. Bloomsbury House.

—Oh?

—They have received lists of . . . names.

—What do you mean?

—You know, from the camps. The victims. They're displaying them Monday week.

—I see.

—Sister has allowed me the morning off, so long as I make up for it.

—I'll come with you.

—You needn't.

—Nonsense. I'll come with you.

—You needn't, honestly. It won't be a very pleasant morning.

—I don't care about pleasant mornings.

There is another pause. Rosa clears a circle in the condensation on the window of the telephone box and looks out onto the bustling Whitechapel Road, the colour of butter in the failing light.

—Are you still there? says Samuel.

—Yes.

—I'll come with you.

—Are you sure?

—I'll collect you at half past six, and we'll go to my house for break-fast first. Then, when you're ready, we'll motor to Bloomsbury House.

—Samuel, I—

Rosa's voice breaks and she bites her tongue.

—You don't have to say anything, Samuel replies. See you next Monday.

Monday arrives before its time. On Rosa's insistence, they have a full and extravagant breakfast. The wireless is playing at a considerable volume, which makes conversation difficult, so they exchange reassuring smiles across the table as they tap the tops of their eggs with the underside of their spoons and slide rough-edged soldiers into the yolks. Rosa makes a Pro's Pudding, the recipe for which a probationer imparted to her during the war: golden syrup, bread, two eggs and lots of milk, placed in a pan and boiled. Samuel doesn't care for it, says it's too sweet for breakfast; Rosa, uncharacteristically, eats most of it herself.

After breakfast they prepare to leave. Rosa has packed sandwiches for the journey as if they are going on a day-trip, and the weather lends itself to that impression, a warm day in early spring; they decide to take their coats just in case, folded in the boot of Samuel's latest car, which is an impossibly narrow Austin 8, smelling of grease and leather, with a bonnet that tapers to a grille, two circular headlamps and scuffed running boards along each side. Samuel has to duck his head to get through the door, his shoulder touches Rosa's as they sit in the cramped, maroon front seats.

The car shudders into life after a couple of false starts, but the journey through town is smooth. Much of the bomb damage has been repaired, yet builders and cranes are frequent. The streets are quiet; a man strolls with his jacket over his arm, a Yorkshire terrier by his side, he is wearing an ill-fitting brown trilby which marks him out as recently demobilised. Two women, secretaries perhaps, walk briskly on stout heels along the pavement, laughing and shaking their heads; a man in a cloth cap sits on a step in his shirtsleeves, holding a bottle of something. Samuel turns a little too fast onto the Marylebone Road, the car lurches slightly, then settles down.

—Are you all right? I mean, are you ready? asks Samuel. We're almost there.

—I'm glad you're coming with me, says Rosa.

There is a pause; the engine clatters beneath them.

—I don't mind telling you, says Samuel, I'm rather jumpy.

The car comes to a halt and they get out, stand side by side on the pavement in the sun, looking up at Bloomsbury House, a smart Georgian building surrounded by black railings, with a prominent porch capped with carved stone and a highly polished black door. Samuel puts on his hat. Then he takes Rosa's arm and starts to walk towards the entrance.

—Wait, says Rosa, just a minute.

He looks at her for a moment, then stops and waits, still holding her arm. Her eyes are fixed on the polished door, and the breeze plays in the curls beneath her hat; her face is unusually flushed. Two men pass by in business suits and bowler hats, walking in opposite semicircles around them; Samuel makes an apologetic face.

—All right, says Rosa at last, let's go in.

They make their way into the foyer and join a sombre group of people standing in irregular patterns on the black-and-white tiles, whispering occasionally in German, Polish, Dutch. Nobody is manning the reception desk but everyone seems content to wait resignedly. As the minutes go by Rosa grips Samuel's arm tighter and her face grows increasingly flushed, tight-lipped. He leads her to the desk and looks around for a service bell, or any sign of life; finally a studious-looking man bustles through a door and takes a seat at the desk, tightening his tie. There is a murmur of recognition from the assembly, but rather than press forward, the people seem to shrink back.

—May I help? says the man, peering at Samuel through wire-rimmed glasses.

Samuel and Rosa glance at each other.

—We received a letter, says Samuel, regarding a certain list of names.

—Ah yes, says the man, if you follow that corridor, it's three doors down on the left. They should all be up there now.

They walk along the corridor followed by others from the foyer. The first door passes, then the second. Their footsteps are unbearably loud now, and brass light fittings on the walls seem to throw them into a spotlight. Other people are around them, a thin woman in a shapeless hat and leather gloves, a portly gentleman carrying a folder bursting with paperwork, a young lad with short trousers and a scampish face. More languages can be heard, Hungarian, Romanian, Yiddish, French. Third on the left, the door is open; they enter a large, square room with high ceilings and broad windows facing the street. The floorboards are covered in a thin Turkish carpet. Groups of people begin to assemble around the room, clustering around the walls, where, above the fireplace, and on either side of the paintings, and in between the windows, and across the paintwork, stretching up almost to the ceiling, there are rows and rows of large cork notice-boards, enclosing the room like a fence. On these are sheets of foolscap, pinned all the way across without the slightest space in between, ruled into columns and filled with tiny writing: names and figures and locations and details, name after name after name.

—Let's hope it's alphabetical, says Samuel drily.

Rosa gazes around her in grim wonderment at the sheer number of names on these lists. Her family could be anywhere among them, any one of these spidery lines of ink could represent Papa, or Mama, or Heinrich, or Hedi, and in a way all of them do; behind each of these little two-word units there is a life, a person, someone who had bonds with their family and their friends and their country, with a job and a house and a preference for sweet tea, or panama hats, or pumpernickel, or strolls in the Grunewald, who was plucked from the apparatus of their day-to-day existence and put to death.

They move to a corner of the room and find all the people who had surnames beginning with 'A', starting off the list and continuing for several pages; then it is 'B', then 'C', Samuel is skimming the names now, leading her towards the letter 'K', stop, she wants to say, go slower, I'm not ready, I cannot look at the list, I cannot, I do not mind this unknowing, I have grown used to it, let me stay, let me stay, let me stay.

—Are you all right? says Samuel.

—Fine, says Rosa.

—I think the 'K's are over here. Are you ready?

Rosa nods. Could it really be that such a flimsy thing as a name, in two words, is sufficient to support the weight of somebody's life? Here, they arrive, and look down the list. Kabakoff, Kacev, Kaciff, Kadar, Kadury, Kagan, Kaganoff, Kahane, Kahn, Kahin, Kaisermann, Kalisch, Kalischer, Kalmann, Kalonymos, Kaluzna, Kamin, Kaminski, Kaminetzky, Kan, Kaner, Kann, Kansi, Kantor, all 'K's, one below the other, people who could never have envisaged, during their lives, that their names would end up here, on a list of victims on the wall of a room in a Georgian building in Bloomsbury, Kapke, Kaplan, Karelitz, Karlinsky, Karlman, Kaskel, Kaspi, Kassiere, Katz, don't look, close your eyes, for these people no longer walk the earth, it is impersonal and stifling, this dry presentation of people in the form of a list, written in columns in black ink, sometimes blue ink, name after name, fate after fate, Kirsch, Kirscheldorf, Kirschenbaum, Kirschner, Kirstein, Kirsten, Kisch, Kisselevich, Kissinger, Kissner, Kivel, Klass, don't look, Klausner, Kleben, turn away, it will be final, once seen it can never be unseen.

Rosa's body shudders slightly. Samuel follows her gaze.

Klein, Hedi, 15974, Auschwitz, died 2nd February 1943.
Klein, Inga, 15973, Auschwitz, died 10th March 1943.
Klein, Otto, 103762, Auschwitz, died 13th April 1943.
Klein, Heinrich, 103761, Auschwitz, died 23rd June 1944.

—That's them, isn't it, Samuel says flatly.

Rosa does not reply. Suddenly she feels at peace. A numbness settles upon her, a sense that all striving and yearning and wishing and praying has come to an end, leaving behind a vacuum, peace. Unsure if Samuel is following, she releases his arm and backs away from the wall, then turns and walks towards the exit, across the black-and-white stone floor. Samuel takes her arm again and helps her down the stairs, and out to the motorcar; they join the traffic in silence, Samuel holding her hand as they drive.

The journey passes in silence all the way down High Holborn until it turns into Cheapside. The world outside the windows of the car is absolutely normal, too normal, yet for Rosa it seems to be passing in slow motion; she knows now, she has reached the end of uncertainty, and she is reeling.

—How are you bearing up? says Samuel.

—All right, says Rosa, a little giddy.

—Shall I stop? Would you like a drink of water?

—Thank you but I'm fine. I think it's the sun. I hope I'm not coming down with something.

—Let me know if it gets any worse.

Rosa nods and looks out of the window at a rag-and-bone man on a horse-drawn cart, flicking his switch against the beast's hindquarters.

—I suppose we can get married now, says Rosa.

Samuel slows to allow the vehicle behind to overtake him, his furrowed brow reflecting in the mirror.

—You mustn't worry about burdening me, he says, you don't need to put a brave face on.

—It's not that, says Rosa.

—Would you mind lighting me a cigarette? says Samuel. I think this has affected me worse than you.

He hands her his cigarette case and lighter; she places one in her mouth, cups her hands round it, lights it and hands it to him.

—Have one yourself if you like, says Samuel.

They drive on without speaking for a while, Samuel breathing smoke over the steering wheel, Rosa gazing out of the window.

—I never imagined it would be like this, she says. Ever since leaving Berlin I've been waiting for my parents, yet now that I know there is no chance of ever seeing them again, I do not feel a thing.

—Give it some time to sink in.

—I suppose there's no reason to go back to Germany now, says Rosa.

For the remainder of the journey they do not talk, and despite a little traffic around Aldgate their progress is smooth. Eventually the street broadens onto the Whitechapel Road, and the London Hospital comes into view. Samuel stops to allow an ambulance to pass in front of him, then turns in to East Mount Street and parks outside the nurses' home. Rosa gets out quickly and closes the door, waves, and walks towards Cavell House. Samuel gazes after her until she disappears indoors, then shakes his head and lights another cigarette. As he starts the engine and looks over his shoulder for oncoming traffic, he wonders if it is actually possible to know someone fully, or if one is only ever shown one mask at a time, even by one's closest friend, lover and fiancée.

4

—They're late, says Samuel.

—No they're not, says Rosa, looking at the clock on the ornate mantelpiece across the room, we've still got fifteen minutes. You're just jumpy.

Samuel takes another sip of tea, the delicate porcelain teacup fitting perfectly back into its saucer as he replaces it.

—Mustn't drink too quickly, he says, this tea cost a fortune.

—Why did you decide to meet them here? says Rosa.

—I didn't, says Samuel, they suggested it. I hate Mayfair. Is that them?

Across the hotel café, which sparkles with a thousand mirrors, can be seen a middle-aged couple entering the lobby.

—That's not them, says Rosa, you're panicking. We've still got fifteen minutes.

—I'm just afraid they might not come.

—They said they would, didn't they?

Time slips by, and Rosa and Samuel sit in high-backed chairs at a table laid with gleaming silverware; piano music flutters around the edges of the room, and a monotone of genial conversation lies like a silk sheet over everything, pierced here and there by the scrape of cutlery, the clink of glasses and porcelain.

Samuel sips his tea again, then flicks open his cigarette case; a waiter appears with a lighter, Samuel prods a cigarette into the flame and inhales deeply.

—It's driving me insane, says Samuel. I'm going to the lavatory.

—They will be here in a minute, says Rosa.

—I shan't be long, says Samuel, getting to his feet.

He threads his way through the maze of tables populated by diners, each of whom is contributing towards the cloud of genial conversation that hangs in the room like opium smoke; he passes various marble pillars, chandeliers, gold-framed paintings and opulently upholstered sofas, and finds the gentlemen's lavatory. Behind the heavy door he finds no privacy; American businessmen of sizeable girth are talking with cigars between their teeth, and two bellhops stand on either side of the doorway, handing out towels, turning taps off and on, and collecting tips. Samuel makes his way to a cubicle where he locks the door and sits on the toilet lid, his head in his hands, cigarette smoke collecting above his head. Five years.

Dear Samuel,

We received your letter with some surprise this week, and thank you for finally making contact with us. These last years have been very hard, due mainly to your unexplained absence which has left us daily wondering if you are alive or dead. Nevertheless we are prepared to meet. We suggest the Dorchester in Mayfair for afternoon tea, at four o'clock on Monday, 20 January. Should this prove inconvenient, please do let us know.

Yours sincerely,
Father and Mother

Samuel folds the letter and places it back in his pocket; familiarity has desensitised him to the nuances of its language. He looks at his watch: seven minutes to four. He takes a last lungful of smoke, stubs out his cigarette, rises from the lavatory seat and unlocks the door, I will just splash some water on my face and then let battle commence; but here is a bellhop, what could he want with – oh, he is entering the cubicle,

306

flushing the toilet on my behalf, how I hate Mayfair. And now – oh, he has turned the taps on for me, I cannot splash my face with his little eyes fixed on me like a cobra, I shall just wash my hands and – oh, a towel, I cannot very well refuse, and now he will be wanting a tip I suppose, well I'm damned if I'm going to give him one, I did not request his services and I will not be bullied into giving away money willy-nilly. Oh very well, maybe just a shilling, I don't want to be miserly, and these people have a job to do after all.

He emerges from the lavatory straightening his jacket and smoothing his hair. Rather than picking out a route between tables across the middle of the hall he decides to skirt the perimeter, moving from pillar to pillar, making his way circuitously in the direction of his table; perhaps he should have another cigarette to steady his nerves, he reaches into his pocket for his cigarette case – then there they are.

For a full minute Samuel stares at his parents. They are sitting with Rosa, making conversation, Gerald is ordering tea from a white-breasted waiter, now Mother is asking for something, gesturing at the tabletop with a sprinkling motion of her fingers, they both look so different. Pain grips Samuel as his father removes his hat, revealing hair and a beard that are almost completely white; and as his mother straightens her husband's collar he sees her lined face, her slight stoop. Yes, they have aged, these five years have not treated them kindly, but there is something else that is different about them now, their clothes perhaps, Father's suit looks expensive, even from this distance, and Mother is wearing an elegant navy jacket with pearls gleaming at her neck. Samuel takes a deep breath and exhales slowly, blowing out his cheeks; then he approaches the table.

For several minutes Rosa has been talking about the hospital, and every one of those minutes has felt like an age, these are the very people who carried out that terrible act against her all those years ago, but so far nobody has mentioned it, the conversation is meandering unbearably around the everyday, every word adding to the pretence that everything is somehow all right. She finds herself wondering if they will ever address the issues that plague them, even when Samuel arrives, or if they will all content themselves with this most banal of communications, and never touch upon the real issues that affect them, for as Papa would have put it, such are the ways of the English. Ah, they look so much older, and rather lonely, she would feel quite sorry for them in different circumstances, but sitting here now she is unable to rouse anything but nervousness and fear. Just as she is running dry on the subject of blanket-bathing, she becomes aware that both Mimi and Gerald are looking over her shoulder; she turns in her seat and sees Samuel, dwarfed by the luxurious backdrop of the Dorchester like a boy in a headmaster's office. She reaches over and takes his hand, guiding him to his seat. He sits down without taking his eyes off his parents. Finally Mimi speaks.

—My boy, she says, my son.

—Mother, says Samuel, you look well.

There is a pause. Gerald gets to his feet, pushes back his hat and walks round the table to where his son is sitting; he places his hand on his shoulder, pats it once, twice, then offers his hand, Samuel takes it, still sitting down, awkwardly, and Gerald says, so, my boy, you no longer get to your feet for your old father? And Samuel gets to his feet, and suddenly they embrace, for many seconds; the diners around them avert their eyes and focus on their food, and Rosa rearranges her cutlery. Gerald holds his son by the shoulders and says, why don't you greet your mother properly, and Samuel walks round the table to his mother, and she gets to her feet, and they embrace, her shoulders jerking and falling beneath her navy jacket as the piano music washes around them. Finally they all take their places at the table, Mimi dabbing her eyes with a napkin; Samuel is pale, his eyes are red-rimmed.

—Look at you, says Mimi, you are already a man. It's been so long.

—I've missed you, Mother, says Samuel.

He looks at Rosa, and she nods. Strength, thinks Samuel, be strong.

—So you're getting married? says Mimi. When's the date?

—Six weeks' time, says Samuel, in the Bevis Marks synagogue.

—So it will be a big wedding, says Mimi.

—No, no, a very small one, says Samuel, they fit us in on a Friday.

—And what are you doing for money these days? asks Gerald.

—I have my own business, Samuel replies, motorcars.

—And it's going well?

—Well enough.

—A businessman and a fully qualified nurse. This makes me proud, says Gerald, this makes me very proud.

—What about you? says Samuel.

—I am retired now, says Gerald. Zeidi's inheritance has kept us going nicely. One day we shall pass it on to you.

Samuel exchanges glances with Rosa.

—When the war ended we decided we liked life in Norfolk, says Mimi, after all London is frightfully frantic. But Northrepps is rather rural if you haven't got the Germans to worry about, so we moved to

Norwich to be closer to the synagogue. It was bombed, of course, but there's still the community.

There is an uncomfortable silence, broken only by the waiter arriving with another pot of tea; then he disappears again, and the silence is intact.

—I'm sorry, says Mimi, I'm not sure I can talk about the past. I'm not sure I can do it without bursting into tears.

—We can't simply ignore everything, says Samuel.

—It's been such a very long time, says Mimi, wiping her eyes with the napkin, it's been horrid.

—Did you see action again? asks Gerald.

—No, Samuel replies, not abroad anyway. I was injured in a bomb blast near Liverpool Street and that put me out of action for the remainder of the war.

—Oh, darling, says Mimi, why didn't you write?

—It wasn't too bad, says Samuel. My arm is a bit gammy even now, but other than that no lasting damage.

—And you have some scars on your forehead, says Mimi, and your cheek.

—I didn't think you'd be able to see that, says Samuel.

—A mother sees everything, says Mimi.

—We're looking at buying a house, says Samuel, for after we're married.

—Do you hate us still? says Mimi, interrupting.

—Of course not, Mother, says Samuel, and looks down at his teacup.

Gerald clears his throat and starts looking around the room as if he is suddenly interested in the architecture; Mimi raises her teacup and puts it down again. Rosa is struck by the impulse to get to her feet, take them each by the shoulders and shake them, you cannot afford to hold back, she wants to say, no matter how terrible it is, you must shake off the weight and build a future together, for who knows how long you might have left?

—Has there been any word from your family, Rosa? says Gerald.

—I'm afraid, she replies, they are no longer with us.

He looks uncomfortable.

—May the Lord comfort you amongst the mourners of Zion and Jerusalem, he says.

Rosa bows her head; she is starting to feel a little dizzy, she needs to get away from the claustrophobia of the hotel, she needs to breathe fresh air. The waiter glides back to the table with a cake-stand brimming with sandwiches, with deft movements he arranges it on the table, refills Rosa's teacup, asks if there is anything further; Gerald dismisses him with a small sweep of his hand.

They continue to talk, nobody touches the sandwiches, and no more is said about the past, and after a time Gerald pays the bill and they leave. On the pavement outside the Dorchester they shake hands, and Gerald says, good luck with the wedding preparations, we shall be as supportive as we can from afar; then, as Samuel and Rosa walk towards their battered Austin 8, and a little sunlight filters through the clouds, picking out highlights on the curves of the motorcars, the shop windows, the leads of the dogs, the spectacles and necklaces of the people on the pavements, the overhead poles on the trams and trolley-buses, Rosa says, that went as well as could be expected; and she looks at Samuel and sees that his eyes are burning, his jaw is set and his hands are clenched. Supportive from afar, he says, supportive from afar.

7 March 1947, London

The square outline of the Bevis Marks synagogue rises against the afternoon sky. The heavy doors are resplendent in the sunlight, crowned by an ornamental lantern and engravings of Hebrew calligraphy; a prominent black-faced clock extends its history with golden hands. Inside a chandelier illuminates a building sombre in colour and tone. Dark panelling on the walls resonates to the sound of liturgical singing coming from the main chamber, at the far end of which a silken wedding canopy, open on four sides to symbolise hospitality, has been raised. Each of the synagogue's hanging candelabras has been lit with wavering candles; the carved pews all around host a smattering of men, Samuel's friends and business associates, a little family and members of the congregation; in the ladies' gallery above, supported by twelve great pillars of cream marble, stand the womenfolk, and prominent amongst them is a collection of fresh-faced nurses who have managed, despite Sister's protestations, to synchronise their precious days off.

The choir swells in harmony as the double doors open and Samuel is seen silhouetted against the grey light, flanked by his mother and father; as they step onto the carpet the men in the pews turn to face them, following the groom with their gaze as he walks along the aisle under the great high ceiling of the synagogue, his feet falling in time to the music, and approaches step by step the wedding canopy where the rabbi stands; he looks left and right and sees nothing but smiling faces, he looks upwards and sees the heads and shoulders of the women gazing down from the gallery above, and then, all at once, the shade of the canopy has fallen upon him, and the rabbi has taken him by the elbow and manoeuvred him into position; and as the candlelight glimmers in the polished façade of the intricately carved ark, and the choir's voices fall and rise in interlocking melodies, all heads turn once again to the doorway, waiting expectantly for the bride.

In a small anteroom smelling of wine and sawdust, Rosa adjusts her hair beneath her veil, straightens her back and looks at the door, trying to quell her racing heart. Her mouth is dry, her palms are sticky and she is glad of the veil hanging before her face; and she is tired, for last night she was once again kept awake by an overpowering dread; she knows that as soon as she falls asleep she will be vulnerable to whatever dreams choose to make their appearance, and this alone keeps her awake, for just as Samuel's parents are coming back into their lives, Rosa's parents have been breaking through the wall of her numbness, slipping round it, appearing as if by magic on the other side, nightly, during her dreams. She has begun to see them vividly, sometimes with breathtaking clarity, entering her room at Cavell House, walking alongside her through the wards; sometimes she dreams simply of daily life in Berlin, school and her bicycle and the Grunewald and family meals, and awakes disorientated, murmuring in German. By day the atmosphere of her dreams lingers, and snapshots flash into her mind when for the occasional moment she sits down to rest; from time to time German words slip into her conversations. Her dizziness has worsened too: when thoughts of her family break into her mind, inevitably they are accompanied by a reeling sensation, as if she is standing vertiginous upon a ledge. Every day tectonic shifts are taking place on a level of which she is unaware; her parents' fingers are slipping under her armour and prising it away. But they are gone; Rosa shall walk to the wedding canopy alone, all the way along the aisle, alone, to the accompaniment of nothing but music. Be strong, Rosa, be strong. She closes her eyes, and on her left is Papa, dressed in the shiny black morning suit and top hat, his moustache waxed and gleaming above a broad smile, and on her right is Mama, wearing a mauve hat boasting a large ornamental flower, they are taking her arms and leading her towards the door, two ushers doff their hats and open the double doors leading to the main chamber. Rosa appears, a lonely figure at the end of the aisle, the men all turn to face her, and the women far above; she is carrying an arrangement of flowers and is trembling. As she steps onto the scarlet carpet she cannot feel her feet, she remembers Mama saying once that angels have no feet, they simply glide along without them, and that is how she feels, not like an angel as such, of course, but footless, yet her feet must be there for they are carrying her along the carpet leading to the wedding canopy, past rows of smiling men standing in the pews, and there is Samuel so elegant and dapper in the morning suit that he bought from the Fifty Shilling Tailors, and there are Mimi and Gerald beside him, and in the gallery above the nurses have gathered; Betty Robinson is waving.

Another step, and another, with Mama on her right and Papa on her left, filled with pride on her wedding day, and behind are Heinrich and Hedi, both vital and full of life, smiling at the onlookers as they walk to the sound of a heavenly chorus, there – Baron de Rothschild, how kind of him to come; ah, two more steps, and the shade of the wedding canopy is falling on her shoulders, and with her parents beside her she walks round her beloved seven times, feeling lighter than air, her head bowed, looking at his perfectly polished shoes from beneath her veil, she can see the golden glint of Papa's watch on his wrist, nestling under his sleeve; she walks round him and round him, her beloved, her groom, mirroring the seven times that Joshua circled the walls of Jericho, causing them to miraculously collapse, symbolising that Samuel's heart has been disarmed by her love; she takes her place beside the rabbi, and her family congregate behind her, Mama and Papa sharing solemn smiles. The rabbi is intoning the prayers, somebody raises her veil slightly and a goblet of wine appears, it is thick and sweet like blood, her lips tremble as they touch the liquid, more prayers are being chanted, her hand is being taken, she looks up into Samuel's eyes, open and dewy, he is saying something in Hebrew, it is familiar, they practised it, he is slipping onto her finger a ring, she glances over her shoulder at her parents – they are not there, they never will be, and now the breaking of the glass is approaching, more prayers, the glass is being placed on the floor, it is inside a napkin, she never thought it would be inside a napkin, the breaking of the glass symbolises that their happiness shall never be complete because their temple was destroyed and Jerusalem was sacked, the flames licking from the roof of the Rykestraße synagogue, the window breaking and the person tumbling through onto the street, the broken windows of their apartment in the Arbeiterviertel which Mama boarded up, looking out of the window of a train, seeing the closed door to the waiting room, wishing that Mama and Papa would open it and wave to her one last time, the door does not open and the train pulls away, and their letter, their last letter, now we must say a very painful goodbye, we will love you always and are so proud of you, we will be with you always, you are in our thoughts, never forget us, please be strong, my darling. Be strong. Rosa is feeling dizzy, and the congregation is singing a mournful psalm – if I should forget thee, O Jerusalem, let my right hand wither, let my tongue cleave to my palate if I do not remember thee, if I do not set Jerusalem above my highest joy; the glass is about to be broken, what is happening to her? Something is welling up inside, a fist in her stomach pushing up towards her chest, a pressure threatening to break the surface, Mama and Papa and Heinrich and Hedi, names on a list under 'K', her numbness has evaporated, the world is in sharp relief, it is too clear, it is unbearable, it has been stripped naked and she has been thrust into life afresh, the singing is blaring in her ears, if I should forget thee, O Jerusalem, now we must say a very painful goodbye, Samuel is raising his foot, and the fist is pushing up into her throat, and Samuel brings his foot down – there is the sound of breaking glass, the glass is broken—

Mazel tov! shout the crowd, again and again, and music is playing, and people are dancing, and Samuel is reaching for Rosa's hand, and she struggles against the unbearable pressure, and she sees Mimi and Gerald standing side by side, clapping, and she tries to smile, and she is vaguely aware that Samuel is saying something, but she cannot make out the words, the world has gone silent. The synagogue and guests are like objects seen through a telescope, everything is distant, hissing somehow, she falls to her knees, her hands grasp at her veil as if tearing away cobwebs, and finally the pressure is released, it bursts out of her mouth, and from the depths of her soul a sound comes, a primordial, human sound; the sound – at last – of her grief.

Samuel crouches beside his new wife, people are closing around them, a forest of legs and shoes and voices, has she fainted? Is she ill? Samuel moves the veil aside, Rosa's face is contorted in a way he has never seen, Mama, she cries, Papa, Mama, Papa; people are closing around them, the music has stopped, somebody is saying in a grave voice, the doctor is on his way, in the meantime we should raise her feet above her head. Samuel, making a decision, stands and lifts her into his arms, her white dress fanning out below her; he carries her through the crowds, back up the aisle, asking the onlookers to move out of the way, to give them a little time alone, Otto Klein's golden watch glinting on his wrist. In the foyer he pauses; at the bottom of the synagogue steps he can see the Daimler ready and waiting, the chauffeur reading the newspaper, he could get in and instruct the man to drive; Rosa is hiding her face in his chest, her legs hanging limply; he hesitates for a moment then changes his mind, backs into the anteroom, closes the door and sets her down gently on a chair.

For many minutes he holds her as she cries. Gradually the sobs subside, and she sits there, spent, in silence. He hands her his handkerchief, and she wipes her eyes, then he removes the golden watch.

—No, she says, I want you to wear it. Please. Put the watch back on. Papa would have wanted you to wear it.

Slowly Samuel obeys. Rosa removes her veil and tiara and places them on the floor.

—I'm sorry, she says, I'm sorry, it all just came out.

Her face begins to crumple again, and he takes her in his arms.

—I've ruined everything for you again, she cries.

—No, you haven't.

—It's just, I almost saw my parents, I almost saw them.

—It's all right, it's all right. You've been bottling it all up.

Rosa wipes her face again, gets to her feet and crosses to the mirror, dress rustling.

—I quite understand if you can't face the dinner, says Samuel, we can go home and leave them all to it.

—No, says Rosa. My parents would have wanted me to be strong. I want to be strong. I want to build a proper future with you, and I want it to start today.

Samuel takes her hand and feels her fingers slipping over the strap of his golden watch; her wedding ring scrapes softly against it.

—I can do it, she says, I'm not going to abandon our wedding. We shall take our seats at the top table, and lead the dinner, and take the first dance, and celebrate. I can do it if I know you are there.

—Very well, says Samuel, but if it's all too much, let me know.

—I will, says Rosa.

They take a deep breath, leave the anteroom and walk hand in hand into the foyer of the synagogue. As they rejoin the throng and reassure the guests, and the music starts again and festivities resume, a sense of acceptance arises in Rosa, one quite different from the numbness that has enfolded her for so long. Suddenly she understands that these scars will never go away, her life will forever be a wounded one; yet she also knows that there is a future filled with promise that is there to be lived, and her parents would want her to embrace it.

3

For the first year of marriage, Samuel does not feel as if he ever comes to rest. Days and months slip into one another, unified by a stream of work, chores, weekends and evenings and breakfasts, repairing the roof of the house and washing the car and mowing the garden lawn. His business reaches a comfortable plateau, and although they are not short of money Rosa chooses to continue with her career. For her part, she is the perfect wife; as one of the few married nurses at the London she is not given special treatment, she is not even exempted night duty, yet she is still able to make time for her husband, always providing the meals and keeping the house spick and span. They make local friends, not many but a few, entertain them once a month at home over sherry. As the months build like bricks, cemented and unmoving, and each season gives way to the next, Samuel fears that despite the routine, despite the money and the meals and the friends and the garden, something, somehow, is not right.

It is a Friday in the middle of June 1948, and Rosa has the day off work. Samuel has taken the day off as well, leaving the business in the hands of his new manager, Ronnie Bawden. Rosa has been out all morning doing chores, leaving her husband at home to read, listen to the wireless and polish his shoes; now she is back, cooking lunch while he sits at the kitchen table brooding upon last night, which they passed, as usual, on opposite sides of the bed, with a stretch of cold mattress between them, a no-man's land. Rosa, exhausted from her work at the hospital, appeared to fall instantly asleep, and for a long time Samuel lay awake looking up at the faint column of moonlight on the bedroom ceiling, struggling with a tangle of emotions that he was not able to understand, feeling as if Rosa was not simply on the other side of the bed, but countless miles away, aloof and inaccessible. And as he lay sleepless amongst tangled blankets, his thoughts turned to the week before, when, one morning, about to leave the house for work, he had seen an envelope on the mat with his father's handwriting unmistakably etched upon it; he stopped, crouched, turned the letter over in his hands, and his heart was beating a little faster, he knew it was stupid but he was always nervous when he received a letter from his parents, or even a telegram, he was never confident that it would not contain a rebuke, or a final decision that the years of silence would be reinstated. So he had turned the letter over immediately, slit the envelope with his penknife and removed a single folded piece of foolscap, inscribed with a brief missive in his father's small, high-spiked writing:

Dear Samuel,

It is with great regret that I must notify you of the tragic death of your friend Esther Cailingold, who was killed in action on 23 May while defending the Old City of Jerusalem against the Arab Legion. Esther had been a full-time soldier in the Haganah since January, and was acting as a Sten gunner in the Jewish Quarter at the time of her death. Your mother and I wish to send our deepest condolences.

With best wishes,
Father

Samuel's reaction had been to pocket the letter, leave the house, get into the rattling old Morris 8 that he was driving at the time and make his way to work, telling himself that after all he hadn't seen Esther since he went to war nine years ago, and they hadn't kept in touch, so it did not affect him personally. It was only later that the matter began to play on his mind, and last night, lying in bed with nothing but the moonlight on the ceiling for company, he found himself thinking of Esther, shuddering at the circumstances of her terrible death, recalling how they used to ride on a motorcycle out of London and through the countryside; as these memories bloomed into his mind and faded into the darkness, and flickered and died, and lived again, he looked across at the slumbering form of Rosa, so far away from him, hunched against the wall on the far side of the bed, tiny and remote amidst the blankets, and he found himself wishing that he had been with Esther in her final hour, fighting alongside her in the defence of Jerusalem.

—Boiled? says Rosa.

—That would be fine, Samuel replies.

The door slams in the neighbouring house, footsteps fade down the path and onto the street.

—Nice not to be going to work, says Samuel, turning over the page of his newspaper.

—Isn't it? says Rosa, lowering an egg into a saucepan of water with a spoon.

—There's not much here about Palestine, says Samuel, not on the front page at least. People get used to war, after a while it just carries on in the background. Especially if it's not involving our own troops.

—Everyone's sick of it, says Rosa.

—Ah, there's something on it here, on the inside pages, says Samuel. The truce is holding, apparently, although it is fragile, and violations are occurring on both sides. I have to admit, part of me wishes I were there.

—Would you like a cup of tea while you're waiting? says Rosa.

—No thank you, says Samuel absently.

—I think the war is a little pointless, says Rosa, as if we haven't had enough of war over the last decade.

—It's not pointless, says Samuel, we must fight for a homeland. We need a Jewish state. You should know that as well as anyone, with your background.

—I've enough trouble with being German and English, says Rosa, I couldn't possibly manage with a Jewish nationality as well.

317

—Nonsense, says Samuel curtly, if there had been a Jewish state during the war things would have been rather different. You would have had somewhere to run to.

—I had somewhere to run to, says Rosa. I came to England.

—Many Jews weren't so fortunate, says Samuel, his temper rising.

Rosa turns sharply and faces him.

—I know about the misfortune of Jews, she says.

He clears his throat.

—All I'm trying to say is that fighting for a Jewish state is a noble and worthy cause, he says, not a pointless one.

Rosa turns away and turns down the flame on the stove.

—I know you are thinking about Esther, she says quietly.

—What are you talking about?

—I've seen how you react when I mention her, says Rosa. You never stop going on about her, morning, noon and night. You're pining for her. You talk about nothing but her.

—I am entitled to grieve.

—You said you had forgotten her.

—She was a hero, says Samuel.

Rosa removes the saucepan from the heat and drains it into the sink.

—Dead people are easier to love, she says.

Samuel gets to his feet.

—You take that back, he says.

—You take back your comments about my family, says Rosa.

—What comments?

—About Jews who were not fortunate.

—I wasn't talking about your family.

—Then who were you talking about?

Samuel, trying to swallow his rage, looks up at the ceiling.

—What do you expect? he says finally. These days you and I are nothing more than friends.

—Friends?

—Yes, friends. Not man and wife.

Rosa turns back to the saucepan.

—I am tired all the time, she says. I am working many night shifts.

—You don't have to work, you choose to. Have you grown to hate me?

—I do not hate you, says Rosa.

Something in her voice causes Samuel to stop. She sits heavily at the kitchen table and Samuel, after a pause, draws up a chair to join her.

—There is something I need to tell you, she says.

Samuel looks at her intently, concerned by her expression, her voice.

—Go on, he says.

She takes a deep breath.

—I have been to the hospital for some tests.

—What kind of tests? Why didn't you tell me?

Rosa looks up, and for an instant he glimpses her vulnerable, exposed, without a mask.

—They don't think I am capable of having children, she says.

There is a silence.

—Not capable? says Samuel.

—Something to do with . . . Norfolk.

Another silence.

—When did you hear? asks Samuel.

—Recently.

—Why didn't you tell me?

—I wanted to. I couldn't.

Samuel gets to his feet and walks to the window. Outside the summer breeze is tousling the grass and the trees, lifting tiny birds high on swelling thermals.

—I think I need a drink, he says. I know it's early, but if you'll excuse me?

Rosa nods and he leaves the kitchen, goes into the sitting room and opens the drinks cabinet; the bottle of Bristol Cream has just been started; he pours himself a generous glassful. Then, replacing the bottle in the cabinet, he takes a gulp and returns to the kitchen.

—Are they sure? he asks. I mean to say, shall we get a second opinion?

—They are sure, says Rosa.

He clears his throat and raises his eyes to look at his wife; suddenly he is filled with an overwhelming tenderness, as intense as his anger of a few moments ago.

—It's all right, he says, it's all right. He takes her hand and embraces her.

—Perhaps we might consider alternatives, he says.

—Alternatives?

—Yes. I don't know, adoption.

—It wouldn't be the same.

—I know.

They sit quietly, the wind maintaining a texture outside.

319

—Everybody needs children in their lives, says Samuel. Perhaps we could grow to love an adopted child as if it were our own.

—Perhaps, says Rosa. Perhaps.

4

Several months later Rosa rises for work early. Neither she nor Samuel has slept well; filled with anticipation, they were too excited to sleep, they talked into the small hours, and eventually, though sheer exhaustion, dropped off. Another winter is approaching, and the morning is rather cold; she untangles herself from her husband's arms and swings her feet out of bed onto the chilly linoleum.

—Not morning already? Samuel mumbles into his pillow.

—Don't worry about getting up now, says Rosa, it's early.

Already her heart is beating with nerves. Samuel seems to fall asleep again, and she moves quietly through the shadows, dressing, readying herself for the big day. Then, with an exaggerated yawn, he rolls onto his back.

—I never thought this day would arrive, he says, his voice deepened by sleep. I truly never did.

—I'll be waiting on the hospital steps at lunchtime, says Rosa. Everything is prepared and ready here. If you make any mess, be sure to clean up after you. We can't have it looking messy, not today.

—Yes, Sister, says Samuel.

Rosa smiles.

—Don't forget to bring the documents, she says.

—Of course.

—And bring a map.

—But I've driven there scores of times.

—Bring a map.

Rosa kisses him then goes downstairs. On the table beside the front door is a large package in brown paper; she picks it up carefully and tucks it under her arm. Then she leaves the house, embarking upon her usual morning journey to Whitechapel.

Today everything is somehow imbued with significance; it is as if all creatures in the world and every object in it are working together seamlessly to carry her into the future. A tingle of excitement spreads up her spine as she takes a seat on the upper deck of the tram, wipes the condensation on the window with her sleeve and looks out into the chilly streets. She remembers the first time she went on a London tram, all those years ago, from Liverpool Street to Hackney, accompanied by Mimi and Gerald; it was a cold day like today, colder in fact, with thick smog outside the window, she remembers the smog. And she could speak no English then, barely a word, she was a timid German girl who knew nothing at all about life; it seems like an age ago now that she is looking into the glare of a future, dawning as she approaches; she feels elated, perhaps, but nervous, for today is the day when their own family will begin.

When Rosa arrives at the hospital she makes her way not to the wards, but to the quarters of the deputy matron, her nervousness increasing step by step. She has only been to Matron's wing a few times before, most recently when she received the news that she was to be blued and issued with a brown parcel of material which she was to take to Miss Duggan, the dressmaker; the very same material that now, having been made into a uniform, is folded inside the parcel under her arm. She knocks politely, twice, and waits in the early morning shadows in the corridor. The door opens without a sound, and Rosa enters; a home maid shows her to the deputy matron's cloakroom where, a little nervously, she parts her curls in the middle, pulls her hair back from her ears and forms a bun on top of her head, in the manner that has become so familiar to her; then she takes out her new dusky blue uniform and puts it on. The starch has made it rather stiff; Miss Duggan is a devil when it comes to starch. And here are the blue sleeves to be attached above the elbow, I haven't worn detachable sleeves since I was a probationer, for some reason Sisters still have to wear them. There, how do I look – she regards her reflection in the mirror – as if I am dressing up, not me at all. I suppose I shall get used to it. Ah, I am trembling with nerves; why did they choose to blue me today of all days? I should have applied to take the day off, prepare for this afternoon. Can't be helped. Now, ready – oh, just one more thing, a good handful of hairgrips, I have heard about the weight of those caps.

She leaves the cloakroom and indicates to the home maid that she is ready – prepared to be blued. Within seconds there is the sound of footsteps approaching, and Deputy Matron herself appears; in her hand is a crisp white Sister's cap, complete with three-foot-long frilly streamers. She regards Rosa haughtily, she is a short lady and Rosa stands above her, so she tilts her head back to allow her line of sight to nevertheless fall along the length of her nose.

—You have not breathed a word about this to a single soul?

—No, Deputy Matron, I have told no one.

—Good, she replies, the butterfly must not be seen to shed her chrysalis.

She makes a motion with her hand, and Rosa stoops, then bends, then kneels, awkwardly, on the floor.

—It gives me particular pleasure to award you the status of Sister, Mrs Kremer, she says. As you may be aware, Matron, being somewhat old-fashioned, is of the general opinion that it is impossible for the married lady to look after her home and work at the hospital at the same time. She believes that no married lady can survive in full-time nursing beyond a few months. You, Mrs Kremer, are happily proving the exception to the rule.

—Thank you, Deputy Matron.

—Right, now let's get on with it, says Deputy Matron, composing herself. I beseech Thee, O Lord, to bless the hand of this new Sister of the London Hospital, to protect her and guide her in all her duties, to help and inspire her to always keep the welfare of her patients foremost in her mind. Amen.

With the Amen she places the cap over the bun on Rosa's head – it is heavier than she expected and requires her to straighten her neck and back, and tilt her head forward; Rosa reaches up and spends some time pinning the cap to her hair, while Deputy Matron looks on in silence. Then she gets to her feet, feeling rather unbalanced.

—Very good, Sister, says Deputy Matron. She raises the watch that is pinned above her left breast.

—The time is twenty-three minutes past eight, she says. Accompany me to the wards, if you please.

Rosa, now walking with a Sister's upright gait, follows the deputy matron out of Matron's wing, across an echoing iron footbridge and into the hospital. She is surprised that the people she passes do not acknowledge that she has within the last few minutes shed the chrysalis of the staff nurse and been reborn as a fully fledged Sister; then she passes a small group of probationers, and one of them catches sight of her, looks away, looks back, recognises her, grins, nudges her companions, points; and Rosa feels a mixture of pride and humiliation, torn between the world of the nurses and that of the Sisters. Then they turn a corner, and the probationers are gone, and Deputy Matron pauses, and Rosa pauses behind her; they have reached the double doors of the Rowsell Ward. Rosa is surprised at the noise that can be heard within, the sound of frantic activity. She knows exactly what has been going on this morning: the night reds have been removed, folded and replaced with the day reds, the patients have been bathed and served their break-fasts, the probationers have washed the dishes, balancing bowls on the coal box and the washstand, the ward has been swept with tea leaves to lay the dust, the ashes from the fireplace have been raked by a middle-aged cockney ward maid, the junior probationers have emptied and replaced the bedpans, the locker tops have been scrubbed, a high sweep has been carried out on the ledges, the aspidistras have been brought out in vases with leaves polished with castor oil, the hassock has been brushed and placed in the centre of the ward, the bell and prayer-board have been placed conveniently to hand, Sister's inkpot and pen tray have been polished, and a final flick of the duster has been carried out over the reds. Yes, Rosa knows exactly what has been going on, but she had never appreciated the noise it all made, or how far that noise can carry outside the ward. Deputy Matron turns, looks at Rosa along the length of her nose and says, are you ready, Sister Kremer? And Rosa thinks of her papa, Herr Doktor Otto Klein; she remembers him in his doctor's white coat, regarding his ward with an easy authority, and in imitation of his manner she draws herself up and says, yes, Deputy Matron, I am ready. She pushes open the double doors, and a hush falls immediately upon the ward; the staff nurse and her probationers line up ready to receive their new Sister, and after checking and locking up the ward stock of morphia, Rosa walks along the line, inspecting them. When she reaches the staff nurse they catch each other's eye – it is Betty Robinson. Her mouth drops open, she looks as if she is about to keel over from shock, and a broad smile spreads across her face. Rosa selects the probationers who are to be on duty and sends the others away.

A junior probationer steps forward, performing her task as usual.

—The temperature of the ward is as it should be, please Sister.

Rosa nods gravely as she has seen ward sisters do hundreds, maybe thousands of times before. Then Betty Robinson speaks her staff nurse's lines, the grin still spanning her face, her eyes moist:

—Please Sister, nothing special to report, the ward reports are on your desk, please Sister.

—Will there be anything else, Sister Kremer? says Deputy Matron.

—No thank you, says Rosa, that will be all.

—Sister Kremer, she says with a flourish, your ward.

With that she turns on her heel and leaves. Rosa takes her place on the hassock; the nurses and probationers kneel behind her, and the patients bow their heads; then, in perfect imitation of all the Sisters who have come before her, Rosa leads the ward in the London Hospital prayer:

—Almighty and Everloving God, Who didst send Thine only Son Jesus Christ to be the Saviour of men, we pray Thee as earnestly as we can to bless the work done at the London Hospital. Bless all those, whether rich or poor, who have denied themselves to help the Hospital. Help all those who are nurses to have always present to their minds the example of our Blessed Saviour's love and sympathy for the poor and suffering. Give them grace and patience faithfully to fulfil their holy calling, doing all as unto Thee, and we pray Thee to crown their work with success and happiness. We commend, O God, the patients to Thy loving care. Soothe their pain; relieve their anxiety; lead them to a knowledge and love of Thee; give them patience under their sufferings, and a happy ending to all their trouble. We pray Thee also to remember the wives and children of the men here, and to help them in their trouble and distress. Grant this, we humbly beseech Thee, O God, for Thy Son Jesus Christ's sake. Amen.

After a pause Rosa gets to her feet, followed by the nurses and proba-tioners, and work begins in the ward, the hum of ordered activity filling the air. It was a little strange leading a Christian prayer, but Rosa knows that few people pay attention anyway. As she approaches the Sister's desk, Betty takes her aside and whispers excitedly:

—Goodness gracious, Rosie, I cannot believe it. Why didn't you tell me you were going to come out in blue?

—I was forbidden, Rosa replies. Matron would have sent me packing with a ferocity second only to Miss Lückes's.

Betty smiles and wipes her eyes on her apron.

—Who would have thought that you would be blued first, she says, out of everyone in our set? Out of all the Speedy Susies?

—Don't worry, says Rosa, you'll be next, I'm sure of it.

For the remainder of the morning Rosa is surprised to find that she falls naturally into her new role. At lunchtime she automatically walks towards the nurses' dining room; she is halfway there before she remem-bers that she is no longer a staff nurse and makes her way instead to the Sisters' dining room, where a place has been set for her complete with her own napkin ring, a place that she knows she may occupy for years, even decades. As soon as lunch is concluded Rosa changes back into mufti and hurries to the hospital entrance, her nervousness returning. Samuel is waiting for her in his best suit, leaning on the side of his motorcar and huffing into his hands, for the day has become very cold. Rosa joins him, and they kiss; then they get into the motorcar and thread their way nervously into the traffic.

5

Willesden Lane is a spacious, grand sort of street. Distinguished trees, stripped of their summer finery, stand at regular intervals along the pavement, and behind walls and gates large, rambling houses lie couched in grassy grounds. Rosa and Samuel swing open the doors of the old Riley Samuel is driving, step out outside number 167 and stand arm in arm looking up at the house. Its high façade, rectangular and whitewashed, hosts a porch supported by thin pillars, and stone balconies outside the first floor windows. A flight of steps leads up to the door, and the semi-circular driveway is bordered by perfectly tended flowerbeds. The house and grounds seem imbued with an atmosphere of almost uncanny peace and decorum.

—Well, says Samuel, are you ready?

—Did you bring the documents? asks Rosa.

—I did, you've asked me that already.

She grips his arm tighter.

—It's going to be grand, says Samuel, the future is going to be grand.

They walk along the driveway, climb the steps and knock on the door with a smoothly swinging brass knocker. Within seconds the door glides open, and a nun in a black habit beckons them in; they step onto glistening floorboards. The building is filled with a rarefied quietude and smells faintly of incense.

—Sister Jane, hello, says Samuel.

—Welcome back to Bellview, says the nun, please come this way.

Something in the movement from the sunshine to the shade, something in the smell of the flowers perhaps, or the furniture polish, or the quietness of the house, causes a memory to surface in Rosa's mind with such vividness that she lets out a gasp. She remembers a childhood holiday in Wiesbaden, remembers scrambling up the Neroberg hill, her legs hurting from the climb. She remembers pausing for a moment, stretching and turning round to look at the view. Hey, comes a voice from further up the hill, don't look round till you're at the top, you'll spoil it. She makes a face, turns and continues to climb – not far now, comes the voice again, one last effort and you'll be at the top. Her curls bounce like the hair of a clown from beneath her blue felt hat with the big flower on the side which butterflies will land on come summer, and she has that strange sensation of being hot even though the weather is cold, it is a clear, crisp winter's day, the first week of the Weihnachtsferien holidays, and her face is red with both heat from inside and chill from outside. She pulls at her scarf to loosen it and, despite being tired, breaks into a run, dashing up the last few yards of the hill and collapsing on the grass, laughing and panting and blowing her cheeks.

—Come on, says the voice, don't just lie there, get up and look at this damn view.

—Pfui, Heinrich, we don't use such words, says Inga.

—Don't chastise the boy, says her husband, he is simply exuberant, that's all.

Rosa raises herself on her elbows and sees, silhouetted against the sunlight, her parents, standing side by side on the edge of the Neroberg hill, and Papa has the fat little Hedi on his shoulders, and Heinrich is doing star-jumps, waving his father's hat above his head, his scarf flicking in the air like a tail.

—Come on, Rosa, he shouts, just look at this damn view.

Rosa gets to her feet, brushes the grass off her coat, shields her eyes from the sun, and the panoramic view of Wiesbaden is revealed, sprawling and magnificent, houses and churches and trees and buildings, spreading across the landscape to the horizon. She runs to join her family, and Heinrich drops Papa's hat on her head.

—Now, says Inga, crouching on the ground and opening a bag, who would like some bread and Damenkäse?

—Wonderful, says Papa, setting Hedi on the ground and smoothing his hair and moustache, let me just light my pipe.

The nun leads Samuel and Rosa across a large, square foyer. Piano music can be heard from the drawing room, where the flicker of a coal fire can be seen. A little girl walks past them at a subdued pace, nodding maturely as the adults catch her eye. A child's laughter can be heard upstairs, a mischievous hysterical laugh, followed by a female voice demanding silence. Sister Jane shows them into her office and closes the door.

Rosa squints her eyes against the sunlight from the window, the nun lowers the blind and the office is cast into muted shadow. Rosa shuffles her feet on the floorboards and tries to compose herself; she hasn't been this nervous since her interview at the London all those years ago.

—Now, says the nun, the documents, the documents. I trust you are both well?

As Samuel replies, fine thank you, Rosa thinks, I wish we could just get on with it. They answer the questions, read the declarations, provide the paperwork, sign document after document, fill out forms. Finally the nun says:

—Now if you wouldn't mind waiting for a few minutes, I will go and see if Julian is ready. You know to call him Julian, yes?

—Of course, Rosa replies, affronted.

—Good, good, that's good, says Sister Jane. Very well, I won't be long. Would either of you like a cup of tea?

They both shake their heads, and she leaves the room. On the hard wooden seats they sit in silence, exchanging nervous glances, Samuel feeling uncomfortable in his best suit and Rosa checking her make-up in a little Bakelite mirror. After a time Samuel gets to his feet and slowly paces the room. Somewhere in the building, in a staffroom maybe, a wireless is playing; from time to time children's voices can be heard, as well as frequent footsteps. It has taken so much effort to get to this moment, and now the end is in sight, these few moments are like a ring through which the multiple threads of their lives must pass; as soon as the little boy enters the room they can start to weave the tapestry of their future.

As Rosa sits and waits, her mind wanders back to Wiesbaden. The family sit down to eat beneath the turquoise sky, Mama passing round chunks of rye bread, Damenkäse and salami. They eat contentedly, then Papa suggests a game of tag; he takes off his tie and gets to his feet, followed by Rosa and Heinrich, and while Mama sits with Hedi on her lap, feeding her pieces of cheese, Papa chases after his children, in and out of light and shadow, bellowing and laughing, running one way then the other. Within minutes he ends up on his back in the grass, there is a great grass fight, and after a while they all lie looking up at the sky, giggling and catching their breath.

The door opens hesitantly.

—Hello, Julian, says Samuel.

In the pale light stands a boy of around ten, with a cloth cap bundled over black, curly hair, dressed in a coat done up with a belt; Sister Jane carries a little suitcase in behind him.

—Ready, little man? says Samuel.

The boy nods timidly; Rosa takes his hand and Samuel takes his suitcase.

—Once we're home, says Rosa, we're going to give you a lovely mug of cocoa.

—I like cocoa, says the boy.

Samuel, Rosa and Julian each shake Sister Jane by the hand.

—Goodbye, Julian, says the nun, you be a good boy now, do you hear?

—I'm sure he will, says Rosa defensively.

—And be sure to say your prayers.

They leave the building and step out onto the pavement. Samuel stashes the boy's suitcase in the boot, and with a rev of the engine they move off down Willesden Lane.

—Where do we live? asks Julian.

—Not far, says Samuel.

—Is my room ready? he asks.

—Yes, my darling, says Rosa, we've painted it blue as you wanted. I'm sure you're going to love it.

Rosa catches sight of the boy in the mirror and remembers the tiny baby on the dark train from Berlin. She remembers the steam, the carriage, the basket, the weight of the baby in her arms; she remembers holding him inexpertly, feeding him all the milk, slipping him under her seat to protect him from the SS, bringing him safely out of Germany. She remembers him being taken from her. Could this really be the same face? The same person? The years have changed the boy unrecognisably, yet she feels in her heart that this is him. There can have been no mistake. Not after the many long hours spent tracing his identity, all the letters, the documents, the records. The breakthrough came when Samuel managed to contact Norbert Wollheim, who had survived Auschwitz and returned to Germany. With his assistance they discovered the baby's name, Joachim Levin, who alone, amongst all his relatives, had survived. Joachim had been fostered by a middle-aged Catholic family in Essex, they discovered, and christened Julian; towards the end of the war, when his foster mother died, he was entrusted to the nuns of the Crusade of Rescue. And now he is here, really here, in the back seat of their car. After all these years Rosa is caring for him again. Minute by minute the first delicate threads of tapestry are being woven. Rosa rests her head against the car window and closes her eyes.

—Come on, children, says Papa, we must start making our way back to the hotel.

—But what about the damn view? says Heinrich.

—All right, my boy, that's quite enough. Come along.

As the light deepens and the shadows lengthen, Papa and Mama lead their children down the hill towards the road where the driver is waiting with the car. Hedi is on Papa's shoulders again, her hands patting his forehead, and Heinrich is walking beside, talking non-stop about his upcoming handball tournament at school; Mama and Rosa follow arm in arm.

—Did you have a nice day? asks Inga.

—Yes, Mama. How about you?

—The hot springs were especially good, says Inga, I still feel as if I'm glowing somehow.

—Yes, says Rosa, me too.

For a while they walk in silence, their feet whispering through the grass.

—Mama, says Rosa suddenly, when we are grown up, do you think I will have children before Heinrich, or him before me?

—What an odd question, says Inga, whatever makes you ask that?

—I don't know, just thinking.

—Well, girls tend to get married earlier than boys, so who knows?

—I want to have lots of children, says Rosa, at least four.

—God willing, replies Inga. As they say in religious circles, God willing.

Julian sits forward in his seat.

—My mother and father are dead, he says suddenly. Sister Wendy told me.

Samuel and Rosa exchange glances.

—Yes, says Rosa, we believe that to be the case. They're in heaven.

—Did you know them?

—Not really, says Rosa, I saw your mother once but that was all.

—What was she like?

—It's difficult to say. I only saw her for a moment.

—How come?

—She was putting you on the train to England. You were only a baby.

—Why didn't she come with me?

—She wanted to, very much. But she wasn't allowed.

There is a pause, and Julian goes back to looking out of the window. Cars slip by outside, each containing complex and multi-faceted lives, each with thousands of stories contained within fragile walls. Shadows wheel across the boy's face as the car turns a corner; after a time his eyes narrow and his head begins to nod to the rhythm of the engine. He didn't sleep very much last night either. Before long he is slumped in the leather seat, asleep.

—He's a bright one, isn't he? says Rosa.

—Indeed, says Samuel, and he's got rather good manners, too.

—That's nuns for you. They're like nurses.

Samuel reaches over and takes her hand. The engine throbs gently around them, and the wind blows ripples of cloud across the sky above the endless grey roofs.

—I feel as if I am caring for myself by caring for Julian, says Rosa. And for my family.

There is a pause. A lorry rumbles alongside them for a while before turning into a side road; a flock of sparrows passes overhead. Rosa turns to Samuel, squinting her eyes against the sunlight.

—Can I ask you something? she says.

—Of course, says Samuel.

—Well, it's not a question really. I want you to promise me something.

—Go on.

Rosa looks over her shoulder, checking that Julian is still asleep.

—In the future, she says, if there should ever be another war, and if we were faced with the same choice as my parents, promise me we would never send Julian away. Promise me we will keep him with us whatever happens, even if that means to the end.

Her voice breaks slightly and falls into silence as the car winds slowly through the streets of London. Samuel looks at the road, looks at the people moving on the pavements, looks at the buildings and the sky.

—Yes, he says slowly. Very well. I promise.

Afterword

I was extremely fortunate to have been able to draw upon the advice of many insightful and generous readers while working on this book. Foremost of these was my wife Isobel, whose combination of a startlingly perceptive intellect and earthy common sense makes her the consummate adviser. In addition, my good friends Haydn Middleton and Danny Angel provided me with regular feedback, as did Andrew Cowan, Giles Foden and Trezza Azzopardi at the University of East Anglia. My formidable agent, Andrew Gordon, brought his full editorial powers to bear upon the novel as it took shape, and acted as a tireless sounding board whenever I needed him. Judy Moir, my editor, helped at the vital 'polishing' stage. My father-in-law, Michael Sallon, was a creative rudder who set me on a true course at crucial moments, and my sister-in-law, Zoe Sallon, read an early draft and delivered her thoughts with élan.

My uncle, the sometime playwright David Del Monté, offered an invaluable perspective on scenes involving dialogue, helping me appreciate the difference between dialogue that is genuine and dialogue that is cramped by the plot. Afua Hirsch, an old and valued confidante, helped me arrive at a key creative decision during a lengthy conversation on the way back from Nottingham to London (we had been to see the Dalai Lama). My only regret is that the other idea we came up with, for a healthy breakfast nut bar called 'Get Up And Glow', never materialised.

I was also fortunate to be able to turn to some good German friends for detailed advice. Chiefly, the magnificent German novelist Jan Brandt went through the Berlin chapters several times with a fine-tooth comb, saving me the humiliation of having made countless schoolboy errors; he and his girlfriend Danni also hosted me in Berlin when I visited to carry out research. Janek Schmidt of *Sueddeutsche Zeitung* read these sections very thoroughly as well, and painstakingly elucidated the difficult theory involved when using German words in an English novel. The Anglo-German journalist and writer Philip Oltermann was a constant presence, dealing with my on-the-spot technical queries via pithily worded SMSs. Dr Jo Catling at the University of East Anglia helped by double-checking the material.

In addition, a number of experts in various fields were kind enough to make themselves available for consultation on what increasingly became questions of minute detail. These included the historians Sir Martin Gilbert and Dr Colin Shindler; the novelist Clive Sinclair; Jonathan Evans of the Royal London Hospital Archive; Rachelle Mortimer-Mattingham of the Cromer Museum; Keith Farrow, Hugh Taylor and David Bradley of trolleybus.net; Mike Handscomb and Richard Adderson of the Norfolk Railway Society; Dr Hermann Simon and Ingrid Schramm of the Stiftung Neue Synagogue Berlin Centrum Judaicum; various people at the Sachsenhausen Museum; Julia Feast and Jenny Lord of the British Association for Adoption and Fostering; and my grandparents, Ruth and Tony Simons, who shared with me memories of their honeymoon in Jersey and my grandfather's post-war second hand car business.

Over the years, I have had the honour of speaking with many people who escaped from Europe on the Kindertransport. Four in particular granted me extensive interviews: the extraordinary Bertha Leverton, Walter and Herta Kammerling, and Ann Meyer. I owe them a great debt. I would also like to offer my profound thanks and admiration to Emmy Mogilensky, who escaped from Munich on a Kindertransport as a teenager and cared for twin babies who had been placed on the train in secret. Clearly this inspired a key aspect of Rosa's story, and I am grateful to Emmy for allowing me to take her experiences as a starting point in this way, and also for reading the relevant sections of the novel and giving me her thoughts.

Finally, of the many books that I studied closely, these were the most important (in roughly chronological order): *The Berlin Stories*, by Christopher Isherwood; *Before the Deluge*, by Otto Friedrich; *Defying Hitler* by Sebastian Haffner; *The Pity of It All*, by Amos Elon; *Peeling the Onion*, by Günter Grass; *Berlin Alexanderplatz*, by Alfred Döblin; *Mr. Brecher's Fiasco*, by Martin Kessel; *The Past Is Myself*, by Christabel Bielenberg; *Jews in Berlin*, ed. Andreas Nachama, Julius H. Schoeps and Hermann Simon; *Into The Arms of Strangers*, by Mark Jonathan Harris and Deborah Oppenheimer; *The Tiger in the Attic*, by Edith Milton; *Kindertransport*, by Olga Levy Drucker; *Other People's Houses*, by Lore Segal; *Berlin Mosaic*, by Eva Tucker; *Norfolk in the Second World War* and *Norfolk at War*, by Neil R. Storey; *Betty's Wartime Diary 1939–1945*, by Betty Armitage; *Shir-Ella: Remembrances of Two Sisters Evacuated from London to a Norfolk Village, World War II, 1939–1945*, by Ella Grimmer, et al.; *The*

Norwich Hebrew Congregation, 1840–1960: A Short History, by Henry Levine; *London at War 1939–1945,* by Philip Ziegler; *Patients Come First* and *Patients Are People,* by Margaret E. Broadley; *London Pride, The Story of a Voluntary Hospital,* by A. E. Clark-Kennedy; *The Children of Willesden Lane,* by Mona Golabek and Lee Cohen; and *An Unlikely Heroine,* by Asher Cailingold.

It's a notoriously tricky business to write novels about the Holocaust. Ultimately I believe that fiction, if done properly, has a special power to bring these events alive in the minds of future generations. But doing it properly is not easy. For my own part, I felt a keen sense of duty towards the Kindertransport children and their families throughout the writing of this book. To avoid historical travesty I wanted to make it as accurate and realistic as possible; at the same time, I did not want to stand accused – as Peter Hall so memorably put it – of 'bumming a ride on the Holocaust'. This phrase haunted me throughout the writing process, and I can only hope that I have achieved the right balance in the novel that you hold in your hands.

Index of real-life characters in the novel

Apart from the people listed below, all other characters in the novel are fictional. The only exception to this is the patients and staff of the London Hospital. Although many of these characters were inspired by real people, the author had to use fictional names in accordance with a declaration he signed while working in the Royal London Hospital archives.

Alexander, Clare: Matron of the London Hospital from 1941 to 1951. She resigned her position to marry Sir John Mann of the brewers Mann, Crossman & Paulin Ltd, who was chairman of governors to the London Hospital. With characteristic modesty, Matron Alexander kept news of her forthcoming resignation a secret, going to work as normal on her final day and disappearing after lunch.

Altmann, Ludwig: Organist at the Neue Synagogue, Berlin in the late 1930s and early 1940s.

Baeck, Rabbi Leo: Eminent rabbi and scholar in the Progressive Judaism movement, he acted as an army chaplain for the Germans during WWI and became head of the Jewish community in Berlin during the Nazi era. Some criticised him for encouraging Jews to cooperate with the Nazis. Nevertheless when he was deported to Theresienstadt in 1943 he became a spiritual figurehead for incarcerated Jews. He survived the camps and died in London in 1956, head of a large family. He was also the mentor of Norbert Wollheim.

Broadley, Margaret: Prominent figure at the London Hospital from 1923 onwards, she worked her way up from student nurse to assistant matron. Describing her vocation to the Queen, she said, 'It's a jigsaw puzzle that never stands still.' She remained at the London well into her eighties, working on the archives. Author of two autobiographies and other books, she died in Epping in 1999, aged ninety. Like most nurses of her generation, she never married.

Cailingold, Esther: A strictly religious British schoolteacher who volunteered to fight with the Jewish forces in the Arab–Israeli war of 1948 and was killed in the battle for the Old City of Jerusalem. She was twenty-three.

Duggen, Mrs: A dressmaker from the East End to whom nurses from the London Hospital entrusted their uniforms.

Ehrenfreund, Jacob: A young German member of the Zionist youth group Makkabi Hatzair who tore down a swastika flag and, as a result, was beaten so badly that he had to be admitted to a mental institution.

Fabritz, Reverend Maurice: Rabbi of the Norwich Synagogue during the war, which was bombed in the Baedeker raids. In a gesture of solidarity, after the synagogue was destroyed local churches offered to share their premises with the Jewish community.

Fehr, Oskar: German Jewish ophthalmologist and internationally renowned eye surgeon who fled Nazi Germany in 1939, and lived in London until his death in 1959, at the age of eighty-eight.

Jonas, Regina: The first woman ever to be ordained as a rabbi, she practised in Berlin. In 1942 she was deported to Theresienstadt where she survived for two years lecturing and working with Viktor Frankl, the renowned psychologist and author of *Man's Search for Meaning*. Her role was to treat inmates for shock and work to reduce suicide rates. She was deported to Auschwitz in 1944 and was murdered two months later. She was forty-two.

Katznelson, Siegmund: Well-known Berlin publisher and editor of the Weimar period. In the pre-war years he was commissioned to assemble an encyclopaedic record of Jewish contributions to the Reich entitled *Jews in the Realm of German Culture*, with the intention of stemming the prevailing anti-Semitic sentiment by pointing out Jewish achievements to the wider public. An appendix featured a list of non-Jews often regarded as Jews, which included such diverse characters as Johann Strauss and Charlie Chaplin. The entire edition of the book was destroyed by the Gestapo; the manuscript survived the war, however, and was subsequently reprinted.

Knutsford, 2nd Viscount (Sydney George Holland): Eldest son of the Conservative politician Henry Thurstan Holland, 1st Viscount Knutsford, he was the chairman of the London Hospital House Committee until 1931. He acquired the nickname 'Prince of Beggars' as a result of his tireless fundraising, producing millions of pounds for the hospital.

Krützfeld, Berta: The wife of Wilhelm Krützfeld. She survived the war.

Krützfeld, Wilhelm: Police lieutenant, chief of Precinct 16 at Hackescher Markt, Berlin. He had jurisdiction over the main orthodox Jewish district known as the 'Scheunenviertel', or 'barn quarter', and is best remembered for his actions of 9 November 1938 in which he saved the Neue Synagogue from destruction at the hands of the Nazis. From that point on he faded from prominence in the police, opting for early retirement in 1942. He survived the war, dying in Berlin in 1953 at the age of seventy-three.

Landsberger, Hermann Artur: German Jewish novelist and critic of the pre-war period. He is particularly remembered for his 1925 novel *Berlin Without Jews*, a satire on anti-Semitism in which Germany eventually returns to its senses and relinquishes its prejudices. The novel was published contemporaneously with *Mein Kampf*. Landsberger died in 1933, the year that Hitler rose to power.

Lückes, Eva Charlotte Ellis: Legendary matron of the London Hospital. Appointed at the age of only twenty-four, at the time she was thought by many to be 'too young and too pretty'. Nevertheless, she retained her position for thirty-nine years and became renowned as a fearsome reformer. Miss Lückes, as she was known, died in 1919.

Pfeifenkopf, Bernhard: Contemporary of Jizchak Schwersenz. His first name is unknown and was provisionally invented by the author.

Rothschild, Baron James Armand Edmond de: French-born philanthropist and politician who fought as a private in the French Army during WWI and then as a major in the Jewish Battalion of the British army. From 1922 he lived in Waddesdon Manor, which he had inherited from his great-uncle, Baron Ferdinand de Rothschild, a Liberal MP. He did much to rescue Jews during the war, including many members of the Kindertransport, and donated generously to key establishments in Israel. He died in 1957 aged seventy-nine.

Schwersen, Jizchak: Berlin youth leader and teacher. Upon receiving his deportation orders in 1942 he was persuaded by his girlfriend, Edith 'Ewo' Wolff, to go underground. They formed an illegal Jewish youth movement called Chug Chaluzi which met late at night in the parks of Berlin and aimed to hide its members from the Gestapo and evacuate them to Palestine; thirty-three of its forty members survived the war. In 1944, after Ewo was arrested, he disguised himself as a member of the

Luftwaffe and escaped to Switzerland. He later emigrated to Haifa in Israel where he was reunited with Ewo, who had herself survived the concentration camps. He later adopted a German boy, and in 1991 moved back permanently to Berlin where he educated children about the Holocaust. He died in 2005.

Solomon, Mr: A member of the Norwich Synagogue Committee during the 1940s.

Warschauer, Rabbi Malvin: Linguist, scholar and rabbi of the Neue Synagogue, Berlin, in the pre-war years. A close friend of Rabbi Leo Baeck, in 1939 he escaped from Germany to England, also rescuing some synagogue treasures. For the rest of his life he lived in London, working with refugee communities in Guildford. He died in 1955, aged eighty-four.

Willstätter, Richard Martin: Nobel Prize winning German Jewish biologist, widely recognised as the father of modern biochemistry. In protest against burgeoning anti-Semitism, he announced his premature retirement in 1924 and resisted all subsequent calls to continue his work. In 1938 he fled the Gestapo and, with the help of a pupil, made his way to Switzerland. He died in 1942 at the age of seventy.

Wolff, Edith 'Ewo': Half-Jewish member of the German Resistance. Although brought up a Christian, she converted fully to Judaism in 1933 in protest against the Nazis' anti-Jewish policies. When the first deportations started in 1941, she and her boyfriend Jizchak Schwersenz assisted Jews seeking to flee or go underground. In 1943 she was arrested by the Gestapo for this activity and went on to survive several concentration camps including Dachau and Ravensbrück. In 1950 she emigrated to Switzerland, and from there to Israel where she was reunited with Schwersenz. For the rest of her life she worked in the Holocaust Memorial Centre Yad Vashem, as well as for organisations committed to fostering Jewish–Arab understanding. She died in 1997 in Haifa, aged ninety-three.

Wollheim, Norbert: Professional accountant and functionary of Jewish organisations. He played a key role in the organisation of the Kindertransport, often accompanying the children to England and returning to Germany himself lest the transports were stopped. In March 1943 he and his family were deported to Auschwitz, and his wife and child were murdered. Wollheim himself survived and escaped during one of the notorious death marches at the end of the war. He emigrated to America and in the 1950s spearheaded definitive legal action against I. G. Farbenindustrie, winning millions of Deutschmarks in compensation for slave labour on behalf of himself and others. He died in 1998 at the age of seventy-nine.